Anaphylaxis

alan anson wanderer

Anson Publishing Inc.
Box 10998
Bozeman, MT 59719

This book is a work of fiction. Names, characters, places, and incidents either are the product of the author's imagination or are used fictitiously, and any resemblance to actual persons, living or dead, business establishments, events or locales is entirely coincidental.

ISBN-10: 147815943X
EAN-13: 978-1478159438

Library of Congress Control Number: 2012913995
CreateSpace Independent Publishing Platform
North Charleston, South Carolina

"Anaphylaxis is the opposite condition to protection (phylaxis). I coined the word in 1902 to describe the peculiar attribute which certain poisons possess of increasing instead of diminishing the sensitivity of an organism to their action..."

CHARLES R. RICHET, ANAPHYLAXIS, THE UNIVERSITY PRESS,
LIVERPOOL, 1913

Charles R. Richet, M.D. was awarded the Nobel Prize in Medicine and Physiology for discovery of anaphylaxis in 1913.

Pronunciation: an-ah-fill-ax-iss
Definition: An exaggerated, life threatening allergic reaction following re-exposure to a foreign substance, e.g., food, bee sting, drug.

Dedication

For my nephew Kurt, who despite extraordinary efforts by his family and friends, could not be saved from the abyss of cocaine addiction, with the hope that society will combat and overcome this global enemy.

For physicians who raise the standard of care in the specialty of allergy, asthma and immunology by participating in fellowship training required by the American Board of Allergy & Immunology.

And for my family who provided me with encouragement during the writing and publishing my first novel.

List of Main Characters

Frank Stevens, Ph.D.	Researcher at COADD
Leonard Haberman, M.D.	Denver Allergist
Elizabeth Finch, R.N.	Nurse in Dr. Haberman's office
Denise Stevens	Wife of Dr. Stevens
Jimmy Barone	Head Technician at COADD
Peter Doren, M.D.	Denver Physician
Jacqueline Doren	Dr. Doren's wife
David Sabatha, M.D.	Denver Psychiatrist
Sol Feldman & Ole Bettman	Officers of COADD
Ted Larkin	Colorado Senate Majority Leader; brother of Denise Stevens
Mark Persons	Malpractice attorney for Dr. Haberman
Ed Tucker & Josh Cutter	Attorneys for Stevens' estate
Glen Carthage	Attorney for Elizabeth Finch
Charley Blackwood	Private Investigator
Ben Locke	CBI Field Agent
KC	Member of Bronx mob
Tommy Pazzoni	Head of Bronx mob
Jack Haberman	Haberman's son
Elaine Haberman	Haberman's wife

Prologue

The small gathering of friends and cast sat transfixed as they listened to her sing arias from *Madame Butterfly*. This was her final rehearsal in preparation for the opening performance at the Boulder Opera House. Each note was perfectly focused; her voice so rare and pure, it stood apart from multitudes of aspiring vocalists. Physically she was stunning: milky-white complexion, large captivating blue eyes, dimples, long straight golden hair and an hourglass figure. All of it miniaturized in comparison to an inner beauty expressed by her humility and grace.

When she finished the rehearsal, some of the audience rushed onto the stage to hug and kiss her. She received their praises gratefully and then departed to rest up for the opening performance the following evening. Feeling a combination of elation and exhaustion, she collapsed into the leather seat of the VW Golf that her fiancé had given her as an engagement present. She tilted the seat as far back as possible, closed her eyes, and pursed her lips breathing slowly to release the heightened tension in her body. Visions of her struggles to succeed came forward: exhausting voice lessons from early childhood, frequent auditions, and fending off bitchy competitors who tried to undermine her success.

Being naïve and trusting, she didn't always recognize dirty tricks being played on her. Early in her career, she recalled one particular incident while trying out for an opera group in Denver. She had arrived for the audition on a frigid wintry evening, shivering and voraciously hungry, having not eaten lunch or dinner because of nervous anticipation. A seemingly friendly competitor offered her warm soup. The soup had a delicious appetizing aroma and was so inviting she quickly gulped down a full cup. Instantaneously copious drainage poured out of her nose, followed by flushing of her face, choking, coughing and a raspy voice. Someone gave her a bottle of water which she guzzled but the distress persisted and she had to forgo the audition. When she departed, tears flowed to release her personal disappointment and the rage she felt having learned that Tom Yum Goong Soup contained extremely hot spices—chili paste and spicy Thai galanga root. The friendly competitor who gave her the soup could be heard giggling in the auditorium, knowing a formidable rival had been eliminated.

Despite this and other nasty obstacles along the way, she had finally reached a pinnacle of opportunity; scouts from the Metropolitan and La Scala would be present for the opening performance. Tomorrow would be the biggest day of her life.

Driving home, she flipped on a recording of *Madame Butterfly* to rehearse *"Un bel dì vedremo"* one more time. To a trained listener the voices appeared duplicated and superimposed. While crossing an intersection, a sudden flash appeared in the corner of her eye, followed by a dissonant, crunching, screeching, metallic, crescendo sound. Then came heat, steam, and silence, except for one soprano singing an aria.

She laid there dazed, and after several moments opened her eyes to face a blinding cyclops-like headlight protruding through the broken window of her door. Pinned behind the steering wheel, she could feel pain in her chest but none in her lower body. She moved her hands slowly down to her legs which were covered by crunched pieces of hot metal, shards of glass and plastic. There was no feeling when she squeezed her thighs; it was if her limbs were of another person. Moving her head slightly, she was able to focus on warm fluids enveloping her hands. Dark violet and spurting bright red blood were mixing together in swirling whirlpools; an alarm signal that accelerated her panic. Trying to calm herself, she tried to sing again, but managed only tones of anguish. Then lapsing slowly into unconsciousness, she watched bubbles surfacing from rubric currents, wondering if they were her final breaths.

Chapter One

Twenty years later

IN DENVER, THERE are years when summer thunderstorms roll in daily for weeks at a time; they can be mild to violent, always unpredictable. The storms this year were scarce and the city was experiencing a drought with unusually high temperatures. Dr. Leonard Haberman looked out his office window at the promising billowing black clouds moving into metro Denver, but he also knew this might be another dry lightning storm that could make matters worse. As he watched, cracking thunder followed closely after z-shaped lightning bolts, indicating the storm was coming in fast. In the distance he was able to make out what appeared to be sheets of rain. *Maybe this could be it… Finally… cleaner air.* He was hoping the rain might wash out some of the smog that was triggering asthma flare ups for his patients.

He returned to his paper work until he was interrupted by a call from one of his elderly asthma patients. The patient wanted to thank Lenny for saving his life so he could continue to "play with the band." Lenny had always admired the old guy's wisdom, especially his Titanic metaphor. *"We're all on the top deck of the Titanic. You can spend your time anxiously watching the rising waterline or go play with the band. I decided to play with the band. Enjoy every moment."*

After hanging up, Lenny searched for the patient's chart in a pile on his desk. When he found it, a copy of an operative report was clipped to the front of the chart waiting for his review and signature. He had been treating the patient for ten years, but two months ago his asthma had worsened and became unresponsive to conventional therapies. Lenny had become convinced he was missing something. It kept troubling him until he decided to order a high definition CT scan to rule out a lung tumor. The unexpected finding surprised him; an aortic aneurysm ready to burst. Without surgery it would have meant sudden death. Lenny whistled a sigh of relief, and murmured, *"This is one I'll never forget."*

The intercom buzzed.

"Dr. Stevens is on the line for you."

Frank Stevens, Ph.D. was the head researcher at Colorado Addiction Disorder Laboratory (COADD), a biotech company developing vaccines for cocaine and other addictions. He and Lenny had become close friends after Lenny came on board as the medical director of COADD.

Lenny answered. "Hi Frank, what's up?"

"Lenny... wow! Just got an email from Jimmy, the results are in! This is it! If the vaccine works we are solid. I'm on my way to COADD to read them....Hey I just remembered I need to come over for an allergy shot. We can review the results then."

"Hey, that's great. I'll have time to meet."

"OK, see you soon."

✶ ✶ ✶

Frank parked in the COADD space marked for Research Director and grabbed his briefcase out of the backseat. As he opened the car door, he fought resistance from fierce whirling winds. He stood up and without warning, marble-sized hail started to bounce around him. Covering his head with the briefcase, he sprinted toward the building's entrance. Thunder grumbled as he lurched inside the lobby. He struggled for breath, muttering, "Fuckin' asthma!" Now in his forties, Frank had long since lost his college athlete physique. He now carried an extra forty pounds on his six foot frame. He'd had asthma since he was a kid, but the extra weight was making it worse. *Shit! I totally need to start working out again…maybe I can if the vaccine trials are a success…* He shook his head, but smiled at the thought that they might actually have something. He placed his briefcase next to his desk, dropped into his chair, and reached in the top drawer for his inhaler. He took a couple of puffs and leaned forward to open his email. The first one was from Sol Feldman, President and CEO of COADD.

Frank, just a reminder. Board meeting tomorrow at 9AM. Be ready to present status on the vaccine trials. The board members have been hounding me all week to make sure you and the results are on the agenda! See you tomorrow. —Sol

Frank grimaced. This was the third email from Sol this week about his presentation. Everyone was on edge, waiting for the results. Frank, however, had more to lose than any of the board members or other executives of COADD. He had left his cushy academic job seven years ago to take a chance on this risky commercial research company. If he failed to get the vaccine results and the company folded, he might have to resort to taking a dead end job doing research at a big drug company.

He clicked on the email he had previously read from his chief lab technician, Jimmy Barone. He wasn't sure if Jimmy mentioned where he had left the results.

Dr. S:

Good news. Johnson CRO has analyzed data from CMV trials. Should be able to get printout by 3 & will leave it near or on your desk...assuming space is available! Hope results look good. Need to leave early. Got a busting headache.

Jimmy

P.S. PLEASE, PLEASE. REMEMBER TO BRING OTHER SET OF SPECS SO I CAN MAKE CHANGES.

Frank glanced around and found the data printout lying on the chair adjacent to his desk. His heart started pounding with anticipation. Finally, after seven tedious, frustrating years of research, this set of experiments could validate his work. He knew if today's results demonstrated efficacy of the cocaine vaccine, he, Dr. Frank Stevens, would be catapulted literally overnight to professional fame, something he had worked for since earning a Ph.D. in immunochemistry.

Immunologists had speculated that an immune stimulating technology could effectively treat cocaine addiction. The key obstacle was that cocaine did not stimulate an immune response because of its small molecular size. In his research, Frank had attached cocaine to a larger proprietary molecule that induced an antibody immune response in mice. Then, with technical maneuvering, he altered the cocaine antibody so it could be tolerated in humans. Theoretically, the cocaine antibody would bind cocaine in the blood, preventing it from crossing the blood-brain barrier to release pleasure sensing chemicals in the brain, and if it did that, it could potentially decrease cocaine addiction. His lab was racing against other scientific groups investigating a similar approach to treat chemical addictions. He already knew of one company ready to announce the launch of a vaccine antibody treatment for nicotine addiction.

Frank was hopeful that the human trials approved by the Cottonwood Institutional Research Board (IRB) would answer key questions, but it was too late to second-guess the study since all the funding had virtually been used up.

He read the results of the first group of subjects who had received low dose cocaine monoclonal antibody vaccine (CMV). He felt deflated when he saw the cocaine use was no different from the placebo group, but his anticipation rose when he read the results using mid-range doses of CMV. Blood cocaine concentrations were twenty-five percent lower in this treatment group compared to placebo. He flipped over to the data for high dose CMV. It indicated cocaine levels were undetectable in twenty of the subjects, and the remaining thirty had significantly lower concentrations compared to their initial levels. Even more impressive, average cocaine consumption was reduced by 75 percent. After reading the results several times, Frank pushed himself out of the chair, raised his arm and exclaimed quietly, "Yes!"

What these results meant began to sink in. Thoughts of acclaim from respected academic colleagues made Frank feel giddy. It could mean the Lasker Award for his medical research contribution. His mind raced with all the potential ramifications. It could also mean immense wealth from his stock ownership in COADD, which would allow him the luxury of returning to academia to do more basic research.

Glancing at his watch, he realized he had only fifteen minutes to get to Lenny's office for his bimonthly allergy injections. Fortunately, the office was located nearby at the Strong Medical Office Building, part of a large complex including a hospital, medical offices, research labs and pharmaceutical companies.

As he sprinted toward Lenny's office, he stopped briefly to drop the trial results in his car so he could bring them home to show his wife, Denise, and maybe take her out for a surprise celebration dinner. He was beside himself; years of built up tension seeking release. Increasing his pace, he intermittently jumped with his arms raised, landing intentionally in small puddles, splashing and laughing shouts of joy that echoed off walls of nearby buildings. Arriving at the office building, he climbed two steps at a time to the second floor and ran down the hallway to the office with the sign:

Allergy & Asthma Specialists of the Rockies, P.C.
Leonard T. Haberman, M.D.
Walter Oliphant, M.D.

When he entered the waiting room, the receptionist, Holly Brown, greeted him with a nod. He took a seat but his breathing was labored from the run, so he walked over to get a drink from the water fountain. It took several minutes before his breathing slowed down.

Elizabeth Finch, the nurse in charge, had finished giving an injection to another patient and then glanced up. She motioned to Frank. "Dr. Stevens, I'm ready for you." At age thirty-nine, Elizabeth maintained a striking figure, although slightly thin for her five foot five frame

Familiar with the routine, Frank walked into the injection area and rolled up his sleeve. On the counter he noticed there was a new photograph of two smiling preteens.

"Hey, Elizabeth, those are two beautiful kids. Are they yours?"

"Yes, they're mine," she said, turning away abruptly to draw up his vaccine. "Were there any problems with your last injection?"

He was accustomed to her abruptness. She always seemed just shy of rude, but he just ignored it. "There was some swelling and a little soreness for about a day."

Concerned, she asked, "What size was the swelling?"

"Oh, about the size of a silver dollar... and I also had a nasty migraine headache after the last shot, but the new migraine med seems to be keeping my headaches under better control."

"That seems like a pretty large reaction. I'll lower the dose and let's see how you do this time."

He waved it off. "Whatever. By the way, is Dr. Lenny available? Need to chat with him about some personal stuff, and let him know I had a little tightness in my breathing during the week."

"He's next door. I'll let him know you're here."

Elizabeth injected the dose into his arm, and as Frank rolled his sleeve back down, she reminded him to wait the usual time following his injection.

Suddenly, a hot flush rushed through his body and he noticed his mouth had a metallic taste. He walked to the nearest chair and sat down. His heart began to pound and his arms started shaking. He tried controlling the trembling in his arms by squeezing them against his chest. An elderly female patient sitting next to him glanced over with annoyance when his jerking movements vibrated the magazine she was reading.

His skin began to itch and he felt a surge of warmth. A tight sensation gripped his throat and chest and he began to wheeze. He tried to get Elizabeth's attention, but she had turned to another patient.

Trying not to panic, he grabbed a *People* magazine. After a scant ten seconds he dropped it because he couldn't concentrate. His nose started running and his mouth filled with saliva, triggering strident coughing spasms that made several patients peer at him with a mixture of annoyance and concern.

When Elizabeth became aware of his distress, she ceased her conversation and rushed over to him. "Dr. Stevens, do you need some water?"

"Yes…feels tight," he gasped, pointing to his chest.

She noticed large welts forming on his neck and arms. "Dr. Stevens, let's go to an exam room so I can listen to your chest."

Weakness permeated Frank's body. He tried to stand, but his legs couldn't hold him up and he fell back into the chair. Elizabeth bent over to grab his shoulders, trying to steady him. He could faintly hear her voice, like distant echoes bouncing around inside his head. His eyes widened and his body jolted, causing his head to jerk upward. He forced out a few unintelligible words, "cnn'th…. bbrrth." In a futile effort, he wrapped his hands around his neck, and then suddenly his body went limp. He fell forward onto the floor with a crash that shook the entire waiting room. A woman screamed, "Oh my God!"

Elizabeth bent over and yelled, "Dr. Stevens!... Can you hear me?...Can you hear me?"

There was no response. He had lapsed into unconsciousness.

"Dr. Stevens! Dr. Stevens! What's wrong?... Please...answer me!"

Frank tried opening his mouth, but couldn't move his swollen tongue. His skin color had turned a dark blue and his face, eyelids, and lips were enlarging into distorted shapes.

Elizabeth felt a barely detectable pulse in his neck. She ran to grab adrenalin, and at the same time she yelled to the receptionist, "Holly, get Dr. Haberman on his cell. Tell him we have a serious emergency and call the ER to send someone over right away!"

Chapter Two

LENNY HABERMAN WAS deep in conversation with his psychiatrist, Dr. David Sabatha. They had been classmates at Columbia College of Physicians and Surgeons, but only had known each other only casually in a large class of over one hundred. They hadn't seen each other for several decades until Dave moved to Denver a year prior to assume an existing practice from a retiring psychiatrist. Lenny had been totally surprised to bump into his old classmate one day in the same office building, and the decision to start therapy with him was an easy one. He recalled Dave was not only an outstanding student who had graduated second in their class, but according to classmate chatter at a recent reunion, he had become an internationally recognized psycho-pharmacologist at Albert Einstein Medical School after discovering a class of medications that became one of the standard therapies for psychosis.

But Dave's intellect was not the only reason Lenny decided to begin therapy with him. He remembered that Dave had an inviting personality and confident demeanor, which was so embracing, that many classmates sought guidance from him. They affectionately referred to him as Buddha because of his body type: pot-belly, premature baldness, moon-shaped face and dark skin of Afro-Asian heritage.

Lenny was somewhat surprised that Dave appeared a lot older than their mutual age of fifty. The self-consciousness that Lenny felt about his own age was occasionally lessened when he noticed furtive glances from younger women checking out his trim body, ebony eyes, olive complexion and curly black hair mixed with accents of silver.

They were engaged in a discussion dealing with Lenny's midlife issues. "Dave, I feel like I'm in a rut. I still like what I'm doing, but I want more. You know, like you had in research. Sometimes I wished I'd stayed in academia. I keep thinking that by now I might have made a few important discoveries, written more publications and found time to just think."

"Lenny, each of us has to find our own path. Don't compare yourself to me. There were times I felt just the opposite when I was frustrated by academic BS and wanted to be more independent and go into private practice. It's the main reason I left the university and moved here."

"I know, but every once in a while I'd like to take a sabbatical, go somewhere for a year with my family, study something different. I'd like to spend some time living on a boat, maybe sailing around the Caribbean. I get so angry sometimes with all the fucking red tape, the insurance companies, hospital meetings, the staff meetings ...it goes on and on. I never have enough time to be with the kids and Elaine."

Lenny's phone vibrated. His office was calling and it had to be important since his staff had been instructed not to interrupt unless there was an emergency. "Hang on, Dave. I need to take this call."

"Hello, Dr. Haberman here."

Holly Brown screamed, "Doctor come now! Please! A patient just collapsed."

Lenny leaped up from his chair and headed out the door. "It's an emergency. I have to leave!"

"Go, I understand," Dave said as Lenny rushed out of the office.

Although in good shape from running three miles every other morning and working out with a martial arts instructor, Lenny could feel his heart race as he ran down the flight of stairs. His staff had pulled him out of an exam room on two previous occasions for patients who had fainted. One of the patients had hit his head on a tabletop, causing a mild concussion. Lenny hoped this was just another fainting spell. A glance at his watch showed it was 5:16 pm as he entered his office.

He immediately recognized Frank Stevens lying on the floor. Elizabeth was kneeling at his side, encircled by terrified patients. She was pressing her fingers on his neck trying to detect a pulse.

"Elizabeth! What happened? What's going on?"

"I gave Dr. Stevens his allergy shot about five minutes ago. He sat down and started choking and coughing, and then he just collapsed and fell."

"Is he conscious?" Lenny's mind was racing. *My God, don't let it be anaphylaxis, please!*

"I don't think so. I only get a faint pulse."

"Did you call for help?"

"Holly called the ER and I gave him a shot of adrenalin."

"Good, get the crash cart and oxygen tank!"

Elizabeth ran to fetch it while Lenny rolled Frank over onto his back. When the cart arrived, he took some Kleenex to wipe away mucus from Stevens' mouth and nose. Then he tried to insert an oral airway inside Frank's mouth.

"Frank, can you hear me? Open your mouth." There was no response. "C'mon, help me. Open your mouth!"

Again, just silence. Lenny grabbed a tongue blade and tried forcing it inside Frank's mouth. He met resistance from a swollen, bulging tongue, unlike anything he had ever seen. That meant only one thing to Lenny. Frank was experiencing anaphylaxis, a severe allergic reaction.

He extended Frank's head backward while bringing his chin forward to reduce the airway obstruction. Respirations were becoming more rapid and shallow, and the skin overlying his windpipe retracted deeply with each effort, signifying labored breathing. Lenny placed his fingers on the side of his neck and couldn't feel a pulse. Suddenly, Frank stopped breathing.

"Elizabeth, CPR...now! Where's Jane?" He glanced around the room for her.

"She left earlier because she was sick," Holly said anxiously.

Groaning inwardly, Lenny grabbed a ventilation bag from the emergency cart, placed it over Frank's mouth, and began squeezing the bag. Each time he squeezed the bag, he could feel air wafting away. Lenny realized Frank's swollen tongue was obstructing the air flow.

Looking up, Lenny saw Elizabeth standing frozen, gazing toward the hallway. Her hands were shaking violently and tears ran down her cheeks.

"Elizabeth, help me, now!" Yet she didn't budge. Lenny looked over to the patients. "Does anyone know CPR? ...Anyone!"

A young man in his late twenties wearing worn jeans raised his hand.

"Doc, Phil Bellows here. I can help." Lenny remembered that he was a fireman for Denver County.

"Great. Let's go, Phil. Start chest compressions and I'll squeeze the bag."

They became a synchronized team. Despite vigorous efforts, Frank's chest did not rise with each squeeze of the bag. The color of his lips and fingernails remained blue. Recognizing the need for oxygen, Lenny tried attaching the ventilation bag to the oxygen tank, but couldn't reach the tubing with one hand.

"Elizabeth, get over here and attach this," Lenny shouted while pointing to the tubing hanging from the oxygen tank.

She didn't respond, still paralyzed. Another man knelt down to attach the tubing and followed Lenny's instructions to turn on the oxygen tank. Lenny tried squeezing the bag more forcibly, but still encountered a wall of resistance. He barked out orders while drawing up another dose of adrenalin that he injected deep into Frank's arm.

"Someone get coats, jackets, anything ... prop them under his legs. That'll help blood flow into his heart and brain. Phil, do you know how to start an IV?"

"I do."

"OK, let's get one started."

Phil noticed Frank's veins had collapsed due to shock. "I can't find any veins...Should I keep trying?"

"No, take over chest compressions ... I need an oximeter! It's over on the shelf near the door. Does anyone know what I'm talking about?"

A woman yelled out, "Yes, I use one for my child's asthma." She ran to get it and handed it to Lenny, who placed it on Frank's fingertip. The readout was 63% saturation, a number confirming that Frank was severely deprived of oxygen.

Lenny knew he had only a few more minutes to save him. He recalled if you couldn't get an IV started, it's possible to inject adrenalin under the tongue where it can be absorbed rapidly into the blood circulation. Frank's swollen tongue was so large that Lenny could barely hold onto it with gauze, but with some effort he was able to inject diluted adrenalin into its underside.

While Phil compressed Frank's chest, Lenny assembled equipment to help guide a plastic tube into Frank's trachea which would allow him to breathe for Frank. He snapped the laryngoscope together and glanced at Elizabeth who continued to shake and sob profusely while two female patients tried to comfort her. He didn't have time to contemplate the absurdity of their reversed roles.

"OK, Phil, stop compressions. I want you to give him intramuscular adrenalin every 5 minutes until I say stop. Dose is 0.3 cc of 1:1000. Right now I need to intubate him."

Frank's huge tongue bulged out of his mouth as Lenny started probing with the scope. Lenny moved the tongue to the left with the scope's curved blade, then lifted the blade forward and upward at a forty-five degree angle, trying to view Frank's vocal cords; the sentry to the lungs. While he probed Frank's mouth, he began to count out loud as a reminder that he had only a short time to get Frank breathing again to prevent brain damage.

"One, two, five, seven, nine, ten, eleven," He paused and mumbled to himself, indifferent to the presence of patients in the room. "Damn it! I can't see a goddamn thing...Fifteen, sixteen, seventeen, eighteen, nineteen, twenty."

Frustrated and unable to get the tube into Frank's trachea, Lenny replaced the mask over Stevens' mouth and nose and then resumed squeezing the bag while Phil proceeded with chest compressions.

He needed to relieve the airway obstruction and realized the quickest way to accomplish it was by cricothyroidotomy, a procedure in which a hole is created in the upper trachea. He searched the cart for a large bore needle and a scalpel and then recalled he had forgotten to add them to the cart.

He yelled out, "Holly, did you get hold of the ER?"

Holly ran to him. "Doctor there was a problem."

"What!"

"They couldn't leave the ER unmanned... They told me to call 911. I did that and the paramedics should be here soon."

Lenny clenched his teeth tightly. *Shit, how fuckin' stupid is that...The ER that's literally next door, won't respond to this emergency.*

Realizing he still needed to do the cricothyroidotomy, he turned to patients standing around. Several had walked out of the waiting room to huddle in the hallway. The rest formed a circle around Lenny, remaining curious and wanting to help if called upon.

"Does anyone have a pocket knife?"

The patients looked at each other, but no one answered.

Lenny remembered there was a sharp knife in the staff lounge and shouted, "There's a knife in the staff lounge down the hall. It's in a drawer next to the refrigerator. Someone get it, now!" Holly ran to get the knife. Lenny took a deep breath while waiting for her to return, his mind racing, wondering what in the world could have caused Frank's collapse. He had known Frank for several years. They were colleagues and friends, much more than doctor and patient. If the worst happened, what would he tell Denise, Frank's wife?

Holly hurried back to him with the knife. Lenny felt Frank's neck below the Adam's apple for a soft notch pinpointing the cricothyroid membrane. Dark blood gushed out as he began cutting into the skin. Phil reached for gauze from the emergency cart and dabbed away pooling blood, making it easier for Lenny to see. Lenny nodded, acknowledging Phil's help, as he continued to push the knife deeper until it hit resistance. He pushed slowly until he felt the membrane give and air suddenly hissed out under pressure. By widening the incision, Lenny was able to insert the plastic tube into the trachea and then connect it to the ventilation bag. He squeezed the bag several times and for the first time Frank's chest moved unimpeded as his lungs filled with oxygen. The color of his skin instantaneously pinked up.

All at once Frank's arms and legs contracted into a fetal posture and his body started to thrash around. His jaws and teeth clenched together, saliva began frothing from his mouth; all signs that Lenny recognized as a grand mal seizure. As Lenny stood up to fetch tongue blades from the crash cart, sounds of rapid footsteps approached the office signaling the arrival of the paramedics. One of them, apparently the senior member of the team, began asking a series of staccato questions. Lenny filled him in while turning Frank over to his left side and then forced two tongue blades between his tightly clenched teeth.

The senior paramedic yelled orders. "Get an IV started and a tracing," referring to an ECG. "Doctor, I'll take over the breathing end."

"I just did a cricothyroidotomy. His tongue is huge. I couldn't intubate him. It was just impossible. At least he's getting oxygen now."

"OK, fine, we'll take over."

Frank continued to have seizures while the paramedics tore open their packs. Suddenly the spasmodic contractions slowed down and finally halted. The senior paramedic recognized the opportunity. "Let's go... start the IV now! Get the pads on."

One of the paramedics moved quickly to start the IV and withdrew blood into several tubes. He hooked up a bag of saline and glucose fluids, while another paramedic cut away Stevens' shirt and attached ECG pads to his chest. The third took over the chest compressions while the senior paramedic continued ventilation by compressing the bag attached to the endotracheal tube. The paramedic watching the electrocardiogram on a monitor yelled, "OK, we got v-fib!"

The ECG revealed ventricular fibrillation, an abnormal rhythm associated with impending death. The paramedic prepared to defibrillate Stevens with a series of electrical shocks. "Step back. I mean everyone, now!"

The paramedic activated an electrical shock but the ECG did not change. One of the paramedics yelled out, "It's v-fib with v-tach!" a combination of deadly abnormal rhythms. The senior paramedic barked orders to inject several medications into the intravenous line to treat the abnormal heart rhythms.

Over the next few minutes they repeated the series of electric shocks followed by more IV medications. To Lenny's dismay, the rhythm transformed to a flat line. No pulses were palpable and blood pressure was undetectable.

Lenny was the first to acknowledge the obvious. "It's over."

The paramedics continued their maneuvers despite Lenny's comment, but after another few minutes, they simultaneously looked at each other, and nodded in agreement.

With total disbelief, Lenny stared blankly at the patients, some sobbing, others covering their mouths with their hands and a few muttering what sounded like prayers. Lenny bowed his head, as he couldn't fully grasp what had happened.

Frank Stevens, his good friend, was dead.

Chapter Three

LENNY'S LEGS AND back began to cramp after being crouched down for a long time. He got up to stretch and walked over to sit in a chair facing away from his patients. Feeling overwhelmed, he closed his eyes in a vain effort to shut out the horror of what had just happened. He couldn't help wonder if he had done his best. He had treated many others with minor reactions from allergy injections or more severe allergic reactions from other causes, like bee stings, and food or drug reactions, but nothing had come close to the rapid onset and severity of this episode. He kept shaking his head as he thought about the magnitude of Frank's death.

He headed over to the senior paramedic. "I need your help... There's going to be an inquiry. I saw you draw blood from him during the resuscitation. Can you let me have a few tubes? There are tests that may help explain what happened. Also, do you know if the police have been called?"

"Doc, I'm glad to help. I'll call the police and get you some blood tubes."

"Thanks. I need to call the family. I just don't know what I'll say."

The paramedic nodded, and Lenny went to retrieve Frank's chart to get his home number.

He dialed the number slowly, trying to gain clarity on how to explain Frank's death to his wife, Denise. When Lenny joined COADD as its medical director, he and his wife Elaine had become close friends with the Stevens family. Their families celebrated birthdays and holidays together.

The phone rang four times and went to voice mail.

"Hello, this is the home of Frank and Denise Stevens. We'd love to hear from you, but we're currently not available. Please leave a message and the time and we'll call you back. Please make your message brief as possible because life is so short. Thank you and have a great day."

"Denise, it's Lenny Haberman. Please call me. It's important. It's about Frank. Call me back on my cell as soon as you can." He left his cell number and hung up. In an odd way he was relieved that no one was home. His thoughts focused on Denise's disturbing comment: *"Life is so short."*

He paused to look around the waiting room and noticed two female patients sitting next to Elizabeth, trying to comfort her.

"Elizabeth, I need to talk to you. Let's go to my office."

She looked up slowly, holding a bundled Kleenex. Her skin was mottled and flushed with patches of makeup washed away by tears. "Dr. Haberman, I'm so, so sorry. I never thought this would happen. Please forgive me." She sobbed as she squeezed his hands.

Lenny needed to know why she couldn't function during the crisis. It made him wonder if she might have made a mistake, maybe injected the wrong vaccine into Frank. If so, he needed to approach the subject gingerly. "Elizabeth, please... calm down. I'm sure this isn't your fault. We need to figure out what happened."

Elizabeth quietly shook her head. "Dr. Haberman, I need a few minutes." As she stood, Holly took Elizabeth's hand and led her toward the women's restroom in the hallway.

As Elizabeth left, the senior paramedic walked over to Lenny. "Doc, I called the police and they'll be here shortly. Can you sign these forms?"

He perfunctorily signed four sets of triplicate forms and handed them back. "Thanks for all your help. Before you leave, do you have those tubes of blood I asked for?" The paramedic reached into his pack and handed them to him.

A police officer arrived and began questioning the paramedics, who were repacking their equipment. Lenny could overhear parts of the conversation as he read the forms he had just signed.

"When we arrived, the subject was unconscious and experiencing a grand mal seizure. Dr. Haberman had just completed a cricothyroidotomy. We took over but it was too late. Time of death was 18:00."

"OK and the cause of death?"

"Can't say for sure but looks like a reaction from his allergy vaccine."

"Got it. Thanks, guys."

After finishing his notes, the officer walked over to Lenny. Looking up, Lenny saw a towering blur of dark blue with leathery weapons screeching against each other.

"Dr. Haberman, I'm Officer Tyson with the Denver Police. I need to ask you some questions. I'll try to be brief as possible."

Lenny answered a list of personal questions followed by a recount of the incident. After forty-five long minutes, the interview was over and everyone had left, including the paramedics with Frank's body.

He remembered that he still wanted to talk to Elizabeth and realized she hadn't returned. He walked out of the office toward the women's restroom.

"Elizabeth. Are you there?"

There was no answer.

"Elizabeth, I need to talk to you!"

"Is anyone here?" He entered slowly, looked around and under the privacy door to convince himself she was gone.

He walked back out murmuring. "Where the hell did she go?" He felt a mixture of anger and confusion, wondering why she would just walk off and not come back to talk to him. As he entered his office, the phone was ringing.

"Dr. Haberman."

"Doctor, this is your answering service. Mrs. Stevens is returning your call. Shall I patch her through?"

Suddenly his pulse raced and he had to catch his breath. "Yes, go ahead."

"Hello, Lenny ...it's Denise. Are you and Frank planning to go out for a drink? It's perfectly fine with me."

"No, that's not why I'm calling. Denise, I—I need to talk to you about Frank. I'd rather come there."

"What's it about? ...What's the matter?"

"Denise, I really need to talk to you in person. I can come right now... Is that OK?"

"Lenny, what's wrong?"

"Look, ah… this is extremely difficult to discuss on the phone. Is there anyone there with you?"

"Well, my kids are here, but why does that matter?"

"Denise, is there another adult around?"

"No, but Frank should be home soon. Lenny! What's happened? You're scaring me!"

Lenny paused.

"Lenny, are you there? What's going on?"

"Denise, it's about Frank. He—he had a reaction in my office. Denise, I'm so sorry. He died."

"What?!" There was a shrill scream and then silence. "He died? What do you mean he died?"

"He had a reaction after his allergy injection."

He heard more screams and then a thump.

"Denise! Denise!" In the background, he could hear uncontrollable sobs and suddenly the phone went dead. He dialed 911 for assistance and described what had just happened. The 911 operator informed him an ambulance would be dispatched to the Stevens' home immediately.

Realizing he needed to do something to calm down, he went back to the lab, centrifuged the blood given to him by the paramedic and separated off the serum and plasma. He placed the tubes in the freezer and put all the vaccines back into the refrigerator, including Frank Stevens' allergy vaccine. As he closed the refrigerator door, he noticed litter on the floor; crumpled paper and a piece of scrap wire shaped like a ring. He stuck the trash into a side pocket of his jacket, and then walked over to a counter to write a note to the morning nurse:

Jane, please remove the frozen tubes of serum and plasma from the freezer with Dr. Stevens' name and send to the lab for two tests: tryptase and histamine.

Later, as he got out of his car, he realized he couldn't remember leaving his office or driving home.

Chapter Four

AFTER READING THE results of the recent human trial, Jimmy Barone, COADD's chief lab technician, realized that Dr. Stevens had succeeded in developing a very effective treatment (CMV) for cocaine addiction. He left the printout of the results for Frank and decided to leave, feigning a headache. He drove to a coffee shop near COADD and sat pondering his next step. His thoughts returned to a conversation he had with his handler two days ago.

"KC. I'm calling about the experiments. They're positive. They can vaccinate against cocaine."

KC's response was short. "OK, we'll deal with it. Are you able to get the specs?" He was asking if Jimmy could destroy all the specifications for manufacturing the drug.

Jimmy replied, "Sure, I can take care of the ones at COADD. But there's still a problem. I know there's another set outside the lab, and I'll need time to find them."

"You know, Jimmy, here's my advice. You get the specs, yesterday! Someone else will take care of the rest. This can't be another mess-up. Do you get what I mean, Jimmy?"

Jimmy responded, "Sure, I—I understand." A surge of nausea rose into his throat.

"Good. I expect you'll take care of everything for us!"

Jimmy pulled himself out of the anxiety-ridden recall and decided to go back to the lab to finish some work that he had left behind. Everyone was gone so he felt more relaxed not having to talk to anyone, especially Frank. As he was finishing up, his office phone rang. When he answered he recognized the voice of Pete Doren, a friend he had known since his childhood in the Bronx. Pete was now a medical doctor who had moved to Denver to start a private practice.

"Jimbone, my God, where have you been? I didn't think you'd be at work this late. Did you hear about Stevens?"

Jimmy became very still. "No, what are you talking about?"

"Jimbone...did you have anything to do with it?"

"Stop. For Christ's sake Pete, just tell me what going on!"

"Jimbone. Stevens is dead. He died from an allergy shot in Dr. Haberman's office. It's all over the news. I owe you man."

Jimmy paused to think, *My God they took care of it quicker than I had planned.* He needed to get off the phone to get the rest of the specs. "Then you shouldn't have any more problems."

Pete said with enthusiasm, "My problem is solved. I'm moving on, actually have plans for dinner with Jacqueline at Louie's. We're having a special date, so I'm hoping she hasn't heard about Frank yet."

"Look, Pete, I've got to run and finish some work. I'll call you later."

"OK, Jimbone, thanks. You deserve a bonus. I'll wire it to your account."

"Pete, please that's not necessary."

"Still doing it. Remember to call me when you have a minute."

After hearing the news, Jimmy knew that he had to accelerate his plans. He was the only other scientist at COADD who knew the entire manufacturing process. Having planned ahead, he moved quickly, gathering everything Dr. Stevens had on the cocaine trials: written records, computer hard drive, back-up drive and CDs detailing the method of manufacturing CMV. He couldn't find the printout data he had left Dr. Stevens, but decided it wasn't worth worrying about. He figured it would take COADD years, if ever, to get back to square one after all the records had disappeared. As he was leaving, he snapped his fingers. There was still a duplicate set of specs that Frank had told him he kept in a safe place off campus. His exact words were: *"They're stored safely from acts of God."* Jimmy figured they had to be in a lockbox at a bank or in a safe at Frank's home. That meant he had one more important stop to make before leaving town.

Jimmy first went home to pack and then drove over to the Stevens' home. He figured that with any luck he would locate the backup specs. A dozen cars were parked around the lit-up, red brick mansion on 6th Ave Parkway, a neighborhood of past and now renewed, stately prominence. Jimmy had always admired the colonial look that reflected old-money eastern influences that had been so prevalent in prior decades. He rang the bell and high-pitched chimes announced his arrival. An elderly man dressed in a conservative suit opened the door.

"Hi, I'm Jimmy Barone. I worked with Dr. Stevens and want to pay my respects."

The man smiled sadly. "Yes I'm Pastor Anderson." Before he could finish, two small children ran to the door yelling, "It's Uncle Jimmy! Uncle Jimmy's here!" They grabbed his legs, pulling him across the threshold.

"Hey, kids. How ya doing? " He scooped them up for hugs. No matter how hard he tried to avoid it, he had been drawn into the Stevens' family circle. The Stevens knew he was a bachelor and had no family in Denver, so they'd invited him to many family functions.

The kids were laughing and chattering, so he assumed they had not been told of their father's death. Holding their hands, he walked into the living room where a small group of people were talking quietly. He didn't see Denise and no one looked over to greet him so he whispered to the kids,

"Hey, guys, I have to get some work from Dad's office." They ran off and he edged out of the room toward Frank's study where he and Frank had met many times to discuss technical issues on the project.

He knew he had only scant minutes to find the other set of specs. Looking around to make sure no one was close by, he gently closed the door to the office and swiftly moved to Frank's desk and computer. When he jiggled the mouse, he found the files on COADD were already open. *Frank, how nice of you to make this easy,* he thought. *Ok here's a file that says CMV.* As he opened the file, he suddenly heard someone walking down the hallway. In a flash, he knelt down behind the desk and waited, listening attentively. He could hear a gravely male voice talking angrily on a cell phone.

"I'm pissed. Not only me, but Ted will be too if the deal falls through. Tell them we're still buyers, but we want a price adjustment and call me back in the morning." The voice faded as the caller moved away.

Jimmy remained still for a few more moments and then crawled back into the seat. Waking up the computer, he scanned the CMV files. Oddly, he couldn't find any documents that pertained to CMV manufacture. There were extraneous files containing discussions with the board of directors, something about Frank's benefits and stock options, another document dealing with market projections for sale of an effective cocaine vaccine and a file that had something to do with Frank's purchase of a Jeep. Jimmy stopped and smiled as he thought, *That's exactly like Frank. He always mis-filed things, sometimes on purpose.* It made him realize that for security reasons, Frank may have placed the specs in an unrelated file. He decided to search the hard drive and typed in "CMV." An icon of a Sherlock Holmes cartoon-like character popped up with a magnifying glass.

While the computer was searching, Jimmy was acutely aware that he had been there for several minutes. At any second, someone could walk in. He started to rummage around in Frank's desk. He found a cache of CDs and thumb drives, stuck them into his pockets and then moved over to a file cabinet, where he found several pages in a file labeled CMV. He placed the contents in an inside jacket pocket and then peered around the room searching for a safe. None was obvious, so he explored behind books, photographs and a prized oil painting of a Cape Cod sailing vessel. Frank had purchased the painting because it reminded him of happy childhood summers when he learned to sail with his grandparents. Frustrated, Jimmy returned to the computer, where no results had been found from his search.

"Shit, Frank, where's that fuckin' file?" he muttered. In case Frank had hidden the specs with a different nametag, he decided to delete all files by opening a command prompt and entering the command *del* **. Then he realized this would take more time than he had. Taking out a screwdriver he'd brought along for just this purpose, he opened the computer casing and removed the hard drive. Then he unhooked the external backup drive, stuffed them in the side pockets of his jacket and checked for bulges. Quietly he slipped from the room and strolled back into the living room.

He passed an older man whose gruff voice identified him as the person who had been on the cell, talking about some deal. Just then, a middle-aged woman walked over and introduced herself to the older man.

"Mr. Larkin, you may not remember me, but I once bought a house from you when you started your real estate business in Denver."

"Really?" he said as he stood up to shake her hands. "May I ask your name? I'm getting a little forgetful these days."

"Why certainly. I'm Janet Bloom. You may know my husband, Senator Gary Bloom. He's in the Senate with your son, Ted."

"Why, of course. Forgive me for not recognizing you. My son often talks kindly of your husband. Please call me Conrad."

"Thank you, Conrad. I want to express our sincere regrets about your loss. I knew Frank at our church. Just a wonderful person."

"Thank you, Janet. We all agree with that."

Denise was sitting nearby, dabbing her eyes with a handkerchief. She was talking to the minister who'd met Jimmy at the door. Jimmy walked over and put his hand on her shoulder. When she realized it was him, she stood up and gave him a hug. He carefully kept his hips back, keeping the hard drive at a safe distance.

"I'm so sorry, Denise. What can I do to help?"

She didn't answer, just continued to sob on his shoulder.

"Jimmy, why? I can't believe this happened. Why?" She kept asking the same question, waiting for an answer.

"I don't know, Denise. I'm so sorry."

He let her run on for a while longer before he whispered, "Denise, I know this will sound inappropriate, but Sol Feldman just called to ask me to temporarily take charge of the research." He paused as Denise started to shiver. He grabbed her shoulders and gently helped her sit down.

"Denise, I need to find some important papers and disks related to Frank's research. They're technical specifications on a CD or thumb drive. Do you know where they might be? I'm sorry to bring this up, but it's really important."

She looked confused. "Jimmy. I can't think about that now. I don't know anything about them... Frank never shared that kind of thing with me. I'll look later."

Jimmy knew it had been a long shot and the more he thought about it, the more unlikely it was that the CDs and thumb drives he had taken would have the specs. Then it occurred to him *that Frank may have put them in a place that no one else knew about, and now that he was dead, they might never be recovered.* He went out to his car and tossed his jacket with all the records from Frank's office into the back seat. He would just have to assume that the backup specs were lost forever. Once he explained it to the guys, he could still get his reward.

✱ ✱ ✱

He stopped at a gas station to pick up some snacks, threw his wallet on his jacket, turned onto I-70 and drove east toward the Kansas border. Trying to push back guilt feelings about Frank, he muttered, "Well, it was his own fuckin' fault! I tried to stop him, but he would never give up. God damn it!"

After crossing the state line, Jimmy stopped at a rest station and headed for a picnic table around the back to make sure he was alone. He reached into his shirt pocket and took out a small plastic bag of white powder. His habit was well controlled; he only used it for special occasions. He never understood why people were so weak that they abused this magical medicine and could not confine their use to special times like he did. He opened the bag, tapped out two lines on a notepad and quickly snorted them one after the other. The immediate rush buoyed his mood.

He hopped back in the car, invigorated. He yelled out loud, "Life is great!" He smiled about the million dollars that would be wired into his Caribbean account. Then he thought, *It could've been two million, if only I could have sabotaged things, but that damn Johnson CRO made it impossible and now the guys are gonna be angry cause they had to stop Frank.*

The drive to Chicago was going to take several days, so he'd brought along his favorite CDs. He turned the sound up to a deafening level and began to sing along, "I like it, I'm not gonna crack. I miss you, I'm not gonna crack. I love you…"

It was a perfectly clear summer night. He opened his sun roof to view the constellations and bright full moon that whitewashed the road, adding to his exhilaration. He pretended he was snowmobiling through deep powder, swaying the car in rhythm to the tune. He just loved that song, so he leaned over to push the CD player to repeat.

As Jimmy fumbled with the stereo button, a large dark blur appeared out of the corner of his eye. "What the hell…" He reflexively jerked the steering wheel to avoid a huge buck as it collided with the right side of the Subaru. The car tipped and careened over onto the driver's side. The impact knocked Jimmy out, and the car rolled several times before it stopped, lying on the passenger side. Steam rose from the engine while the wheels continued to rotate. Airbags inflated and then deflated immediately. Jimmy was restrained by his seatbelt, hanging down and unconscious.

A semi-trailer roared over the hill and the driver saw the wreckage. He pulled over sharply and ran to see if he could help. He climbed up onto the car to peer through the driver's window. The person inside was unresponsive to his repeated yelling and pounding on the car. He tried to open the door, but it was locked. The strong odor of gas permeated the air. Knowing the car could explode any minute, he kicked on the window with the back of his shoe but the window merely cracked. He found a fist-sized rock and pounded out the window. Reaching in he managed to unlock the door along with the seatbelt and with incredible strength, grabbed Jimmy under his head and arms and pulled him out. He was able to carry Jimmy from the wreckage and laid him down gently on his back. Fortunately, he knew enough first aid to put pressure on the bleeding. The only other first aid he could offer was the Lord's Prayer.

As the truck driver dialed 911, Jimmy's car exploded, billowing black acrid smoke into the clear night sky.

Police, ambulances and firefighters arrived shortly. They sprayed retardant on the remains of the vehicle. Incinerated auto parts and contents were scattered for hundreds of yards. Even the license plates were destroyed and they found no identification on Jimmy.

He was taken by ambulance to the local hospital, where the ER doctor recognized he would require multi-specialty trauma expertise. He placed a call to Denver Memorial Hospital, recognized as the best tertiary trauma center in the Rocky Mountain region. The chief surgical resident received the call.

"This is Dr. Patterson."

"Hi, Steve Bronson here. I'm the ER doc at Burlington. Got a real bad one here."

"OK."

"For starters, the guy's about 30 without ID, brought in an hour ago from a car accident on I-70. Car hit a deer. He was pulled out of the wreck by a truck driver who saved his life before the vehicle exploded. He's in hemorrhagic shock. Already received four units along with Ringers to keep his BP from falling through the floor." He paused. "He's in coma, on a ventilator, has a left hemopneumothorax with a chest tube draining pure blood, slightly distended abdomen with bowel sounds but no air in the abdomen based on a CT and no red cells in urine. There are open fractures of left humerus and left tibia and a closed fracture of the right radius. We've slowed the bleeding with splints and compression dressings. CT of the skull and spine show no fractures, but I suspect there's brain swelling, so I started decadron just in case. In my judgment, he's unlikely to survive unless we get him to you guys."

"Got it. We'll accept him. I'll send a helicopter ASAP."

"Thanks. Appreciate the help."

Still unconscious, Jimmy was soon loaded up in the life flight helicopter and unwittingly returned to Denver.

Chapter Five

LENNY WALKED INTO his living room and found his wife, Elaine, reading. She waited for his customary kiss, but looked up when Lenny didn't approach her. He was staring at her with a look on his face she had seen only one other time when he'd told her that her mother had suddenly died of a heart attack. Elaine had never forgotten that look. She stood and embraced him for several minutes. Her instincts told her something was seriously wrong. Finally, he spoke.

"Honey, Frank Stevens died in my office today from a reaction to an allergy shot."

Elaine pulled back, gripping both of his arms. "What?"

"I just can't understand it! He was on his regular dose and never had a problem with it. Elizabeth gave him the shot and within minutes he was convulsing violently, like nothing I've ever seen. I tried everything, but nothing worked. Paramedics tried too, but we just couldn't reverse it. It was horrible."

Elaine pulled him down onto the couch, holding his arms tightly. She began to cry as the impact of what he told her sank in.

"Elizabeth was a wreck. She fell apart and couldn't do anything." He paused and turned away from Elaine to contain the anger that was building inside of him. Then he turned back and went on. "I'm not sure what the hell was wrong with her. I needed to talk to her afterward, but she just disappeared. I have to call her."

"Lenny, maybe you should wait until tomorrow. She must be upset."

"I know you're right, but I feel I should do something, talk to Elizabeth to figure out what happened...And poor Denise. She's our friend, Elaine!"

"Lenny, please. Listen to me. Take a hot shower and think this through. You have to talk to Walt." She was referring to his partner. "And you should notify your insurance company before you do anything."

He pulled away, feeling calmer, knowing Elaine's advice was usually correct. She had been raised in Iowa and in his experience, Mid-westerners had a lock on common sense.

After cleaning up, Lenny decided to follow his wife's advice and placed a call to his insurance carrier. He left a message about an emergency and requested someone call him at his home. He doubted anyone would be available after hours, but just as he was about to make a drink for himself, the phone rang.

"Hello, I'm Colette Andrews with Rocky Mountain Malpractice Insurance."

"Ms. Andrews, thanks for calling right back. I have some bad news. A patient died in my office this afternoon."

When he finished detailing the incident, she advised writing everything down and placing his notes in a file separate from Dr. Stevens' chart. She promised to call him back in the morning with further information.

Vodka martini in hand, Lenny went to the living room and flipped on the TV. The early evening news on Channel 15 had been on for ten minutes, so he wasn't sure if he'd missed a report on Frank's death. Elaine came in to sit next to him, placing an arm around his shoulders. They remained silent as they listened to a female newscaster talk about forest fires and national news highlights. Nothing was mentioned about Frank Stevens. Then, just as he started to relax, the anchor announced a breaking news story and cut to an attractive reporter.

"This is Margaret Jensen reporting some very sad news… the sudden death of Dr. Frank Stevens, a prominent Denver researcher who was recognized internationally for his efforts to develop a vaccine to control cocaine addiction. Dr. Stevens was director of research at COADD, a start-up biotech company in Denver dedicated to developing therapies and vaccines to control drug addictions. He died unexpectedly in the office of his physician, Dr. Leonard Haberman, a Denver allergist. According to another patient who was present at the time, Dr. Stevens collapsed and died after receiving a routine allergy shot. The cause of death will be investigated by the medical examiner's office, which had no comment at this time."

When the anchor finished with a few more comments, Lenny groaned. "Elaine, this is just the beginning. I need to give Walt a head's up."

He pulled out his cell phone and dialed his partner.

"Walt, it's Lenny. Have you heard the terrible news?"

"No, what happened?"

"Frank Stevens died this afternoon in the office."

"What? My God, what happened?"

Lenny went on to describe the events, including Elizabeth's hysteria, her inability to help and then her disappearance.

"Lenny, what can I do to help?"

"Nothing right now. I need to talk to Elizabeth, but the malpractice rep advised against it until I talk to the attorney."

"Best to take their advice," Walt said crisply.

He finished the call and Elaine asked if he wanted dinner.

"Oh honey, I can't think of food right now. I just need to clear my head. I'm going to take a walk." When troubled, Lenny had two outlets: walking by himself or going to the target range. While serving in the army, he had become a competitive member of the U.S. Army Marksmanship Unit.

After his discharge he had continued to practice and compete, a great stress reliever. It was too late to go to the range now, so he decided to take a walk. He had discovered during walks that if he purposely didn't think about a problem, a solution might spontaneously pop into his head. It worked frequently when he had writer's block with scientific manuscripts, so he applied this approach to other vexing problems.

The walk covered familiar terrain, an illuminated park that even in the early evening hours attracted runners and dog walkers. As he walked, Lenny's mind opened up. *Maybe Frank was having asthma symptoms, didn't say anything about it and when he got the shot it caused the reaction... Or had he started a medication that made his asthma worse or caused hives and swelling? Or maybe he stopped his regular asthma meds. Maybe that made him susceptible too.* He needed to check out these possibilities, so he decided to cut short his walk, and returned home to make some notes.

When he returned, Lenny remembered to call his son, Jack. He needed to speak to Jack before the news spread, anticipating that Jack would be extremely upset. After Lenny's divorce from Jack's mother, Frank Stevens had become the most important person in Jack's life: his mentor, advisor and confidant. Lenny realized he had been displaced, but he was pleased that Jack connected with Frank. There was no answer at Jack's, so he left a message for him to call back as soon as possible.

By then it was time for the late-night news, so he turned on the TV for any report on Frank's death. This time the same news anchor began with the major story of the day: Stevens' death. Part of the report was identical to the earlier one, but the anchor mentioned they were going LIVE to an interview with Senator Ted Larkin, Colorado Senate Majority Leader, who wanted to make a statement about Dr. Stevens' death.

"Good evening, Senator. First, I would like to express our sincere condolences to you and your family for the untimely death of your brother-in-law, Dr. Frank Stevens."

"Thank you, Margaret. I appreciate this opportunity to say a few words for my family."

"Go ahead, sir."

"We have been overwhelmed with phone calls and e-mails from friends, press, and fellow Coloradans. The support has been tremendous, especially for my sister and her children. I want to thank everyone who expressed their condolences. On behalf of my sister and our family, I would like to ask everyone to understand our need for privacy at this very difficult time. I know everyone will respect our request."

"Thank you, Senator, we absolutely understand."

"I have one other comment. Dr. Stevens devoted his life to developing a vaccine to reduce dependency on cocaine. We don't want his life to be lost in vain. I promise all my constituents and the people of Colorado that we will investigate the circumstances of his death. Thank you and God bless."

When Larkin finished, Lenny turned to Elaine. "My God, Senator Ted Larkin. I forgot he's Denise's brother. That can't be good news for me."

Elaine tried to change the subject, but Lenny indicated he needed more time alone. She left to get ready for bed. He walked over to pour himself a shot of brandy, a reasonable excess given the circumstances. As he began to mull over the day's events, a vivid memory that he'd tried to forget sprang into his mind. During Desert Storm he had endured the loss of another close friend, Billy, a medic.

"Doc, Doc...over there, do you see them?" Billy pointed at three Iraqi soldiers staggering as they ran in the sun-scorched desert toward their Huey, which was closing in and hovering over them.

"OK, I see them. Lower down and start dropping out MREs' and water."

Billy opened the door, causing papers and debris to swirl around as heated air rushed inside the cabin. As the pilot began the descent, Billy climbed out on one of the skids to throw out the meals and water bottles. Suddenly Billy noticed one of the soldiers running closer with a hand behind his back.

"Doc, look, he's holding something behind his back! It's a grenade! Do you see it?"

Lenny shouted into his headset, "Abort! Abort! At the same time he pulled out his 9mm Beretta. "Get the hell out now—now!" He reached for Billy's hand to pull him inside the cabin just as the helicopter made a sudden lurch forward and up. Realizing they were still vulnerable if a grenade was thrown, Lenny fired three rapid rounds, hitting the Iraqi in his arm and giving them time to gain enough altitude to avoid the blast zone. The Iraqi soldier fell, followed by a loud explosion.

"Doc, you stopped him. Oh my God, his legs are gone!"

As they ascended they watched the other two Iraqis surround their comrade. One of them held up a white flag to surrender, while the other waved, appealing for help.

Lenny responded. "OK, let's be very careful guys. Hover over them one more time. We may be able to save that guy's life, even if he doesn't deserve it."

The pilots nodded, and just as they brought the Huey down, Billy suddenly fell over into Lenny's lap with bright red blood bursting out of his chest.

"Pull out, pull out! Billy's been hit! Someone shot him... a sniper. Get the hell out, now!"

The words *pull out* snapped Lenny out of the recall, but the association was clear: deep guilt for the deaths of two friends.

If I hadn't directed the Huey back over, Billy would be alive today. Then he recalled his meeting with Billy's parents. He'd gotten a furlough. It wasn't something he had to do; but he knew it would be important for the family and for him. Billy's mom and dad were wonderful, describing letters and e-mails they'd received from Billy saying how Lenny had been a great support to him, training him with kindness and patience, and how Lenny made a difference with injured members of his unit. Billy's parents comforted Lenny with compassion he had never imagined. Their support allowed him to put recurring what-ifs to rest. Lenny was able to move on with his life but only with a scarred memory that would never completely leave. But now he knew this horrible loss of another friend could set him up for more of the same.

After another shot of brandy, he crawled into bed with Elaine, who pretended to be fast asleep, knowing this wasn't the time to reengage about the day's events. Lenny gazed at the ceiling and somehow fell asleep.

Chapter Six

PETE DOREN FINISHED his chicken marsala with a fresh Caesar salad, both a specialty of Rizzuto's restaurant. What made the dinner most enjoyable was being seen with his exquisite wife, Jacqueline. As they passed on the way to their table, other diners assumed that she had to be an actress or a famous model. Occasionally Pete had to shake his head in disbelief that he was married to this extraordinary beauty. All he had to do was invite influential doctors and VIPs for dinners and parties, and the results were startling. The invited docs would regularly refer to his practice.

At first glance they'd appeared to be incongruous. At forty-five, Pete seemed older by ten or fifteen years, although Jacqueline was actually only five years younger. The age difference was made more noticeable by his premature balding and black frame glasses with thick lenses. Some gossiped about what could possibly attract her to him, and the general conclusion was it had to be money. He smiled to himself, knowing they were right, as he eyed her Prada bag and Jimmy Choo heels. He knew what turned Jacqueline on; money and status, and he had boatloads of both. And now he was rid of his past annoyance, Frank Stevens. He wondered when he should tell Jacqueline and decided not to waste this great evening until they were home.

After they finished dinner and paid the bill, Pete walked slowly behind her with his hand on her back, enjoying the envious glances. When they departed from the restaurant, he whispered to himself the famous line of Mel Brooks, *"It's good to be the king."* It had been a great day. In his new metallic green Mercedes Benz CL 550 coupe, he turned on the CD player and sang along to James Brown bellowing "I Feel Good." Jacqueline got in the mood too and sang along with him.

Every evening they watched the news and Pete thought that would be the best time for Jacqueline to discover what had happened to Frank. That way he could act supportive. When they returned home, he turned on the gas fireplace and TV while sipping a single malt scotch. Jacqueline snuggled into his arms as they waited for the ten o'clock news and chatted about the day. The death of Dr. Frank Stevens was the lead story,

Pete stood up, pretending to be shocked, spilling some of his drink on his shirt. Simultaneously, Jacqueline gasped and grabbed the coffee table in front of her for support. Starting to sob, she stood and ran into the nearest bathroom.

Pete's thoughts were mixed with elation and immense satisfaction. His horoscope had indeed been correct when it had predicted this day would be exceptional. He felt personally vindicated that his wife's lover had been eliminated and the blame would fall on his professional nemesis, Lenny Haberman. He reminded himself to wire a bonus to Jimmy the next morning.

Feeling satisfied and content, Pete stared at the flames in the fireplace.

The affair had started when he'd invited Stevens and his wife to one of their Christmas parties, along with influential well-connected society notables, and an artistic group Jacqueline knew from her philanthropic work at the Denver Museum of Fine Arts. Although Pete had never met Stevens, his name was suggested by a previous guest, Sol Feldman, who told him Stevens was one of the most gifted scientists in the region and was working on a breakthrough vaccine that could control cocaine addiction. Pete also learned from another source that Stevens' wife was the sister of Senator Ted Larkin, the Colorado Senate Majority Leader, so the senator and his wife were also added to the invitation list.

The Stevens integrated quickly at the party and were surrounded by many guests who found them interesting conversationalists. Little did Pete realize that Dr. Frank Stevens was particularly interesting to his wife. For months after the party, Jacqueline was glowing not just at parties, but also in her everyday life. Pete responded to her happiness with demonstrative gifts, thinking he had to be the luckiest guy on earth marrying a woman who had five star ratings in all categories. To outsiders, they appeared to be a happily married, perfect couple.

Then one day three years ago, a friend told him he had seen Jacqueline at a movie theater downtown with a good-looking man. His friend first thought that perhaps they were just casual friends, but as the theater darkened it became obvious they were a lot more than that. Pete was shaken. He hired a private investigator, who brought back intimate photographs of his wife with the man whom he recognized as Frank Stevens.

There was no way he was going to lose Jacqueline. He decided to intervene the same day. Pete loved catching people off guard, and this was the perfect situation to apply the tactic, thinking the shock effect would cause her to confess. After a quiet dinner he steered her to the living room and poured her favorite after-dinner drink.

"Sweetheart, we're so lucky to have each other," he said.

Jacqueline responded. "I'm so grateful we found each other too. Just think how fate works. If I hadn't had that appendix attack, we would have never met each other."

He couldn't have imagined a better introduction to what he was about to say. "Fate's really interesting. Out of nowhere it decides to visit. I like to think of it as a person, like someone who sits back to watch vicariously, just to see what happens next." He paused to hug her. "You know, if fate brings adversity, some people can ultimately benefit from it. But for others it can lead to disastrous results. It can destroy relationships, even marriages."

She smiled, "Honey, let's never let that happen to us," and then she kissed him.

"You know, Jacqueline, I agree with that. So I hope what I'm about to show you will benefit both of us."

She looked at him quizzically, not sure what he meant.

He reached into his shirt pocket and without further comment, he carefully placed the photographs on the coffee table. She reached for them slowly, gasped, and abruptly ran up to their bedroom. He left her alone for a while and then walked in. She tearfully confessed, swearing the affair was short-lived and had ended. He also decided to inform Denise Stevens about the affair, hoping she would exert added pressure on Frank to be sure the affair was over.

Pete kept the private investigator on his payroll to watch Jacqueline closely. She resumed her busy social schedule and hosted parties, which continued to make him happy and wealthy. Over the next few years, the P.I. found no trace of infidelity. It was as if the affair had never happened.

One evening, while she was out of the house, Pete was paying bills and ran out of blank checks. While searching for some more in Jacqueline's desk, he discovered a small drawer hidden behind a framed picture of the two of them vacationing in Buenos Aires. In the drawer, he found a letter written in Frank Steven's handwriting. Until Pete read the letter, he had no idea of the depth of their love affair. He copied the letter, and read it periodically, which reinforced his bitterness toward Frank.

The rage he felt continued unabated until he finally decided to do something about it. He contacted an old friend, Jimmy Barone, who he had known since his childhood. Jimmy was connected so he decided to tip him off about cocaine vaccine research at a company called COADD. Jimmy was intrigued because his family received large revenues from cocaine, and would want to stop development of an effective vaccine. Pete explained he needed to get rid of Stevens because of an affair Stevens had had with his wife. He emphasized he wanted Stevens out of Denver and explained he hoped Jimmy could sabotage the research. Lack of results could get Stevens fired and then he'd have to move to another city for employment. Jimmy agreed and relocated to Denver where he was hired at COADD as the principal laboratory technician.

Now that Stevens was literally gone, Pete's elation made him pull the letter out and read it one more time.

Dear Jacqueline:

I know there is no way for us to be together, but I wanted you to know that you have touched me in ways no other woman has ever done. I remember the first time we saw each other. It was as if we were the only two present in a room filled with a hundred people. We tried to ignore realities as we found moments to enjoy together. I treasure the times we had and wish we could have found each other earlier in our lives. I know I will always consider you the love of my life.

Love,
Frank

He read it slowly, enjoying the knowledge that Frank was no longer a threat to his perfect life. Then he tossed it into the fireplace, smiling broadly, as he watched the ashes rise up the chimney. The love of his wife's life had just floated away in smoke.

Jacqueline's emotional reaction to the news of Frank's death infuriated Pete, but he decided to say nothing about it. He only hoped it would not become an issue again. Having made that decision, he confidently walked up the stairs to comfort his most cherished asset, his beautiful wife.

Chapter Seven

AFTER SHE READ the morning headlines, Elaine's first impulse was to hide the paper but she realized Lenny needed to know everything. The storyline was similar to the television reports, but with a new twist. It mentioned that Denise Stevens was the daughter of Conrad Larkin, an affluent and influential real estate developer. Denise's brother, Colorado Senate Majority Leader Ted Larkin, said the family was in a state of shock and would demand a thorough investigation into the death of Dr. Stevens.

Lenny sighed, "Larkin's already turning on the pressure. I'm sure this'll mean going after a huge malpractice award."

Before he left, Elaine gave him a hug, but Lenny pulled away quickly, not wanting her to recognize the stress he was feeling. Even in that fleeting moment of contact, though, he knew she detected the tightness in his body.

Lenny arrived early at his office but three patients were already waiting at the door. A Hispanic male reporter in his early thirties was holding a microphone while talking to his TV cameraman for Channel 15 News.

When Lenny approached his office, the reporter pushed in front of the patients and began peppering him with questions.

"Doctor, would you tell us what happened?"

The video light was blinding Lenny, but he stuck to what his malpractice insurance agent had told him to say. "I have no comment."

"But Doctor, please, just a short explanation of what happened."

"I told you, no comment." He turned away from the reporter, unlocked the door, ushered in the patients and relocked the door.

"Please, everyone, just take a seat. My staff will be in shortly. I'm sorry for the disturbance."

Without waiting for their response, Lenny walked into the back to his office, shut the door, and sat down, trying to calm himself.

When he saw the bank of telephone lights turn on, he knew his staff had arrived. He straightened his tie, took a deep breath and walked into the front office where his staff stood quietly talking to each other. They turned when Lenny walked in, and nodded greetings. His office manager, Annette White, and his nurse, Jane Cross, had worked in his office since he opened his practice. Although they were not related, patients often mistook them for each other. They were both in their late-fifties, with short brunette hair and brown eyes. Holly Brown, the receptionist, had just joined the staff a couple of months earlier. She was twenty-seven and petite, with youthful energy.

They were clearly nervous and unsure of what to say. Lenny asked them to come into his office and shut the door. They all sat, each woman on the edge of her chair.

He turned first to Holly, "You were there, so you know what happened yesterday."

She nodded.

"I assume the rest of you know too."

Jane answered, "Yes and we all feel so horrible about it. I wish I'd been there to help, but I wasn't feeling well."

"I know Jane, that's OK. The way it worked out, I'm not sure anything would have made a difference. Look, I need to ask all of you not to talk about this to anyone. By that I mean no one…not patients, press and your families. It's really important because of the legal liability issue." They nodded again.

"I'm sorry if I appear distracted today. Don't take it personally," he continued.

Annette responded, "Doctor, we understand and we'll do all we can." The others nodded in agreement.

"Thanks. I'll need you to call patients and reschedule them for next week. One other thing…I plan to continue allergy injections."

A surprised look appeared on their faces as Lenny went on. "I want you to take each patient into an examination room before their allergy injection so I can talk to them. They may be upset and have questions, and I want time with each of them."

They nodded in unison.

"Just one point, in case you're asked by a patient. What happened is very rare and has never occurred in my practice, but we need to remind patients of important precautions."

Jane knew he was referring to standard precautions explained to patients before starting allergy injections. No patient should get an allergy injection if they had a cold, fever, wheezing, or had just exercised. Patients had to be reminded to report any new medication. And most important, they had to remain in the office for observation after an injection.

Lenny asked if Elizabeth had called. Holly and Jane looked at each other and shook their heads.

"Holly, you left with her. What happened?"

"I took her into the bathroom and left. I came back to calm the patients and walked out with them sometime before the paramedics finished."

"Did Elizabeth say anything to you before you left?"

"No, not that I can recall."

"Jane, can you call Elizabeth? If you don't reach her at home, call her relatives and friends. Try to find her." Jane nodded.

"Finally, please screen my calls. I only want to talk to my family, Elizabeth, Dr. Oliphant, my malpractice insurance and Sol Feldman from COADD. Just take messages from anyone else."

Once they all left, Lenny found a legal pad and started making notes of what he remembered about the incident. On a fresh page he made a list of questions that needed answers. He started when he entered the room and found Frank unconscious on the floor. He listed all the resuscitative measures he'd tried that ultimately failed. He couldn't keep his thoughts from turning to issues that might become legal ones, like not having a large bore needle or a scalpel on his emergency cart to open Frank's airway and why the ER couldn't come to his office for an emergency. He then remembered reading a recent hospital newsletter that the ER couldn't send an emergency team into the office building because it would leave them at potential legal risk if they were understaffed to handle other emergencies. He thought, *Another example of medical liability bullshit that's suffocating the medical profession. Could the delay have resulted in Frank's death?*

The more Lenny thought about his resuscitative procedure, the more comfortable he felt, especially since he had recently passed the Advanced Cardiac Life Support course that certified his ability to handle common medical emergencies. Still he had many questions that needed to be answered and he jotted them down:

- *Could Elizabeth have given a wrong dose or even the wrong vaccine to Frank?*
- *Was Frank wheezing before he received the injection?*
- *Did he have a reaction from his last dose that wasn't recorded?*
- *Did he run into the office or was he overheated before getting the injection?*
- *Did he have other medical conditions that might have affected the outcome?*
- *Did he start any new medications for other conditions?*
- *Why was the reaction so fast and severe???*

Lenny knew it was exceedingly rare for patients to have a fatal reaction from allergy shots. He was aware of recent surveillance data compiled by his academy indicating there were no fatalities associated with allergy injections over the past four years. Prior to that period, rare fatalities occurred mainly from giving an incorrect dose of vaccine. His office had the most advanced system to prevent shot reactions. They used a program with barcodes on a personalized card and vaccine vials which identified patients with their photograph. It assured the correct vaccine vial was selected for each patient, listed dates of prior doses, recorded any changes in medications, pertinent medical issues or reactions, and indicated the next dose to be administered. If a reaction to prior injections was entered, the system warned to repeat or lower the dose. It also tracked how long patients remained under observation; a key issue for surveillance of early signs of anaphylaxis that could require immediate treatment. All of this corroboration helped eliminate the chance of giving an incorrect dose or the wrong vaccine to a patient; a fail-safe system that he was glad he had in place. Despite the built-in safety of the software, Lenny knew there was no such thing as a one hundred percent fail-safe system in medicine.

Extremely bothered that this had happened to his friend, he decided to spend the day reviewing Frank's chart and injection records. Frank's original history indicated that he'd experienced chronic nasal congestion and intermittent asthma since childhood. His asthma symptoms occurred more frequently during the summer and with exercise. During childhood, Frank's asthma was frequently treated with oral steroids and an older drug, theophylline. He was hospitalized for asthma at age thirteen, requiring an overnight stay but not intensive care treatment. He'd also been hospitalized for injuries resulting from an automobile accident in his twenties. Frank had a history of sulfonamide drug sensitivity that had caused hives during treatment for a urinary tract infection. Occasionally he experienced lip swelling for unknown reasons. His previous allergist thought it was caused by oral allergy syndrome. That meant he could have developed food allergies from being sensitized by pollens. A series of diagnostic blood tests indicated he was allergic to celery, apples, pears, almonds, peaches, peanuts and walnuts. He was advised to avoid these foods and prescribed an emergency self-administration adrenalin kit to be used in the event he inadvertently ate one of those foods.

Lenny made a note to ask the medical examiner to check Frank's stomach contents and his clothing, just in case he might have accidentally eaten one of the foods he needed to avoid. Frank had some other notable medical problems, such as treatment with Imitrex for migraine headaches and an early cataract in his left eye, probably a side effect from past steroid treatments for asthma. Lenny specifically searched for mention of chronic recurring nasal polyps, chronic sinusitis, and asthma, which together were occasionally associated with aspirin or ibuprofen sensitivity that could trigger life threatening asthma. Although there was no indication Frank exhibited this rare type of asthma, he made a note to find out if Frank had taken one of these medications before he received the allergy injection.

Frank's list of current medications included an inhaled steroid for control of asthma, an albuterol inhaler for asthma flare-ups, and allergy injections for pollen sensitivities. His last physical examination six months ago was normal, except for being forty pounds overweight. Allergy skin tests indicated high sensitivity to multiple pollen allergens that plagued him in the spring and late summer. Aside from his pollen sensitivity, nothing in the chart categorized Frank as being high risk for allergy injections. Mostly, Lenny was relieved that Frank's asthma was not rated as severe, based on symptom assessment scores and breathing tests. If his asthma had been severe, it would have meant Frank should not have been on allergy injections.

Lenny then reviewed the allergy injection record. Frank had been tolerating the allergy injections without localized swellings or serious reactions. He had remained on a regular maintenance injection schedule every two weeks and was a compliant patient who always remained in the office for the required observation time following his injections.

Next, Lenny added up the volume of injections administered to Frank based on the allergy injection records. It totaled 2.7 cc, which should have left 2.3 cc in the vial that had an original volume of 5.0 cc. He walked into the lab, pulled Frank's vial from the refrigerator and filled an empty vial with 2.3 cc of water. Strangely, when he compared the vials, it was apparent Frank's vial had less volume than 2.3 cc. He grabbed an empty vial, added water to the vial with a syringe until the level was visibly equivalent to the level in Frank's vial. The total volume equaled 1.2 cc. Frank's vial had 1.1 cc less vaccine than it should have, based on his calculations from the allergy injection records. He stopped to think, *That's weird.*

An ugly thought raced through his head. *Did Elizabeth accidently give him a larger dose of vaccine? Shit, did that cause the reaction? Could that explain Elizabeth's bizarre behavior during the crisis?*

Finishing up, he placed all the vials in the refrigerator and took his written notes to his office to file.

Jane Cross knocked on his door to announce that Colette Andrews, the woman from his malpractice insurance company, had arrived. Having never met her, Lenny had imagined a commanding corporate type, so he was surprised to meet an attractive, charming young woman in her early thirties, wearing a white blouse with visible cleavage and a tight black skirt accentuating her athletic figure.

"Dr. Haberman, I'm sorry to meet you under these circumstances."

"Thanks for coming. I've never had an experience like this, so I appreciate your help. Have a seat."

Seeking her assistance seemed a little odd to Lenny, since he had nearly twenty plus years of medical experience and she was by her youthful appearance, a relative newcomer to the medical field.

"Have you spoken to anyone about Dr. Stevens' death?"

"I talked to the police, but it was very brief. There are some things you need to know." He went on to describe the volume discrepancy in Stevens' vial, and his suspicion that his nurse may have administered a dose that was larger than prescribed. "It could explain the severe reaction. I've tried to reach her numerous times, but she doesn't answer."

"Have you mentioned this to anyone?"

"No I haven't."

"All right, keep your notes in a private folder, and don't make it available to anyone unless you talk to me or your attorney. His name is Mark Persons, a trial lawyer with fifteen years of experience in malpractice litigation. Here's a card with his phone number."

"OK. I have a question. Do you think it's all right for me to attend Frank's funeral and speak to his wife? Just so you know, we were good friends, so this is really tough."

"That's a good question to ask Mark. Give him a call and meet with him as soon as you can. Here's my card with my cell and e-mail. I'm available anytime. Now just to prepare you, I expect you'll be hearing from someone representing the Stevens' family, and when you do, just tell them to contact me or Mark. Don't get into any conversation or offer any information. They may try to provoke you, maybe get you to admit something they can use against you."

After she left, Lenny thought again about calling Denise or dropping over to see her. After a brief mental debate with himself, he decided to take Collette's advice and placed a call to Mark Persons' office to set up an appointment for the next day.

Chapter Eight

SOL FELDMAN, CEO and president of COADD, sat down to preside over the emergency board meeting he had called. As he waited for everyone to settle in, he thought back to the previous evening. He had been enjoying a biography on Winston Churchill until he received a phone call from Ole Bettman, vice-president of COADD.

"Sol, Ole here. I have some horrible news about Frank Stevens. He's dead!"

"What? What did you s-s-say?" He had been sipping a vodka martini at the time and suddenly experienced a choking episode.

"Are you OK, Sol?"

"Yes, yes...wait." Finally he was able to talk. *"Ole, what happened?"*

"He died from an allergy shot given in Lenny's office."

"My God, how horrible!"

Someone coughed, snapping Sol back to the present. He realized everyone had arrived and now they were waiting for him to start. All members of the COADD board were present except Lenny Haberman. Others present included Ole Bettman, Albert Case of Johnson CRO, the organization that oversaw their research, three major investors, and Beth Cohn who had worked with Frank for several years on the project. Ole had tried to contact Jimmy Barone, the chief lab technician, but couldn't reach him.

Sol took charge of the meeting. He was in his early sixties with thin gray hair and wore vintage thin framed glasses. An uncomfortable arthritic posture had his head and neck fixed in a forward arch. "Does anyone know where Jimmy Barone is?"

Everyone looked around and shook their heads.

Ole spoke. "I sent him a high priority e-mail but he never responded."

"OK, let's just go on without him."

Sol brought everyone up to date on Frank's death. He had called Mrs. Stevens to express condolences from COADD. She was unavailable, but her brother, Senator Larkin, filled him on the details.

"It appears Frank had a severe reaction to an allergy injection. Unfortunately, his death occurred in Lenny Haberman's office. As most of you know they were very close friends. I called Lenny to see how he was doing, and as you might imagine, he's in a lot of pain over this, so I excused him from the meeting."

Sol resumed, "Lenny doesn't understand how or why it happened. All he said was that it's extremely rare. He quoted some statistics on fatal allergy shot reactions. It's so rare, there's less probability of it happening than being hit by lightning or a meteor."

Sol let that sink in and then continued. "I'm planning to attend Frank's funeral, and I'd encourage employees to be there to show COADD's support to his family." He stopped to drink water when he suddenly realized that his priorities were wrong. He then asked everyone to take a minute of silence for Frank.

After a moment, he resumed. "We all need to pull together through this tragedy. Frank would've wanted that for sure. Does anyone have anything to add before we continue?"

Ole raised his hand. "How about starting a research scholarship in Frank's name? It could be with his alma mater, and we could contribute to get it off the ground."

"That's a great thought, Ole. Will you call the university and coordinate with them? I'll talk with our corporate attorneys to see how it can be done."

Everyone supported the idea and the motion was officially approved.

"Unfortunately, we have to take care of business. Can someone bring us up to date on the project?" He looked over at Albert Case and asked, "Are results in on the recent trials?"

Albert Case, was the assistant manager of Johnson Clinical Research Organization (CRO), and was in charge of the CMV research project with COADD. At six foot three he had the look of an absentminded professor with gray hair, black overgrown eyebrows, and small eyeglasses on the end of his nose. He wore a dark blue shirt with black pinstripes, yellow bow tie, and fire engine red suspenders.

The CRO was located in Denver and had monitored COADD's study according to Food and Drug Administration (FDA) guidelines. Its mission was to ensure high ethical standards for the study. They secured the study drugs at their headquarters across town, contracted to supervise administration of the study medications in two local drug dependency clinics, and analyzed the clinical data.

Case spoke. "Mr. Feldman, I brought a printout of the latest results from the cocaine vaccine trials. He paused, obviously trying to control his excitement. "I don't want to appear inappropriate at this time of mourning, but I reviewed the data early this morning and the results are incredible. I believe you have a winner! At the highest dose of CMV, there's an astonishing reduction both in cocaine addiction and blood concentrations of cocaine."

Everyone sat up with total focus on Albert.

Sol asked. "Albert, are you absolutely sure of those conclusions?"

"Sir, statistical analysis of the data is very convincing. I believe you'll be able to proceed to the next phase with the FDA."

He was referring to the FDA process for new drug approval. The next trial would study the efficacy and safety of CMV in a larger population of patients. Once all the trial phases were concluded, the company could then submit a new drug application to the FDA for approval to market the vaccine.

The board members had a flurry of questions seeking confirmation that the data was valid. Sol assumed control of the discussion.

"These results should attract interest from a venture capital group, and gather lots of interest from big pharma. Beth, you worked closely with Frank. Do you have access to the formulations and manufacturing details?"

Beth Cohn was a Ph.D. in immunology, in her mid-forties, small in stature, with a gaunt runner's physique. She stood to answer.

"Sir, unfortunately I was never permitted access to the CMV formulations. Frank kept it locked up on his computer. He was always very concerned about security," she noted. "That made sense but I never understood why I wasn't permitted access, even though I was involved in the vaccine development."

"Beth, do you or does anyone know the password to that information?"

"I don't, but maybe Jimmy Barone does. Frank confided mostly in him."

Sol sat back thinking, while other members waited to see what he would do. "OK, I'll get IT involved and find out how this information can be retrieved from Frank's computer. Ole, find Jimmy and set up a meeting as soon as possible. Let's adjourn and, everyone, be available for another meeting on short notice."

Sol entered his private office wondering why Frank had locked up the specifications and kept them from Beth. He called the IT department and asked the manager to meet him in Frank's office. They arrived at the same time.

"Thanks for coming, Richard. Here's the problem." Sol brought him up to date on his need to access Frank's computer to obtain the manufacturing specs.

"Let me take a look." The IT tech tried turning on the computer but nothing happened. He made sure everything was plugged in and when nothing worked, he started to examine the CPU tower.

"Well, here's the problem. The hard disk is missing."

"What? It can't be gone. Show me what you mean."

Richard brought the tower onto Frank's desk and opened the back door panel to reveal an empty space. "That's where the disk should be, but it's gone."

"Well, God damn it, are there backup files?"

Richard looked down and saw that the backup disk was also gone.

"I hate to tell you this, but whoever took the hard disk and backup disk was computer savvy and knew our system."

Sol said, "What do you mean?"

"We never had the go-ahead for a backup server, so unless you have other copies, there's nothing to retrieve. Everything was just stored daily on the backup drive. No data went out to a secure server. Whoever took the disk and backup drive must have known that."

Sol's heart began pounding. The IT department had requested funding for an elaborate computer update for the entire corporation, a budget of over two hundred thousand for new software, hardware, and servers to back up all the operations, but because of budget shortfalls, every available dollar went to complete the current trials. He knew immediately what a colossal mistake the board had made by not agreeing to the computer upgrade.

"Richard, are you telling me someone stole all the CMV files?"

"Yes sir, that's what it looks like."

Chapter Nine

DENISE STEVENS WAS asleep, awash in a series of nightmares. Her brother Ted sat next to her bed, deep in thought. As she opened her eyes, he spoke to her.

"Denise, how are you?" Without waiting for a reply, he continued. "We're all worried about you,...the entire family."

Denise couldn't deal with that. "Can you just leave me alone? I don't want to talk about anything. Not now."

"Well, we're concerned. What can we do to help you?"

"I don't need any help, please!"

"OK, but the kids are downstairs with Dad and some friends. Would you like some coffee?"

"Ted, do you not get it? I'll come down in a while."

"All right, Sis, I'll wait downstairs, but remember, the kids need to see you. They still don't know about their dad."

"I told you I'll be there. Please leave me alone!"

Ted sighed and left the room.

As she staggered into the bathroom, Denise purposely avoided looking in the multiple mirrors, not wanting to confirm what she imagined. She suddenly remembered her nightmares...*All about Frank's affair with that slut! I wanted him to die... and now it happened.* With that thought she suddenly felt faint and sat down on the edge of the tub.

She recalled the good times, falling in love with Frank when she first met him at a church gathering. He was handsome and engaging when he introduced himself. She could tell immediately that he was extremely smart. After a long courtship, mostly because she was still in college and he was completing his Ph.D., they decided to marry. The wedding was in Charleston where her family was prominent. It took place in the Southern Evangelical Church in front of her God with her favorite pastor. Frank went along with it because he wanted her to be happy, even though as a scientist, he leaned toward agnostic beliefs.

She sat up, feeling calmer, recalling their move to Denver when Frank was offered the top research job at COADD. A smile appeared on her face as she thought about the fun things they had done together in those days. Hiking, skiing, and all the society functions they attended through introductions from Ted and connections from her father's influential real estate company.

Their lives had seemed perfect then, *at least until that bitch entered our lives.* Denise's facial expression changed as she remembered the call from Dr. Doren. She could never forget it.

"Mrs. Stevens, this is Pete Doren calling. I'm a doctor here in Denver."

"Why yes, Doctor, we've met a few times, at Mr. Feldman's home and at your Christmas party, if I'm not mistaken. Is that right?"

"Yes. Mrs. Stevens, I have some very uncomfortable news."

"What is it?"

"There's no nice way to tell you this, but your husband and my wife have been having an affair."

She gasped. "What? What do you mean an affair?"

"Just as it sounds."

"Why—why would you accuse Frank of that? I don't believe it!"

"My wife has already confessed. She told me they were involved for almost a year. I have photos that were taken of them together. Do you want to see them?"

"I— I guess."

Denise recalled slowly opening the envelope, finally overcoming her instinctive revulsion, then the sick feeling that overwhelmed her when she saw the incontrovertible evidence. *They seemed so blissful together, holding hands, smiling, kissing, hugging, sharing ice cream cones.*

The photo that angered her most showed Frank and Jacqueline leaving the Broadmoor Hotel in Colorado Springs, one of the places she and Frank had celebrated several anniversaries. *I hated him so much when I saw that.*

She'd confronted Frank with the photos and he readily confessed. She told her brother Ted about it and threatened to file for a divorce. Ted told her he didn't think it was a good idea and suggested counseling with their minister. Frank agreed to work on their marriage, but Denise needed more than counseling. Raised in a Bible-quoting Southern evangelical family, she turned to her faith, participating in prayer meetings and Bible study. Nothing seemed to work, though, and she continued to feel rage and embarrassment, believing that everyone was talking about the affair.

She jumped up and entered the shower as a surge of anger overwhelmed her. As the warm water pelted her back, she started praying intensely.

"Sweet Jesus, oh dear Jesus, please save me from my sins."

Suddenly she felt faint again and fell, hitting her forehead on the tiled floor and slumping unconscious in the shower stall. After several moments, she came to and gingerly rose to her feet. Blood dripped from her forehead, which was tender and swollen. She washed it off and stepped out of the shower, trying to regain her composure. After getting dressed and applying cosmetics to cover her puffy eyelids and injured forehead, she was ready. Feeling wobbly, she walked downstairs to meet everyone.

Ted was standing at the bottom of the stairs. Anyone could see they were brother and sister, with identical fair complexions, blond hair, pale blue eyes and similar slightly turned-up noses, all physical attributes of their Anglican ancestors who'd owned plantations before the Civil War. Ted took her hand and led her into the living room, where friends and her children had gathered.

Denise's six-year-old daughter, Tara, ran over and hung on her skirt.

"Tara, stop it! Now!"

Tara pulled away and started to cry. Her ten-year-old brother, Bradley came over to comfort his sister. Denise, realizing that everyone had stopped talking, bent down to hold both children.

"Sweethearts, I'm sorry. Mommy is very tired. Can you please try to understand?"

Tara continued to cry and then impulsively lashed out and scratched Denise's face.

"Damn it!" Denise pushed Tara away and stood to her full height, putting her palm over her cheek.

She called to the nanny. "Maria, please take the children into the playroom. I'll be there soon."

Everyone was staring at her, but she didn't have the energy to care. She excused herself and went to the powder room to calm down.

When she returned, Sol Feldman extended his hands to express condolences from the entire COADD family and organization. She nodded acknowledgement and then responded without inflections, similar to a robot-like voice. "Mr. Feldman, Frank's death makes me realize how important it is that people believe in our Lord Jesus Christ. I want you to reconsider our previous conversations, and again ask you to come as my guest to our Sunday church meeting."

Denise felt empowered to proselytize anyone of a different belief, especially Jews, because her minister had declared this to be a primary mission of their church. When opportunity knocked, she faithfully tried to take advantage of it.

Sol looked completely taken aback by her request. "Denise, I know these are trying times for you. I want to reinforce that everyone at COADD is available to help you and your lovely family."

He shook her hand and backed away.

Denise, calmed by her attempt to save Sol's soul, sat on the couch and accepted condolences from the other guests. Within a few minutes, everyone had left. Ted sat down next to her, and their father, Conrad, joined them. Conrad was in his mid-seventies, with a bulging abdomen, rounded shoulders and a face scarred from skin cancer treatments. He had recently retired as chairman of his very successful multi-state realty company and his wealth was estimated to be in the half-billion range. After his wife died, he had moved from Charleston to Denver to be close to his children and grandchildren.

Conrad spoke. "Denise, you're under a lot of stress. We all want to help. Let Ted and me tell the children about Frank."

Ted added, "Denise, I could get advice from a therapist. You know, just to be sure we handle it correctly."

"I'm not sure. It should be me...," her voice trailed off.

Ted looked at his father with concern. "Sis, this is very hard on you. Please let us do this. You can talk to them later when you're in a better frame of mind. Let me call a therapist. I'm sure it could be helpful."

Denise felt overwhelmed and started to cry. "OK, I know you have to do that."

"Denise, I'll also talk to Tucker for you," Ted said. Ed Tucker was the family attorney. "We need to get him in the picture and figure out what to do next."

She looked at Ted, trying to understand what he said. "I guess so. You know I'm feeling so tired, I'll just let you handle all of it, but now I need to lie down."

She struggled to her feet and trudged upstairs to her bedroom. Flinging herself on the bed, she began sobbing. She kept repeating, "I killed him. I killed him! Jesus, please forgive me for my sins, please, please! What have I done?" Finally exhausted, she fell into a deep sleep.

Downstairs, Ted and Conrad shook their heads.

"We have to get her some help," Ted said.

"Either that or have her committed," Conrad replied grimly.

Chapter Ten

LENNY AND ELAINE had just finished dinner at home when the phone rang.

"Dr. Haberman, it's Elizabeth. I need to talk to you. Would it be OK if I came over?" Lenny covered the phone. "It's Elizabeth, she wants to talk to me ...here."

Elaine raised her eyebrows. "I guess so. I'll just make myself scarce."

"That's fine, Elizabeth. I'll see you soon."

Remembering Colette Andrew's directive, he tried to call her but she wasn't in the office, so he left a voice mail to call him back. When Lenny opened the door a half hour later, he was surprised to see Elizabeth standing with a man he didn't recognize. She immediately introduced him as Glen Carthage, her attorney. He was slightly built, in his mid-fifties, dressed in a dark blue suit, a pale gray striped shirt and dull pastel tie.

Carthage spoke first. "Dr. Haberman, we're here voluntarily to clear up any issues you may have regarding Elizabeth's involvement in Dr. Stevens' death. Also, this isn't a proper legal venue. Do you want to have your attorney present? If you do, we can reschedule."

Lenny knew he should postpone the meeting, but he couldn't resist the urge to talk to Elizabeth. "No, I understand, let's talk."

"Despite my advice not to have this meeting, Elizabeth was adamant. I'm only going along with this if I can be with her while she talks to you. You should also be aware that anything mentioned will be hearsay and cannot be used in any litigation."

Lenny was taken aback by the tone set by Carthage, feeling disadvantaged because he had little knowledge of legal proceedings. Trying to weigh his options, he decided he had no alternative but to pursue this opportunity. He started by asking if they would like coffee. They both declined and sat down on a sofa in the living room.

Lenny asked, "Elizabeth, what do you remember about Frank when he came in that day?"

"Well, he seemed normal. Very chatty as always, and in a good mood. He said something like it being a great day. Otherwise, there was nothing out of the ordinary that I can recall." Her voice shook, and got a little higher as she talked.

"Did he seem out of breath, maybe from running to the office?"

"I didn't notice that. When he talked, he didn't sound winded or wheezy or anything and he wasn't sweating or flushed."

"Did he mention anything about not feeling well? Anything unusual?"

"He did mention that he wanted to talk to you because he had some problems with his asthma earlier in the week."

"Wait...what? No one told me about that!" Lenny shook his head slightly to clear his thoughts. The SOP was to always have symptomatic asthma patients checked by a doctor before they received an allergy injection.

She quickly explained. "But I asked him if he was fine then and he said yes. He said something like his asthma was bad during the past week, but he wasn't having problems at the time I gave him his shot."

Lenny noticed her voice cracking several times, making him wonder if she was leaving something out. He made a mental note to return to it.

Elizabeth continued. "I asked him if he had swelling from his last shot, and he said it had swelled to the size of a silver dollar. I told him I would reduce the dose, which I did. His normal dose was 0.5 cc and I cut it back to half of that."

"Was there anything he mentioned around the time of the injection, like his medications, other symptoms, or anything else you can remember?"

Carthage listened intently, ready to intercede, if necessary. He was about to interrupt during the last exchange, but sat back when Elizabeth qualified what she meant.

"Well, he apparently had a migraine headache when he received his previous injection, and he mentioned his new migraine medication was helping."

That comment caught Lenny's attention. "Did he mention the name of the new migraine medication?"

"No, only that it really helped. Could that be important?"

Lenny ignored the question and asked. "Did you get the idea that he had taken the migraine medication before he came in?"

"No, just that it was helping."

Carthage interrupted. "Dr. Haberman, is this important?"

"I don't know," Lenny said slowly. He didn't want to mention it, but he wondered if Frank may have been on a beta blocker medication for migraine control. He knew the presence of a beta blocker would prevent adrenalin from working, and could explain why Frank didn't respond to resuscitation attempts. He decided not to pursue it, but he thought it might be important if this ever went to litigation. "I need to know every drug he was on since many of them can cause anaphylaxis."

Carthage seemed to accept the answer and they continued.

"Elizabeth, are you sure you gave him the correct dose?"

Carthage interrupted, this time with an edge to his voice. "Dr. Haberman, I'm advising my client not to answer that."

Lenny sat back, not sure how to respond. He knew this might be the only opportunity to get to the truth until there was an official deposition.

"Elizabeth, I'm not inferring anything with that question, I would just..."

"Stop right there, Doctor. I will not have my client answer any question related to the dose of the allergy injection."

Lenny sat back, wondering what that was all about. "All right, Elizabeth, what happened once you gave him the injection?"

Carthage gestured his approval, and Elizabeth described the events as they'd occurred. Her description was interesting because she left out any mention of her failure to help him.

Lenny wondered what she was not telling him. Something didn't add up here. He thought about taking a different approach, as he recalled an experience in medical school when he had to question a patient with an obsessive-compulsive disorder in front of a psychiatrist and classmates. His questioning had led to a roadblock and the patient had stopped talking when asked an emotionally charged question. Out of instinct rather than experience, Lenny guided the patient back to being cooperative by changing the subject, and then gradually returned to the issue that caused the roadblock. He decided now to try this approach on Elizabeth.

"Elizabeth, Frank had been tolerating his injections well up to this time. Do you have any idea why this happened now?"

"I've thought about it a lot...I honestly don't know. I lowered the dose because of what he said about swelling from the last injection." She opened her hands toward Lenny. "I'm just as baffled as you are. Could he have taken some medication that he reacted to? I just don't know. This has never happened to me."

"I understand.... So you're certain you gave him the correct dose. Right?"

Before Carthage could interrupt, Elizabeth answered, "Absolutely! I know I gave him the correct dose!"

Carthage's face flushed with anger as he turned to Elizabeth. "I'm advising you not to answer any more questions."

Ignoring Carthage, Lenny pursued his questioning. "Elizabeth, why didn't you help me? I needed you. You kept saying you were sorry. Why?"

Her head suddenly dropped to her chest and tears rolled down her cheeks. She muttered something under her breath, but before Lenny could ask her to repeat what she'd said, Carthage stood up abruptly and took her arm.

"Doctor, this conversation is over!"

They left the house in a hurry.

Elaine came back downstairs. "What did she say?"

Lenny was as perplexed as before. "It was strange. She's not telling me something, and she brought a lawyer with her. I need to write this all down so I can remember what she said, and didn't say."

Lenny sat at his desk and made notes on the meeting.

- *Elizabeth didn't have me check Frank before giving him a shot, knowing he had been experiencing chest tightness during the prior week. Why didn't she do that?*
- *Frank had taken a new medication for migraine control. What was it? Could it have been a beta blocker?*
- *What did Elizabeth mutter when I asked her to explain why she didn't help?*
- *What was she sorry about?*

When he finished, he decided that on balance the meeting had been helpful. He had extracted new information that might explain the reaction. He had also learned an important lesson about legal proceedings. Carthage had controlled what Elizabeth told him and interfered with answers to important questions. Lenny made himself a promise that he would have his own lawyer present next time-if there was one.

✻ ✻ ✻

The next day, Lenny walked into the law office of Burns, Outer and Jansen to meet his attorney, Mark Persons. The waiting room was classic neo-attorney with floor-to-ceiling windows, great views of the Rocky Mountains, and several large paintings of skylines, countryside and cowboys. Several large, elegant leather sofas and chairs were tastefully placed around the waiting room.

After a ten minute wait, the secretary escorted him to Persons' office. Mark Persons stood up to introduce himself and his paralegal. The first thing Lenny noticed was that Mark had a significant tremor in both hands, which was more noticeable when he talked. Lenny estimated Mark's age slightly older than himself because his hair was totally gray, including his eyebrows.

"Dr. Haberman, sorry to meet under these circumstances, but I'm here to help you."

"Thank you, I appreciate all the help I can get."

"I received a call from Colette Andrews, and she gave me a briefing about the death of your patient, Dr. Stevens. I understand you gave details to Colette and she faxed over the information, which we'll use as the beginning record for your defense."

When Lenny didn't reply, he continued. "This will most likely become a lawsuit. You may receive a request from the family or their attorney for a copy of Dr. Stevens' records. You need to let me know about this or any communication from his family or their attorney. Also, advise your staff not to talk to anyone about this."

"I understand all that," Lenny affirmed. There's something else you need to know. Last night, Elizabeth Finch called me and came over to my house. She's the nurse who disappeared after Dr. Stevens died from the allergy injection reaction. She came over with her lawyer, Glen Carthage."

Persons narrowed his gaze. "I hope you're not going where I think you are."

"I guess I should've known better, but I did ask her a number of questions, and..."

Persons interrupted. "May I call you Lenny?"

Lenny nodded.

"Lenny, I wish you hadn't met with her and her attorney without legal representation. That wasn't wise. In the future I must advise you to never, and I mean never, do that again. You must heed me on this. Carthage doesn't care about you or the truth; he has one mission, which is to protect his client. I don't want you to feel bad, but I need to emphasize how important this is."

Lenny could have done without the lecture, but he simply said, "You can't make me feel any worse than I already do."

"OK. Now, I'm sure you're aware that Mrs. Stevens is Ted Larkin's sister. He's the Colorado Senate Majority Leader and a member of a powerful and influential family in Colorado. Larkin indicated in the press he plans to sponsor a new bill to raise award limits on negligent medical care, so we must assume this case will be used to promote his cause."

Lenny replied, "I know that can't be good for me."

"Lenny, I promise I'll do everything possible to provide you with the best defense, but I need you to follow my advice. Let's talk about your thoughts on what could have caused this tragedy. I assume you've been thinking about it. Do you have any explanation of why it happened? Tell me any concerns you might have about how you handled the emergency."

That request opened the floodgates. Lenny proceeded to describe some of the issues, and handed over the list he'd made after his talk with Elizabeth. He spoke about not having equipment for a cricothyroidotomy, and that his biggest concern was the volume discrepancy in Stevens' vaccine and realizing Frank might have somehow received an overdose. He also mentioned that he had not been in the office at the time of the incident, but he was in the same building, and it took him less than a minute to get to his office after his receptionist called him.

Mark made a notation on his pad. "That could be a concern."

"Yes, but Frank stopped breathing just as I arrived, so I was there at the critical time."

"You're probably right, but I can assure you the plaintiff's attorney will do everything to argue that by not being there, you delayed Dr. Stevens' treatment."

"But there couldn't have been more than a ten second delay starting resuscitation."

Mark waved for him to calm down. "Lenny, it's important for me to know these issues in advance. By the way, do all doctors have equipment in their emergency carts to do a crico, or whatever you called it?"

"I don't know if they do, but frankly, I should have had it."

Lenny remembered to ask if it would be appropriate for him to attend the funeral.

"Lenny, there's no legal prohibition to going, but it could have two effects. It might show your compassion, but it could also be construed by the Stevens' family as being manipulative. By being there, they might think you're asking for forgiveness with the implication not to sue you. I'd prefer you not attend, and instead send a note of condolence to Mrs. Stevens and her family, but I'll leave the decision to you."

"If I go, it won't be with any agenda," Lenny said, angry at the logic of what his lawyer was saying. "I've lost a close friend and feel responsible."

"Lenny, you need to keep thoughts like that to yourself. If someone overheard you saying that, it could be used against you. We have enough of an uphill battle without giving the opposition more ammunition."

Chapter Eleven

JIMMY BARONE REMAINED in critical condition in the ICU at Denver Memorial Hospital, where he was listed as an unidentified person. The Colorado Bureau of Investigation (CBI) was called in to assist in his identification. Most of his fingers were not injured, so they were able to obtain prints.

Two emergency operations had been performed on the first day to repair multiple fractures, a collapsed lung, hemorrhaging spleen and bleeding inside his skull. Multiple tubes drained blood from his chest, abdomen and skull. A ventilator mechanically assisted his breathing through a tube inserted into his trachea. Sophisticated computer systems monitored his condition, and round-the-clock nurses and surgical residents tracked his vital signs, fluid input and output. Replacement of blood loss was ongoing, and now totaled ten units.

Because of his uncanny resemblance to Albert Einstein, even with facial swelling, the nursing staff taped posters of Einstein in his room. Typically, the staff remained emotionally detached from critical patients without identification, but over the years the staff had cared for several unidentified trauma victims, and when they could provide a poster of a famous individual who most resembled the unidentified person, the outcomes always seemed better. No one could explain why it worked, although some believed providing identity, even if not true, inspired dignity and respect for unidentified victims. The staff spent extra time checking on Jimmy instead of dispassionately viewing monitors in the nursing station.

Buried in the *Rocky Mountain Tribune* was a small article describing the accident.

An accident occurred on I-70 caused by a nighttime collision between a Subaru and a deer. One person involved in the accident, an unidentified adult Caucasian male, approximately thirty to forty years old, lost large quantities of blood, and was in shock. The victim was transferred to Denver Memorial Hospital and is listed in critical condition. The car was totally demolished by an explosion and subsequent fire. The CBI has been asked to assist in the victim's identification.

The CBI investigator assigned to the case was Field Agent Ben Locke, a veteran agent and a member of the identification department. In his mid-forties, Locke retained the intimidating look of an MP from his Desert Storm days. A strong jawline with wide neck and shoulders, softened by a short graying beard, gave him an Ernest Hemingway look. He had become well known intra-departmentally when he was able to identify a middle-aged male who was found wandering in downtown Denver, suffering from amnesia. Information from a label on his clothing helped identify a manufacturer in the Midwest. This information led to publishing the man's photograph in a small Kansas newspaper. A family member recognized her uncle and came forward to identify him. By default, this and other successes made Ben the "go-to" CBI expert for unidentified persons.

This case particularly frustrated Ben because he thought he might have met the victim in the past, but couldn't jar his memory to connect a name to the face. This was unusual, since Ben had an uncanny recollection for faces and names. Photographs of the victim were being readied for future press release in the event fingerprints didn't identify him.

After viewing pictures of the accident, Locke was amazed that the victim had survived at all. He called the state patrol and was able to locate the remains of the vehicle. He had it moved to Denver so he could personally inspect it for clues that might help identify the victim.

He decided to call in his junior associate, Alice Holten, to help with the inspection. Alice was in her thirties, with a plump figure and curly thick black hair. She was infatuated with her newfound career and eager to learn the practical aspects of investigative techniques. Ben never enjoyed teaching trainees. When she first arrived he had given Alice one of the tougher cold cases to keep her busy, thinking she'd go nowhere with it. Surprisingly, she'd gained his respect by tracking down insiders in a jewelry robbery committed several years before. Passing that test was significant, but Ben considered this to be a more important challenge that would determine her future value to the CBI.

When he saw the remains of the vehicle, he was even more surprised that the victim had survived. The devastation reminded him of another accident he had handled when a gasoline truck had collided with a small Honda FIT. The fire had left a metal skeleton of the vehicle and a black ink silhouette of the passenger, totally carbonized.

Ben and Alice spent hours looking over the remains of Jimmy's vehicle along with debris gathered at the accident site. She brought a flashlight and magnifying glass to search for identification numbers on the chassis, engine, dash and driver's door. She called over to Ben, who had been inspecting remains of contents found in the car.

"Agent Locke! I may have found something."

Ben dropped what he was doing and came around to look at the dashboard near the windshield. "See there. They're barely visible, maybe four to six characters. Two are numbers and the others are letters."

He looked intently but he couldn't see what she was referring to. He took the flashlight and brought it closer. Now he could see a faint outline of some characters. "Alice, you have great eyes. I have to admit, I would've missed it."

The accolade made her smile.

"Let's get forensic to take a look at it. Maybe they can do some of their magic and pull out the VIN number."

She responded. "Yes sir, I'll call over and get them here right away."

He went back to his office to determine if anyone resembling the victim had been reported missing. Nothing turned up, but he thought maybe the remnants of the VIN number would help identify the mystery man.

Chapter Twelve

LENNY CALLED THE Medical Examiner's office to find out if they had made a determination on the cause of Stevens' death. The ME's office was under the supervision of Dr. Robert Short, a well-known forensic pathologist in the Rocky Mountain region. Dr. Short was often quoted in the news, and occasionally served as a forensic expert in murder trials. Lenny had never met him, and wasn't sure of the response he would receive as a potential defendant in a probable malpractice case. He finally got through and explained who he was and why he was calling.

"Dr. Haberman, as you know, we don't take sides in potential litigation. Our job is simply to record the results of the autopsy. Nothing more."

"I understand Dr. Short and I'm not asking anything more than a copy of the autopsy results. I was wondering if you could fax them to me."

"Sorry, but you must realize we need to go through proper channels and get authorization to release any information. Is there anything else I can do for you?"

"Actually, there's something odd about this case. As you probably know, the presumption is that Dr. Stevens died from an anaphylactic reaction to an allergy injection—"

The ME interrupted. "Dr. Haberman, there has been no determination at this time and I can't tell you any more than that. I'm sorry, but I need to get back to work."

Lenny hesitated, wondering if what he said could be used against him in some bizarre way in court.

"I'm sorry. I don't want to affect your involvement in this case. I just want to let you know some information that might be helpful."

"Well, what is it?"

"I've been reviewing Dr. Stevens' case record and noticed he had a history of oral allergy syndrome, which suggests he had food allergies that could cause mouth and lip swelling. He had a long list of foods he was supposed to avoid based on allergy test results, called IgE cap-RAST. I was wondering if there was any food in his clothing, possibly some food he had eaten, that could have caused the reaction."

"I can tell you that his clothing was thoroughly checked, and our staff didn't find any food or medication."

"Can you check stomach contents for evidence of foods?"

The ME now seemed more interested in Lenny's questions. "The stomach contents were completely liquefied, which would imply that he hadn't eaten for several hours. Since there were no solid foods in his stomach, would you still believe a food could have caused the reaction?"

"Actually, I do. There is another possibility-exercise-induced anaphylaxis with underlying food allergy."

The ME paused for a beat. "I'm not familiar with that."

"Some patients will only experience anaphylaxis if they eat a particular food prior to exercising, and the oddity is that they tolerate the same food without exercising. They have evidence of allergic antibodies to these foods by skin tests or allergy blood tests, but they still tolerate the food as long as they don't exercise. One theory is that exercise accelerates absorption of the food into the circulation, which then leads to anaphylaxis."

"Go on."

Lenny continued, knowing he had his attention. "When we suspect this type of anaphylaxis, we advise patients to avoid exercise around the time they plan to eat. Dr. Stevens' lab is in a building within walking distance of my office. He was late getting to my office, and may have run to get there on time. For most people that would have been an insignificant amount of exercise, but he was out of shape, and maybe just the run to get to my office on time was enough to accelerate a reaction, assuming he had eaten one of those foods earlier."

The ME was intrigued by this novel hypothesis. "I'll look into it. I'll ask our forensic chemist to test for specific food contents in his stomach. I know we freeze gastric contents for a year after an unexplained death. Can you fax me the list of foods?"

"Of course, thanks again for your help."

They hung up and Lenny wrote a note to tell Persons about his conversation with Dr. Short, and to request a copy of the autopsy report, along with the food tests he suggested be done on Frank's stomach contents

Chapter Thirteen

THE MOOD AT COADD was like a prairie dog colony on high alert. The news of the missing manufacturing specifications had somehow leaked out. Employees were standing around anxiously, talking about whether the leadership would impose a layoff if the specs could not be found.

Sol Feldman, was meeting with Ole Bettman, to get an assessment on what was missing. "Ole, where in the hell could they be?"

Ole responded. "Not sure, but it looks like Frank might have moved them. It's a puzzle," he said, scratching his head. "It doesn't make any sense. Why would he remove everything just before he died? ... Unless he was worried someone might steal them, especially after seeing the great results. Sol, maybe we should call the police."

Sol was concerned that if the news got out to the public, it would cause panic with investors. "Look Ole, if we call the police, it'll create bad publicity, and no one will invest with us if they find out we can't make the vaccine... No, not yet. We need to wait a few more days. Maybe all of this'll work out."

Ole said, "OK, but what about Jimmy? We still can't find him. Maybe I'll ask Beth to go over to his house. What if he's sick, unable to call? He's kind of a recluse and I don't think he has family around here."

"I like that idea. Yeah, see if Beth can do that."

After Ole left, Sol looked out of his top-floor office window, staring at the bustle of traffic. Those people are fortunate, he thought. If COADD couldn't recover the specifications, he would have no purpose in life, especially since his wife died, they had no children and he had no one else to share his life with.

He stopped his depressive thoughts to avoid letting the emergency overwhelm him. Situations like this catered to his strength. Sol was known in the pharmaceutical industry as a sharp, steady and clear-thinking manager, especially during crises. His last post was vice-president of Dall Pharmaceuticals, a large company that had to recall an obesity drug because it had caused blood clots in a few patients. The recall was resolved with alacrity under Sol's command. A few lawsuits were handled quietly and the problem disappeared. When Sol decided to take the helm of COADD, the CEO of Dall did everything he could to keep him, even offering to increase his salary by thirty percent, but other considerations were driving Sol's decision. Being sixty-two, and a widower, he decided to accept the COADD opportunity because it would not require 24/7 oversight, or so he'd thought. His future now seemed bleak unless he could keep the company viable.

An idea suddenly popped into his head. He searched his contact list on Outlook and made a call to a private detective he knew.

"Charley Blackwood speaking."

"Charley, Sol Feldman calling. Haven't talked to you in a while."

"Hey Sol, how you doing these days?"

"Good until recently. Look Charley, I have a job for you. Can you come over to COADD sooner rather than later? We've got an emergency that requires your skills."

"Sure, I have a short appointment, but I could make it later this morning. Will that work?"

"That'll be fine."

Charley was known as a specialty sleuth for pharmaceutical companies. Sol had hired him before to investigate medical backgrounds of the people who had claimed Dall's obesity drug caused clotting problems. Charley's investigative skills had discovered that some of the patients had lied about not having clotting problems before taking the obesity drug. That information had saved millions for Dall.

Sol was hopeful that Charley could employ some of his talents to find the missing hard drives.

Beth left the lab and drove over to Jimmy's condo, only three blocks away. She rang the bell several times, but no one answered. After waiting several minutes, she peeked through a side window into the condo while leaning over a large juniper hedge. The drapes were open and she was able to get a good view of a barren living room. There were no pictures, paintings or ornaments, and it was empty except for an old sofa with padding coming out of the pillows, and a coffee table with a broken leg, causing it to slant to one side. The floors were covered by faded pale green carpet with noticeable holes from wear and cigarette burns. Takeout food cartons and pop cans littered the floor. She wondered why someone so intelligent would live in these awful conditions.

She walked to the condo next door and rang the bell. A frail lady in her seventies opened the door slightly while keeping the chain lock attached. The neighbor was wearing a bathrobe and her hair was up in rollers.

"Yes? What do you want? I don't talk to solicitors."

"I'm sorry to disturb you, ma'am, but I'm not a solicitor. I'm looking for Mr. Barone. I rang and knocked on his door, but there was no answer. Do you know where he could be?"

"I don't. I'm not in the business of snooping around like you, so leave me alone!"

She slammed the door, leaving Beth slightly stunned and not sure of her next move. As a last effort, she returned to Jimmy's front door, knocked again several times and tried the handle. To her surprise, the door opened and she walked into the repugnant odor of filth and rotting food. There were open cans of tuna and milk cartons, old partially eaten pizza, and dishes piled in the sink. Cockroaches scattered as she moved through the kitchen and the rest of the apartment. She hoped she wouldn't find Jimmy's body, and was relieved when there was no sign of him. She searched for the documents and computers, but found nothing of interest. Having completed the search, she quickly left the apartment and took some very deep breaths of fresh air.

She returned to COADD and reported her findings to Sol and Ole Bettman, who were both waiting in Sol's office for Charley Blackwood. Knowing that Jimmy had moved out made Sol think, *Did Jimmy have something to do with the disappearance of the specs?*

When Charley arrived, Sol introduced him to Ole and they sat down to discuss the situation. Charley was a black man in his late forties, bald with extra flab in places that made him appear lumpy in his well-pressed khaki pants and short-sleeve blue shirt.

Sol started by recalling stories of how Charley had ferreted out the con artists who thought they'd hit pay dirt with their claims against Dall. It triggered Charley's characteristic booming laugh.

"Well, gents, how can this ole black guy help?"

Sol quickly brought him up to date. "We need your help, Charley. We don't know where to go with this. Should I call the police?"

"Hold off. I need to start by talking to everybody who worked with Dr. Stevens. Do you have a list?"

"The person who had the closest relationship to Dr. Stevens has disappeared. His name is Jimmy Barone, the chief lab technician who worked with him. One of my staff went to his house today and found it empty. We have no idea where he is."

"OK, that's a start. Give me some time to look into it." He paused to think about the situation, and then reiterated his caution. "Sol, you know calling the police will make it a newspaper story. That'll cause problems for your company. Give me a week to get back to you."

"Charley, I have another idea. Maybe Stevens took the specs home, possibly for security once he realized the vaccine worked. I don't want to bother his wife right now, but we may have to."

"Yeah, maybe later, after I do some investigating."

Sol stood to shake hands. "Thanks for coming on such short notice. Call me when you have something."

After Charley left, Sol said nothing but looked helplessly at Ole, feeling like a patient who was just told he had one month to live.

Chapter Fourteen

FRONT RANGE SOUTHERN Evangelical Church was overflowing with family, relatives, friends and professional colleagues. Those who did not know Frank Stevens personally were there to pay respect to a prominent scientist because they or a family member were affected by cocaine addiction. Organ music drifted throughout the church as people filled the pews. A large screen magnified the pulpit.

The church choir began singing hymns. After they finished, the minister entered, and a lay reader stood to recite a passage from the New Testament. The congregation stood to sing, "A Mighty Fortress Is Our God." After they were reseated, the minister began his eulogy, describing Frank first and foremost as a solid family man, a supportive member of the church and a good Christian. He mentioned Frank's contributions to science and mankind. Several in the audience murmured quietly, *Praise the Lord.* After he finished, he asked those who wanted to speak to come forward.

Lenny had entered the church dressed in a conservative gray suit and dark sunglasses. He remained quietly in the back and sat in a pew occupied by several COADD employees. A few of them turned their heads to whisper hello and Lenny nodded back. He cautiously scanned the congregation and noticed Denise sitting in the front row with her two children. She was sobbing while a relative had an arm around her. The sight of her grieving triggered his own profound sadness and tears came to his eyes.

After a few minutes, he resumed scanning faces and stopped when he recognized a good friend, Dr. Hernando Ramirez, who was president of the Denver Medical Society. Lenny had become friendly with Hernando, a Mexican immigrant, who overcame prejudice and poverty to become a successful orthopedist admired by his peers. He and Lenny had worked together to develop a free medical clinic for families without insurance. Lenny noticed Hernando had turned toward him and was whispering to an attractive woman, probably his wife. Lenny turned back to the front of the church, wondering if Hernando was judging him somehow. The thought that a respected friend and colleague might be singling him out, caused Lenny intense discomfort.

Ted Larkin rose and walked slowly to the pulpit. He shuffled papers around and then turned to look at the large screen that projected his face.

"Dear Denise, family, friends, and people who have gathered to pray for the soul of our brother Frank Stevens, who has gone to our Lord Jesus. Frank was more than a brother-in-law. He was a special friend! He was a loyal member of the Larkin family and proud to be part of it. His love for my dear sister was an example of faithfulness that should be an inspiration to all of us. He adored his children. He was, without any question, a true family man."

He paused to emphasize the next part of his eulogy.

"All of us will miss this great man whose life ended prematurely because of a medical mishap. The Stevens family has lost a husband and a father, and the community has lost a promising scientist."

Larkin paused for emphasis again.

"We live in very difficult economic times. Many are struggling to make ends meet. Think now if this medical calamity had affected a bread winner in one of these struggling families. Their chance to survive economically would be gravely impaired. Acts of medical negligence are not tolerable and should not be acceptable to the people of Colorado," he proclaimed.

He waited for this to sink in. "Colorado is the only state that makes it very difficult to get punitive damages for grossly negligent medical acts. It is my solemn promise to all of you, to the entire state of Colorado, and to the memory of Frank Stevens, to make it my personal goal to enact new legislation to change this injustice."

The entire congregation sat up and murmured in agreement. Larkin nodded with a slight smile to acknowledge the congregation's response.

Lenny found himself also sitting straight up. *This bastard is incredible. He knows how to connect to the average guy who's angry with his lot in life.*

Larkin resumed. "I will personally set in motion a bill to be named the Frank Stevens Memorial Legislation to remediate the gross injustices of the medical malpractice system in our wonderful state. My love goes out to all of you who have taken the time to support our family. Please ask your legislative representatives to support my reform medical malpractice act in Frank's name. God bless all of you."

Several other friends gave eulogies, praising Frank's intellect, his service to humanity, and especially his work on cocaine addiction, as well as simply being a good person.

Sol Feldman then walked up to the pulpit. He surveyed the faces in the church, most somber, many crying, and others with their heads bowed. He recognized Denise with a nod.

"My name is Sol Feldman. I am CEO and president of COADD, the biotech company where Frank was in charge of research to develop a treatment for cocaine addiction. I admired Frank for his friendship, his intellect and for his fairness to all who worked with him. Frank was truly a very special friend, and one whose memory will remain with me. I have many fond memories and stories about Frank. He was not only a scientist, but had many talents, particularly music. I understand he took up the fiddle when he was in his Ph.D. program and turned out to be very gifted. One evening he was at my home for a dinner party. At the end of the evening I asked Frank to play a few tunes. He started to play some Irish jigs, and everyone including me, and I am hardly Irish, just started dancing. We couldn't help it! His music was contagious, except for one little old woman who remained in her chair. She had severe arthritis and couldn't stand by herself, but she was having fun too, clapping her hands and tapping her feet along with the music. Frank was watching her the whole time he played."

Sol paused to sip some water. "After he finished, Frank walked over and helped her stand. It was tough for her because she was really bent over. Frank got her up to dance a common waltz with him while he sang the words. After they finished, it made her so happy that for a few minutes she hummed and high-stepped an Irish jig. That, ladies and gentlemen was Frank Stevens, the person we all so admired and loved."

When he finished there wasn't a dry eye in the entire church.

When the service ended, Denise left first with her children, followed by Conrad and Ted, and other members of the family. They walked slowly with their heads bowed while the congregation stood in respect. Lenny slipped out, trying to be as inconspicuous as possible, walking close to a corridor that led to the exit doors. He was able to see Denise talking to several people on the other side of the church. Suddenly something distracted her as she dropped the hands of her children and rushed out of the church like a crazed person. Lenny watched her race towards a woman wearing a black veiled hat. She roughly grabbed the woman's arm, and both fell forward against a railing. Denise literally leaped onto the woman's back, pulling on her hair with one hand and slapping her face with the other.

She started yelling, "You slut... you bitch! Frank died because of your sins, you filthy whore!"

The woman being attacked also began screaming. She fell down on her knees, yelling and struggling. "Help! Help me. Someone, please!"

Ted Larkin heard the commotion and when he realized Denise was involved, he ran over and pulled her off of the woman. Denise continued to scream, as Ted and another man firmly escorted her into a waiting car and drove off while she screamed and pounded on the windows of the car. Stunned by the outburst, Lenny turned to catch a glimpse of the attacked woman. A church member walking close to him whispered loudly to her neighbor, "That's Dr. Doren's wife," while pointing at the woman who was still bent over the railing, catching her breath.

The eruption seemed so bizarre, but to Lenny the bigger question was what Denise meant when she'd screamed, *"Frank died because of your sins."* None of it made any sense and he wanted to ask someone in the crowd if they knew what was going on, but curious as he was, he decided to leave before he was recognized.

He returned to his office and called his partner, Walt, to tell him about Denise attacking Doren's wife.

"Walt, it was so weird. She literally leapt onto the woman's back."

"I guess you didn't know Doren's wife had an affair with Frank a few years ago."

Lenny was shocked. "You're kidding!"

"Yeah, I heard about it over a coffee break in the doctors' lounge. They had quite an affair until Doren discovered it and told Denise. The scuttlebutt was that Denise never got over it."

"Walt, besides attacking her, Denise yelled out, 'Frank died because of your sins.' What do you think she meant by that?"

"It could have been a religious reference. You know Denise. She's a religious nut and believes in the literal interpretation of the Bible. Maybe she was saying Frank died because of God's wrath against his adultery."

Lenny saw the sense in that. "I suppose that's what she meant. You're right about her extreme religious beliefs. I've had some personal experience. She keeps trying to convert me."

"Lenny, she might talk to me. Do you want me to try and find out what she meant?"

"Sure, but be careful. If she gets upset, I'll hear about it from my attorney and probably Ted Larkin. By the way, the attorney representing me and our corporation seems like a very competent guy."

"Oh, what's his name?"

"Mark Persons. The only concern I have is he has a resting hand tremor that gets worse when he talks. Makes him look nervous and makes me nervous."

"Lenny, not to worry. I know a successful CEO with a hand tremor and no one thinks about it when he does public speaking. It's not important."

"I guess you're right. Anyway, let's stay in touch."

After they ended the call, Lenny's thoughts returned to the bizarre scene at the funeral. Denise had been angry enough to kill that woman. *Why was she so angry? Was it the affair? And if it was, could she have done something to punish Frank? Maybe she substituted placebos for his asthma meds. Maybe that's why his asthma worsened and it could have made him susceptible to the shot reaction. That thought might be worth pursuing.*

Chapter Fifteen

AFTER HIS CALL with Walt, Lenny realized he was late for a therapy appointment with Dave Sabatha. He arrived just as Sabatha finished a phone call.

Dave started, "Lenny, I heard about Frank Stevens' death. I'm assuming it had something to do with the call from your office. Right?"

"Yeah, he collapsed after he got an allergy shot. I just can't believe it happened. He was a very good friend." He went on to describe what had happened, walking in circles as he talked nonstop for a half hour. He abruptly sat down.

"Lenny, losing a patient who was also a close friend is tragic. Isn't it rare for someone to die from an allergy injection?"

"Extremely…I've never seen it before."

"Do you have any idea why it was so severe?"

"Not entirely. It's probably too early to jump to conclusions, but my nurse was of no help. She was totally out of it, unable to assist."

Dave frowned. "Lenny, are you telling me your nurse panicked? Aren't they trained for these situations?"

"Yeah they are, but she behaved as if she was paralyzed."

"To some degree, that doesn't surprise me. I've seen firemen and cops unable to respond to a life or death crisis. Later on they needed a lot of psychological support to deal with their guilt feelings. I suspect your nurse will need help too."

"I guess. But there's other stuff. She might have made an error that caused the reaction. It's too early to say for sure. Maybe she could use your help. I'll mention your name when I see her again."

"Whatever, but it's more likely she just panicked. What's her name in case she calls?"

"Elizabeth Finch."

"OK. Lenny, let's talk a little about your response to this. Do you feel depressed?"

"Well, my appetite's fair, but I'm not sleeping. I'm waking up after just a few hours."

"Then it sounds like you may need a little help. Before you leave, I'll write a low-dose anti-depressant, one of the serotonin uptake inhibitors, and something to reduce your sleep anxiety."

"You know, on top of everything, I just left Frank's funeral. It was incredibly difficult. What made it worse was Ted Larkin's eulogy. Turns out he's Frank's brother-in-law."

"Really? Isn't he the Colorado Senate Majority Leader?"

"Yeah, that's him. He gave a political speech with his eulogy. Even mentioned that he's going to sponsor a bill in Frank Stevens' name to raise ceilings for medical negligence. He's planning to use this case to get support for his malpractice reform bill."

Dave considered this new development. "Lenny, keep this in perspective. Larkin's doing what he was elected to do. He's a classic politician. You have enough on your plate without worrying about changes in malpractice laws."

"But I don't know if I have enough coverage," Lenny exclaimed. The jury could award millions to the Stevens family. I have a million dollar limit, and if the case goes to a jury and they think it was gross negligence, I may not have enough insurance. If there's any possibility of his legislation being passed retroactively, I'm royally screwed Dave. To be honest, it scares the crap out of me."

Dave modulated his voice down to calm Lenny. "You're jumping to conclusions. First of all, have you actually received notice of a lawsuit?"

"No, not yet, but it'll come."

"Well, you need to wait. See what happens. Larkin's bill may never get passed. It takes a long time to approve new legislation, and I'm sure it'll get a lot of opposition from the insurance lobby. I wouldn't go there yet."

Lenny had to agree. "I know but it's hard not to think the worst. Dave, this whole thing is turning into a soap opera. After the funeral, Frank's wife went nuts and assaulted a doctor's wife. The doctor's name is Pete Doren. Anyway, Denise said something weird like, Frank died because of sins committed by Doren's wife. I have no idea what that's all about, other than maybe she was referring to the affair they had. But the way she said it makes me wonder if there is more to it."

"You'll probably never know everything. But let's stop now and get you on anti-anxiety meds along with an anti-depressant."

"OK, I'm sure I can use help."

"Lenny, I want to see you back in a week. You're under a lot of stress."

Lenny agreed and left for the day.

Chapter Sixteen

AFTER THE FUNERAL, Denise remained in her bedroom most of the time, in part to isolate herself from her children, who hung on her whenever they saw her. There was no other place to deal with her grief, and be alone to pray. She asked for sleeping pills and took more than prescribed, making her exhausted and lethargic. There was no way she could handle her daily chores, so Ted hired a second nanny, a housekeeper and a cook.

Ted was concerned about his sister's mental health, but his real focus was to keep her condition a secret, which was now more difficult after her outburst at the funeral. Any mention in the papers would have been bad for the Larkin name and certainly not good for his political plans. He decided to drop in unannounced to see how she was doing. He spoke to Maria, a Dominican who had been the Stevens' family nanny for many years.

"Maria, how's she doing?"

"I think she not doing well, sir. She cry all the time."

"Has she seen the children?"

"No sir, she don't."

"Damn it! Do you think she's getting worse?"

"I think maybe. You know she pray a lot and cry a lot too."

Denise had to keep it together. He went up to the master bedroom. The drapes were closed and a light from a small candle silhouetted the sad figure of his sister, who was on her knees by the bed reading a passage from an open Bible. She was disheveled with no makeup, and noticeably thinner.

She seemed unaware of his presence. Ted walked over and laid his hand lightly on her shoulder. Denise jerked, and when she recognized him, she smiled softly and kept reading aloud from her Bible: "I am the resurrection and the life."

Ted stood transfixed, candlelight flickering on his face, wondering how to get her to stop. As she bent down to pray, dropping her face to her folded hands, she started weeping with loud wracking sobs. She stopped suddenly, and with renewed energy she read the next passage: "He who believes in me will live, even though he dies." She shouted, "Yes…yes, yes!" Each yes was louder than the previous one, and then she fell forward, sobbing softly.

Ted decided he needed to find help for her right away. He walked into the hallway, pulled out his cell, and called the family internist to describe her behavior. The internist referred him to Dr. David Sabatha. Ted immediately made the call. He had to leave a message with the answering service, but Sabatha called him back within minutes.

"Dr. Sabatha. Thank you for calling me back so soon. This is Senator Ted Larkin."

"Yes, Senator, what can I do for you?"

"I assume you know who I am." He continued without waiting for an acknowledgment. "I'm calling about my sister, Denise Stevens. Her husband died recently, and she's having terrible problems, severe enough that our internist suggested I call you."

"What's going on?"

"She's out of control, sobbing, praying incessantly, depressed, won't eat, and hasn't left her room in days. She also won't see her children. I'm really worried about her."

"Is the behavior getting worse?"

"Yes, and she's become aggressive."

Dave interrupted. "What makes you say that?"

"At her husband's funeral she attacked a woman who had an affair with her husband several years ago. She made a terrible scene."

"Well, if she's violent and depressed, she probably needs observation. It would be difficult for me to assess her mental state without seeing her. Has she been suicidal?"

"I don't know, but she seems groggy, and prays all the time. She's been taking sleeping pills. It's possible that she's taking too many."

"All right, call an ambulance. Get her immediately to the ER and have them call me. They'll need to check for an overdose."

Ted didn't want any part of that. "Doctor, look, there's another concern. We need to be sensitive here. My sister's reputation is important. I'm concerned about going over to the ER and someone recognizing her or me. We need to keep it out of the press."

"Senator, my first concern is to make sure your sister is alive tomorrow. If you want me involved, take her immediately to the ER and have someone call me when you get there."

Scowling, Ted gave in and called an ambulance, which took Denise to Denver Memorial. He also called the president of the hospital, who assured him she would be protected from the press. When she arrived, she was taken to a private room and given a pseudonym. A drug screen revealed a low blood concentration of the prescribed sleeping pill, not high enough to be of concern.

Ted called Sabatha for advice on what to do next.

"Dr. Sabatha, Senator Larkin calling. The ER doctor told me he had called you with results. She wants to go home, but I'm concerned that she might hurt herself. What do you think?"

"Yes, the tox screen turned out OK, but I'd like to keep her for an observation period."

"I don't think she'll go for that. At least that's what she told me."

"Well, if it's necessary to keep her from injuring herself, I can order a hold on her. It'd be better if she would agree, but if she won't then I need you to talk to your attorney. He'll know the procedure. Assuming you're her closest relative, you can file an affidavit for a court order to keep her under observation. I'll submit a supporting document, and usually the court agrees when a psychiatrist concurs. There's more to it if we have to keep her for an extended stay without her permission."

"OK. I understand. Thanks, Doc."

Ted immediately called his attorney, Ed Tucker, and asked him to handle the court order procedure. Denise was transferred to Rocky Mountain Psychiatric Pavilion, a private facility, managed like a hotel, with plush furnishings and gourmet food. It maintained a code of strict confidentiality. Names of patients were never used. If family or friends wanted to talk to a patient, they had to know the patient's alphanumeric code. All costs were paid in cash, keeping insurance companies out of the loop to ensure patient privacy.

The next morning, Dr. Sabatha found Denise sitting up in bed, appearing very groggy. She looked up, realizing he was someone she didn't recognize.

"Who are you? Leave, now!"

"I'm Dr. Sabatha, a psychiatrist. Your brother Ted asked me to talk to you. He believes I may be able to help you."

"I'm not going to talk to you! Just leave, now!"

"Mrs. Stevens, I understand you're upset. I'm very sorry about your husband."

"I want to be left alone. If you don't leave now, I'll call security."

"Can you just tell me how you're feeling today? Are the medications helping?"

"I told you to leave. I need to pray."

David realized he had only a short time to engage her. "Mrs. Stevens, the nurses have told me you're always talking about Jesus."

She suddenly seemed more interested. "Well, now that you bring it up, are you a Christian? Have you accepted the Lord Jesus Christ as your savior?"

"Mrs. Stevens, we need to talk about you, not me."

"Well, I'm a Christian. My faith is in the Lord Jesus Christ."

"Having a strong faith is wonderful, Mrs. Stevens, but why are you so concerned about others knowing Jesus?"

There was a long pause, and then she fell back onto the bed and covered her face with her blanket. "I don't want to talk to you anymore. Leave me alone. Help! Someone help me!"

Realizing the interview was over, Dave left the room and called Larkin.

"Senator Larkin, this is Dr. Sabatha. I just saw Denise."

"Well, what do you think?"

"It's too early to know what's going on. I'll need more time with her. Frankly, it concerns me." Dave was concerned that she was severely depressed. Her incessant praying was obsessive and mixed with delusional thoughts. However, he couldn't tell Larkin any details because of confidentiality issues.

"What do you mean by that?" Larkin cried. If his sister's condition was serious, it could create bad publicity for his family.

"She needs to remain under close supervision to make sure she's not suicidal. And I need to add some medications to help her. Did you get the court order to keep her in the facility?"

"My attorney called, and it's been approved."

"Good. Hopefully she'll voluntarily stay until she feels better."

"Thanks, Doctor, and please do everything possible to keep this under wraps."

When he finished the call, Dave wrote orders while wondering what kind of person would be more concerned about his own reputation than his sister's severe illness.

Dave went back to his office to create a chart on his new patient. When he finished his notes, he placed the chart into the files mixed with active and less active patients. When he first assumed the practice, he'd made an effort to read all the charts and get familiar with the ones who might need more attention. The chart next to Denise's was on Frank Stevens. He was one of the patients whom he'd categorized as less active, only needing an occasional visit to deal with a pressing problem. Even though Frank was dead, he thought the information in his chart might help him understand Denise's psychiatric condition. He knew he had to be careful and keep the information confidential from Denise.

Frank had been in intensive psychotherapy at the age of nineteen following an automobile accident. He had been drunk, ran a red light and crashed into another car causing serious injury to the passenger in the other vehicle. The judge placed Frank on probation, but a jail sentence loomed if he didn't attend AA meetings and remain under the supervision of a psychotherapist. It appeared to make a difference. He became a better student and voluntarily gave lectures to other college students about his bad experience with alcohol. His life stabilized, he got married, finished his Ph.D. and everything went smoothly until he was caught having an affair with the wife of a prominent surgeon. Frank's wife threatened a divorce after the affair, but stayed with him after having counseling with her pastor. She became more religious, spending many hours at church participating in prayer meetings and Bible study groups. Frank mentioned that he'd found crumbled up notes written in Denise's handwriting containing explicit descriptions of how much she hated him and wished he was dead.

After reading the chart, Dave exhaled slowly while thinking about what he'd just read. *Why did she continue to be so angry about the affair that had been over for years, and what made her continue with her extreme religious views? It's going to take me more time to develop her trust and get to the bottom of this.*

While engaged in intense thought, Sabatha sensed dryness in his mouth. He poured himself a drink of cold water and splashed some on his face. He was ready now to greet his next patient with practiced coolness.

Chapter Seventeen

AS SOON AS he left Sol's office, Charley went to work on the COADD case. He was given carte blanche to investigate any and all angles regarding the disappearance of the specs. First he called the security company to ask for videotapes of the premises. He was informed there was no video surveillance, but the system could identify persons entering and leaving based on pass codes. Based on the assumption no one would take a chance to remove items during daytime, he asked for a list of all persons who had gained entry to the company after routine hours on days just before or immediately following Frank Stevens' death. The company sent him the list, which contained two entries. One was the janitorial service, Universe Cleaning, and the other was Jimmy Barone.

Universe had a contract with COADD to clean labs and offices three times a week. According to the manager, the same personnel had done the cleaning for the past two years. Charley couldn't rule out the possibility that someone in the cleaning company had removed the documents, but that someone would've had to know which lab books contained the specs.

That meant having intimate knowledge of their location, since most of the lab books looked alike and were only identified by code. They also would've had to know Frank's passwords at different security levels, and be familiar with all computer folders that contained key files. Only one person possessed that access and familiarity, and that was Jimmy Barone. Charley asked for a background check on Universe employees, but he was sure he had his man.

Next he interviewed all personnel who had worked with Frank, in particular those who were familiar with CMV formulations. That was easy, because Beth Cohn and Todd Bigelow were the only others who were directly involved with the project. Charley met with them separately.

"Beth, I've been asked by Mr. Feldman to find the specs that disappeared. I need your help with anything you might know."

"Sure Mr. Blackwood, but I have to tell you I know nothing more than I told Mr. Feldman. Frank never let me have access to them."

"I gathered that from talking to Sol, but can you think of anyone who would know about the specs?"

"The only people Frank confided in were Jimmy and maybe Jack Haberman. Jack no longer works here, but he worked part time while he was in high school. You may know his father, Dr. Lenny Haberman. Jack is his son and you must know, Frank died from an allergy shot reaction in Dr. Haberman's office."

Charley perked up his ears. "Yeah, I knew that, but I didn't know about his son. Do you know how to reach him?"

"The last I heard he was in college in Boulder. I think he's studying chemistry, and premed."

"Do you know if Frank made copies of the specs?"

Charley could tell that Beth was sharp of mind and seemed honest. "I think he kept another copy, possibly at his home."

"Great, thanks Beth, you've been really helpful."

He spent another hour interviewing Todd, who had just been added to the staff in the past few months doing patent research for Frank. He hadn't worked directly in the lab, and had no involvement with the CMV specifications.

Later, Charley dismissed both as suspects when their background checks came back clean.

Over several days while thinking about all the possibilities, a thought occurred to him that someone at Johnson CRO could have been involved. They supervised the study and would have known the positive results of the recent trial. Maybe a person there had an opportunity to sell the information to an outsider for big bucks. He was given a list of the CRO employees involved with the project, and then submitted them to his friend at the CBI for background checks. Everyone came back clean, except one- Alonzo Gonzalez, a Hispanic kid from L.A. Gonzalez had a misdemeanor ten years ago for driving off from a gas station without paying. He was fined, and had his driver's license revoked for a year, but had a clean record since the offense. His supervisor was not familiar with his misdemeanor history, but she never had reason to doubt his honesty. In fact, he was up for a raise and promotion because his work was excellent.

That left Charley with one suspect, Jimmy Barone. The CBI background check on Jimmy also came back clean. It described his scientific education and tracked his past employment. Comments from past employers indicated that he had been an excellent, trustworthy employee.

Within a few weeks Charley submitted a summary of his investigation to Sol. Although Jimmy was the chief suspect, he could not state unequivocally that a crime had been committed, since Jimmy could have secured the specs for safekeeping after something happened to Frank.

The obvious goal now was to find Jimmy. Charley obtained his cell phone number and called the phone company. No one would provide him with voice mail messages without a court order, which would take time. Then he had a better thought, and called Sol to get the name of the IT manager at COADD.

Charley made the call. "Hi, Richard, I'm Charley Blackwood. Did Sol Feldman tell you I'd be calling?"

"Yes sir, he just got off the phone. How can I help?"

"Well, you probably know all the manufacturing specs to make the vaccine are missing. They suddenly disappeared after Dr. Stevens' death. The primary suspect is Jimmy Barone, and he also disappeared after Dr. Stevens' death. I'm trying to find Jimmy, and it would help if I could get a copy of his voice mails. They should be on the company servers."

"No problem. If the calls were on company phones, the information belongs to the company. I'll retrieve them right away."

"Richard, you've made my day."

Charley then decided to track Jimmy by accessing his credit card usage. That turned out to be a dead end when he discovered that Jimmy always paid in cash.

He asked Beth for directions to Jimmy's condo. Like Beth, he was repelled by the decay and rotten food odors when he entered the unit. Walking around with gloves, he carefully placed several items into evidence bags, thinking fingerprints might identify acquaintances that could lead them to Jimmy. He included scraps of paper with handwriting and scribbled notes of apparent bets on football games. There was no telephone in the home. Apparently he did his calling on his cell phone, but that was also missing. Even with the food and trash, Charley got a weird, impersonal feeling about the condo. Nothing suggested Jimmy had ever lived there except for labels with his name and address on science journals.

As he was about to leave, he checked one other wastebasket containing newspapers and discarded food. While reaching deep inside he found a one-way Greyhound bus ticket to Chicago. He wondered who or what was in Chicago, and made a note to ask Sol and Beth if they knew if Jimmy had a vacation planned to visit someone, maybe friends or relatives.

Then he took out his cell and placed a call to Sol.

"Sol, Charley here."

"Yes, how's it going?"

"I just visited Jimmy's place. Beth was right. It's a disgusting dump. Looks to me like Jimmy had planned his exit very carefully. He left no trace of his existence."

"What do you think? Should we call the police?"

"No, not yet. I took items that should have prints. I'm sending them to a friend at CBI. With some luck they may lead us to Jimmy. Who knows? He may have other aliases."

"Charley, if anyone can figure this out, I know it'll be you."

"Your confidence can get you in trouble, Sol, but I'm doing my best to find the bastard."

Chapter Eighteen

DAVE WAS IN his office reading a psychiatry journal when Lenny arrived for his appointment at the end of the day.

Dave began. "Lenny, how are you doing?"

"I'm still having trouble sleeping, but overall I think I'm adapting as well as can be expected."

"That's good. It may help to talk more about Frank's death. You mentioned you and he were good friends."

"Yes. I got to know him when I joined the board of directors at COADD. He helped my son Jack, and I was very indebted to him." He paused as he thought about how much he would miss Frank.

"When I got divorced, Jack was only twelve. He withdrew from me, became moody even with his mother, had a sudden change in personality. He lost interest in school and started hanging out with a bunch of losers in middle school. I tried everything to get in touch with him. It got worse after I remarried and he turned thirteen. He didn't like Elaine's kids or Elaine. Basically he didn't want to spend time with me or my new family.

As he got older I kept trying different ways to break through the wall he'd built around himself."

Lenny paused to sip from a water bottle. "I kept thinking of a science analogy because that's how my brain works. The one that worked for me was thinking of water in an ice tray, watching the water crystallize and eventually morph into a different physical state, and yet the composition was still the same, water... now in a different form. I thought metaphorically that all I needed to do was warm the ice cube and it would melt back to water. But nothing I did seemed to help. Jack has remained distant from me."

"Lenny, who was he living with at that time, you or your ex-wife?"

"Sorry. I didn't mention that his mother and I shared custody, but Jack decided to live with me most of the time. Elaine and I brought her two children, a fifteen-year-old daughter and sixteen- year-old son, and Jack together. For the first year things seemed OK. Then he started to complain that we weren't fair. He wasn't getting his fair share of whatever. You name it, material things, time with me alone, love... anything you could name. Regardless of how hard we tried, Jack would see it as being unfair. I tried everything, even took him on several fishing trips, just the two of us. But nothing changed. Then I got calls from his high school; he wasn't going to classes. He was caught smoking on campus and got into a fight with another kid. I took him to a child psychiatrist, but that wasn't much help. We simply couldn't communicate, although God knows I tried."

Lenny shook his head in disbelief while thinking about his next remark. "One day Jack mentioned that he was having headaches, and they were getting worse. That's when the alarm bells went off. I took him to see a neurologist and he worked him up. It never occurred to me that his behavior change could have been from something physical. Up until that time he never mentioned his headaches, but anyway we found out that he had a benign brain tumor, a meningioma. I couldn't believe it! The neurologist said he was fortunate because the tumor could be removed by surgery. That was when he was fifteen, and there's been no recurrence."

Dave interrupted. "Lenny, that had to be one hell of a relief. Did his personality return to normal?"

"Well, he had to drop out of school for a year, and he still seemed moody. He had no interests or hobbies, and when he went back to school he remained a loner. I remember saying to him, 'Jack, you're not acting like yourself. Is there anything I need to know?'

"He said no, but anyway I said, 'Jack, you're not making good grades, you seem uninterested in everything. Elaine and I are trying to help, but we need to know what's wrong. Would you rather spend more time with your mother?' He said no, that he was OK at our house. I kind of kept after him. He would say things like, 'I don't know why I feel so down. Maybe, because all my friends are a year ahead of me... I need time to make new friends.'

"I thought about getting him more psych therapy but then I came up with the idea of introducing him to Frank and having him work at COADD. I said, 'Jack, I talked to friends at COADD. You remember they're studying a vaccine to prevent cocaine addiction,' and then he screamed, and went off. Thought I was accusing him of using cocaine. I told him I wasn't, and that COADD just needed computer and chemistry lab help and they were willing to have him work part time in the lab. I even mentioned he'd make a few bucks.

"In the end, he started working at COADD. After a few weeks, he'd come home bursting with excitement, talking endlessly about what he was doing. He said, 'Jimmy taught me to use this incredible mass spec machine. You just can't believe what it can measure, and how little it can detect! And Dr. Stevens lets me work on his programs and he has me writing code for him too. It's the best!' When he said, 'It's the best,' I felt that he'd found his passion. He got close to Frank. Probably became a father figure to him.

"From then on, Jack was a changed kid. I couldn't keep him away from the lab, and you know he's now a premed student at University of Colorado and loving it. But we still have a relationship problem. He's continues to be moody and stays away, doesn't call much either. I keep wondering if the brain tumor is recurring or whether it caused permanent changes to his personality, but overall, I feel lucky. At least he found something that matters to him."

Dave smiled. "Now I can see why Frank meant so much to you."

"Yes." Lenny suddenly felt the sadness again as his words trailed off, and his eyes welled up. "Dave, this is really helping. I'd like to schedule another session later this week."

Dave nodded, and made a note in his book.

Both stood up. Dave said, "Hey I'm done for the day, let me walk out with you."

As they walked down the stairs, Lenny started to relax. "Dave, how do you like Denver so far?"

"Well, this town is so different from New York, but we're getting adjusted. We live out in Lakewood. I don't think I'll ever take the amazing views for granted. It's so very different from office buildings! Instead of honking taxis, I get honking geese."

Both men grinned. Dave continued, "We do enjoy it, and we're starting to make friends as well. Plus, my wife has family here."

"Great, I'm so pleased you came when you did. I'm not sure what I would've done without you here."

"Lenny, I'm doing nothing special but I'm glad to help."

They walked into the parking lot and realized their vehicles were parked next to each other. Dave went to open the door of a large van.

Lenny remarked, "Dave, I can't imagine the gas bills on that one."

"Oh, it's a matter of necessity. I need it for a member of my family who has difficulty getting into small cars."

"Well that makes sense. Have a nice weekend. I'll see you next week." As they departed, Lenny realized that was the first time Dave mentioned anything to him about his private life.

Chapter Nineteen

JACQUELINE DOREN REMAINED secluded in her home after Denise attacked her. Mostly she was concerned that Pete would find out she had attended Frank's funeral. She sat sipping a glass of brandy, gazing out into her backyard watching a pair of yellow finches, and thinking back on her life.

She had seen a lot - too much - and she knew the players in this present drama all too well. The operative word was *knew*.

She had grown up in Salty, Nebraska, a town of two thousand situated in the center of the state. Those were not fond memories.

At age eleven she had experienced signs of precocious sexual development, with breasts and menstrual periods. In high school, she avoided the boys and would repeatedly turn down offers to date. Because of her unusual beauty, some thought she was stuck up, but she had a dirty secret; there was trouble at home.

Her parents drank excessively. Her father sexually assaulted her during one of his alcoholic binges, while her mother slept off a hangover. That happened a few more times before she decided to work late as a waitress to avoid him, hoping he would be asleep in a drunken stupor by the time she returned from the cafe. Finally after more nightmarish rapes, she left home at seventeen to try a modeling career in New York City.

Nothing had prepared Jacqueline for the thousands of beautiful girls who had the same plan. At every agency she heard the same rejections: *"Yes, you're really beautiful, but so are the last one hundred girls,"* or *"you have no experience,"* or *"you don't have good head shots,"* and on and on.

One day while sitting in a row of candidates waiting to be interviewed, she started talking with the girl next to her about her frustrations. The girl eyed her speculatively and then said, *"You know, there are other kinds of agencies looking for pretty girls. I work for this high-end one if I'm really broke. They treat you pretty well and the guys are rich and not too creepy."* Jacqueline shook her head, but she took the girl's number anyway.

Later as she cooked a packet of ramen noodles in her fifth-floor walk-up, she listened to her roommate having sex in the next room. She was at her wits end-no money, nothing left but her looks. She picked up the phone and dialed the girl's number.

It wasn't that bad. Carol, a hard-eyed blond, owned the escort service with her strangely effeminate husband Ron. They screened their clients pretty well, keeping their girls safe from strange sexual fetishes and predators. Jacqueline was popular from the beginning, with her extraordinary beauty and sweet demeanor. She was paid a lot of money, which she saved and later used to get an art history degree at the City College of New York.

Having sex with strange men took some getting used to, but Jacqueline decided early on to treat each encounter as a learning experience. She carefully copied mannerisms and preferences of her clientele, many of them regulars, and other escorts became jealous of her growing reputation. She increased her appeal by learning basic Spanish and Arabic, making her more popular with influential Hispanic and Middle Eastern clients.

Not all the men were nice, and some just wanted sex, not the socializing. One guy in particular, who visited regularly from out West, wouldn't tell her his last name, only his first name and told her to refer to him as *"Just Ted."* He had a terrible problem of premature ejaculation, which she tried her best to help. Nothing ever worked, but Just Ted returned every time he was in town.

Finally, by age twenty-five, she was ready to call it quits, having amassed over three million dollars, and with sound investment advice, she had a nice stream of income. While she was considering her future, she suddenly developed severe pain in her belly. She went to an emergency room at a New York City hospital, and met Dr. Pete Doren, a young family practice resident. He diagnosed her condition as acute appendicitis, requiring surgery.

Pete was smitten with her, and after she recovered he asked her out, willing to deal with the prohibition of dating patients. He realized right away that besides being strikingly beautiful, she was also very intelligent. Initially, she did not find him to be physically attractive. After several dates, though, she realized that he was becoming more fascinating to her. She never tired of listening to his medical stories. What really turned her around was his appreciation of her intellect, not just her good looks, and the realization that she would no longer have to want for anything. Pete never asked about her past, and she never told him. After dating for just three months, he proposed and she accepted. Following a small wedding, they moved to Denver where Pete accepted a position with a family practice group. They found a beautiful house in the exclusive Cherry Hills neighborhood and settled in to enjoy new marital bliss.

But after just six months, Pete decided he was unhappy with his specialty because of the long hours, relatively poor pay for the large number of patients he had to see, the need to kiss bureaucratic asses of young cocky insurance administrators with MBAs telling him how much he would be paid and having to practice defensive medicine to prevent lawsuits. Jacqueline knew he already had one lawsuit filed against him, and they'd sit long hours discussing his unhappiness. She supported his need to change, hoping he'd have more time for her.

After some careful deliberation he decided to combine several specialties: allergy, laser aesthetic surgery with liposuction and weight loss. He considered these disciplines easy to learn and practice, so he rejected the time honored path of board qualified education and mentorship, and elected a quicker path: weekend courses taught by businesses promoting their products and services. He set up his clinics with technicians to run the allergy clinic and weight loss center, and hired nurses to perform simple laser procedures and administer Botox injections. His new plan was to get paid in cash for his time, phone calls, and procedures, and have less administrative bullshit.

Jacqueline was proud that Pete was proactive and willing to make a drastic career change to improve their lives. She saw her role as being part of a team she privately called the dynamic duo. They hosted parties at their Cherry Hills home, inviting socially influential people and doctors. All of her efforts helped get referrals for Pete's rapidly growing practices. She became a local celebrity in her own right, and was often asked to help with charity fund-raising events.

There was no reason for Jacqueline to think about her past until one day when she recognized "Just Ted" at a charity social event. She hadn't seen him for years and was surprised to learn he was Colorado Senate Majority Leader Ted Larkin. She tried to slink away, hoping he hadn't seen her, but he recognized her and discretely came over.

"*Jacki , what brings you to Denver?*"

"*Hi Ted! I actually live here. I'm married to Dr. Pete Doren. Do you know him?*"

"*Vaguely. Isn't he a plastic surgeon or something?*"

"*Something like that,*" she said.

Ted moved very close to her. "*Jacki, I'd love to see you.*"

She whispered, "*I told you. I'm happily married,*" but when she started to move away, he grabbed her arm and pulled her toward him.

"*I know what you are, so stop this socialite crap. I can change your comfortable life with a leak to the press. They would love to find out who you really are.*"

She shook him off and pushed her face right up to his. *"Ted, if you want to play hard ball, you might want to rethink playing it with me. I'll tell all if you ever threaten me again."*

He didn't expect her tough response. *"Bitch, you have the gall to threaten me. Don't you know who I am?"*

She spat back. *"I'm not afraid of you. I told my husband all about you and me. He knows everything."*

Ted dropped her arm and took a step back, staring at her in disbelief. He knew of several powerful politicians who had their careers derailed when something like this became public. *"You—you told Pete?"*

A wry smile appeared as she responded. *"Yes, Ted, that's right. Pete knows, so maybe you need to think seriously about interfering in my life."*

He knew Pete better than he let on. He turned away, realizing he had a new problem. He had to keep Pete quiet!

When Jacki finished the brandy, she remembered the powerful feeling of having Ted's balls in a tight grip. She also knew he was a wily SOB, and she would have to keep her guard up against him using the vacuous threat that Pete knew about him. It would be a delicate balancing act not to tell Pete about her past and keep "Just Ted" at bay. But she knew she was up to the task, having proved to herself that she could deal with difficult situations like controlling sexually aggressive johns in her past.

Chapter Twenty

EACH TIME HE visited the ICU, Agent Locke was informed that the accident victim was still in a comatose condition. Fingerprint results from the CBI and FBI returned with no identification. Results on the incomplete VIN number were still being processed. Locke was about to ask the press to print a photograph of the unidentified patient when an odd coincidence occurred. The CBI lab director called to tell him another set of fingerprints sent in by a private investigator matched perfectly with the fingerprints of the unidentified man.

Ben immediately called the P.I.

"Charley here."

"Hi, Mr. Blackwood, I'm Agent Ben Locke with the CBI. I've been trying to ID a patient in a local hospital."

"Sure. How can I help? Oh, and call me Charley."

"Charley, we have an odd coincidence. The fingerprints you sent in match an unidentified male at Denver Memorial who was in a bad car accident. It looks like we're dealing with the same guy."

"That's great news! Then you have Jimmy Barone, who worked at COADD. They're the company that hired me. I've been trying to track him down since he disappeared weeks ago, about the same time some important company documents went missing."

"Oh, what's that about?"

Charley brought him up to date on the events at COADD.

"Is that the researcher I read about in the papers, the one who was working on cocaine research?"

"Yup, that's him. We don't know why the documents were taken, but we suspect Barone took them."

"Well, he won't be able to help right now. He's in a coma and they're not sure he'll make it. If he does, they think he may have significant brain injury."

"Damn!" Charley exclaimed. By the way, were there any personal items recovered from the car?"

"None. Everything inside was burned up...Couldn't believe it." Ben gave him the low-down on the accident.

Charley whistled, "That's going to be a real mess for COADD."

"Charley, your name and voice sound familiar. Any chance we might have crossed paths?"

"Not that I know of."

"Wait a minute. Were you an MP during Desert Storm?"

"Hell, yes. Why do you ask?"

Ben responded, "Well, then maybe we might know each other. I was an MP in Desert Storm too, and your name sounds familiar. What do you look like? Maybe I'll remember you."

"At that time in my life, I was on the large side, so to speak, and some of my friends think I was born with a dark tan. Actually, kidding. I'm really a big black guy."

"I think I remember you. That's great. Hey, wanna get together sometime for a drink?"

"Sounds great! Let's do it."

When Charley got off the phone he called Sol. "Hey, it's Charley. I have some good and bad news for you."

"What is it?"

"Well, the good news is, we know where Jimmy Barone is. The bad news is he's in Denver Memorial ICU after a rollover accident. His car hit a deer and he's critical in a coma. My source tells me he was on I-70 near the Colorado-Kansas border when the accident occurred."

"How bad is he?"

"Very bad, real bad. They don't think he'll survive."

"Did they find any papers, disks in the car?"

"That's more bad news. The car and everything in it was destroyed. The car actually blew up. The cops told me there was nothing left at all."

There was a long pause. "How in the hell could this happen? The Colorado-Kansas border! What in the hell was he doing there? I have to think Jimmy stole those documents-for whatever reason only God knows-and now they're gone. So unless Frank kept a copy, our company's history."

"Look, Sol, this story isn't over yet. I need to do more work. If it's OK with you, I want to talk to Mrs. Stevens and find out if Frank left a copy somewhere, maybe in a safe deposit box or in their home. And I still wouldn't say anything to the police or investors. I just need more time."

"Fine, but keep me up to date, day or night. Is there any way I can find out about Jimmy's condition?"

"Sol, they won't tell you anything unless you're a family member. But maybe the CBI agent might be able to help. Actually, we may know each other. I think we were MPs at the same time during Desert Storm." He paused and then had another thought. "But there may still be a problem if he's off the case now that Jimmy's been identified. Let me see if I can find out anything. One of the nurses there is a friend of my wife. Maybe she'll tell me how he's doing."

"Good, keep me posted. I'll also ask a doc I know who might be able to help. Oh, and yes, give Mrs. Stevens a call."

After they hung up, Sol sat quietly in his office, wondering what the hell Jimmy had been doing. Each time he thought about it, he returned to the same conclusion. Losing the documents, for whatever reason, could be lights out for COADD.

Chapter Twenty-One

LENNY WAS BACK into his normal routine. Patients were returning for their allergy injections, and the whispering about the incident in doctors' lounges and offices was reduced to an occasional quip. The one that was most hurtful was a riddle told by one doctor to another in the hospital cafeteria. *"How many allergists does it take to treat an allergy shot reaction?"* The answer was, *"None, because they're never around."*

He tried to get on with his life, and started attending grand rounds at the hospital and going to Denver Allergy Society meetings. Numerous colleagues commiserated with him, and several offered to be an expert witness if it came to litigation. Patient referrals hadn't decreased; in fact he'd experienced an increase in new patients. Everything was going smoothly until one day an imposing sheriff served him with a civil complaint to appear in the Denver County Court. It listed defendants Leonard T. Haberman, M.D., Allergy & Asthma Specialists of the Rockies, P.C., and the plaintiffs as Mrs. Denise Stevens, her children, Tara and Bradley Stevens and the estate of Frank Stevens. The attorney for the plaintiffs was recorded as Ed Tucker, Esq.

He called Mark Persons immediately. "Mark, it came today. A subpoena was handed to me in my office by a sheriff. The bastard did it in my waiting room, in front of my patients!"

He read the complaint aloud and Mark responded. "All right, it's what I expected. I'll call Tucker. I know him from other cases. Just send me the complaint so I can file an answer."

Not knowing what any of it meant, Lenny said, "Mark, it only took a few months for them to file. That can't be a good sign."

"It just means they want to get on with it, nothing more. Don't read anything into it. You have to figure Larkin is probably accelerating it so he can leak the filing to the press, and use it as his celebrity case to get support for his medical reform legislation. Lenny, this will be the beginning of the discovery phase, and I'll need a list of anyone who might know anything about the case."

"I'll put it together. By the way have you heard anything from the medical examiner?"

"Not yet, but I'll have someone call. Lenny, stay cool. I need time to put it all together."

Before leaving the office, Lenny called the reference lab for tryptase and plasma histamine levels on Frank's blood. They were just what he had predicted. Both levels were sky high, compatible with anaphylaxis. At least the cause of death was verified. But he had one major concern, something he learned at a conference on medical malpractice. It made no difference if a staff member caused the reaction; the overriding rule was the captain of the ship principle. That meant he would be ultimately responsible for Elizabeth's actions if she inadvertently overdosed Frank.

As he drove toward home, he could feel his guts twisting with the stress. He decided to change course and head to the target range. Shooting off a few rounds would relieve some of the tension. When he arrived at the range, one of his fellow team members came over to chat. "Hey Doc, give me a crack at getting back the money I lost to you last month."

"Not today, Bud. I'm feeling rusty, just need to practice." He could hear the cracking in his voice. "Hey, do me a favor and ask the setup guy to arrange the plates."

He was referring to shooting colored plates; red plates represented *foes* and blue *friends*. Each was attached to a pendulum, and arranged so a *friend* and a *foe* were hung one behind the other. All the plates moved sideways at different speeds. The object was to knock out *foes* without hitting *friends* while they moved. The other object was to shoot quickly, as the competition measured both time and accuracy.

Lenny stood with legs wide apart, arms extended and parallel. Both hands gripped his 9mm Beretta steadily. The plates began to swing at slow speeds. He took his time warming up, requiring twenty seconds to shatter three *foes* without damaging a *friend*. He repeated several sets, each faster than before. At times, when the edges of red and blue plates were almost superimposed, an illusion of purple appeared, making distinction of the plates even more difficult. He shot with almost perfect accuracy, hitting only two *friends* out of a total of forty rounds. His best effort was a time of ten and a half seconds with one hundred percent accuracy, and it occurred when the plates were moving at their maximum speeds.

His teammate watched with amazement, realizing he had just witnessed something very special. Lenny's score was just three seconds off the national record for the event, which he had set a year ago, and only six seconds slower than the world record set by a Russian. When Lenny walked away he felt better, and the team member who'd watched his performance was very thankful that Lenny hadn't taken him up on the bet.

Chapter Twenty-Two

TED LARKIN'S PR team promoted him as a highly moral Christian, a believer in family values and right to life, largely to maintain support from the religious right. It also meant he had to keep his personal dirt underground. His concern was Denise's mental status, especially her assault on Jacki, Doren's wife, who he also knew intimately. He couldn't afford to have the press find out about her breakdown, and make it public. And he especially didn't want anyone to investigate Jacki's background, and in turn reveal his history with her. All of it made him uneasy. If any of it were to come out, the smear on his name could be irreparable.

Ted could never quite understand Denise's intense anger over the affair between Frank and Jacki. It had been over for several years. He had witnessed Denise breaking china, glass, anything in view, shouting that she hoped Frank would die and she was ready to make it happen. Now with her increased depression, he was concerned something else was causing her behavior, something beyond the anger she had expressed over the affair. She was seriously disturbed and very unpredictable. He called Sabatha twice a week for an update, but the shrink would not share information. He was frustrated with Sabatha's stonewalling, and decided to see what he could find out for himself.

Denise was at home, having been discharged from the hospital on sedatives and anti-psychotic medications. She was spending a little time with her children. Tara, age six, had the Larkin blond hair, blue eyes and mimicked some of Denise's impulsive displays of emotion. Bradley was a ten-year-old with the Stevens' black hair, blue eyes, and an outgoing personality like his father. Bradley had already developed precocious social skills, which he used frequently to amuse and placate his feisty sister. He had become quieter and more withdrawn since his father's death and seemed to have taken on the task of caring for his sister.

Tara missed her daddy and had become more querulous. She crawled onto Denise's lap and asked, "Where's Daddy?"

Denise said, "Maria, please, will you take them outside?"

Bradley ran over "Sis, come play on the computer with me." Tara started to cry, repeating what she had heard her mother say so often: "No, no, leave me alone!" He tried picking her up, but she struggled against him and continued her tantrum.

The phone rang and Denise rose to answer it, but before picking up she asked Maria again to take them outdoors.

Ted spoke. "Denise, how are things?"

"Not well, the kids are just too much for me. I can't bear ten minutes before I start screaming at them. They're going to hate me!" Her voice trembled. "And I feel so bad, they miss Frank so much."

"The weather has cooled down this morning. Let's take a ride to the park and walk around. It'd be good to get some fresh air."

The idea seemed to cheer her up, and she agreed. The park was bustling with energetic joggers, kids with iPods, and skateboarders. The sky was quintessential Colorado blue and a cool breeze sifted through giant cottonwoods, making conditions ideal for a morning walk.

They started walking slowly, avoiding runners on their left.

"Sis, how are you doing?"

"Ted, please. I just want to enjoy the moment and not think about anything. Can we just do that?"

"Sure, understood."

They walked a one mile circuit in silence. She appeared relaxed, gazing at people and young squirrels playing tag. After a few circles around the park, they sat down in a covered pavilion.

Denise dropped her head in her hands and mumbled, "Ted, I did a bad thing. I can't tell anyone,...except you."

He wondered what a "bad thing" might be. Knowing her mental state, he decided it was probably some imaginary issue that she had magnified out of proportion.

"Whatever, we can work it out."

"I'm not sure I should tell you. You have enough on your plate right now."

Ted coaxed her. "Why don't you just tell me so we can fix it? I'm sure it'll help just talking about it. Sis, you can't keep beating yourself up over this."

"I think I killed him."

He knew it wasn't possible. All of this had to be part of her delusions. He sighed, "Come on Denise, you know that can't be true. We both know he died from an allergy shot reaction."

She started to cry softly. "About two months ago he was having these horrible headaches. It was clouding his vision, so he went to an urgent care center when he was having one, and the doctor prescribed a drug for migraines."

As Ted listened, he grew concerned that she was about to tell him something he didn't want to know, maybe a mitigating issue that would make their case against Dr. Haberman more difficult.

"Our regular pharmacy was closed, so they sent a prescription to another pharmacy, one we never used. I went over to the other side of town to get it, and the pharmacy aide told me to read the information about warnings and side effects. Frank was sleeping when I got home, so I just left it on the bathroom counter and forgot to read it." She paused and sipped some water.

"The headaches stopped when he took it, and I didn't think any more about it until he died. Sometimes he complained about his asthma flaring up, but Frank's asthma was like that. It just flared at different times, especially when the pollens were high. He was going to talk to Dr. Haberman because he was wheezing more, and he wondered if his meds and shots were doing any good." Her voice became more fragile. "The day after he died, I found that brochure when I was looking for some sleeping pills. After I read it, I realized the drug probably caused his death." She turned directly to face Ted. "It killed him! Not the shot!"

"Now, Denise, stop! Frank's death had nothing to do with you."

She ignored him and kept talking in a monotone. "I thought about how I wished he would die after the affair. I know I caused his death. Ted, I'm so sorry. I really am. I didn't really want him to die. I didn't want my children to grow up without a father." She leaned into his shoulder and sobbed.

Ted let his sister cry it out. "It's not your fault, Denise, and anyway he died from a reaction to an allergy shot. I don't see how this has anything to do with his death."

"But you don't understand...It caused his death!"

She reached into her purse and pulled out a small piece of paper.

"Read this. It's the brochure on that headache medicine."

He unfolded the brochure, which listed information on the medication.

Propranolol hydrochloride: <u>*Indications*</u>*: hypertension; angina pectoris; migraine prophylaxis.* <u>*Contraindications*</u>*: Propranolol is contraindicated in 1) cardiogenic shock; 2) sinus bradycardia; 3) bronchial asthma; 4) congestive heart failure.*

He stopped reading and looked up. "I don't see the connection. What's the problem? OK, he had asthma and he died from an allergic reaction to a shot."

"No, no, keep reading."

While taking beta blockers like propranolol, patients with a history of severe anaphylactic reaction to allergens may be more reactive to repeated challenges, either accidental, diagnostic or therapeutic. <u>Such patients may be unresponsive to the usual doses of epinephrine used to treat allergic reactions.</u>

All the medical lingo was irritating him. "I don't get it. What the hell's the issue?"

"I called the pharmacist and asked what epinephrine was. They told me it was adrenalin and it's used when someone has a severe allergic reaction, like anaphylaxis." She paused dramatically. "I'm sure they gave it to him when he collapsed. I read on the internet it's routinely used to treat ana-phylaxis. Don't you understand? That headache drug kept adrenalin from working…from saving him. And it could have been why his asthma was worse, and maybe made the allergic reaction worse too! He died because of me, Ted, because of me!"

He wasn't sure what to say, but he knew this information had to remain just between the two of them. If true, it could potentially destroy their case against Haberman.

"I still don't buy it," he said smoothly, but let me check with another specialist to get a better idea if it could have had anything to do with his death. In the meantime, please try to get some rest. We'll work this out somehow. And don't tell this to anyone else before I check it out, even to Dr. Sabatha."

She continued to cry softly. "I won't, Ted."

"Let's get you home."

Ted needed to know more about this new complication, and he figured the person who could answer this was his friend and medical advisor, Pete Doren.

✳ ✳ ✳

Ted first met Pete at a medical society meeting where he gave a talk to gather support of the medical profession for his re-election to the Colorado Senate. Pete came over to introduce himself as a Denver doctor with specialties in allergy and aesthetic surgery. They became casual friends, playing racquetball on a few occasions at Ted's country club. Months later when Ted attended a charity, he noticed Pete with an attractive woman. As he drew closer, he recognized the woman was Jacki from his past, and then he learned she was Pete's wife. When he confronted Jacki, she told him Pete knew about her past with him. He wasn't sure if she had told him, but he decided one way to find out would be to develop a stronger friendship with Pete. Ted began to invite Pete to lunch meetings. Over time they became co-investors in commercial real estate and land development projects. Most were initiated from contacts with the real estate company owned by Ted's father. The deals proved to be very lucrative for Pete.

As it turned out, he genuinely liked Pete. Now he was glad he and Pete were friends because he needed a prominent doctor to endorse his medical malpractice reform legislation. Ted invited Pete to the state capitol to hear the debate on the legislation. It fed Pete's ego and was helpful in gaining his support. Ted told him the new legislation would be applying basic principles of market economics. Bad doctors would end up paying higher insurance premiums and, by the process of natural selection, be forced out of practicing medicine when their premiums became too high. Pete saw the logic immediately and agreed to testify in favor of the legislation. After all, he considered himself to be one of the best doctors around, so he would benefit.

When Ted called, he was put through immediately.

"Pete, it's Ted. Got a minute?"

"Sure, what's up?"

"I've got a family medical question. You do allergy as part of your practice, right?"

"Absolutely, how can I help?"

"I have a cousin living in Washington, D.C., and we were getting caught up on family matters when she mentioned her asthma problems. She's getting injections from an allergist there. Lately, she's been experiencing migraine headaches. She had seen her family doc, and he prescribed a drug called…let me see if I can pronounce it, pro- pran—o-lol. Does that sound right?"

"Sure, propranolol is a beta receptor blocker. It's used for conditions like heart problems and migraine headaches."

"Well, her allergist advised her not to take it because it could cause her asthma to flare. Was his advice correct?"

"Yes, that's right. In fact, she shouldn't be on it at all if she's on allergy shots. If she ever has a severe allergic reaction, it can interfere in treating the reaction with adrenalin."

Ted felt his heart start to pound. *My God, it's true.* Then he said casually, "That's good to know. By the way, she's not happy with her allergist. Got any suggestions?"

"I don't know anyone out there, but she should look into their background. She really needs to avoid those academic snobs who call themselves clinical immunology allergists." Pete was so scornful, Ted figured Pete had been snubbed by such a doctor in the past. "Tell her to find someone who's less academic and more practical. They don't need to be fellowship trained, just trained by people with experience. She'll be a lot happier, and they're a lot cheaper."

"Super. Hey, let's get some court time," he said, referring to racquetball. "How about next Wednesday at ten? Then lunch, I'll bring you up to date on the legislation."

"Sounds great, and by the way, Ted, let me share my condolences to you and your family."

Knowing the history between Pete's wife and Frank, Ted was temporarily taken aback by his comment. He recovered quickly, though.

"You know, Pete, life has a strange way of handling things. I very much appreciate your kind thoughts. I'll pass them on to Denise."

Chapter Twenty-Three

A NURSE HURRIED out of Jimmy's room to make a call to the ICU resident. Jimmy's eyes had opened, and he appeared to be struggling against the endotracheal tube, coughing and choking. His oxygen saturation levels had fallen to eighty one percent, dangerously low. The ICU nurse was concerned the tube might have moved, preventing the entry of air into Jimmy's lungs. When the resident assessed the situation, he decided to remove the tube. It appeared Jimmy had regained consciousness, and he might be able to breathe on his own. When the tube came out, Jimmy kept breathing just fine.

His recovery was considered one of the most miraculous in the history of the ICU. The director congratulated the residents and nursing staff for their vigilance and expertise, and suggested one of the residents write the case up because Jimmy's survival had been considered highly unlikely. The next stage would require long-term rehabilitation for his orthopedic injuries, but the major concern was whether he would have memory problems from residual brain swelling and injury.

Dr. Harry Finkle, a well-known neurologist with a specialty in brain trauma, was brought in to consult. He was in his early sixties and could easily have been mistaken for a Talmudic scholar with his bushy dark beard and mustache. He was stern and uncommunicative, with no detectable sense of humor. When asked to consult on patients with coma or amnesia, he would write down his assessments and recommendations and leave as quickly as possible to avoid talking with residents and relatives.

Dr. Finkle determined that Jimmy had signs of significant brain injury; the question was whether it was transient or permanent. The most obvious issue was his total loss of memory. Jimmy couldn't remember current events, and had no recall of the accident or his past, including his name. Radiological studies showed there was still evidence of swelling, which if reversed, might improve his memory. For that reason Dr. Finkle was hesitant to predict permanent brain damage, although he was certain the memory center, called the hippocampus, was affected by the trauma.

Jimmy's rehab was slow, but he started to recognize the faces of hospital personnel. Sol and Ole showed up one day to ask him if he knew where the documents might be. He strained trying to recall their faces, and he shook his head with a look of confusion, not knowing what they were talking about.

On a subsequent visit Sol tried talking patiently to him.

"Jimmy, do you know who I am?"

Jimmy stared at him with a dazed look. "Sure you're a friend."

"You're right, I am your friend. Sol's my name. You worked in our company called COADD. Do you remember?"

"Oh …I think I do. I was fixing something, wasn't I?"

"Not exactly, Jimmy. We're looking for computer discs and files you took. Do you know where they are?"

He looked confused. "Don't know anything about them, don't know."

After working with physical therapists, he was able to stand with support, and move with a walker while keeping pressure off a full leg cast. He remained confused, couldn't recall recent events, but some of his past was starting to return. An orderly had just finished bathing him when suddenly Jimmy blurted out, "Call Pete."

"Pete who? Do you know his phone number?"

"Just call him... now!"

"But I can't unless you tell me his phone number."

"Damn it. I told you, call Pete... God damn it, now!"

"OK—OK, calm down."

After getting him back to bed, the orderly reported what Jimmy said. The charge nurse recorded a note in his chart and called Charley Blackwood, who was listed as the contact for COADD to report any new developments.

When Charley arrived, Jimmy again became agitated when he was asked who Pete was. On another occasion, he blurted out, "Beth, stay away from it!" The nurse asked him who Beth was, and again he became frustrated, angry, and unable to elaborate.

His physical strength improved, enough for him to be transferred to Walnut Rehabilitation Center. Dr. Finkle dropped in to see him periodically. The nurse said Jimmy was mentioning first names, although he didn't remember last names or who these people were. Dr. Finkle noted that radiological studies confirmed Jimmy's brain swelling had subsided significantly. However, he remained guarded as to how much memory improvement would occur.

Speech and occupational therapists worked daily to improve his cognitive skills, which still remained rudimentary. He relearned simple tasks, like identifying an apple, shoes, and toothbrush. The therapists were hoping Jimmy might eventually be able to live in an assisted-living facility. Despite all these efforts, progress remained slow.

✳ ✳ ✳

Sol began to realize the only chance of finding the specs was getting law enforcement involved. He placed a call to Charley.

"Charley, it seems Jimmy isn't going to recover. What's the name of your contact at CBI?"

"Agent Ben Locke."

"Is it possible to build a case that we may have been robbed by Jimmy, and get the CBI or the police involved? COADD's future is at stake, and I can't keep the hyenas off much longer."

"Let me call Ben and see if he has any ideas. I'll get back to you."

Charley and Ben had that drink together and subsequently many more. They were now good friends, and working together again was an unexpected benefit. Charley called Ben to explain COADD's predicament.

"Ben, COADD is at a critical stage. Everything seems to point to Jimmy stealing those documents. Sol asked me to talk to you to see if the CBI would get involved."

"What makes you think he stole them? The evidence seems awfully slim."

"Well we finally got access to Jimmy's voice mail. Besides calls from COADD people, we uncovered a call from someone named KC, who sounded like a New Yorker. The number was blocked."

"So why is that important? Was Jimmy a New Yorker?"

Charley answered. "I don't know. But the other call was even more interesting. Some guy called, and let me read what he said." Charley held a small paper and read, " *'Hey Jimbone. Just letting you know I wired 50K to your bank account.'* The call came in the day after Stevens died and wasn't blocked. We're trying to find out who the caller was."

"So you think the wired money could have been a payoff for stealing the specs?"

"Well, that's certainly one possibility."

Ben said, "I see. Let me think about it. Just tell your boss to stay cool."

"I will. Oh, one other thing. Got anything on the Chicago bus ticket that I found in Jimmy's condo?"

"Nothing yet, but I'm still working on it."

Charley said "OK, let's stay in touch. I got a hunch Jimmy Barone may soon be in good enough shape to confront him about the missing specs."

Chapter Twenty-Four

ED TUCKER MET with Mark Persons to present interrogatory requests, schedule depositions and expedite discovery. There was no overt animosity, just two lawyers trying to move things along smoothly. When they finished, Ed had a few items to talk about.

Ed was five foot five inches, rotund with a slight beard and full head of short-cropped black hair, a bowl cut that would make a small town barber proud. It had the appearance of a bad hairpiece and Mark had to control his urge to pull on it to see if it was real. Ed's outfit was right out of the 1950's: a checkered jacket in combination with a large, bright yellow tie and brown-white saddle shoes. He may have looked odd, but juries loved him.

"Mark, you should know my clients are going for the gusto on this one. They believe there was gross negligence, and they're looking for significant damages."

"C'mon, Ed, you know how hard it is to prove gross negligence." Mark wasn't in the mood for bluffing. "I don't think you understand how serious my clients are about this case. You know me, Ed. I'll do everything possible to defend Dr. Haberman and his practice."

Tucker kept pressing. "We're willing to consider arbitration to avoid the time it takes to go to trial." He was referring to voluntary arbitration before a panel consisting of physicians, lawyers, and occasionally a retired judge. It was rarely offered to settle cases, and it was understood by all that the determination would remain confidential and non-binding.

Mark was puzzled. Tucker derived no benefit offering it. He figured it had to be a ploy, having heard from other malpractice defense attorneys that Tucker used it to get a defendant's hopes up, then dropped it the last minute to get them to accept settlement at a higher number. Still, Mark realized he had no choice but to consider it. "We're interested in all settlement options. If you're willing, I'll talk to my client."

Tucker understood the word *"interested"* since he figured Mark preferred keeping this case from a jury that might impose higher damages.

Tucker tried to switch gears back to the original discussion. "Good. By the way, if you want to make this even shorter, we could go directly to settlement talks."

Mark waved off the thought. "Why in hell should we consider settlement? We don't believe you have a legitimate case. We think this lawsuit is being accelerated by Larkin because he needs support for his legislation. He'll do anything to ratchet up his political agenda."

"That isn't what this is about!" He then rubbed his head vigorously. Mark watched carefully to see if there was any movement, but he was disappointed.

Tucker angrily picked up his briefcase, nodded and walked out.

✳ ✳ ✳

When Tucker returned to his office, he called Ted and told him about the conversation with Mark. Ted laughed when he brought up the issue of using this case to get political support.

"He's full of crap, Ed. Where do you think we're at?"

"I think it's just part of the normal jockeying in cases like this. If I had to guess, deep down he's worried. We could be talking five to ten million."

"There'll be no minimum settlement if I have anything to do with it," Ted growled. "I'm really pushing my legislation to increase ceilings. When it passes, he'll lose his shirt, I guarantee it. There's a clause to make it retroactive to the first of this year for cases with proven gross negligence."

He added, "Just so you know, I decided not to name it the Frank Stevens Bill. I don't want the opposition to tie the legislation to that case. It looks like it'll pass the Senate and I got Representative Bill Scott to sponsor the same bill in the House. He owes me a favor. The insurance lobby will oppose me, but this bill will get through. You know, Ed, people are damn tired of bad medical outcomes. People want reform, and they want pressure on the medical profession to clean up their act. I know the governor will sign it. He's on his way out next year and he's always had a dislike for the insurance industry."

Unseen, Tucker rolled his eyes at the speech. "Yes, Ted, and it'll put a lot more pressure on Persons. I started the discovery process and talked about the pre-hearing arbitration. My recommendation is to forgo it and just move ahead to plan for trial. So here's the next step. We'll need an allergist to sign off on a certificate of merit that an expert was consulted, agrees the case has merit, and is willing to express a supportive opinion. Do you know an allergist who would be willing to do that?"

"Yes, actually, I do. I'll call my friend Pete Doren. He's a local allergist and I'm sure he'll do it for me."

"Great, let me know what he says."

When they finished, Ted immediately called Pete.

"Pete, Ted here. How're things?"

"Couldn't be a better day, Ted. What's up?"

"Dr. Leonard Haberman. Do you know him?"

"Sure do. He's an arrogant asshole who thinks he's the premier allergy expert in Denver. I'm trained differently and know a lot more about this specialty."

"Great! Pete, I need you to sign what's called a certificate of merit to support our case against Haberman. Basically it states you're an expert in allergy and that you believe our case has merit. Can you do that for us?"

"Are you kidding me? I'd love to go up against him. I'll need to review the records, but I'll be happy to sign on."

"Wonderful! I'll let Ed know you agreed to do it. Let's play racquetball next Wednesday. I'll have my secretary set up details. "

"Good to go, Ted."

✱ ✱ ✱

Pete had just finished his surgeries for the day and left his office for a round of golf with another doctor who referred lots of patients to him. He got into his warm weather car, a new Jag convertible, and sped off to his country club.

Just before teeing off, his friend decided to have a little fun.

"Hey Pete, how about some practice putts for a few bucks?"

"OK, five bucks a hole?"

"Sure."

Pete was getting ready to putt when his friend mentioned being at one of Haberman's lectures.

"Say, Pete, is your allergy care scientific…you know, evidence-based, like Haberman's?"

Pete looked up, surprised by the question.

"Are you putting me on? He and his academic snob colleagues push that evidence-based crap to feel superior. It's just another way of claiming everyone else is stupid and don't know what they're doing." His face flushed as he was getting overheated. "Look, they're the ones who are stupid. It takes them two years of special fellowship training to learn what I did in a one week course. They're just pompous asses. Tell Haberman to take his evidence-based BS and stuff it where the sun-don't-shine!"

His friend started to laugh, knowing questions like this would provoke a tirade and affect Pete's game. Pete ended up paying his friend fifteen dollars for their putting game and losing all kinds of bets during their round. Back in the clubhouse, his friend assured him he'd send his allergy cases to him. Still it didn't satisfy Pete, because he knew Haberman was referred many allergy cases that should have been sent to him. He thought, *I would love to see that SOB busted with a big malpractice judgment.*

Chapter Twenty-Five

DENISE WAS FEELING better. Talking to Ted did help, but she was still under the care of Dr. Sabatha. At her next session with him, she skipped the elevator and walked up the stairwell to the third floor of the office building, hoping to avoid anyone she knew who might see her entering a psychiatrist's office.

Dr. Sabatha's small waiting room had up-to-date copies of high-end magazines, *The Atlantic* and *The New Yorker*. Denise didn't care for those, so she sat quietly, clasping her hands on her lap. Finally, Dr. Sabatha opened the door, smiled, and invited her in.

He told her she was making good progress, while avoiding mention that she still needed medications for her severe psychotic depression. She seemed more willing to participate in therapy, which surprised him, given the response he'd received when he first met her. By now he'd become less concerned that she was suicidal. She definitely seemed more engaged and trusting as they talked.

"Mrs. Stevens, tell me how you've been feeling this week."

"I'm feeling better, and praying does keep me calm."

"Do you pray as much as before?"

"I don't think so, but if I don't pray for me, I pray for Frank and for my children, and even for you to accept Jesus as your personal savior." She smiled slightly.

"Mrs. Stevens, we're going to push on today to a new topic. Why don't you start by telling me about your marriage with Frank?"

"I didn't trust Frank."

"Why not?"

"You know he cheated on me, don't you?"

"No, I didn't. Can we talk about it?"

She mentioned details he already knew, having read personal information from Frank's chart.

"How did that make you feel?"

"You know. I was real angry. I hated him. At times I wanted a divorce."

He thought the time was right to touch the edge, see how she responded when he asked a pressing question.

"How did you feel when he died?"

"Very sad. That's why I've been crying a lot."

"Did you have any other feelings?"

"Well, I didn't have to worry any more about that slut taking him away."

"So you felt some relief because she couldn't hurt you anymore."

"Yes I did."

"Is it possible you felt some relief when Frank died, realizing he too couldn't hurt you anymore?"

"Well, no." She suddenly became panicky. "No, no. Why would you say something like that? I was devoted to Frank! I cherished our home and our family."

Her head dropped, and she began crying quietly. "I was a good wife to him. I never cheated on him, but he cheated on me. He loved that slut, that bitch! I hate her." Wiping her eyes, she looked up sheepishly and said, "You know I slapped her at Frank's funeral."

Dave heard about her outburst at the funeral, but decided to move on for now.

"Mrs. Stevens, it's sometimes difficult to admit something like this, but you were very angry at him. Maybe you felt relief when he died and it could explain why you're praying so much for forgiveness."

She shot back emphatically. "No. I don't agree with you."

He felt he was getting close to a critical issue.

"You know, feeling relief when someone dies isn't unusual. When an elderly parent dies from a painful disease, relatives often feel relieved. They don't want to see their parent suffer anymore and they're free from having to care for them. When it's over, though, they may have lingering feelings of guilt. Does that make sense to you?"

"Well, yes, I guess."

"In your case you were so angry with him you wanted him out of your life, so feeling relief after his death would be a normal feeling. Can you accept that concept?"

There was a long pause. "No, but I did hate him and wished he would go away. He embarrassed me. My friends knew about it, and I hated him for doing that to me."

Sabatha pursued the thought. "Do you feel your wishes made you responsible for what happened to him?"

She became utterly still. "Dr. Sabatha, I can't talk about that. My brother doesn't want me to say anything about it to anyone, especially you."

Dave paused, mulling over what she had just said. His voice became more emphatic. "Mrs. Stevens, you're my patient, your brother isn't! Whatever you tell me is confidential. I want to help you, but you need to be able to tell me anything you feel about your husband's death."

"I can't, Ted will be very angry if I do. Please—please don't ask me to say anything more."

He could see that her back was up. Pushing her would do no good. "For now let's just set up another appointment and we'll talk more about it then."

After she left, Dave thought this was the best session he'd had with her. He sat at his desk and made a few notes. *I need to get her to open up. Why is she praying for forgiveness? What is it that she can't tell me? Could it be important for Lenny?* When he finished, he realized he was treading on treacherous grounds, hovering on boundaries of confidentiality.

✶ ✶ ✶

Denise walked down the stairwell, again trying to avoid meeting someone she might know on the elevator. When she reached the first floor, Lenny was walking into the building. They literally bumped into each other. Lenny stopped and turned to her.

"Denise, how are you?"

"I'm fine, Lenny, thanks, but I'm in a hurry."

"Denise, please, just a minute. I'm so sorry. I've wanted to call you, but you know the lawyers. They didn't want..." His voice trailed off. "Is there anything I can do? Anything at all?"

"No, nothing." She started for the exit door.

"Denise, please. Could we just talk for a few minutes, maybe over a cup of coffee?"

"Lenny, I have to get back." She faltered suddenly, realizing she needed to appear normal, especially if he had heard about her outburst at Frank's funeral.

"Maybe a cup of coffee," she allowed.

They walked to the hospital cafeteria, making small talk about her children, his family and about COADD. After sitting down with their coffee, Lenny spoke.

"Denise, I know how difficult this is for you, but I need to tell you something." He paused, choosing his words carefully. "I am totally baffled about what happened. I keep searching for answers. Do you know anything that could help me understand what happened?"

Her face became pale, drained of all color. "I—I don't, Lenny."

"Was Frank having more asthma symptoms, or had he mentioned any other medical problem? Anything I'm not aware of."

The cup in her hands started to tremble, spilling coffee onto the saucer and table.

"This was a mistake....I have to go." She stood up and bolted from the cafeteria.

Lenny looked at her retreating form. He wondered, *Why had she suddenly seemed so panicked?*

Chapter Twenty-Six

THE DISCOVERY PROCESS was in full swing. Most of the requested documents had been received. Tucker's office had obtained Frank's medical records from Lenny's office, copies of records from his primary care physician, Dr. James Kerlin and reports from the Medical Examiner's office, the paramedics and the Denver Police. Similar records were sent to Mark Persons' office. Additionally, Persons' office requested previous allergy records from another allergist who had treated Frank for five years prior to his move to Denver, and the records from pharmacies close to Frank's home and office.

Tucker had put one of his young associates on the case to analyze the records and search for evidence of negligence. Josh Cutter Jr. was two years out of Yale Law School and considered to be one of the brightest graduates of his class. His interest was in medical malpractice and criminal law, and after interviewing with several Denver firms, he decided to join Tucker & Price because of their malpractice experience and solid reputation.

This would be his second malpractice case, and he was excited to be involved. Some colleagues in the firm called him highly motivated, while others, who were envious of his close relationship with Tucker, considered him an opportunist. He was able to quickly identify those who didn't like him and he deftly avoided them. It was one of his special talents; sensing adversaries even before they were aware of disliking him.

He wasted no time using this as another great opportunity to climb the firm's ladder, and immediately sequestered himself to read the records. The firm's experienced nurse had placed the records into chronological order. Having organized notes was a major time saver.

He opened a Word file and named it *FS Case* to enter notes and questions. Initially he was most interested in the chronology of events, so he pulled out the paramedic record, thinking it would give him the most accurate look at the incident.

He began by reviewing a printout report by the senior paramedic of what happened in Dr. Haberman's office. He made a note to request the handwritten records, just to verify the accuracy of the printout. When Josh finished reading the paramedic record, he typed the following notes into the file:

- *Dr. Haberman was out of the office when the collapse occurred. If he had he been on site, could CPR have been started earlier?*
- *What was his reason for calling the ER? Why did he delay notifying 911? Why didn't the ER send help?*
- *Why did he wait so long to perform the cricothyroidotomy? How many had he done in the past?*
- *Did he have the necessary equipment to perform CPR?*
- *Was his training up to date for medical emergencies?*
- *Interrogatories and depositions to be requested from:*
  - *Elizabeth Finch*
  - *Patients who assisted in the CPR and patients who were in the waiting room.*
  - *Dr. Haberman*

- *Senior paramedic*
- *Dr. David Sabatha*
- *ER manager at Denver Memorial Hospital*
- *Get an expert witness to review these reports. Was the handling of the emergency consistent with the standard of care for allergists?*

He next reviewed the police report by Officer Tyson of the Denver Police. Haberman was interviewed at 6:35 P.M. The narrative was also a typed printout. The details were very similar to the paramedic's report with one exception, namely there was no mention of the delay calling 911. Basically, it didn't raise any new questions. He opened the file and typed in:

- *Order the original written notes from Officer Tyson for comparison.*
- *Interrogatory and deposition: Officer Tyson*

Josh was feeling good that he had uncovered many issues after only a few hours of research into the case. He was ready to move on when Tucker buzzed him to come to his office.

"So Josh, what do you think of the case so far?"

"Well, in just a few hours I've uncovered lots of issues that suggest negligence and maybe even gross negligence."

"Great! Give me an example."

"For one, he was not in his office when the reaction occurred. We might have him on abandonment and delayed treatment."

"Outstanding!"

"And he delayed a call to 911 for unknown reasons. Whatever the reason, it had to delay care for Stevens."

Tucker was pleased with his protégé. "I can't wait to find out more. Get me whatever else you uncover. Maybe we'll be able to wrap this one up without a trial and get a big settlement. Good work, Josh!"

Josh smiled to himself as he returned to his office. He could almost visualize the word Partner after his name.

Chapter Twenty-Seven

JIMMY WAS REMEMBERING a lot more than he let on at the Walnut Rehabilitation Center, but he kept on pretending he was unable to recall names, faces, and details of his past.

That came in handy when Sol and Charley visited again. They walked into his sunlit room at the rehabilitation facility. It had a few flowers and plants, mostly from staff at Denver Memorial and the rehab center. The room was otherwise barren except for a hospital bed, generic table with an inexpensive lamp and a TV. Some old *People* and *US* magazines were scattered on the table.

Sol spoke first, "Hi Jimmy, how you feeling?"

He regarded them with a wrinkled brow. "I'm feeling fine."

"Jimmy, we're here to talk about COADD."

"I remember you were here before."

"Do you remember working at COADD?"

"Sure, why would you ask that?"

"Until recently you had no recall of working there or even knowing Dr. Stevens."

"I sure do remember working with Dr. Stevens. He's a great guy. How is he?"

Both Charley and Sol looked at each other.

Sol responded. "Um... Jimmy, Frank Stevens is dead. He died from an allergy injection reaction. Do you remember hearing about it?"

Jimmy pretended to think. "Maybe I did, yes, I think on TV. I'm so sorry. Gosh, I had dinner at their house. How's his family?"

"As well as anyone might expect."

As Jimmy suspected, Sol started to intensify the grilling. "Jimmy, do you remember taking the CMV specifications with you?"

"What? Oh, you mean the computer?"

"Yes, the hard drive with the notebooks and CDs. Do you remember?"

Jimmy realized he needed to be very careful. "Well, maybe. I remember going to the lab to pick some things up. Maybe I did, it's still fuzzy, but I kinda remember something like that."

"Do you remember what happened to them?"

"I'm not sure. Did it have something to do with the accident?"

"Possibly, can you tell me why you took them?"

"Um... I kinda remember going on a trip to visit my family. For some reason I had to pick them up. That's all I remember."

Sol's facial expression hardened. "We found a bus ticket to Chicago with your name. Do you remember what that was for?"

He paused, trying to figure out how they knew about the bus ticket. He had bought the bus ticket to get to his next laboratory job. He had originally planned to sell his car so he wouldn't leave a trail, but Stevens' sudden death forced him to leave immediately in his car. "Maybe my family wanted me to meet them there."

"Is that where your family lives?"

"I think so." He decided to mislead them just in case they were trying to track down his contacts in the Bronx.

"Jimmy, what's the name of your family?"

He spelled it out, "B a r o n e."

Sol looked at Charley and wasn't sure what else to ask. After thinking about it for a moment, he decided to get to the bottom line.

"Jimmy, is it possible you took them to give to someone for safekeeping?"

Jimmy feigned astonishment. "No! Why would I do that?"

"Jimmy, the company won't survive unless we find them. There was another set. Can you help us find them?"

Looking at Sol, he said weakly, "I'll try. It's just so hard to remember things."

The two stood up preparing to leave. "Thanks, Jimmy. Please call if you remember anything—anything at all. OK?"

"Yes, I'll do that." They left the room.

✱ ✱ ✱

After they left, Jimmy realized it wouldn't be much longer before they caught on. Possibly, they had enough evidence to bring in the police to start an investigation on the missing documents. He couldn't make a slip and let anyone know he was now faking his memory loss.

His major concern was with the Pazzonis. He sat back in a stuffed chair as he remembered how it had started with them. He was in the third year of the chemistry program at Brown when his father died suddenly. Tommy Pazzoni met with him after the funeral and offered him his future.

"Jimmy, you know I loved your father. Marco and me, we were very close. He worked many years for us. He was a loyal soldier." He paused as tears formed in his eyes. "He was an intellectual like you, always reading those science journals. I'd get a kick out of him, when he'd lecture me on things like dark matter, black holes or

the big bang. I'd say something like, Marco, dark matter don't matter to me cause if someone gets in my way, I'd make some big bangs with my Glock and all you'd see would be lots of black holes." Jimmy laughed, remembering his Dad's lectures too.

"And he was so proud of you going to Brown and your brother Johnny being at Rutgers. Both of you have great scientific minds. You know your Dad was disappointed when Johnny dropped out to get into the concrete business with me. But you, he saw you as the special one. You're the one he had the most hope for, getting your chemistry degree and all."

When Tommy described how proud his father was of him, Jimmy got tears in his eyes.

"Look Jimmy. I've got an offer to make. I need somebody with your talent. You see, sometimes I get calls from clients who need help. They have a business, you know, something like gambling, or selling a product that might not be readily available to the public. You get the gist, don't ya?"

Jimmy nodded.

"So anyway my clients get very upset when someone tries to stop their sales with a new treatment or something that could slow down their business. And after all Jimmy, all of us believe in capitalism. Right?"

Jimmy nodded again, wondering where he was headed.

"OK so we're on the same wavelength. Hey now I'm talkin' like Marco, eh?" He smiled. "So I need someone with your talents to work for me, you know, like work in a lab and try to prevent things from happening. Are you getting the idea?"

Jimmy nodded slowly, as he thought about the implications of Tommy's request.

"So here's the deal. You get a job, say in some lab that's developing a drug to prevent people from gambling. Your role is making sure it don't happen in the lab, like screw up their experiments or something. No hard stuff. You leave that up to me and the boys. You'd be set for life. The clients are willing to pay in the millions for a successful job. What d'ya think?"

Jimmy needed time to think about it and told Tommy he'd get back to him. He had really wanted to finish his Ph.D. at Brown. That's what his Dad would've wanted, but there was a part of him that wanted the good life. Some of his friends who had business degrees were now making big bucks working for hedge funds and banks. His colleagues in chemistry remained caught up in their theoretical dialogues, arguing over scientific concepts while not paying attention to practical issues of everyday life, and as a result remained in debt. Jimmy knew it would take years at a university before his salary would permit him to buy a decent car or a house, or for that matter get married and support a family. He decided to accept Tommy's offer. He rationalized that even if the objectives were not high-minded, he knew he would be intellectually challenged by research projects, and he would still be associating with intelligent scientists. And he'd be able to afford some luxuries, maybe a large Chris Craft in San Diego harbor. Life could be good, and he agreed to the offer.

Most of his jobs turned out well. Sabotaging a research group developing a new drug to control gambling addiction was his biggest success. Tommy and the boys really liked the way he destroyed the research and it didn't require family intervention. That one earned him an additional bonus of half a million from the gambling syndicate who paid the contract.

He was still bothered that he couldn't stop the marijuana herbicide research without the death of the head scientist who was killed biking- an unexplained accident that led to an investigation by law enforcement. The family never forgot that botched one. KC sat down with him after the investigation had cooled, and told him, 'Jimmy we don't ever want a repeat. It causes Tommy to get very upset. So remember, never slip up like this again or things might happen. You know what I mean, don't ya?'

Sweat beads from his forehead rolled into his eyes, startling him back to the current harsh reality. He realized he needed to flee and soon. The only thing keeping him in rehab was the slow recovery of his leg, and soon the cast would be coming off. For now he needed to plan. To start off, he decided to call his old friend, Pete Doren.

Chapter Twenty-Eight

MARK PERSONS DECIDED to ask Lenny to review the discovery records, knowing he would be the most vested in doing a good job.

"Lenny, it's Mark. I want you to review the records I received from discovery. I can get another allergist to do it, but I prefer you do it. You have the background, and you're obviously very interested in the outcome. Are you OK doing it, or do you want me to call someone else?"

Lenny eagerly agreed. He would have the opportunity to search for explanations that might help his defense.

Mark continued, "There's a document called the certificate of merit. I'm sending you a copy that was filed with the court. In essence, it verifies that an allergy expert reviewed the case and agreed it has merit to move forward."

"Isn't that great news? I can't believe one of my colleagues would do that. Do you know who signed it?"

"It's kept a secret until the trial, for reasons I'll explain later, but I'll try to find out if I can. Usually it's signed by a peer in this state, but if a plaintiff's counsel can't find someone, they can go out-of-state for an expert."

Once he received the records, Lenny headed for the University of Colorado Medical School Library, located on the old Fitzsimmons Hospital campus. It was beautiful; some considered the building to be representative of a new architectural era for twenty-first century medical institutions, having a unique and friendly combination of expansive areas and small intimate alcoves. The lighting design was particularly avant-garde with pseudo-natural light creating an environment of being in and outdoors simultaneously. During wintery, overcast days it was difficult to find seats, especially when students and faculty with seasonal affective disorder took advantage of this accessible light source.

Lenny was a titled faculty member of the university, which allowed him access to the library, and the privilege to use the academic title of clinical professor when he authored research papers. Over the years he had collaborated with research staff on new advances in anaphylaxis. He thought it ironic that he was an expert in the very mechanism that caused Stevens' death.

He found a small alcove and sat down to review the records. Mark had given him a daunting foot-high stack. He decided to begin with the pharmacy records.

Frank usually used two pharmacies-High Peak Pharmacy, located one block from his home, and a CVS pharmacy close to COADD. There were monthly prescriptions at CVS in his name. The list was long and included prescriptions from Lenny's office for rescue and controller asthma inhalers. Older prescriptions included Zoloft, an antidepressant, and Ambien, a sleeping medication, all from Dr. Albert Rosen, a now-retired psychiatrist. Apparently Frank had used the High Peak Pharmacy mostly for prescriptions from his family doctor, Dr. James Kerlin. Those prescriptions were for antibiotics to treat sinus infections and a pain medication, Tylenol with codeine. Dr. Kerlin had also prescribed Imitrex, a migraine medication, on several occasions and more recently Celebrex, an anti-inflammatory medication. Frank had been diagnosed with carpal tunnel syndrome, pain associated with his wrist, and Lenny assumed the Celebrex was for that.

Most pharmacies recorded drug allergy histories of their clients, and Lenny wondered if it matched with Frank's chart. Both pharmacies listed no drug allergies, but Lenny remembered Frank was allergic to sulfonamides. He thought that was odd, because pharmacists were usually compulsive compiling lists of drug allergies and current medications in order to advise their clients of potential drug interactions and side effects.

He reviewed the drug lists for mention of beta-blocker medications used for a variety of conditions, including migraine headaches. Dr. Stevens had a history of migraine headaches, but there was no mention of his receiving a beta blocker. Pausing, Lenny wondered if the list of pharmacies was complete. He made a note to ask Mark to find out if Frank had used any others.

As he searched the stack of papers for the medical examiner's report, he paused while remembering about drug interactions that might be relevant. He pulled out his Droid and tapped his Epocrates app that helped him easily access drug information. If used properly, the software helped doctors avoid medication errors. He typed in "Celebrex."

Celebrex (celecoxib):

Contraindications/Cautions:

Hypersensitivity to sulfonamides.

There it was: patients shouldn't take Celebrex if they were sensitive to sulfonamides, sulfa containing antibiotics. *Was Frank taking Celebrex on the day of the fatal injection?* He pulled out Frank's chart from Dr. Kerlin's office and leafed through to the most recent office visit. A note dated two days before Frank died showed he had been evaluated for pain in his left wrist. It suggested a diagnosis of carpal tunnel syndrome and recommended treatment with Celebrex. Frank could have taken it the day of the injection, particularly since Elizabeth said that Frank wasn't feeling well and wanted to talk to him. Lenny felt a sudden surge of hope. *It might explain Frank's reaction!* He made a note to mention it to Mark, and to order a measurement of Celebrex in Frank's blood. But he also planned to check with an expert who knew more about drug induced anaphylaxis to see if this was a worthwhile lead.

Next, he moved on to the medical examiner's report. The summary gave an overall view of the findings. Gross swelling known as edema was described involving Frank's tongue, pharynx, larynx and lungs. Complete closure of the upper larynx was specifically noted, also caused by massive swelling. The pathology report showed hyper-expansion of the lungs due to air being trapped because of obstruction of the larynx. The entire airway was filled with thick mucus. Microscopic examination of tissue from the larynx revealed broken mast cells, the very cells that store histamine and other chemicals that cause anaphylaxis. Skin examination showed swelling with hives, also associated with anaphylaxis. The stomach contents were completely liquefied with no evidence of undigested foods. The findings were consistent with death caused by anaphylaxis, most likely from an allergy vaccine injection.

The report was just what Lenny had expected, especially knowing that the tests for anaphylaxis, tryptase and plasma histamine were very elevated in Frank's blood sample. He searched to see if they had tested for the presence of foods in the gastric sample. An appendage at the end of the report listed results from a reference lab. It included the analysis of the gastric fluid for foods that Lenny had requested through the ME's office. None of the foods requested were detected. However, a note at the bottom of the report by the reference lab read:

The detection of food allergens in gastric fluids may not be possible if foods have been completely digested by gastric enzymes and acids, as proteins and complex carbohydrates may have been reduced to small molecular products not detected by this assay.

It seemed the food allergy explanation wasn't going to pan out.

He made a note to ask Holly, his receptionist, to get a list of patients who were in the waiting room around the time of Frank's injection. Maybe one of them had noticed if Frank was short of breath when he arrived.

Maybe someone had seen him running. Exercise could increase body temperature, cause blood vessels to dilate, allow rapid absorption of the allergy injection into the bloodstream and potentially induce a systemic allergic reaction. If he could prove that Frank had done some type of exercise right before he arrived for his injection, it might help explain the severe reaction. Patients were always advised not to exercise before and after allergy injections. This precaution was also contained in the informed consent signed by patients before starting allergy injections.

After Lenny finished his review, he left the library to have a cup of coffee, and think about what he had uncovered. Several possibilities had to be explored. Cross-sensitivity between Celebrex and Frank's sulfonamide antibiotic allergy was a potential concern. The exercise issue also needed to be investigated. But the one that made him most suspicious was realizing that Frank had been treated for migraine disorders. Was he started on a beta-blocker? It was an important question. He would ask Mark to broaden the net, send letters to more pharmacies. If they searched hard enough, they might find the smoking gun.

Chapter Twenty-Nine

FOLLOWING DENISE'S ATTACK, Jacqueline kept a low level of visibility in Denver society. She turned down volunteer opportunities to host charity events, disappointing many who had come to rely on her hosting skills. A concerned friend called to invite her to attend their next book club. Figuring the club members knew what had happened, she attended the meeting and immediately went on the offensive. "*We all know Denise was hospitalized for severe depression after Frank's death. She must have been crazy. Did you hear her yelling that I killed her husband when everyone knows he died from an allergy shot? Well, I hope she gets some serious therapy. Who knows what her next violent act might be?*"

Still, the sting of embarrassment had not disappeared and she was hopeful it would be forgotten quickly so she could move back into her prominent role in Denver's affluent society. There was however, one silver lining; Pete hadn't mentioned the attack, so she remained optimistic he didn't know about it, and that meant he probably wasn't aware that she attended the funeral to pay respects to the love she'd lost.

She flipped on the TV to a local station and caught the middle of an interview with Senator Ted Larkin. He was asked about his future political ambitions by the moderator, Nate Spiller, who was known as a tough interviewer.

"Nate, I need to get re-elected to the Colorado Senate and continue as the Senate Majority Leader to get my medical reform legislation passed. That's my main goal."

"I understand that, Senator, but the rumors continue that you have ambitions for higher office. Would you be willing to tell the public what that might be?"

Ted just smiled and said, "Nate, for now I just want to be re-elected. That's my goal, to represent the good people of Colorado."

"All right, Senator, assuming you're re-elected-and the polls strongly suggest that's very likely, would it be a good bet you might consider the Republican nomination for governor next year?"

"Nate, I never turn down opportunities, but right now my focus is on the current campaign."

"Senator that's a breath of fresh air to finally hear you admit you may have future political goals."

"I'll not comment any further on that."

"That's fine, Senator. I would like to ask about your social positions. You've been a staunch supporter of family values. You're against gay marriage, and if I understand your position, you believe women should return to more traditional roles, being home, taking back their responsibility to give stability to marriage, families, rearing the children. Is that an accurate portrayal of your position?"

"Let me clarify for the listeners. It's true that our societies reflects many different social attitudes, but let's never forget our origins. This country is based on Christian values. I believe in faithfulness in marriage between a man and a woman. It is that strong, trusting bond that strengthens families and helps raise children with good morals. As for the role of women, I am not suggesting we backtrack and take away all the hard fought liberties of women. I simply believe there is a need for women to spend more time at home, to be there when the children get off the school bus, spending the quality time children deserve from their moms. If that means less career opportunities for women, so be it. Parents need to choose between dollars and their children."

"That didn't answer my entire question. Senator, Let me be more specific. Is your definition of marriage one that excludes gay marriage?"

"Again, Nate, let's not frame this in a black and white format; there are gray areas that need to be debated."

"That's certainly a good political response, one that passes over the question, but let's move on to a more pressing issue. Just two weeks ago, another Colorado state senator was accused of unethical behavior. The senator, who is married, has been accused of having an affair with one of his female aides. This is the third time in the past two years that a member of the Colorado congress has been involved in alleged sexual misbehavior. Senator, as the Colorado Senate Majority Leader, is this concerning to you, and if so, what should be done about it?"

"Nate, I will do everything possible to improve the ethical standards of the Colorado congress and to push for immediate sanctions when those ethical standards are violated. I promise my constituency that this will be a top priority when I am re-elected."

After hearing the interview, Jacqueline thought, *What a hypocrite. God forbid, if he became governor. The next step might even be the presidency.* She decided to reacquaint herself with him, rationalizing that she shouldn't cut off ties with someone so powerful. She thought, *Hell, what I know about him could get me whatever I want.* She placed a call to Ted's private number.

"Hi, Ted, it's Jacki."

"Hey… How lucky can a guy be in one day?"

"I just listened to your interview. It made me realize how fortunate I am having a friend who's so politically influential, and one who's so handsome I might add."

"So why are you calling, just to tease me?"

Jackie purred, "Actually, I want to titillate myself, knowing someone so important. It's made me rethink about meeting again."

Ted's heart rate accelerated, anticipating resumption of their relationship. "Jacki, I really want to see you. I've had recurring daydreams about it. I thought maybe you would never call after Denise's attack and I want to apologize for it. You have to understand the strain she's been under since Frank died."

Jacki paused, taken aback by his comment, not sure how to respond. She decided to take the high road, even though she felt a surge of anger that Ted had rationalized his sister's outrageous behavior.

"I understand, but that's history. I've moved on."

He was pleased with her response. "Sweetie, call me back in a week so we can set up a time and place. I just have to be so careful. You know the press is watching my every move and I can't have a scandal. You understand, don't you?"

"Absolutely, and I'll be careful. I'll call you soon."

She hung up and thought more about her plan, one that could control the next potential governor of Colorado. *If people knew, they might consider me to be very patriotic. Maybe Jacqueline Doren will become well known. I might even be added to Wikipedia.* That caused her to laugh out loud as she poured herself a glass of brandy.

Chapter Thirty

———————————————————

THE FIRST DEPOSITION would normally have been given by the plaintiff, Denise Stevens. Recognizing she had some ongoing mental health issues, Tucker and Persons agreed to move ahead by temporarily accepting a written narrative of the plaintiff's complaint and a description of damages on her behalf and the estate of Frank Stevens. The next deposition would be with Dr. Haberman and would take place at Tucker's office.

Mark met with Lenny numerous times to prepare, cautioning him to answer questions succinctly and not meander into areas that could lead to new avenues of discovery.

Before leaving for the deposition, Lenny had coffee with Elaine. He was plenty nervous and he refused the cereal she placed in front of him. "My stomach's killing me."

"Honey, you'll be fine. Just tell them what happened. It was a horrible tragedy, but it wasn't your fault. I know you'll come out of this just fine." She hugged and kissed him lightly as he left.

Although he never had been deposed, Lenny felt it couldn't be any worse than situations he'd faced in Desert Storm. He hoped remembering that time in his life would give him the strength to get through this ordeal.

They met late in the morning. Lenny arrived wearing a dark blue sports coat, white buttoned-down shirt and a bright-colored tie. Elaine made sure he had dressed to project a mixture of professionalism and confidence. Mark was wearing his usual well-tailored dark blue suit, and carrying a weather-beaten leather briefcase. In his other hand was a cup of coffee, which was shaking with his habitual tremor. Lenny wondered again if the tremor might signal anxiety or lack of confidence.

Tucker and Cutter introduced themselves. Tucker wore a light blue suit, while Cutter was dressed in a pin-striped suit creating the illusion of greater height, something he wanted to project after reading that a tall professional received more respect from peers.

The court reporter introduced herself without a smile. She administered the oath to tell the truth, and Cutter began the deposition.

"Dr. Haberman, could you state your full name for the record."

"Leonard Tegart Haberman. Some people call me Lenny."

Persons frowned and turned sharply towards Lenny to indicate his displeasure with his response. He leaned over toward Lenny and whispered, "Keep this on a professional level...no first names." Experience told him that clients, who suggested they liked being called by their first name, were less guarded, and more easily duped into providing self-incriminating information.

Cutter smiled, recognizing the first mistake by the witness. "Fine, could you describe your medical education?"

"I graduated from Columbia College of Physicians and Surgeons in 1984, then completed a medical internship at Bellevue Hospital, spent three years in internal medicine at Cornell, followed by a two-year fellowship in allergy and clinical immunology at the Allergy and Asthma Specialty Hospital in Atlanta, Georgia. After my training, I joined the Army Medical Corps and thought it might become a career. I stayed until the end of the first Gulf War, Desert Storm, and then resigned my commission to start a practice in Denver."

"Are you Board certified?"

"Yes."

"Please state the name of the board."

"The American Board of Internal Medicine and the American Board of Allergy & Immunology. It's known for short as the ABAI." He paused and then said. "I forgot to mention, I keep my emergency skills current with ACLS certification."

"What's that?

"It stands for Advanced Cardiac Life Support. It's a training course required for doctors to maintain hospital staff privileges."

"So, Doctor, you would testify that you're well trained to handle adult emergency medical problems?"

He hesitated, causing Cutter to look up from his list of questions. Lenny was heeding Mark's warning to take his time when answering potentially loaded questions, and this seemed like it could be one.

"I'm trained to handle medical problems encountered in my specialty."

"Would that include the handling of anaphylaxis, such as what happened to Dr. Stevens?"

"Assuming his death was caused by anaphylaxis, yes."

"Aren't you sure he died of anaphylaxis?"

"Based on the ME report, it appears that way, but I don't understand why and how it occurred. It was different; the most rapid, severe case I've ever encountered."

"Well, the ME's report states conclusively that the cause of death was anaphylaxis. Let's mark the ME report Exhibit #1. I have copies for you and the court reporter. For the purpose of our discussion, I will presume the cause of death was due to anaphylaxis. Have you treated anaphylaxis in the past?"

"Yes, I've treated numerous cases of anaphylaxis in my training and practice."

"Have you ever treated someone who had anaphylaxis from an allergy injection?"

"I have, yes, but they were all milder forms. There are degrees of anaphylaxis, the most common being hives. Some reactions are more severe and the patient's blood pressure drops. What happened to Dr. Stevens was an extreme case of anaphylaxis, and I had never seen that before. "

"Can you describe a few examples?"

"One patient who was stung by a bee developed hives and was seen as an emergency in the office. We had to stabilize his blood pressure and treat him with intravenous fluids, blood pressure-supporting medications, adrenalin injections and steroids. The patient didn't stop breathing or have a cardiac arrest. The anaphylaxis resolved over two hours, and the patient was monitored closely in my office for several hours before being discharged."

"Doctor, that's not what I asked. I want examples of anaphylaxis caused by an allergy injection."

Lenny paused. If Cutter was trying to rattle him, it was working.

"Allergy injection-induced anaphylaxis is rare. We never had one that caused death. The only reactions I've really had from allergy injections were mild hives, and those all responded to adrenalin."

"So this situation with Dr. Stevens was different than the other cases you experienced?"

"Yes, it was very different."

"Can you explain what the difference was?"

Lenny wondered where he was going with this, as the obvious difference was the death of a patient. "The difference was the patient died."

"Doctor, this is not a contest of wits. What else made this situation different?"

"Well, nothing worked to reverse it. It was rapid, severe and he died."

Cutter's face turned red. "Again, I am asking what else was different. We all know Dr. Stevens died. What made it so severe?"

"All I know was that it was exceptionally severe and I'm still trying to figure out why."

Josh held up a hand to stop him, and leaned over to ask Tucker something. He requested a ten-minute recess. During the break, Mark told Lenny he was doing great, but he needed to keep his answers short, not to give so much information and above all, stay calm. The deposition resumed.

Cutter continued. "Can you tell us about any other case of anaphylaxis you would describe as severe? Like ones that required your intervention."

"A child was rushed to my office from a day care center because she had inadvertently eaten a walnut and was allergic to it. She had hives all over, but she was conscious, breathing well and had good vitals. We called 911 immediately for help. In the meantime, we couldn't start an IV because her veins had collapsed, but we did administer adrenalin injections, gave her steroids and monitored her breathing, vital signs and oxygen saturation. The paramedics arrived within five minutes and she improved, but she was still hospitalized overnight."

"Do you believe this case and the one you mentioned were handled in conformance with standards of care for your specialty?"

"I guess it depends on what standards you're referring to. I'm board certified, if that's what you're referring to."

"I'm referring to national guidelines of care for your specialty."

"We reference the guidelines written by the Joint Council of Allergy cosponsored by both the American Academy of Allergy, Asthma and Immunology and the American College of Allergy, Asthma and Immunology. The guidelines are referred to as practice parameters for anaphylaxis."

"Good, I'm glad you mentioned that because I have a copy of the practice parameter written by members of that organization. It was printed in JACI 2011, volume 126, #3, 477-480, 480.e1-e.41. This will be Exhibit # 2." That was duly noted.

"Doctor, are you familiar with this practice parameter?"

"Yes."

"Do you agree with the recommendations for treatment of anaphylaxis?"

"As I stated, they're a reference to be used in clinical situations like this."

"OK, let's now turn to your care of Dr. Stevens. I have read the report from the paramedics, which we will mark as Exhibit #3. You have a copy in front of you. Is that correct?"

"Yes."

"OK, you first heard about Dr. Stevens collapse when you were called on your cell phone. Correct?"

"Yes."

"Where were you when you received the message?"

"I was meeting with my psychiatrist, Dr. David Sabatha. I was in his office one floor above my office."

"Doctor, how long did it take you to get to your office?"

"I received the call on my cell from my receptionist at 5:15 and was in my office less than a minute later."

"How do you know it took less than a minute?"

"Well, to be honest, I've repeated the run. I've done it twice from inside Dr. Sabatha's office to my office, running down the stairway. It took 35 seconds one time and 43 seconds another."

"Isn't it important to always have a doctor on location in case this type of emergency occurs?"

Mark moved around in his chair, clearly uncomfortable with the direction of the questioning. "It's important to have a doctor onsite and I believe I was, and I responded within an acceptable time frame."

"The word *'onsite'* seems vague. Let me be specific. Should you have been in your office suite when this occurred?"

"My suite is part of a multistory building. There is a pharmacy on the ground floor and restrooms in the hallways. At any time I might go down to the pharmacy to speak to the pharmacist about a medication, and by my definition I would still have been onsite. For that matter, if I had to leave to use the restroom in the hallway, I would again have been onsite.

By being in a suite one floor above mine, I was still onsite and my response was delayed by less than a minute."

"Doctor, you're not answering my question. Please answer yes or no... Should you have been in your office when this occurred?"

Mark leaned forward to intervene in Lenny's behalf, but before he could, Lenny shot back. "I've given you my answer." Mark sat back, pleased with Lenny's response.

Cutter's face flushed with anger. He sat back and took a sip of water. Collecting himself, he resumed. "Doesn't it take between three to five minutes of anoxia to produce irreversible brain damage?"

"Yes, but I don't believe the thirty odd second delay would have affected the outcome."

"Do you know if Dr. Stevens was having trouble breathing before he received the allergy injection?"

"I didn't know anything about that when I found Dr. Stevens on the floor in my waiting room and took over the management of the emergency." Lenny looked over to Mark, wondering if anything he said now could bite him in the ass later. "Frank made a passing comment to Elizabeth Finch, my nurse, that he had some breathing problems earlier in the week, but not on the day of his injection."

"Still, wouldn't it have been prudent for you to examine him before the injection?"

"No, because he wasn't complaining of breathing distress on the day he received his injection." Lenny felt his pulse speed up, knowing this issue might not be defensible. He continued. "Several days after Dr. Stevens' death, Elizabeth called me and came to my house with her attorney, Glen Carthage. She told me Frank mentioned he had some breathing distress during the prior week, but was fine on the day he received his injection."

"Since you weren't there, you couldn't know absolutely if he was having breathing problems, Doctor, because you didn't examine him. Isn't that correct?"

"If you're asking an absolute, then the answer is yes. I could not absolutely have known that unless I examined him at that time. But most allergists do not listen to the chest of every patient before they get an allergy injection unless they're complaining about breathing distress at that time."

Cutter looked at his notes. "Let's move on. When you found Dr. Stevens on the floor, what was your initial assessment?"

"I recognized he was having difficulty breathing and turning blue. His tongue was extremely swollen and blocking his airway. He also had hives. All indications of severe anaphylaxis."

"Was he in shock?"

"Yes, I couldn't get a pulse in his neck, hear a heartbeat or get a blood pressure."

"What did you do next?"

"I started CPR with a ventilation bag and oxygen and elevated his chin to improve airflow. A patient, a fireman, who was familiar with CPR, helped me with chest compressions. Nothing worked, so I tried to intubate him but couldn't because of his swollen tongue. I also had my receptionist call the ER at Denver Memorial Hospital."

Cutter leaned over. "Why did you need the fireman to assist? Did you have anyone on staff to help you in this emergency?"

"Yes, normally that would have been the case. However, one of my nurses left earlier for personal reasons. Unfortunately, my other RN, Elizabeth Finch, became hysterical and was unable to help throughout the resuscitation."

"Are you saying she was not qualified to help you in the emergency? Is that correct?"

Mark interrupted, "Objection! Assumes facts not in evidence."

"Let me rephrase my question. You apparently noticed she was visibly upset and unable to help you. Is that a correct statement?"

"I guess so, but I don't know why she fell apart. I had no idea she wouldn't be able to handle a situation like this."

"Did you screen her past employment carefully to determine if she had a past history of this type of behavior in an emergency?"

"My office manager does all the screening and we check references."

"You never personally inquired as to her experience and ability to handle an emergency, did you?"

"No, but she met the criteria. She's a registered nurse licensed by the state. Basically, I relied on my office manager, who has experience in these matters."

"All right, so you were essentially alone, although you did have a patient volunteer to help with the CPR, a Mr. Phil Bellows, a Denver fireman. Is that correct?"

"Yes."

"Did you ask him if he had experience with CPR?"

"Yes."

Cutter paused to pull out Exhibit #2. "Doctor let me read Annotation 6 (c). from page 480.e8 of the anaphylaxis practice parameter. It states: 'Establish and maintain an airway.' It goes on to state 'endotracheal intubation or cricothyroidotomy may be considered where appropriate, provided clinicians are adequately trained and proficient in this procedure.' " He turned to Lenny. "Do you believe you are qualified to perform intubation in an emergency?"

"Yes, especially because of my army training in anesthesiology."

"Doctor, you stated before you couldn't perform the endotracheal intubation. Can you explain why?"

"Yes, I mentioned before that Dr. Stevens' swollen tongue obstructed my ability to intubate him."

"Wouldn't you agree that once you had help from Phil Bellows, you should have then performed a cricothyroidotomy as the next option according to the guidelines set by the practice parameter?"

Mark interrupted. "Objection, that's not a factual reflection of the anaphylaxis guidelines. The guidelines do not have obligatory requirements for a cricothyroidotomy."

Cutter took a few minutes to reread that part of the guideline. "OK, if you had the proficiency required to have done this procedure, would you agree that might have been the next option? Yes or no, please."

"Yes, and that's what we did."

"My notes indicate that you sent someone to get a knife from the office lounge and then you were able to do it. Is that correct?"

"Yes."

"Is it customary to use a knife for this procedure?"

Lenny knew where this was headed. He looked over to Mark, who indicated it was OK to answer.

"No, it isn't customary to use a knife."

"What would you usually use?"

"A scalpel or a large-bore needle."

"And why didn't you use them?"

" I didn't have that equipment in the crash cart."

"And why was that, Doctor?"

"I forgot to tell my staff to add them. But if you read the practice parameter, they are not included in the recommended equipment list to treat anaphylaxis in an allergist's office."

"Let me repeat what you just said. You didn't have the necessary equipment in your emergency cart because you forgot to add it. Is that correct?"

"Yes, but you aren't listening. That equipment wasn't a recommended requirement."

"Still, not having the equipment could have delayed performing this essential life-saving procedure. Isn't that correct Doctor?"

"I—I guess that's correct."

"You guess or can we agree it's correct?"

Mark leaned over the table toward Cutter. "My client has answered the question."

A slight grin appeared on Cutter's face and then he continued.

"Doctor, are you convinced the alleged anaphylaxis was caused by the allergy injection?"

"It's difficult to understand why it happened. As I've said, I've never seen anything like this before. But I know it's been reported in patients who've tolerated injections for years. That's why we have patients wait in the office for a period of time after their injections."

"I understand he received the correct vaccine and dose. Correct?"

"Yes, according to the notes made by Elizabeth."

"Is there any other way to prove Dr. Stevens received the correct dose?"

"No, there isn't."

"According to a survey by the American Academy of Allergy, Asthma and Immunology, the most common cause of allergy injection related death is from an incorrect dose of the allergy vaccine. Do you agree with that statement?"

Mark objected. "Are you asking if that is what the survey said or if Dr. Haberman agrees with the results of the survey?"

Cutter responded. "I am asking if he agrees with the statement."

"I think the survey was well done."

"So if Dr. Stevens had received an overdose, would you agree it could have caused Dr. Stevens' death?"

Mark objected, "Form of question incomplete, hypothetical, and assumes facts not in evidence."

Cutter frowned while looking at Mark. "OK, let me rephrase it. Was there any evidence that Elizabeth Finch may have given Dr. Stevens an incorrect dose?"

Mark now realized he had inadvertently created a problem for the defense. He didn't want Lenny to describe the volume findings because the evidence pointed to negligence on the part of an employee. That meant Lenny could get nailed based on the legal theory that a doctor, like a captain of a ship, could arguably be responsible for the actions of his subordinates.

Lenny answered. "I did some volume testing with Dr. Stevens' vaccine. The residual volume in his vial was decreased by about 1.1 cc compared to the volume that was recorded as having been injected."

"Well, if there was a discrepancy, doesn't it suggest that Elizabeth Finch or someone gave him more than he should have?"

"That's possible."

"Is there any other explanation?"

"Some of the vaccine could have been lost preparing a dose in a syringe. When you draw it into a syringe, some vaccine can be ejected in the process of removing air bubbles."

Cutter frowned. "Could that explain a discrepancy of 1.1 cc?"

"I think it would be a stretch, but anything's possible."

"Was Elizabeth Finch the only nurse who gave Dr. Stevens his injections?"

"Yes, according to the injection record."

"Since Ms. Finch is your employee, would you agree you had the responsibility to oversee her?"

Mark interrupted. "Objection, form of question, vague, asking for a legal conclusion."

"Doctor, was Ms. Finch trained to give allergy injections?"

"Yes, she was trained by another nurse, Jane Cross, who has been with me for fifteen years."

"OK, did Ms. Finch know how to give a correct dose of vaccine?"

"Yes, she is a trained registered nurse and she had been giving allergy injections for about a year. I'm not aware of her administering any incorrect doses."

"Do you have any other explanation of why there was a discrepancy in the residual volume of Dr. Stevens' vaccine?"

"I don't."

Cutter pursued. "Then again, would you agree it's possible she may have given Dr. Stevens an incorrect dose?"

"I guess it's possible, yes."

"So to return to my original question, assuming the volume discrepancy represented an overdose, could it have caused Dr. Stevens death?"

Lenny paused to think his answer through, hoping if he agreed, it wouldn't be used against him. "I think it could have, yes."

Cutter paused because the implication was obvious. Haberman would still be responsible for her mistake. He stopped to smile at Tucker, who also had grasped the significance of the testimony.

"Let's move on. Do you have any other plausible explanation for the anaphylactic reaction that caused Dr. Stevens' death?"

"I have a few theories."

Expressing a hint of a sarcasm, Cutter said, "Doctor, please share your theories."

"It's possible he ran to my office and had been overheated. In that case the injection would have been absorbed more quickly and caused anaphylaxis."

"Interesting, but do you have any evidence that he ran or exercised before he received the injection?"

"No."

Cutter grinned slightly again, making Lenny even more uncomfortable. "Any other theories?"

"I recently reviewed Dr. Stevens' medical records from his family doctor, Dr. Kerlin. He had been started on a drug called Celebrex for carpal tunnel syndrome involving his right wrist. It was prescribed the day before he died. Celebrex shouldn't be given to a person sensitive to sulfonamide antibiotics, and Dr. Stevens had a history of sulfonamide allergy."

"Are you suggesting Celebrex caused the anaphylaxis?"

Lenny paused, remembering that he had not confirmed this possibility with a national expert. He hesitated but decided it was still a reasonable concern. "Possibly,...yes."

"An interesting theory, Doctor, but do you know if Dr. Stevens had taken Celebrex on the day he died?"

Lenny knew that Celebrex had not been detected in Frank's blood, having sent a sample to the lab for measurement. He was concerned he might perjure himself if he didn't mention it. He then thought, *If Frank had just taken Celebrex close to the time he came for his allergy shot, it may not have been detected, but just enough of it may have been absorbed to have caused the reaction. I need to talk to Mark about this possibility.*

Cutter added. "Well, Doctor, I'm waiting."

"I don't know."

"Are there any other theories I should know about?"

"None I'm aware of."

"All right, let's move on. Doctor, according to the anaphylaxis practice parameter, it's recommended on the same page and paragraph (d) that an IV should be started when dealing with anaphylactic shock. Phil Bellows, the fireman, tried to start an IV but couldn't. Did you personally also try to get intravenous access on Dr. Stevens, and if you had succeeded, wouldn't it have controlled Dr. Stevens' hypotension?"

Mark protested. "Objection! You're asking a compound question." Mark didn't want his client to answer two questions with one answer.

Cutter responded. "OK, did you try to get intravenous access on Dr. Stevens?"

"No, airway management was what I concentrated on. His veins had collapsed and I didn't want to waste any more time trying to get an IV started when it was obvious that wasn't going to happen."

"How did you intend to treat his shock without an IV?"

"It wasn't ideal, but treating him with a shot of adrenalin could stimulate heart contractions and act as a vasopressor to increase blood pressure."

"You apparently were aware of the need for IV access. You performed one on the patient with the bee sting reaction. Correct?"

"Yes, but there are situations when you can't get IV access. I couldn't start one on the girl with the walnut reaction because her veins had collapsed. In Dr. Stevens' situation, I was able to inject adrenalin directly under his tongue. It's an area that's very vascular and allows rapid absorption into the circulation."

"OK. Can you tell me why you didn't use an AED?" He was referring to an automated external defibrillator, which shocked a patient's heart beat into normal rhythm. "Especially when you realized Dr. Stevens was in shock, possibly caused by cardiac arrhythmias."

Before Lenny could answer, Mark objected. "Objection, the question assumes facts not in evidence. Arrhythmias are purely conjectural at that point in time."

Cutter responded. "But we know Dr. Stevens had abnormal heart rhythms when the paramedics arrived."

"Prior to the arrival of the paramedics, when my client was taking care of Dr. Stevens, there was no evidence to support the existence of a cardiac arrhythmia."

Cutter shook his head and turned a page in his notes. "Doctor, do you have an AED in your office?"

"No."

"And why not? Isn't that essential for CPR? It's pretty common in most public locations. Shouldn't you have had one in your office for a medical emergency?"

"The guidelines don't include it as a necessity to treat in-office anaphylaxis."

Cutter interrupted. "So an AED was not available in your office, because it's not the standard of care for anaphylaxis as stated by the practice parameter. Is that correct?"

"Yes."

"So if a patient collapses because of a heart attack, you don't have the requisite equipment to handle that situation either. Is that correct?"

Mark barked out. "Objection! Argumentative." Mark wasn't going to permit a debate on the standard of care for a heart attack.

Lenny wasn't sure where Cutter was going with this, but he knew it wasn't favorable. Before Mark could stop him he responded, "I'm not set up for that contingency but it's not available in most doctors' offices."

"OK, let's move on. Now you called the ER for help and they didn't come. Do you know why?"

"I do now, but I didn't at the time. There was a notice sent to doctors in the building, that for legal reasons they couldn't have personnel leave the ER to assist in an emergency. We were told to call 911 for office emergencies."

"Did you receive the notice?"

"Yes."

"Then why didn't you comply with the hospital ER directive?"

"I frankly forgot about it and didn't recall it until later."

"You forgot about the memo to call 911. Is that correct?"

"Yes, but it was so chaotic."

Cutter cut him off. "Well, do you think it delayed arrival of paramedics?"

"Some, yes, but the delay couldn't have amounted to more than a few minutes."

"Let's get more specific than that, Doctor. You arrived at 5:16 and then you told your receptionist to call the ER. Correct?"

"Yes."

"According to the paramedic report, your office call was received at 5:20 and they arrived at 5:26. Do you agree?"

"I agree with what's in the report."

"It took them six minutes from the time they received your office call to arrive at your office. However, when you got to your office, which according to your notes was 5:16, you waited four minutes before a call was received by the paramedics. That meant it took a total of ten minutes from the time you arrived at your office to the time the paramedics appeared. Doctor, that difference of four minutes could have made a huge difference in the outcome. Correct?"

Lenny and Mark had anticipated the paramedic time delay issue and had a prepared response. They decided the best strategy was to point out the main issue that needed to be addressed was Frank's breathing, and Lenny had successfully dealt with it.

"It did cause a delay, but in the interim I was able to handle the airway problem with a cricothyroidotomy."

"But you didn't have the proper equipment to perform that procedure. Had they arrived earlier, would you agree they might have opened his airway during that crucial four-minute delay and wouldn't that have improved the outcome? Correct?"

Mark interrupted. "Objection! Again, you are assuming facts not in evidence. Also it's argumentative and compound."

Cutter frowned. "OK, let me ask the first part of the question. Had the paramedics arrived earlier, would you agree they might have opened his airway sooner?"

"I can't answer that because I don't know what they would have done."

"When the paramedics arrived, they took over, and according to their notes they started an IV and gave Dr. Stevens medications for his low blood pressure. Correct?"

"Yes, that's correct."

"Then if they arrived sooner, the next thing they would have done is assessed the airway blockage. Correct?"

Mark interrupted again. "Objection. Once again, assumes facts not in evidence." Mark needed to stop Cutter's repeated attack on Lenny's management of Stevens' airway.

"But counselor, I'm trying to point out that during those four minutes, the paramedics might have been able to do a cricothyroidotomy that Dr. Haberman admitted he couldn't do earlier, because he didn't have the equipment."

Mark knew this was a serious issue, and he didn't want Lenny going anywhere near Cutter's speculation. "I repeat my objection, the question is speculative and there are no facts in evidence that the paramedics even had training to do a cricothyroidotomy."

"OK, I'll defer this question until I can establish the paramedics were trained to do a cricothyroidotomy."

Cutter resumed his questioning. "You said you called 911 for the child with the walnut allergy. Why at that time, and not for Dr. Stevens?"

"Because I felt she needed to be sent to Children's Hospital for care and the paramedics would take her there directly."

"OK. Have you called 911 any other time?"

"No."

"I have nothing further at this time."

After a short break, Mark asked Lenny the questions they had previously discussed for his defense.

Lenny repeated his position that a thirty to forty second delay in arrival from Dr. Sabatha's office was not a significant time delay. He pointed out that if he had been in an exam room with a patient, the time delay would still have been ten to fifteen seconds to get to the waiting room. According to Lenny, that meant being one floor above his office resulted in a net maximum delay of twenty-five seconds, an amount that could not have adversely affected the outcome.

Mark avoided the employment screening issue regarding Elizabeth, and he wasn't concerned about the IV access delay. He thought Lenny had explained it well and medical expert testimony would likely support his position. The issue of whether Frank may have been wheezing at the time of the injection was concerning but difficult to prove. He thought Elizabeth's deposition would validate that Dr. Stevens had not complained about breathing problems at the time of his injection. The ER issue may have delayed the arrival of the paramedics by a few minutes; that and the delay in performing the cricothyroidotomy were the main concerns Mark had.

Mark asked, "Dr. Haberman, is a cricothyroidotomy a procedure all allergists are qualified to perform?"

"No, it's not, and the practice parameter suggests that you should have proficiency in order to perform it."

"How is proficiency defined?"

"It implies having hands-on experience, like watching one performed in person, or by video instruction, or doing one with supervision. Most doctors have never performed one."

"Based on your definition, would you consider yourself proficient?"

"I would not have been proficient by that definition."

"Since the practice parameter states clinicians should only do it if they are proficient, and since you weren't proficient, would it have been required for you to perform it on Dr. Stevens?"

"No."

Mark said, "But you elected to perform a cricothyroidotomy on Dr. Stevens even though you were not proficient. Why did you do that?"

"Because it gave Dr. Stevens a chance for survival that he otherwise wouldn't have had." Lenny thought, *Finally, some vindication for my efforts. Thank you, Mark, for rehearsing that question!*

"I'll reserve the remainder of my questions for trial."

Cutter looked up from taking notes. "I have a few follow-up questions. Dr. Haberman, you described having an extensive background with airway management because of your training as an anesthesiologist in the army. Am I to understand that you never learned to do a cricothyroidotomy in that capacity?"

"When I was in the army medical corps there was a shortage of anesthesiologists. The army offered a course in anesthesiology to temporarily fill the gap. I volunteered and took a four month course learning basic procedures, such as intubation, routine anesthetics and how to monitor patients during operations. But I did not witness or perform a cricothyroidotomy, so I would not consider myself proficient for that procedure."

"So you didn't have expertise to do this procedure? Correct."

"It wasn't part of my experience."

"But you would certainly know the anatomy well enough to do one if it was needed. Right?"

"Yes, since I was able to do it on Dr. Stevens."

"Would you agree the requirement of hands-on experience is your definition of proficiency, and not necessarily the definition implied in the practice parameter?"

"I think proficiency in medicine usually requires some visual teaching of a procedure, either hands-on or by visual prompts. A surgeon performing bypass surgery would certainly not be considered proficient if he or she had not previously participated in that procedure."

"Thank you, Doctor."

When it was over, Mark and Lenny spent a few minutes discussing the deposition as they walked out of the office building.

"Lenny, you did fine. Overall, I thought you handled it very well, especially the crico issue."

"Well, that's because you coached me on the proficiency issue. Do you think it helped?"

"Yes, I do." Mark clapped him on the back. "Lenny, take your wife out for dinner and a movie. Try to relax. We've got a lot of work yet, but we've made a good start."

Lenny realized with a shudder, that the operative word was *'start.'*

Chapter Thirty-One

AFTER THE DEPOSITION, Tucker drove toward his country club to meet another attorney for a round of golf. As he pulled into the late afternoon traffic, a thunderstorm was in progress. Large dark ominous clouds were moving swiftly over south Denver, producing severe thunder with lightning strikes, one hitting just a hundred yards away from his Lincoln Continental. He turned the radio on to get a weather forecast and the announcer advised a strong weather alert with funnel clouds observed in parts of south Denver, Littleton and Castle Rock. Tucker decided golf was a bad idea, and he called Larkin to bring him up to date.

He shouted, "Call Ted Larkin" into his car's voice recognition telephone system.

The robotic female voice responded, "Call Tad Larkin."

"No, damn it, call Ted Larkin!" Tucker paused, getting frustrated as the rain hit the windshield harder.

The flat robotic voice responded. "Call Ted Laring"

"No, God damn it, I said call-", then exasperated, he stopped and said, "Call...oh fuck off."

"Call oh fuck off," came the automated response.

He paused, laughing as he hung up. He decided to direct dial Ted's phone. As the call was ringing, large sheets of rain and hail suddenly hit his car, overloading the capacity of the windshield wipers. He couldn't see more than a few feet in front of him.

Larkin answered. "Ted here."

The phone was crackling badly, but Tucker shouted. "Ted, this is Ed Tucker. Can you hear me? Bad thunderstorm! I'll call later."

"OK"

Tucker hung up just as he hit a car in front of him, throwing him forward, whipping him back in the seat, and wrenching his neck. He tried moving his head around to glance in the rearview mirror, hoping he wouldn't get rear-ended, and was relieved to see cars stopped behind him. He jumped out of his car and approached the car he'd hit, cursing as the rain soaked his clothes. A young woman rolled down the window, gasping, her face expressing distress and pain.

"I'm pregnant... I hit my belly on the steering wheel. Oh, my God!"

Tucker ran back to call 911, but his phone didn't work. Out of desperation, he stood near the front passenger side of the woman's car, yelling and waving for help at cars that had started to move around the accident. Finally, a nurse stopped to help. Feeling relieved, he went back to his car and waited for the police and emergency services. He was issued a ticket, refused medical treatment, returned to his office and immediately called Larkin.

"Ted, it's Ed calling. Christ, what a storm! After I called, I hit the car in front of me and injured a pregnant woman. She had to be air lifted to Denver Memorial. My neck is pretty damn sore."

"Wow, hope you're OK. So how was the deposition?"

"That's why I'm calling. I think Haberman's down for the count. I may let Persons stew for a while and then call to find out if he's interested in settlement."

"Terrific. It's coming at a great time. My legislation just passed in both chambers. We made a few concessions on ceilings and reconciled at five million for gross negligence."

Ted continued before Ed could respond. "Ed, we beat the crap out of the doctors and the insurance lobby, and here's the best part. We made damages mirror every other state. It'll be a lot easier to get higher damages for gross negligence, and it'll be retroactive to the first of the year. The bill is on the governor's desk right now. The opposition is working overtime to get him to veto it, but he told me in confidence that he'll sign it."

"And it'll be retroactive to the first of this year?"

"Absolutely! I pushed hard to have that included. It only applies to gross negligence, but it sounds like everything you're discovering fits that definition."

"Great, I think we've got him on several issues. The fact that he was out of the office when it occurred means we can bring in the issue of abandonment and delayed treatment."

"Nice!"

"The second is the nurse fell apart when the reaction occurred. She couldn't handle the crisis. Haberman admitted to not interviewing her before she was hired. He left the screening up to his office manager. I believe he has exposure there too."

"Great, couldn't be better!"

"And he delayed a call to 911 for reasons I'll explain later. And, and get this; he didn't have essential equipment for a procedure that might have saved Stevens' life."

"Oh my God, what a fuck-up! You've made my day, Ed... Seriously."

"Ted, there'll be more depositions, and when they're finished, I'll put out feelers for a settlement. When the ceiling change is signed, they'll have to look hard at an offer to settle if they don't want to be hung out to dry in a jury trial. I'll stay in touch."

Chapter Thirty-Two

DENISE WALKED INTO Dr. Sabatha's office for her scheduled appointment. She remained silent as she sat down. Rather than look at Sabatha, she let her chin settle onto her chest. Her hands were tightly clasped on her lap. Dave waited a few minutes and then spoke.

"Good morning, Mrs. Stevens."

There was no change in her posture. She remained unresponsive.

"How are you feeling today?"

"I would prefer not to be here, Dr. Sabatha. Everyone wants to talk to me."

"Who's everyone?"

"Lenny...Dr. Leonard Haberman. We had coffee, and he wanted to talk about Frank and what happened to him."

"What would you know about that? You weren't there when it happened."

"I just don't want to talk about it to anyone and I don't want to be here."

"Why?"

"I don't know. I just want to be left alone."

"Mrs. Stevens, we've made a lot of progress and I'd like to continue to help you."

"But you make me feel worse!"

"Can you tell me why?"

"You want me to tell you what I did, don't you?"

"I think it might help if you tell me what's bothering you. That's what I'm here for."

"But what about Dr. Haberman? If I tell you, then I need to tell him, right?"

"Mrs. Stevens, please, you only need to be concerned with talking to me. I'm your doctor and I want to help you. Anything you tell me is held in strict confidence."

"All right, then, I'll just tell you."

She deflated like a heavy weight was coming off of her shoulders. "I killed him, I know I did. It wasn't on purpose, but deep down I hated him for what he'd done and ..." Pausing for a moment, she then finished, "and what I did killed him."

"Why do you think that?"

"I let him take a medicine that hurt him."

"Tell me more."

She told him about the propranolol. "He took it because he was having migraines, and when he started taking it, his migraines got better but his asthma got worse. I found out after Frank died, that the migraine medicine could make asthma worse and it could also keep adrenalin from working. They gave him adrenalin when he reacted to the allergy shot and it didn't work because of that drug! I should have known." Her voice trailed off.

Sabatha's voice was soft. "But why was that your responsibility?"

"I should've read the brochure before Frank took it. He was sleeping off a migraine when I brought it home and I just left it on the bathroom counter. I never read the warnings and I don't think he did either."

"But you didn't cause the allergy reaction. It's possible the propranolol might have made it more difficult to treat, but he would have died anyway from the allergy shot. Mrs. Stevens, you're punishing yourself unnecessarily."

"That's what my brother said when I told him, but he'd be furious if he knew that I told you or anyone else."

"Why would he be angry?"

"He thinks it'll make it difficult to win the case against Dr. Haberman."

"Mrs. Stevens, what's most important is to get you well, and the way we can make that happen is help you understand that you are not responsible for Frank's death."

She looked up, confused.

"I think it's why you're feeling the way you do. I believe if you accept that you've done nothing wrong, you'll stop having so many guilt feelings."

"Do you really think it could be that easy?"

"Well, you've assumed the entire responsibility for not reading the warning label before Frank took the medicine, but he was actually the one who should have read it. It was his health, his body and he was ultimately responsible for knowing about his medications. Doesn't that make some sense?"

"I guess so."

"Here's the issue. He should have read the warnings and then talked to Dr. Haberman about how he was feeling. It was never your responsibility."

"But it can't be that simple. You know, just telling myself I'm not responsible for what happened."

"Everyone has their own way of dealing with guilt, especially unfounded guilt. Mrs. Stevens, you are a Christian, so let's use that to your advantage. You have a tremendous ability to focus with prayer. Let's use that to redirect your guilty thoughts. When guilt surfaces, pray hard to accept that you were not responsible for Frank's death. That way you're not letting your thoughts direct you and instead you gain control of your negative thoughts. Would you try that?"

"That's hard to do. I can't seem to let it go, Dr. Sabatha. It's with me all day, every day, and I have nightmares."

"I understand how guilty you must feel, but try to do it. It may be surprisingly helpful."

"I don't know."

"Mrs. Stevens, give it a try and maybe later on you'll be able to talk to Dr. Haberman about this."

"Oh, I couldn't do that! Ted would be so angry with me, and I could be accused of killing Frank. My children wouldn't have any parent to raise them! I can't do that!"

"Let's take it slowly. At some time you may come to the realization you don't need to carry this burden any longer. It will be your choice when you're ready, but in the meantime, consider my suggestion about prayer and then we'll talk."

Having spent several sessions with him, Denise could tell by his comments that the session was ending. She struggled up out of the chair and thanked him. She considered shaking his hand, but instead nodded, and hurried out of the building.

As she got into her car, she thought more about what Dr. Sabatha had said. *Could it be so simple to pray away my bad feelings? Could this all go away if I just told Lenny everything?* While driving off, the guilt feelings resurfaced. She started praying to ask forgiveness from Jesus, and to accept that she wasn't responsible for what had happened to Frank. She actually thought it made her feel better.

Chapter Thirty-Three

ELIZABETH FINCH AND her attorney Glen Carthage arrived early at Mark Persons' office for her deposition. Mark and Glen knew each other from past litigation and respected each other's legal abilities.

Mark spoke first. "Glen, I would normally be representing Elizabeth since she's a member of Dr. Haberman's staff."

"Yes, I know, but under the circumstances I believe she should have her own counsel."

"I understand, but still...."

Carthage interrupted. "There's no other choice, Mark, she needs her own counsel. Can we get started?"

Outside Mark's office, Tucker and Cutter huddled in a corner. "Just remember," Tucker said, "we need to keep the heat on Haberman. Even if Finch admits she gave Stevens an incorrect dose, mistakes by nurses are common. We need to let it be just that, an innocent error. It's still Haberman's ultimate responsibility and we need to hammer on that."

Cutter grinned. "I got it, Ed."

Lenny narrowed his eyes as Tucker entered. A good friend of Lenny's from the hospital, a neonatologist, had called him the other night. Apparently, the doctor was taking care of a baby who had been born prematurely. The baby was still in the neonatal ICU and showing signs of severe brain damage. It turned out the mother went into premature labor after Tucker rear-ended her car. According to Lenny's friend, the baby was in serious condition, and the mother was already planning to file a major suit against Tucker, apparently for huge damages.

Part of Lenny felt terrible for the mom and baby affected by the accident, but part of him felt satisfaction knowing that Tucker was also having major legal problems. It was classic schadenfreude: sensing pleasure when hearing about misfortune affecting an adversary. He wondered idly if he should have a discussion with Sabatha about it. Was it a normal or abnormal response to feel that way?

The deposition was about to begin, snapping Lenny out of his thoughts. Elizabeth was dressed in a conservative business suit, appearing poised.

The first hour dealt with introductions, medical background and legal formalities. After a brief intermission, Cutter got down to business.

"Ms. Finch, as I recall from your statements, Dr. Stevens was not wheezing or complaining of asthma and seemed in good health when he suddenly collapsed after you administered his allergy injection. Correct?"

"Well not exactly, he did mention he needed to talk to Dr. Haberman because he had some asthma problems during the past week."

"When a patient indicates they've had breathing symptoms, wouldn't you normally have Dr. Haberman check the patient before giving the next injection?"

Carthage interrupted. "Objection. I want my client to understand that the question assumes facts not established. My client has already stated that Dr. Stevens didn't indicate he had breathing problems at the time of the injection."

Cutter decided to move on. "All right, when Dr. Stevens suddenly collapsed, was there any indication that he was having an allergic reaction before he became unconscious?"

"He started coughing; that's why I went over to talk to him. Then I noticed hives all over his face and hands. I asked him to come into an exam room, and he tried to get up. That's when he collapsed."

"Then what did you do?"

"I felt for a pulse in his neck, which was barely detectable, and I noticed his breathing was labored. I told Holly to call Dr. Haberman immediately."

"I assume you're referring to Holly Brown, the receptionist in Dr. Haberman's office?"

"Yes sir."

"How long did it take Dr. Haberman to arrive?"

"I don't know...probably less than a minute."

"Do you think it took him longer than if he had been in the office?"

"Well maybe, but only slightly, because I think if Dr. Haberman was in the office it would have taken just about the same time for me to run down the hall, interrupt him and run back to take care of Dr. Stevens. Calling Dr. Haberman let me stay in the waiting room with Dr. Stevens."

Mark smiled, thinking the answer was good for Lenny, while Tucker frowned and murmured something in Cutter's ear, causing Cutter to nod.

Cutter resumed. "According to Dr. Haberman's testimony and other patients who were present, you were distraught, crying and didn't assist him throughout the CPR. Can you tell me why you were unable to assist him?"

Elizabeth blinked back tears and took some deep breaths. Carthage gave her a supportive pat on her shoulder.

"When Dr. Stevens collapsed, I just couldn't think clearly. I didn't know what to do after Dr. Haberman arrived. I just froze...I'm so sorry." She started to cry.

"Were you trained for this type of medical crisis?"

"I take CPR every two years. And once a year we do a mock emergency in the office on how to deal with emergencies."

"Then why couldn't you help when this happened?"

"I don't know."

"Ms. Finch, you must have some idea."

She looked at Carthage, who nodded his head, encouraging her to answer. She turned towards Cutter and began to stutter. "I—I..." She paused and started again. "When I first met Dr. Stevens, I recognized him from the past. He was a big popular jock when I was in college at CU Boulder, but that was like twenty years ago. He didn't recognize me. I was a freshman when he was a junior. He was a popular playboy, everyone knew him-big man on campus." Her voice became progressively angrier. "Anyway, one of my roommates went to a party at his fraternity. They had that Everclear-strong punch. The next thing she knew, she was in bed with him, and later she-she had to have an abortion. He never took responsibility. You couldn't prove anything." She blinked and shook her head. "And then he hurt Sam in the accident. He never even apologized or anything. Frank Stevens never looked back at the wreckage he left behind... Then I saw him in Dr. Haberman's office, still cocky and self-centered. I-I..." She broke off, shaking.

"Ms. Finch, do you want to take a break?"

She didn't answer. Carthage handed her a glass of water and whispered into her ear. She nodded yes. Carthage rose out of his chair. "I'd like to speak with my client for a moment."

They left and Carthage returned alone five minutes later. "She's unable to continue. Let's reschedule."

Everyone reluctantly agreed.

Chapter Thirty-Four

AFTER THE DEPOSITION, Lenny and Mark walked over to a neighborhood coffee shop. Olympus Restaurant was a classic Greek diner with Formica tabletops, vinyl seats and booths filled with legislators, businessmen, lobbyists and an assorted selection of the downtrodden. Smells of fried foods and secondhand smoke permeated the air. They found an open booth and sat back while a waitress in an apron splattered with food stains wiped the table, brusquely threw down menus, utensils and black coffee, and left, all without a hello or requesting their orders.

Lenny remarked, "Wow that proves the Age of Aquarius has ended."

Mark looked at him quizzically, not sure what he was referring to.

"In the old musical Hair, when they talked about the dawning of the Age of Aquarius, there's this famous line in the song. The end goes something like, *'peace will guide the planets, and love will steer the stars.'* Well, you've just witnessed the end of the Age of Aquarius. No more love and kindness. Her attitude goes along with my life right now."

"Lenny, I'm very optimistic that we'll get out of this with little damage to you."

"Thanks for the support," Lenny said sincerely, realizing he sounded pretty negative. "Sorry, just babbling on. That gets me into a lot of trouble these days." He leaned forward. "Mark, this deposition was really odd. Elizabeth seems to be holding something back, something important. I know it. It may explain the dose discrepancy. She was obviously angry at Frank for the thing that happened in college to her friend, and to someone named Sam. I'm wondering if she intentionally gave him a big overdose and it killed him."

Mark responded. "That's possible. We need to do a background check on Elizabeth and find out more about Sam. Something terrible must have happened for Elizabeth to keep a grudge so long. Let me get a P.I. on it. I'll need her maiden name, assuming she wasn't married then."

"I know a good P.I. who works for COADD. Let me call him."

"Great. Still, if she gave Dr. Stevens an overdose, it'll be hard to prove unless she admits it. That's not likely if today was an example of her future testimony," Mark said with exasperation.

Lenny had also seen how closely Carthage guarded his client. "What's your overall sense of things?"

"Well, let's get through deposing Elizabeth. The Celebrex angle is worth exploring. I'll depose Dr. Kerlin to confirm that he prescribed it, but that's probably not going to help our case since you found out it wasn't detected in Frank's blood sample. Right?"

"Yes, that's right... Mark, what about his pill bottle? What if some of the pills are gone? Could it be used to prove he took some?"

"Tucker will argue against it, unless we can prove it was in his blood system. Plus you wouldn't know when he took them."

"I've thought about this some more. Maybe he'd just taken it and that would explain why it wasn't in his blood. You know what I mean, not enough to be detected in his blood, but maybe a small amount was absorbed, just enough to cause the reaction. Can you get a lab to test for it in his stomach sample?"

"Sure, good thought. I'll get on that," Mark said, making a note to himself. Listen, Lenny, there's one other thing. It's a legal doctrine called *in camera.* It prevents us from knowing the name of their expert who reviewed the records and verified the case has merit. The expert remains anonymous to protect him from retaliation by peers."

"So how do we find out who it is?"

"Well, I think I know, but I'm not supposed to. The expert bragged to someone who told me his name. Remember, this is very unofficial, so I could be wrong, but it seems the allergist they consulted is Dr. Peter Doren. Do you know him?"

Lenny sat back. "You're kidding, aren't you?"

"No, I'm not."

Lenny shouted, "God damn it!"

Several people stopped talking and turned to stare.

"Lenny, take it easy. What's the problem with Doren?"

"That ass! He's not even a properly trained allergist."

Mark was disturbed by this outburst. "Lenny, calm down, you'll have a heart attack over this... I'm confused. What are you suggesting?"

Lenny quieted down, but his voice remained tense as he explained. "Look, Doren hasn't had allergy training that qualifies him to be my equivalent. I know he isn't certified by my Board. It's called ABAI for American Board of Allergy and Immunology. It's the only approved Board that validates quality training in this field."

"So then he's not qualified, right?"

"By his standards, he probably considers himself to be an allergist, but he's not equivalently and adequately trained to judge me." Lenny shook his head vigorously. "Look I spent two years in an allergy immunology fellowship after a year of medical internship and three years of residency in internal medicine. You need to be Board certified in medicine or pediatrics to even qualify for the ABAI board. There are oral and written exams and ongoing educational requirements to maintain the ABAI Board cert. There's no way he's trained at my level in this specialty. Having him as an expert witness makes a mockery of our specialty."

Lenny clenched his teeth and his voice intensified again. "I know his training was originally in family practice. A friend of mine was in a family practice program with him back in New York. When Doren finished, he moved to Denver to join a family practice group. He decided to change his career after only six months when he didn't like the long hours and claimed he couldn't make enough money. He took weekend courses in liposuction, aesthetic procedures, weight loss, vein laser treatment, and then went into practice. He added allergy as an afterthought, boasting all of it was easy to learn. He really doesn't care if he's providing the best medical care for his patients. It's all about the bucks. The truth is he's breached the Oath of Hippocrates for an oath of hypocrisy."

Lenny was becoming indignant again. "Anyone, medical doctor or not, can get into allergy because the barrier to entry is low. The specialty is being overrun by docs who view the allergy specialty simplistically. They think it's only about allergy tests and shots, but it's no longer just about shots. We know so much more about asthma, bee stings, anaphylaxis, skin diseases, food allergy-you name it. It takes more than just giving shots to treat these conditions. You have to know what causes them, what the best treatments are, how to best monitor them, provide patient education, and even more importantly, how to rule out masquerading conditions. All of that takes training and experience."

Mark tapped his shoulder to remind him again to quiet down. "OK-OK," Lenny said, "but here's the problem. Buck-driven docs dismiss the importance of allergy training and instead hire technicians to do the work-ups. They don't consider the importance of medical or drug histories. They misread negative tests as positive. They don't correlate allergy histories with test results and then they makeup vaccines with irrelevant allergens. Almost all patients, allergic or not, end up on allergy shots. They formulate vaccines with dilute concentrations that are ineffective, and then have patients give themselves shots at home."

Lenny paused for a moment to slow down his breathing and then resumed. "Mark, let me give you just one example of what happened in this town. A severe asthmatic was worked up by one of these technicians and started on allergy shots. The patient experienced a life threatening asthma attack at her home immediately after giving herself allergy shots, and had to be air-lifted to an ICU. Our guidelines are clear. Severe poorly controlled asthmatics shouldn't be treated with allergy shots, especially at home, because they can have life threatening reactions. Techs just don't have the judgment and knowledge. They shouldn't be making these clinical decisions."

Mark didn't respond, sensing that Lenny needed to finish his tirade.

"And now, alternative therapists are getting into it!" Lenny raised his eyebrows for emphasis. "There's an apparatus that supposedly detects auras on a computer screen. If a patient's aura is asymmetrical they're told a specific organ may not be functioning, and then advised to avoid certain foods. I've seen kids literally placed on starvation diets after having their auras analyzed, and to top off this bizarre crap, patients are given a so-called immune booster made of sheep thymus extract. Now get this; there's a prion disease in sheep called scrapies that looks like mad cow disease. No one can say with absolute certainty that humans can't get it. These prions can't be inactivated by heat, ultraviolet light, or chemicals and they concentrate in sheep thymus. Mark, they're giving this to kids who could end up forty years from now with dementia that'll be misdiagnosed as Alzheimer's disease, and no one will make the connection. It's criminal!

"And now massage therapists are offering allergy care. All of this is just incredible, and no one-not the FDA, the state medical boards, my own board, or boards for alternative medicine give a damn, or if they do, they're paralyzed by fear of lawsuits or intervention from the FTC, claiming that we're interfering with the livelihood of these practitioners. We're hogtied-unable to stop any of it. As far as I know Doren doesn't do any of that weird alternative crap, but he's not fellowship trained in allergy and he's not an ABAI certified allergist. No way is he qualified to judge my care!"

Mark shushed him again. "Lenny, you've made your case. Let me get the Colorado statute definition of an expert witness."

Mark called his office and wrote down a volume of notes: "OK, here's the definition." He read from his notes: " 'Experts must be licensed to practice in the state.' I assume Doren qualifies there, but I'll verify it."

He read on. " 'The witness must be familiar with the applicable standards of care and practice as they relate to the act or omission which is the subject of the claim on the date of the incident. The court shall not permit an expert in one medical subspecialty to testify against a physician in another medical subspecialty unless the expert shows substantial familiarity between the subspecialties and the standards of care and practice in the two fields are similar.' Lenny, what do you think? Would he be familiar with the standards of care in your specialty?"

"No, he's not equivalently trained!"

"Lenny, I get it," Mark said thoughtfully. "I think they may have shot themselves in the foot with Doren. Once we go to trial we can challenge his credentials. They'll need to find another expert, and that'll affect the credibility of their case."

Then, in an attempt to lighten up the meeting, Mark said with a smile, "Relax now, before I have to do CPR on you, and since I'm not certified by the ABAI, I'm sure you'll die!"

Lenny left the meeting, still seething, and decided it was time to head to the range for some target practice. He smiled bitterly as he pulled into the shooting gallery. *Maybe I can hang a picture of Doren to improve my score.*

Chapter Thirty-Five

OPENING HIS MAIL, Lenny was surprised to see a letter from Denise Stevens. He briefly considered calling Mark as he slit open the envelope. The letter was handwritten.

Dear Lenny:

I am writing to you because I think there is something you should know. Ted and Ed Tucker, my attorney, don't want me to tell you, but I can't keep silent any longer.

Frank was taking a drug for his migraines and it was helping his headaches, but I think it killed him. I didn't get the drug at our usual pharmacy, so they didn't know him there, and they didn't know he had asthma. I was supposed to read the warning brochure before he took the drug, but I forgot to do that, God help me. The drug's called propranolol, and according to the brochure, it could prevent adrenalin from treating a serious allergic attack. Ted told me not to say anything, but Jesus won't let me keep this from you any longer. I feel this was my entire fault, not yours.

Forgive me, Lenny,
Denise

Lenny sat immobile, realizing the immensity of what he'd just read. He placed a call to Mark.

"Mark, it's Lenny. I just got a letter from Denise Stevens."

"Really? What'd she say?"

"I'll fax it to you, but let me read it."

When Lenny finished, Mark blew out a long breath. "Wow, you've been right from the beginning. At least now we have a better explanation for what happened," he said. "It would be great if we could prove propranolol was in Frank's system."

Lenny said, "I still have a small sample of Frank's blood."

"Good. I'll have it picked up, and while we're at it, I'll order the tests on the Celebrex and propranolol. I'll also ask the ME's office to send postmortem blood and stomach samples over to our independent lab."

Lenny cheered up at these positive steps. "Great. Maybe we can get some good news."

Mark had some other news. "Lenny, let me bring you up to date on some other developments. Your P.I. Charley Blackwood has been very helpful. Elizabeth's maiden name was Hurdle, and she has a sister, Samantha, who is apparently called Sam. It seems that Sam was a very promising opera soprano until she was severely injured in an auto accident when she was only twenty-two. Get this! Frank Stevens was responsible for the accident. He was drunk, but he was only convicted of reckless driving. Elizabeth's sister ended up a paraplegic."

Lenny responded, "That explains why Elizabeth was so angry at him. Maybe she was punishing him, giving him more vaccine than she should have. My God, do you think she meant to kill him?"

"It does change things. This could actually turn into a criminal investigation."

"Mark, I think we have a much better idea of why Frank had such a severe reaction. We know Elizabeth was angry at him, and she probably gave him a large dose. And then the reaction couldn't be reversed with adrenalin because he was on propranolol." Lenny paused to think about what he'd just said. "Mark, am I off the hook?"

"Possibly, but let me backtrack a little. We need to make sure we can prove two things: first, that Elizabeth intentionally gave Frank a large dose of his vaccine, and second whether propranolol was actually in his system or at the very least in his stomach. Still, they can claim the reaction was caused by the allergy injection and you know there are other outstanding concerns. On top of it all, we could get a fickle jury who might be swayed in favor of the widow. My best answer is that we're in a much better situation than we were before. After we finish Elizabeth's deposition and get proof from the lab, I'm hoping we can get it resolved."

Lenny was deflated by Mark's assessment. "I guess you're telling me there's still a good likelihood that I'll have a trial."

"Less of a chance now than before we learned all of this." Mark hesitated. "Lenny, there's something else."

Lenny winced. He knew when Mark started with that prelude, he was about to hear bad news.

"I received a call from Tucker. He and his clients have decided to proceed to trial without arbitration. They believe their case is solid and they're looking for a big award."

"That a-hole! You know, Mark, I found out that Tucker is also involved in a lawsuit, and I'm glad he's experiencing some of the same crap that I am."

Mark decided not to comment and get Lenny back on track to deal with the problem at hand. "Lenny, it's what I expected. Tucker used that strategy before in other cases, so we simply need to move on. Look, with the letter from Denise, and what we've found out about Elizabeth, we've got a far better chance to win." He paused to change the subject. "By the way, as long as I'm telling you the bad stuff, you're going to hear the rest in the press. The Larkin-Scott bill passed. It raises ceilings, and they were able to include retroactive punitive damages for gross negligence." He qualified that by adding, "However, to be honest, I think there'll be lots of challenges. Retroactive laws are usually unconstitutional, but this is where we're at for now."

"Do you have any other good news?"

"As I said, I like our chances that we can get this settled. I'll call the ME and have the samples sent to our lab."

After hanging up, Lenny wondered what Mark meant by, *Liking our chances. Did he mean settling within the limits of my insurance? That would at least mean there was an end in sight. Or did he mean I'd have to accept a larger judgment against me? Gotta keep a positive attitude – like remembering my patient's advice to play with the band and not worry about the rising waterline.*

Chapter Thirty-Six

JIMMY BARONE SAT with the social worker, who was preparing him to move from the rehab center to an assisted living apartment, especially since COADD's insurance policy might run out. When the social worker left the room, Barone felt a rush of anxiety and decided to place a call to Pete Doren.

"Pete, Jimmy here."

"My God, Jimbone, where the hell have you been? You fell off the map! What happened to you?"

Jimmy briefly told the story of the accident and his long recovery. "Pete, can you come over to Walnut Rehab so we can talk? I'm in 416."

"Sure, I know where it is. I need to finish up with some patients and I'll come over this evening. Why did you leave? Did it have anything to do with Stevens' death? That was some ending, and it sure solved my problem."

"It's a long story. Just come over."

"I'll be there."

Jimmy still felt anxious despite talking to a familiar voice. He knew his problems were just beginning. Now that execs at COADD suspected he took the specs, they would put more pressure on him, and might even ask the police to investigate. All of it made him very uneasy.

Pete arrived still dressed in blue scrubs. He couldn't believe how much weight Jimmy had lost. "Christ almighty, Jimbone, you look anorexic. What the hell happened to you?"

"Pete, close the door."

"OK."

He laid out in detail everything that happened, from the time Stevens died, the accident, his recovery, and admitting to COADD execs that he had taken the specs. "I don't know, Pete. If COADD gets the police involved, the family for sure is gonna hear about it and then I'm totally screwed or dead."

"Jimbone, I'll help anyway I can. Just tell me what you need."

"I need to get out of town, even out of the country."

"Don't you think you're being a little paranoid about the family?"

"Pete I've dealt with them most of my life. They'll want absolute assurance that I won't talk."

"I understand, but let me call them and see if they can get you papers with a new ID." Jimmy waved off that suggestion. Pete continued, "Look, I get you're worried, but you should have enough money in case you need to leave. Do you remember where it is?"

"Yeah, I know where my money is."

"Good, and, you also have another 50K that I wired your bank as a bonus. I tried calling you on your cell about it, but you never answered, so I left a message at COADD."

"Thanks, but you didn't need to do that."

"It was more than payback. You gave me my wife and life back. Hey, let me talk to KC and let him know you're OK. I really think the family will understand. Think about it."

Jimmy thought about this option. *The family was going to find me eventually. Why not take Pete's suggestion?*

"OK, let's do it. Thanks bud."

They hugged, kissed each other on the cheeks and Pete parted.

★ ★ ★

Later that day, Doren informed KC about Jimmy's whereabouts. KC immediately contacted his boss, Tommy Pazzoni.

"Tommy, it's KC. I heard from Pete Doren. You remember him, he ran with Jimmy and some other guys back when they used to hang out at Bonante's cigar store. Anyway, he's a doc in Denver and he just called to tell me Jimmy has surfaced."

"Oh yeah, where is that little prick?"

"All this time he's been in a Denver hospital. He was in a bad accident-in a coma a long time, and then he was, how do you say, amnestic or shit like that?"

"KC, what the hell are you saying?"

"You know, he can't remember anything."

"Oh, you mean he's amnesic."

"Yeah, that's what I mean. Well, he woke up but pretended not to remember anything, like who he was and stuff. I guess they're onto him about the specs, though. They know he took them. The owners of the company are questioning him, but Pete says there's no police... yet."

"That isn't good for us. He could strike a deal to save his ass."

"Got any ideas?"

"I think you need to pay him a visit. Talk to him. Get some idea of where he's at. Maybe take along Jimmy's famous nose spray."

"Tommy, I like that idea. I'll pay him a visit."

The nose spray was Jimmy's own invention. He had read about a natural female hormone, oxytocin, which is released during labor. It turned out oxytocin had some other interesting effects in humans; it encouraged trust. Studies were done with volunteers who took a nasal spray of oxytocin in an investment game. Those who received a placebo were cautious investors while volunteers who received oxytocin were very trusting and much more willing to hand over their game money for others to invest.

Jimmy's genius took it one step further. He figured if oxytocin increases trust between people, it may do this by enhancing bonding between those same individuals. He based that assumption on the observation that oxytocin is released during labor, and may actually enhance the natural bonding between a mother and her newborn infant. Then he made a giant leap of faith; oxytocin might encourage individuals to tell the truth by increasing their sense of trust and bonding. He tested it with family low-level soldiers, gaming each other with lies. Surprisingly, it worked. The family started using it to see who was stealing from them, and actually discovered a snitch who worked for the police. He mysteriously disappeared. Jimmy thought his discovery could be patented, but Tommy Pazzoni wanted to keep it a secret to ensure loyalty in his family.

Attempting to assure his boss, K.C. said, "We'll find out soon enough if he's telling the truth. Otherwise I'll take care of him."

Chapter Thirty-Seven

MARK PERSONS CALLED the M.E.'s office.

"Dr. Short speaking."

"Hi, Dr. Short. Mark Persons here. I'm representing Dr. Leonard Haberman. You remember, he's the doctor involved in the death of Dr. Frank Stevens, presumably from anaphylaxis to an allergy injection."

"Yes, well, the word *'presumably'* may be an inappropriate word based on our pathology findings that were consistent with anaphylaxis. I assume you received them. Did you not?"

"Yes, we did. I'm not calling to challenge the diagnosis."

"Then what can I do for you?"

"We have information indicating that Dr. Stevens may have been on medications that could have had something to do with his death. They're propranolol and Celebrex. Can you send samples of his stomach contents and post-mortem blood to our private lab, so they can be tested for these drugs?"

"I assume you have good reason to make this request."

"Yes." Mark explained the new discoveries.

"I see," said the M.E., agreeing that they could change the cause of the anaphylaxis considerably. "You'll probably need to send samples to the drug manufacturers. They usually have assays set up to measure their own drugs. Send me the written request and I'll send the samples over."

Mark faxed the request. If the results were positive for even one of these drugs, he thought he might have leverage to settle the case for a reasonable amount and avoid trial.

Lenny gave Mark the names of five colleagues to contact as potential expert witnesses. They all agreed to participate. He selected two for the trial and met with them to review the case. Although they agreed with the overall handling of the situation, both had a few concerns.

One was worried about Lenny's delay in calling 911. He thought it might have made a difference in the outcome.

The other was focused on the delay in the cricothyroidotomy. She thought most allergists knew how to do it, although she agreed most had never done one. Still, even if they weren't required to by the practice parameter, she believed Lenny would have been obligated to perform it as quickly as possible. However, she was mostly concerned that Lenny didn't have the appropriate equipment available in his crash cart.

All these thoughts were helpful to Mark and reinforced the areas where he thought Lenny was most at risk.

A few weeks later, Mark received a letter from the private lab. He held his breath while reading it. *Propranolol was detected in both post-mortem blood and gastric samples. Celebrex was undetected in both.* Mark pumped his fist in victory.

He called the two expert witnesses. They both agreed the presence of propranolol was very significant since it helped explain the severity of the anaphylaxis and lack of response to adrenalin. Both said that if Lenny had known Dr. Stevens was on propranolol, he might have reversed the blocking effect of propranolol by administering an antidote drug, called glucagon. One allergist asked if Lenny's informed consent for allergy injections mentioned that patients should not be on beta-blockers. When Mark said the consent included that, she responded supportively, "Well, there you go!"

He called Lenny, who always answered immediately when Mark's name came up on his cell.

"Lenny, I think we've finally caught a big break."

"What is it?"

"The post mortem blood and gastric samples came back positive for propranolol, but negative on Celebrex. You were right about propranolol! Now I've got some leverage to go back and negotiate a reasonable settlement with no punitive damages. Even if they want to go to trial, I'm convinced this will keep damages within the limits of your insurance. Let me call Tucker and get back to you."

"Great news. I guess it means my intuition is still intact...You really think you can get them to be reasonable?"

"I'm hoping they will settle now. This is just an incredible malpractice case. Lenny, it ought to be used in law school—all the twists and turns."

"Please just get it done. As far as I'm concerned, you can do anything you want. I just want it over with.

"Lenny, I'm sorry," Mark said. "Just getting carried away. I know this has been hell for you. I'll call you the minute I know something."

"Mark, one more thing. I realize now that if Celebrex was detected in Frank's system it wouldn't have explained his reaction. When I read the warning information, it indicated Celebrex shouldn't be used in someone with a history of hypersensitivity to sulfonamides. I just assumed that meant Celebrex could have caused the anaphylaxis. I finally talked to an expert and he pointed out there has been no valid report of anaphylaxis with Celebrex in patients with sulfonamide sensitivity. The issue has more to do with Celebrex causing a severe skin reaction. Anyway I apologize. I have egg on my face-rather embarrassed about it. Sorry for misleading you."

"Hey it's of no significance. We're all human. Anyway we now have a great defense. Get some good sleep."

Chapter Thirty-Eight

KC ENTERED JIMMY'S room without knocking. He was an intimidating giant with a distinctive bass voice. "Hi Jimmy."

"KC, how'd you know where I was?" Jimmy asked, trying not to look alarmed. "Oh, I guess Pete told you."

"Yeah. Tommy knows you're here too. We've been looking for you. You just fucking disappeared, man!"

"Hey, I was in a coma for a long time, and when I woke up I couldn't remember shit."

The henchman didn't waste any time. "So, what have you told them?"

"Nothing! I swear! C'mon, you don't need to worry about me."

"Tommy is worried. He thinks you might make a deal if they pressure you."

That comment sent a surge of fear though Jimmy, but he knew he couldn't show it. Instead he sat up straight and looked KC directly in the eye. "Look, what I need is a new ID. I need to disappear, maybe go to the islands. Live there for a year or two until everything blows over. Can you help me?"

KC drummed his fingers on the end of the bed. "I think so, but you need to take the test." He reached into his pocket and brought out a small spray bottle.

"Great idea! Let's do it."

Without hesitation, Jimmy sprayed both sides of his nose, and they waited fifteen minutes. During the wait Jimmy talked incessantly about old times, trying to conceal his anxiety.

Once the time was up, KC started with some easy questions. "Jimmy, what's your real name?"

"Jimmy Bonante."

"How long have you worked for us?"

"Eight years."

"Where did you work before COADD?"

"Colorado Innovation Institute"

"What kind of work did you do there?"

"I was a research scientist."

"What happened to the guy who was working on destroying marijuana plants?"

"He died in a bike accident."

A gleeful smirk appeared on KC's face. "Did you destroy all the specs at COADD?"

"KC, I really tried to get the other set, but you guys made the hit before I got them from Stevens."

KC was puzzled by that response. "Jimmy, you know we always hire these things out. We never know when or how they'll happen. So you're telling me you couldn't destroy the other set?"

"Yeah, that's what happened. I tried. I looked everywhere in Stevens' home office, but couldn't find them."

"Do you know where they could be or who might know where they are?"

"Well, maybe. I think Dr. Stevens might have told Dr. Haberman and his son, Jack. They could know something about it."

"Who are they?"

"Haberman is the medical director at COADD. He's also the doc whose allergy shot caused the fatal reaction that killed Stevens. By the way, that was an interesting way to handle it."

KC's lips twisted slightly. "Remember what I said, we have nothing to do with how it's done. Now, how can we find this doctor and his kid?"

"I know Haberman lives in Denver and his kid goes to school in Boulder, but that's all I know. I haven't spoken to the kid since all this happened. He'd always call me about bullshit stuff, like advice on girls, chemistry and other stuff. For a while we were tight."

"Find him. Find out if he knows anything."

"I'll do it, but I need to get out of here first. Go to another country. Lay low. You know what I mean, KC?"

"All right, let me handle it, but first I have some more questions," KC said, wanting to make sure Jimmy wasn't suckering him. "Did you get a Ph.D. in chemistry?"

"No, I have an M.S."

'Did you tell anyone about the family?"

"No one! Only Pete knows, from the past."

KC nodded. "Did you tell anyone at COADD about the family?"

"No, absolutely not!"

"Are you thinking of talking to the police?"

"No!"

"If they offered you a deal, would you accept one?"

"No!"

"Would you like to kill Tommy or me?"

"No, I never want to kill anyone, especially my family."

"Where do you have your money stashed?"

"In the Bahamas."

"Would you recommend I learn to play the flute?"

"Are you kidding, KC? With those ham hocks of yours, you couldn't even pick your nose."

KC laughed with his loud bass voice and slapped Jimmy on the shoulder.

"You passed, Jimmy. I'll tell Tommy to get you a new ID. You'll see. Everything will work out just right."

Chapter Thirty-Nine

MARK LEFT TUCKER a voice mail asking him to call back. In response, Tucker waited a few days before returning the call, hoping to increase Mark's anxiety.

"Mark, it's Ed Tucker. What's up?"

"I've got some new information I think you should know about."

"What is it?"

Mark told him about the letter from Denise Stevens in which she admitted that her husband had been taking propranolol, and the tests verifying that propranolol was detected in Stevens' blood and stomach contents.

Trying to consider what this meant for the case, Tucker was silent for a moment. "Let me see the docs. Can you fax them over? I'll let you know what I think." Then he hung up.

After reading what Mark sent to him, Tucker called Pete Doren, their resident expert. Pete confirmed that propranolol could interfere in the adrenalin treatment of anaphylactic shock.

Tucker knew damages for the defense would be greatly diminished with this new information. He weighed the pros and cons. He still thought he could prove Haberman was liable for mishandling the reaction. Elizabeth's deposition had not been completed, but he wasn't sure he wanted to hear any more from her. If she did admit to accidentally giving Stevens an overdose, it might keep Haberman on the hook, but it could also confuse the jury. On balance, after judging all the factors, he decided it was time to call Ted Larkin and talk settlement. Also, his own lawsuit was heating up and he needed time to focus on it.

Tucker braced himself for Ted's reaction. "Ted, there's a new development in the case, and it's not going to make you happy."

"What are you talking about, Ed ? What development?"

"Your sister sent a letter to Dr. Haberman about not reading a safety pamphlet on propranolol. It's a drug Frank took for migraines. After Frank died, she found out the drug might have interfered in treating Frank's allergic reaction."

"Denise did what?"

"I have a copy of the letter signed by her."

"God damn it! I told her to keep her mouth shut." Ted stopped abruptly, realizing his mistake.

"What? You knew? Why the hell didn't you tell me?" Tucker said, enraged.

"Ed, get off my back. It wouldn't have helped, because I just found out about it. I thought I was doing the right thing after she told me. God damn it! I told her not to say anything."

"Well this seriously weakens our case, and the defense has an independent lab report stating the drug was found in Frank's stomach and post mortem blood. That proves he took it."

"Now what?"

"Well Haberman's isn't off the hook completely because he was still out of the office, delayed calling the paramedics, and didn't have the right equipment, but there's another potential problem." Tucker explained about the possibility that Elizabeth had given Stevens a higher than prescribed dosage of his allergy vaccine, and that could muddy the waters even more.

"So we're screwed, is that it?"

"To be honest, Ted, I think we need to change directions. We may be able to add other doctors as defendants. The one who prescribed propranolol should have known Frank had asthma. I can also add Dr. Kerlin, who gave him Celebrex without checking on his sulfa allergy. Haberman may want to settle just to get past this, but we're not going to get the big bucks now."

"So you're suggesting a settlement?"

"Unfortunately, it may be the best solution."

"Then get the most you can, God damn it! She'll need it to raise those kids."

Chapter Forty

JIMMY WAS MOVED to an assisted-living apartment to continue his rehab. He was anxious to get going soon, but he still needed physical therapy on his leg. Charley and Sol kept hounding him about the missing set of specs and the whereabouts of the other set. He kept up the amnesia ploy. Helping his cause, Dr. Finkle saw him several times and concluded he had permanent amnesia from irreversible damage to the hippocampal region in the brain.

Jimmy hadn't received a new ID. It made him anxious. Maybe the family had something else in mind, like a Jimmy Hoffa ending.

The best way to demonstrate his loyalty to the family was finding out what Frank had done with the other set of specs. He still thought either Haberman or his son, Jack, might have an idea where they could be. He called Jack, who was excited to hear from him, and they agreed to meet the next day to catch up.

When Jack walked into the room, he gave Jimmy a big hug. Jimmy stepped back, pretending he felt more pain than he actually did.

"Jimmy, I didn't come earlier because I heard you had amnesia. I really missed talking to you."

"Thanks, Jack. I'm getting to the point that I can almost remember things."

"Jimmy, so much has happened since Dr. Stevens died. It was just awful, and losing you too. Then finding out you were in the hospital with amnesia. And wow, when you called...I just can't believe you're back!"

Jimmy talked slowly to accentuate his disability. "You've changed, grown up. What's up with you?"

"I dropped out of school. I needed time to figure out what I want to do with my life."

Jimmy put on a frown. "I'm not happy you did that. You're good in science. I know Frank would have been disappointed to know you dropped out."

"I know, but I needed time away from school and shit like that, and well...losing Dr. Stevens. I'm pissed at my dad. You know Dr. Stevens died in his office."

"I worked with your dad at COADD. He seemed like a good guy."

"I don't care. I'm still pissed. I think it was his fault. You know, he's being sued by Mrs. Stevens and her family."

"No, I didn't know that." Jimmy was getting impatient. The only reason he cared about Lenny Haberman was to get the specs he might have in his possession. "Anyway, Jack, like I said on the phone, I have something to ask you."

"Sure, Jimmy, what's up?"

"From what they tell me, I had a set of specifications with me when I had the accident, and they were destroyed. COADD desperately needs them to make more vaccine. Do you remember if Dr. Stevens had another set?"

"Sure, I know he did."

Jimmy's anticipation heightened. "Do you know where he kept them?"

Jack pursed his lips. "Don't know that. But Dr. Stevens told me he had an extra set."

Jimmy paused, and then asked. "Would your dad have any idea?"

Jack's expression changed to one of upset, having to think about his dad. "I don't know. We don't talk."

"Jack, COADD really needs to find them. Think for a minute, do you have any idea where they could be? You were pretty close to Dr. Stevens."

"Probably at his office or his house. I think he said something about keeping them in a safe or some place at his house."

Jimmy suddenly had a flash. What Jack had just said triggered a memory of Frank telling him they were in a place *'to keep them from being destroyed by an act of God.' That's it.* He then realized the disks he found on the desk in Frank's home office couldn't have contained the specs, because they weren't in a secure location. He needed to call KC.

Jimmy told Jack he was getting tired and had a headache. Jack left, promising to be back in a few days.

Jimmy picked up the phone and dialed.

"KC, it's Jimmy. I've moved to a different place for my rehab."

"Where is it?"

Jimmy wondered if he was signing his own death certificate, but decided he had no choice, and gave KC the address. Then he asked, "KC, where's the ID?"

"Tommy was out of town, but he's back. I'll send it to you soon. Let me know where you're headed."

"I'll do it as soon as I get the ID. Oh, I met with Haberman's kid, Jack, the one who worked at COADD. You remember, the kid who was real friendly with Stevens? He told me Stevens definitely had another set and kept it locked up somewhere, probably at his house."

"So you think the other set is still out there."

"Yeah, I do, and I think Jack knows more than he's saying. I gotta believe that Jack or his father, Dr. Haberman, may know where they're at."

"OK, Jimmy, you've done what you could," KC said gruffly. Remember to call and tell me where you're going. We'll be in touch soon about the next job."

"For sure, KC. Absolutely, I'll let you know." Jimmy hung up, relieved that the *'next job'* meant the family didn't plan to terminate him.

When the ID arrived he made arrangements to leave. His new name was Jimmy Lerrona. The only issue holding him back was his leg rehab, so he made an appointment to meet with his physical therapist one more time. He decided that the next time he did therapy would be on a beach with a knock-your-socks-off island girl. Then he called Pete to let him know he was leaving, but something in Pete's voice raised his anxiety. Without calling KC back, Jimmy left the next day on an early flight.

Chapter Forty-One

A SETTLEMENT MEETING was scheduled at Tucker's office to include only Tucker, Josh Cutter and Mark. Their clients would not be present, but were available by phone to get their response to the offer and counter-offer, assuming the latter was necessary.

Mark placed a call to Lenny to make sure he understood why the settlement meeting made sense at this time. "Lenny, we may not be able to get Elizabeth's deposition completed soon, and it could get too close to the trial date. We can't prove she did something wrong with the vaccine dose, and more than likely her attorney will keep stalling. More importantly, I think Tucker knows the case is less persuasive in view of the propranolol evidence. They might be willing to settle for less."

"So what should we do?"

"As much as I'd like to put all the blame on Elizabeth, I think you'll be better off trying to get them to settle under a million. Remember, they still have a couple of ways to argue your negligence."

Lenny didn't feel he was responsible at all, but he also lived in the real world. "I guess. If you can keep it under my limits, then I'll agree."

The three lawyers settled in a conference room in Tucker's office. Their legal assistants stayed in an adjoining room, available to set up calls to their respective clients. Each side brought an outline of their position on the case. Most of the presentation was a repeat of what each had told the other in past meetings or conversations, except Mark mentioned there was one other explanation for the reaction.

"Witnesses have substantiated that Dr. Stevens had been running when he arrived to get his injection. Dr. Haberman believes that running could have set Stevens up for a severe reaction."

Tucker looked annoyed. "So you have witnesses who can verify that?"

"Yes, we have three patients who will testify to that."

Tucker asked Josh to make a note to verify those statements. Tucker continued, "Can we talk about a settlement?"

"Without admitting negligence or gross negligence, we're ready to consider an offer."

"OK we need two million dollars for complete settlement."

Mark immediately rejected the claim. "C'mon Ed, you know that's over Dr. Haberman's policy limit."

"Do you want to run it by your client before we pull up stakes?"

Mark went out of the meeting room and called Lenny to inform him of the offer. Lenny told him absolutely no. He instructed Mark not to settle for anything above the one million dollar limit on his policy.

Mark returned. "Ed, the answer is no, but I think he'll agree to the limit on his policy, one million."

"I doubt that'll work for us, but I'll call Larkin."

Tucker called his client. "Ted, their counter offer is final. It's one million, the max for his policy. I think you should take it."

"Don't settle!"

"That's crazy, Ted. This case isn't going to get any better. You're making a big mistake," Tucker warned.

"I need time to think about it and to talk to Denise."

"OK, I'll let them know."

Tucker walked back into the conference room to tell Mark that Ted still wanted to go for the higher amount.

Mark sighed. "OK, then I guess we're going to trial."

Mark called Lenny to let him know what happened.

"Those pricks, I can't believe this."

"Lenny, stay cool, I think they're just posturing. The facts are now on your side. Even Larkin has to realize that."

Chapter Forty-Two

DENVER WAS EXPERIENCING a spring heat wave, and Ted Larkin decided to leave the legislative session early to drive thirty minutes to Three Bridges, a small township located on the South Platte River, a pristine blue ribbon trout stream. He had a planned escape route through tunnels under the senate floor to get to his car, which was already loaded with his gear.

River's Edge Fly Fishing Club was a very exclusive one. Ted arrived just as a light cloud cover appeared- a good sign for emergence of a fly hatch. After putting on the latest style Orvis waders and a matching multi-pocketed fishing jacket filled with fly fishing paraphernalia, he checked in to find out what flies were working. Abe Conklin, an old-timer of eighty-five years, was sitting at the registration desk.

"Ted ole boy! How ya doing these days? Making any more laws to complicate my life?"

"You know, Abe, if you weren't such a strong old fart, I'd arm wrestle you, but I'm afraid if you beat me, I wouldn't be able to cast."

"Let's get it on, Teddy boy. Come on!"

Ted smiled as he wrote his name in the registration book. "I need all my strength to bring in some of those four pound rainbows out there. How's the fishing today?"

"Darn good! The water level is still down, but the snow melt is about to begin, so this is a good time to be here. I'd use a sixteen caddis. Throw the fly right off the bank and you'll get em."

"Great, Abe. We'll arm wrestle next time."

Ted walked upstream, trying to stay far enough from the river to keep his shadow from spooking trout near the bank. He waded into the current to his knees, feeling some gentle resistance as he moved into sandy gravel for better footing. He cast a smooth loop with his four- weight bamboo fly rod. Most of the members owned handmade bamboo rods, signifying fly fishing expertise as well as old wealth.

He landed his fly above some large boulders, about thirty feet upstream. It moved slowly down into a patch of foam, where a rainbow trout splashed violently and swallowed it. Ted kept light tension on the line and steered the fish away from drifting logs and other debris. The fish ran upstream and Ted played it until it began to fatigue. Just then, two bees landed and stung Ted on his face and neck. Shaking off the twin shocks of pain, Ted netted the fish, released it and moved back to the shoreline.

As he climbed the bank, he felt a sudden surge of nausea combined with a strange sensation of lightheadedness and shortness of breath. Realizing he might be in trouble, he moved rapidly to a shaded area to cool down. He reached a large cottonwood tree and placed one hand on the trunk, turned slowly and slid down while feeling faint. He wondered if he was having a heart attack.

Fortunately, two fishermen were walking by and recognized him. One of them yelled, "Hey Ted, how's the fishing?" Ted laid there, completely immobile. The one who yelled came closer, thinking the senator might not have heard him over the sound of the river. He approached and spoke louder, but Ted didn't respond. Realizing Ted was in serious trouble, he told his friend to call 911.

By the time a helicopter arrived, Ted was unconscious and receiving CPR from his two friends, who thought he was having a heart attack. The paramedics immediately saw that Ted's face and neck were extremely swollen and realized he was experiencing an allergic reaction. They injected him several times with adrenalin. Miraculously, Ted responded and was stabilized after intravenous fluids were started. He was air lifted to Denver Memorial Hospital for ongoing treatment of anaphylaxis.

* * *

Lenny was just leaving the office when the ER called and asked him to consult on a patient. The doc described the history and handed him the chart.

Recognizing Larkin's name, he sat down to decide what he should do. He couldn't believe how fate had a way of intervening in his life. Ethically, he knew he had to treat Ted, since he was the on-call allergy consultant for the ER. He walked into the curtained-off area and found Larkin sleeping with beeping monitors measuring his oxygen saturation, vital signs and fluid intake. The screeching curtain rings sliding along the metal rods stirred Larkin, and he opened his eyes.

"Mr. Larkin, I'm Dr. Haberman. I happen to be the on-call allergy consultant. I'm sure you recognize my name."

Larkin was still slightly confused, but the name Haberman woke him up.

"Why, yes, Doctor, of course I do."

"Let me make sure you're stable, and then you can call in the allergist of your choice."

Larkin frowned. "What happened to me?"

"You experienced an anaphylactic reaction, maybe from a food or an insect. Do you remember any details before you collapsed?"

"Yes, I remember now. I got stung by something on the river," he said, still not sounding all there. "Anyway, thanks for taking the time to consult. Please do what you can. I understand it's uncomfortable for you. I'll ask them to call Dr. Doren."

It was difficult for Lenny to avoid reacting to that choice, but he decided to let it go. "Did you recognize the kind of insects that stung you?"

"No, but they were damn fast. I saw them fall into the river after they stung me."

Lenny decided to look closely where Larkin indicated he was stung and noticed protruding stingers. He removed them carefully with tweezers.

"I removed a few barbed stingers that remained at the sting sites. Only honey bees have barbed stingers which they lose when they sting. Then they die immediately which explains why they fell into the river. You're apparently very sensitive to honey bee venom. Has this happened to you before?"

"No, never."

"Well, I think you're extremely allergic to bee stings, particularly honey bees. You can get tested to be sure, but wait a month for that. If you're allergic you can get allergy shots to build up immunity. That can eventually give you ninety-nine percent protection."

"That seems like the treatment for me," Ted said gratefully.

"Mr. Larkin, there's another medical issue you should be aware of."

"What's that, Doctor?"

"I noticed from your medication list that you're being treated for high blood pressure with a medication called lisinopril. Is that correct?"

"Yes, why does that matter?"

"There's evidence that this class of drug, called an ACE-inhibitor, can make anaphylaxis worse, especially from bee stings. You need to talk to your primary care doctor about getting off this medication." Lenny looked up from his chart. "Oh and before you leave the hospital, you should receive a prescription for an emergency adrenalin kit that you can self-administer, just in case you get stung again. Make sure you have it on you at all times. Next time you may not be lucky as you were today."

Larkin realized this guy really knew his stuff. "All right, I'll talk to my internist." He hesitated a moment and then said, "Doctor, thanks for helping me, especially under the circumstances."

Lenny thought it best not to say anything further. "I'll let the staff know you want Dr. Doren to consult," and then he left the room.

Chapter Forty-Three

THE NEXT DAY, Ted was recuperating at home. He was thinking about his meeting with Haberman in the hospital, and decided to tell Tucker about it.

"Ed, I had the weirdest thing happen yesterday." He described his severe reaction to the bee stings and being air lifted to Memorial. "Here's the weirdest part. Dr. Haberman was on call and he came to see me in the ER. He was actually very nice and seemed very knowledgeable."

"Wow, what an incredible coincidence."

"Well, it's made me rethink the case. He's a good doc and especially considering all that stuff with my sister, I'm thinking I want to settle this thing. Go ahead and call his attorney, and let's get this over with. Let's settle for one million."

"OK, Ted, I really think that's the way to go. You know, we could've lost this completely at trial."

Tucker called Mark and they agreed on a one million dollar settlement.

Mark called Lenny in turn. "Lenny, it's over. We agreed to one million. I'll get the documents ready and send them over for you to sign. Then you'll be done with it."

"That's a surprise. Did Tucker tell you I took care of Larkin yesterday for a bee sting reaction that almost killed him?"

"No, he didn't." Lenny described what had happened. "My God, that's really something. Maybe it's why Larkin agreed to settle."

"I really had no choice, but if that made it happen… great! Though I have to admit, I had an evil thought."

"What was that?"

"I'm actually kidding, but I had a moment's thought about not removing the stingers. The ER docs missed them. If you leave them in, they sometimes cause a delayed allergic reaction, but the better part of my nature took over."

Mark laughed, "I always knew you were a good guy. If it was me, I would have left them in."

"See, Mark, that's why you're a calculating attorney and I save lives." They laughed.

Lenny said, "Anyway, thanks for helping me get out of this mess, Mark. The only part I'll miss is talking to you every day."

Mark laughed again as they hung up.

Driving home, Lenny began to think about the consequences of accepting the settlement. For the next five years he would have to list this result every time he reapplied for hospital privileges, renewed his medical license, and updated his malpractice insurance. His malpractice rates would go up for sure and the settlement would be reported to the National Practitioner Data Bank. The data bank had been set up by Congress to help state licensing boards, hospitals and other medical entities investigate qualifications of doctors seeking employment, licenses or hospital privileges. Yet, he pushed those negative thoughts out of his mind because, at long last, he could get back to a normal life.

Chapter Forty-Four

BEN LOCKE HAD become more interested in COADD's problems, despite Barone's claim that he wasn't sure why he took the specifications and couldn't remember pertinent details. Ben thought he could make a circumstantial case of theft based on Charley's finding that Barone had a voice mail indicating money had been wired into his bank account just at the time the specs had disappeared. He needed to track down the name of the person who called Barone about the wired money, and if possible, the name of the bank that received the money.

Ben sat back, letting his mind wander without any particular focus. The Barone case was floating around in his thoughts when suddenly something clicked. He recalled a cold case he'd been involved in five or six years ago, that involved the death of another research scientist. The coincidence of two research scientists dying in Colorado seemed too much to ignore. He went out to the desk of his junior associate, Alice Holten.

"Alice, I need you to find some old files for me."

"Sure. Do you have the dates and name of the file?"

"Not exactly, but I remember the time. It was when I started at CBI, sometime around 2004 or 2005. The name of the case isn't clear, but I know it involved the death of a scientist who was working on curing something...No, that's not it. What the hell was it?" He frowned, trying to remember the details.

"To start with, just look at all the cold cases from 2004 to 2006."

She nodded. As he started to walk away, he suddenly recalled another detail.

"I know! It had something to do with destroying marijuana plants. That's it! Let me know when you find it."

Within an hour, Alice was back with two large boxes that she placed on Ben's desk.

"Fantastic, you found them!" He opened the boxes to reveal information on a cold case involving the death of Dr. Sanford Sontag, chief research scientist at the Colorado Innovation Institute in Fort Collins, Colorado.

He first read the summary narrative. Dr. Sontag was working on an herbicide that would selectively destroy marijuana plants. His hobby was riding road bikes. His family had a condo in Vail and he planned to meet them for dinner one summer afternoon after riding from Copper Mountain to East Vail, a grueling high-altitude ride up and down a steep mountainside. As he descended, witnesses reported the bike was gaining speed, moving from lane to lane, trying to avoid vehicles in its path. The bike eventually hit a median and flipped upside down, killing Sontag. CBI was asked to investigate when it was discovered that someone had tampered with the brakes of Sontag's bike. What happened was considered to be very odd because Sontag was a stickler about keeping his bike in good condition. He had gotten his bike checked out at a local Ft. Collins bike shop just one day before his fatal accident.

It had been one of Ben's first cases with CBI, which puzzled him because he should have remembered it, especially since it involved the death of another scientist. Every possible lead was run down. CBI learned that Dr. Sontag had increased his life insurance about six months before his death.

His wife had been pestering him to increase it because their savings were meager and she was concerned that if something happened to him there wouldn't be enough to support her and their children. The insurance company was suspicious, but their investigation couldn't find any evidence that she'd had anything to do with the circumstances surrounding the accident, and they paid her the face value of the policy. The CBI investigation included interviewing staff at the bike shop, but everyone had checked out. No one had a trace of prior criminal activity or association with criminal elements. It eventually became a cold case.

Ben started on the box of files, which weren't arranged in any order. He reviewed interviews with relatives, co-workers, friends, and colleagues some of whom worked elsewhere but knew Sontag and his work. Everyone had admired Sontag's keen scientific mind and most had considered him a good friend. Scientists at CII mentioned that before his death, Sontag was very excited because he thought he'd discovered an effective herbicide against marijuana. Months after his death, the company announced that their herbicide could selectively kill marijuana plants, but the testing material had been completely used up and they were unable to duplicate Dr. Sontag's findings. The company then announced that it was unable to continue operations due to lack of funds.

After several hours of reading, nothing jumped out at him. He was about to take a break when he came to an interview in the second box. Ben was startled to see the name Jimmy Barone. There was the mystery man himself. A photograph revealed a heavier person with a full blond beard and mustache, enough camouflage to confuse anyone who saw him today. He was among thirty or more technical people working in the lab. All were questioned and everyone had come up clean.

Ben compared the Ft. Collins and COADD cases. In the earlier case, Jimmy was a technician in a research project involving an herbicide that could selectively destroy marijuana plants, and the head researcher died from a suspicious bike accident. In the COADD case, Jimmy was the head technician in cocaine vaccine research and the lead researcher died from a reaction to an allergy injection. Regardless of the cause of death, two threads held the cases together: one was Jimmy Barone and the other was stopping research that would interfere in sales of street drugs. Ben was too experienced to believe in coincidences. He called Charley immediately.

Charley was finishing his workout when Ben called his cell.

"Yo, it's Charley."

"Charley, Ben calling. I was free associating about Jimmy Barone and somehow it made me think of a cold case from a few years back. You'll never believe it, but Jimmy Barone worked at a lab several years ago that developed an herbicide to kill marijuana plants, and in that case the research scientist died from a weird bike accident." Ben then brought Charley up to speed on more of the details.

"Are you suggesting Barone may have been involved in Doc Stevens' death?"

"I don't know, but you have to admit it's more than a coincidence. Two researchers died who were working on how to rid the world of street drugs, and Barone was involved in both projects."

"Wow! So how're you going to prove it, especially now when everyone believes that the allergy shot killed Dr. Stevens?"

"What's the name of the allergy doc?"

"Dr. Leonard Haberman. I can tell you from my fleeting contact that he was real upset about what happened to Stevens. I think his case finally got settled, so he might not be happy to hear from you, now that's all over with."

"I understand, but I can't ignore this. I'm giving him a call. "

"OK, but you gotta tell me what you find out. That sure is something!"

Chapter Forty-Five

BEFORE LEAVING FOR a well-deserved vacation in Hawaii with Elaine, Lenny received congratulatory calls from colleagues and friends who had read in the paper that the case was settled. He couldn't reveal details of the settlement because of a confidentiality agreement, but he thanked everyone for their support.

When Ben found out that Lenny was on vacation in Hawaii, he left a voice mail identifying himself as an agent with the CBI and a brief description of why he was calling. A week later, Lenny was back in his office, tanned and relaxed, catching up on correspondence, e-mails and listening to voice mails. He listened to the voice message from the CBI agent and immediately stopped what he was doing to call Mark.

"Mark, I just got a call from the CBI. They want to talk to me about Frank's death. Why would they call me? What the hell's going on?"

"I have no idea. Let me call the agent and see. I'll get right back to you."

Later, Mark called him back. "They're investigating a possible criminal conspiracy that may have something to do with Frank's death."

"What? Am I a criminal suspect or something?"

"No—no it's not you; it's someone else. I told him we could meet later today because I'm leaving town tomorrow. I think we'd better talk before I leave, so I set it up for 5 pm at your office. Will that work?"

"I guess."

Ben Locke arrived at Lenny's office just as the last patient was leaving. After introductions, Ben got down to business. "Dr. Haberman, we're investigating the disappearance of manufacturing specifications at COADD, and there may be a connection with Dr. Stevens' death."

Lenny was puzzled by his suggestion. "You do know that I settled the case already, so this doesn't make any sense."

"I completely understand." Ben went on to tell him about the death of Dr. Sontag at CII, and the particular coincidence that Jimmy Barone worked at both CII and COADD.

Lenny broke in. "Agent Locke, I've known Jimmy Barone for years. We met when I came on as a board member and medical director at COADD. We were all friends. Even though Jimmy didn't have a Ph.D., Frank thought he was a top researcher. I have a hard time believing that Jimmy had anything to do with this."

"Doctor, we look for patterns. When I realized both cases involved deaths of scientists who were researching illegal street drugs, and Barone was a technician in both labs, it seemed more than a coincidence. Yesterday I was informed that Barone left his apartment weeks ago and has literally vanished."

Lenny frowned. "But all of it might be just a coincidence."

"I don't think so. The day Dr. Stevens died, Barone took off without telling anyone, and the drug specifications went missing. When some of his memory returned after the accident, he told COADD officials that he recalled taking them, but couldn't remember why."

Lenny couldn't help becoming irritated by these revelations. He finally answered. "I do remember Sol Feldman was suspicious of a robbery when the documents and Jimmy disappeared at the same time. But there's another explanation that Sol discussed. Frank and Jimmy knew the vaccine was effective and there is the possibility Frank asked Jimmy to move the specs to a secure place."

Ben thought about that possibility but then added more damaging evidence. "I forgot to mention another interesting piece of information. Barone's phone at COADD had a message confirming that a large amount of money was wired to his bank account. We're trying to track down the name of the person who sent it to him and the name of the bank."

Lenny shook his head in disbelief. "Are you suggesting he was paid for stealing them?"

Ben shrugged. "Yes, that's a likely possibility. Here's the other element that I'm thinking about. Stopping research on illegal drugs at COADD and the Fort Collins lab makes a strong circumstantial case for involvement of organized crime."

Lenny murmured, "I can't believe it. You think Jimmy had something to do with Frank's death, but how?"

"Was the allergy injection reaction unusual?"

"Unusual would be putting it mildly. The reaction was immediate and he was unresponsive to adrenalin. His heart stopped within minutes, maybe two to three minutes following the injection."

"Why do you think it was so rapid and severe?"

Lenny brought up the propranolol issue, plus the volume discrepancy in the vaccine vial.

"Could the nurse and Barone have known each other, maybe conspired to kill Stevens? Oh, by the way, what's your nurse's name?"

"Elizabeth Finch," Lenny said, startled by this possibility. "I have no idea if she knew Barone."

Ben made a note. "Let me do some checking on that. Even if they did know each other, can you think of a way that Barone might have murdered Stevens with an allergy injection?"

Lenny swiveled his chair back and forth for several moments. "Well, for sure by giving him a very large dose of his vaccine... Also they could have added something foreign to his vaccine." Lenny spoke his next sentence slowly, as if he needed time to grasp the full significance of what he was saying. "Like something... he was allergic to."

"Well, like what?"

"Well, he was allergic to sulfonamide antibiotics, and lots of foods, so it's possible they might have added something like that into his vaccine. Maybe even a toxin, like snake venom."

"How would they find out what he was allergic to? Isn't that confidential?"

"Yes, of course, but - oh my God - Elizabeth had access to his chart and all the testing that had been done." His voice trailed off as the unthinkable was becoming clearer. "Maybe she told Barone what he was allergic to."

"Yes, that's definitely a possibility. Do you have the vial here?"

"Yes, after he died I stuck it back in the fridge."

Ben didn't like that. "I don't know if we could use it for evidence in a criminal case if it's just been sitting there all this time."

"Do you still want the vial?"

"Yes, I think it's still worthwhile looking into. Can we find out if something's been added to it?"

"I could have it analyzed by a reference allergy lab. I'll send them standards of what should be in it. They should be able to determine if something extra is in it, but how would that be admissible?"

"We'll cross that bridge when we come to it. First let's find out if something was added to Dr. Stevens' injection."

"Agent Locke, I have another thought. I can prepare a vaccine with Dr. Stevens' formula and reduce the volume to the same amount that was in his vial. That would be the control for comparison."

"Good. Call me when it's ready. Where's the analysis done?"

Lenny responded, "I don't know, but I'll find out."

"I also need any information you have on Elizabeth Finch."

Lenny went to his computer and printed out Elizabeth's employment records. He also mentioned that Charley Blackwood, the P.I. for COADD, had some additional information that might help shed some light on Elizabeth and her past.

After Ben left, Lenny had a few questions for Mark.

"Mark, what does this mean for me?"

"If they prove a criminal conspiracy occurred, then your liability in the case would be officially erased from your record."

That would be terrific! If it turns out there was a crime, then the settlement funds would go back to the insurance company and my malpractice rates shouldn't increase. Right?"

Mark hesitated, knowing his answer wouldn't be well received. "Unfortunately that's not what happens since both parties didn't know about a potential crime when they settled."

"You're kidding. That's unreal!"

"Lenny if this pans out, your medical malpractice record will be cleared, but unfortunately you need to stay involved, because it happened in your office. My advice is to cooperate with the CBI."

After Mark left, Lenny sat alone in his office. His thoughts dwelled on what he'd just heard. *My God, a possible murder?* Questions about why, how and who kept reverberating in his head.

The next day he called Agent Locke to let him know he'd found a reference lab willing to do the tests on the vaccine. The lab director, intrigued by the forensic problem, suggested they use high-pressure liquid chromatography (HPLC) to separate the allergens, as each component would show up as a distinct peak on a graph. He requested samples of known allergens that had been added to the vaccine preparation to identify the peaks. Just in case something showed up, Locke decided that he would make sure all procedures going forward met legal requirements to assure a chain of custody for criminal case evidence.

Lenny still couldn't imagine the possibility that Jimmy and Elizabeth conspired to cause Stevens' death. He decided to do some personal investigation. He called Walt to ask him to cover the practice, and then drove over to Elizabeth's neighborhood, and parked down the block from her house. On her front lawn, two young children were playing while two women watched. One woman was standing and the other was in a wheelchair, motionless as the one standing talked continuously. Lenny noticed that the woman in the wheelchair would occasionally nod her head, but very slowly.

He pulled out a pair of binoculars, scanned their faces, and realized the one standing was Elizabeth. He didn't recognize the woman in the wheelchair, but her facial features strongly resembled Elizabeth's. He thought, *That has to be her sister, the one injured by Frank in the car accident. That's why Elizabeth has been so angry all these years.*

Chapter Forty-Six

WHEN LENNY ARRIVED at his office, he found an urgent message on his desk to call Ben Locke.

"Ben, Lenny here. What's up?"

"Lenny, this case is becoming more and more interesting. Apparently, the wired payment to Barone was from someone in Denver."

Lenny felt all his muscles tighten. "Do I need to sit down?"

"Maybe, if you know him. We tracked the voice mail back to a doctor in Denver...Dr. Pete Doren."

"What? I can't believe it! You're kidding, aren't you?"

"No, I'm not. Do you know him?"

"Well, yes. He's an allergist of sort. Why would he send Barone money?"

"Not totally sure but we have motive. I found out that Doren's wife had an affair with Stevens."

Lenny grasped that link instantly. "Yes, that's well known. Frank's wife Denise remained angry with Doren's wife over the affair. She even attacked

Mrs. Doren at Frank's funeral. But why in hell would Doren harm Frank after so long? God, nothing makes any sense."

Lenny followed up by saying he had seen Elizabeth and a woman in a wheelchair, obviously sisters. "Elizabeth had to be involved. Her motive is pretty obvious after seeing her injured sister."

"Lenny, I agree. Elizabeth also remains a prime suspect if we can prove that Stevens was murdered. By the way, have you heard anything on the vaccine analysis?"

"No, let me call and see where they're at with it."

"Lenny, one other thing, I've talked to a district attorney and she believes this could lead to a grand jury investigation. We'll likely need your testimony, but only to corroborate some of the facts."

Lenny thought with an unvoiced groan, *Will this never end?* "That means I have to remain involved, right?"

"Well, to be truthful, yes, but more importantly, we may need your medical expertise to get to the bottom of this."

After the call, Lenny realized that he was back to square one, trying again to discover the cause of Frank's death. He figured he might as well get started by calling the reference lab.

He reached the lab director right away.

"This is Dr. Clarkson."

"Hi, I'm Dr. Lenny Haberman. Do you have any results on the allergy vaccine that was sent over?"

"Oh yes, actually, I'm glad you called. I do have some rather interesting information. The patient's vaccine had an extra protein peak, but we can't identify it with the standards you sent. I have no idea what it is without something to compare."

Lenny paused, realizing the impact of this. "Dr. Clarkson, it must be something he was allergic to, or maybe even a toxin."

"Let's stay with horses on this one," referring to a standard maxim in medicine. When evaluating a diagnostic problem, the hearing of hoof beats would more likely suggest horses rather than zebras.

Lenny got the message. "OK, I'll send reagent samples of all allergens he was sensitive to."

"Good, I'll let you know what I find."

✱ ✱ ✱

Dr. Clarkson was intrigued by the case, and when the test reagents arrived, he made the analysis a top priority. The unknown peak in the HPLC matched, of all things, the peanut standard. Using a sample of Frank's vaccine, he performed a specialized confirmation test called RAST inhibition, which proved conclusively that peanut was the extra component. He called Lenny to let him know.

After Clarkson told him the news, Lenny called Ben Locke right away.

"Agent, it's Lenny Haberman. I just got off the phone with the forensic lab. I—I can't believe what they discovered. Frank was definitely murdered! Peanut was found in his vaccine. He was highly allergic to peanuts, and that no doubt caused the violent anaphylaxis. That in combination with the propranolol made the reaction both severe and untreatable."

"My God, you figured it out! So Stevens was murdered, for sure. This is what I needed. It's enough evidence to move forward with a grand jury investigation."

After he hung up, Lenny sat back, thinking about who could have done this and why. The most plausible suspect was Elizabeth, who had a real motive, knew what Frank was allergic to, and had access to the testing vial for peanut. However, he knew other possibilities needed to be explored, like the payoff from Doren to Barone. He wondered if Doren had paid Barone to kill Frank because he was still angry over the affair. Barone was now a real suspect because he had worked in another lab researching an illegal drug, and the head researcher there had also died mysteriously. *Could Jimmy be involved in a criminal conspiracy, like being part of a mob it sabotaged research on illegal drugs?* That thought concerned him, because that meant that Frank's murder involved organized crime. *What does that mean for me and my family? Do I need protection?*

Chapter Forty-Seven

BEN DECIDED IT was time to contact Dr. Doren. When he called, Pete was having a cup of coffee in the OR lounge. When Pete's secretary called to inform him that a CBI officer was on the phone, he knew it could only mean trouble.

"Dr. Doren," he said with a physician's dry calm.

"Dr. Doren, I'm Agent Locke with the CBI."

"Yes?"

"We're investigating the death of a researcher, Dr. Frank Stevens. I believe you knew him."

"Casually, yes."

"Doctor, we'd like to ask you some questions, either at your office or ours."

Pete could feel his heart rate increasing. He wasn't sure if he should continue the conversation or hang up, but his instincts told him to remain cooperative. "I don't understand. I thought Dr. Stevens died from a reaction to an allergy injection. Wasn't it some kind of malpractice case?"

"Regardless, we still have some questions."

"Well, OK. Let me check my schedule and get back to you."

"Fine, Doctor, but it's important. Please let me know right away. Here's my number."

Pete hung up and sat contemplating his next move, but then remembered he had a patient scheduled in the OR. He walked back into the surgical unit to begin a laser resurfacing procedure on the face of a middle-aged woman. As he moved the laser from region to region, his mind raced as he thought about the call from the CBI agent. Suddenly the hand holding the laser moved away from the treatment area while his foot remained on the power source. The erratic movement startled him, causing him to swiftly return the laser to the treatment area. Hoping the nurse had not witnessed what had just happened, he expressed a sigh of relief when he realized she had momentarily turned her head around to cough. He glanced back to the area he had just zapped, wondering if the injury was deep enough to have caused a third degree burn.

After he finished, he called Ed Tucker, whom he'd met during a pretrial session on the Haberman case. He explained the situation and Tucker agreed to represent him. Tucker mentioned that for the time being, until he finished up another trial, his associate, Josh Cutter, would handle it.

Doren called Agent Locke to set the meeting at his clinic.

When Ben Locke was escorted into Doren's office, Doren introduced himself and then Cutter. "I asked my attorney to be here."

Once everyone took a seat, Cutter asked, "Agent Locke, can you tell us why you're bringing Dr. Doren into this investigation?"

"Our investigation into the death of Dr. Stevens has taken a new turn. We have solid evidence that he was murdered."

Doren shifted uncomfortably. "What does that have to do with me?"

"Well, we've been searching for motives." Locke paused to emphasize his next statement. "And I discovered that you were very angry with Dr. Stevens over an affair he had with your wife...."

Cutter interrupted, "Before he answers, I need to know where this is heading."

Ben responded, "We believe Dr. Doren may have had reason to want Dr. Stevens dead. Maybe he'd rather come to my office for questioning and..."

Cutter stopped him. "You might want to rephrase that remark in kinder words, Agent. They sound very threatening to me."

Ben continued with a stone face. "Take my words however you want. I'm just looking for answers."

Cutter looked over at his client and then spoke. "I need to speak with Dr. Doren privately before we continue."

They left the room and Cutter turned to Doren. "What the hell is he talking about?"

"It's nothing. I do admit that when Stevens died I wasn't sorry, because the son of a bitch screwed my wife... but I didn't kill him."

"Look, Dr. Doren, I need to be absolutely certain you had nothing to do with this."

Doren raised both his hands for emphasis. "I didn't kill him."

"Do you know who did?"

"No, like I said, I don't know anything about it."

Cutter seemed satisfied, and they returned to the office.

Doren began by responding to Ben's previous question. "I admit I was angry with Stevens for a long time over his affair with my wife, but not enough to kill him."

Ben switched to another topic. "Do you know Jimmy Barone?"

Doren glanced at Cutter as he answered. "Yes, we've been friends since childhood. Why?"

"Did you have a nickname for him?"

241

"Oh sure, my nickname for him is Jimbone."

"Was that your private nickname for him, or was it commonly used by friends and family?"

"As far as I know, I'm the only one who used that name. If I had to leave a voice mail, I'd say, *Hey JimBonante, haven't heard from you in a while, so give me a call*. That way he knew it was me and he'd call me back when he had a minute."

Pete suddenly realized that he had just made a grave mistake in mentioning the name Bonante. He needed to correct it immediately. "I, uh, meant Jimbone Barone. I have two friends named Jimmy and I got confused. I'd say, Jimbone Barone, how's your ass these days." He stopped again, realizing how lame that sounded.

Ben realized this slip could be important. He wrote down the name *Bonante* for follow-up. He said, "OK. Do you know if Jimmy has or had any connections to organized crime?"

Cutter interrupted. "OK, let's stop right there. Where are you headed with this?"

"I'm asking if Dr. Doren knew whether Jimmy Barone had any connections to organized crime."

Cutter's face flushed and his voice rose. "What does this have to do with Dr. Doren? You need to explain why you're asking."

Ben's voice hardened. "I don't have to explain. I get to ask the questions and your client gets to answer them."

"So who are you investigating for the death of Dr. Stevens, Barone or my client?"

"Right now it's Mr. Barone, but I need to find out more about his connection to Dr. Doren."

Cutter responded, "I don't like the direction of this, but Dr. Doren can tell you what he knows about Jimmy Barone."

Ben nodded. "Fine, you're doing your job and I need to do mine. Doctor, can you tell me anything about Barone? His past, his occupation, anything that might help us?"

"Jimmy and I were always great friends. We grew up in the Bronx together, and coincidentally we both ended up in Denver. He came from a poor Italian family, got a scholarship to Brown, and became a research chemist. That's all I know."

"So when he lived in the Bronx, was he connected to organized crime in any way?"

Cutter started to object, but Pete interjected. "I want to answer. No, I wasn't aware of any association."

That's when Ben decided to throw out the dynamite stick. "Doctor, we were able to track down a voice mail on Mr. Barone's telephone at COADD. Let me read it to you." He retrieved a piece of paper from his jacket. " *'Hey, Jimbone. Just letting you know I wired 50K to your bank account.'* " Ben stared at Doren and said, "Since no one else used the nickname Jimbone, I shall assume that it was you who left the voice mail. Can you explain why you sent Jimmy Barone - Jimbone, fifty thousand dollars?"

Pete began to stutter, realizing the trap he'd fallen into. He looked over at Cutter for help.

Cutter jumped in. "Doctor, do not answer that! Agent Locke, we're going to take a break here." He stood and motioned for Pete to follow him into the hall again.

"Jesus, what the hell's going on? Why did you wire money to Barone?"

"It was a loan, nothing else."

"Why would you do that?"

"He's a friend, nothing more."

"Well then, just tell this guy that you loaned Barone money and don't answer anything else."

Doren nodded slowly. "But there is something else."

"What?"

"The money transferred about the time when Stevens died. He's going to think I paid Jimmy to kill Stevens."

"You're right about that! Look, when he brings it up, just mention it was pure coincidence."

They returned to the room and Doren resumed. "I lent Jimmy the money. I've done it in the past and he always paid me back. I didn't think anything about it since he's a good friend."

Ben responded. "OK, then why did you send it the day after Dr. Stevens died?"

"Pure coincidence."

"Really?" Ben shook his head. "That's certainly a very odd coincidence. Out of 365 days of the year you just happened to wire him money the day after Dr. Stevens was murdered."

Cutter stood up, fuming. "Dr. Doren stated that he loaned him the money, and assured you it was a coincidence that it was sent around the time Dr. Stevens died. He's told you all he knows and probably a lot more than he needed to, and yet you haven't told us anything about Dr. Stevens' alleged murder, and there's no evidence connecting my client to any wrongdoing. All we know is that money was wired coincidentally after Dr. Stevens died from a reaction to an allergy shot. Agent, this interview is over."

Ben stood as well. "I'll be in touch. Mr. Cutter, do you want me to contact you, or Dr. Doren?"

"Me."

When he left, Cutter reminded Doren not to talk to anyone about the case.

After the interview, Pete felt very hungry. He left his office and headed to a neighborhood restaurant that served breakfast all day. He ordered a stack of pancakes, ham steaks, and fries. As he sat there, his mind raced. *What am I going to tell Jacqueline? If she finds out, she'll think I paid Jimmy to murder Frank for sure, and if this gets out, I'll be ruined. Everything I've worked for will be gone, and she'll probably leave me.*

It suddenly occurred to Pete that he better contact Jimmy. Yet when he called Jimmy's cell, no one answered. All afternoon, Doren left message after message. He had no idea that the phone was ringing inside the dumpster of an assisted-living facility.

Chapter Forty-Eight

THE STEVENS CASE had been occupying most of Ben Locke's time. To clear his mind, he decided to take an afternoon off, which for him was reading about real crime. He had just finished the latest FBI updates on the surging national crime rate. It didn't surprise him that Colorado had recorded a ten percent increase in serious crime. He liked reading details of actual crimes and could never understand the fascination with thriller novels. He had distaste for exaggerated plots, written by authors who needed to dream up gruesome crimes to capture readers - like tying victims upside down and slitting their throats, as if they were slaughtered by a kosher butcher. If crime was a fascination, all you had to do was read about a truly horrific one, like the freak who kidnapped and raped a little girl, and left her to die at the bottom of an outhouse. What could be more terrifying than that real life story? *Why waste time with fiction, when actual crimes didn't need exaggeration, just solutions.*

He had the strong sense that Doren knew more than he let on. He thought it particularly odd that Doren accidentally mentioned the name

Jimmy Bonante. Hearing that Barone had lived in the Bronx, Ben decided to contact an old acquaintance, Ken Ryan, a detective from New York City he'd met at a national police convention that provided educational updates on forensic science and new technologies for law enforcement officials. Ben and Ryan had gone out several times for beers. They kept in touch with annual Christmas cards and updates on their families and careers. He made the call to Ryan's precinct.

A gruff New York voice came on line. "Detective Ryan, what can I do for ya?"

Trying to be funny with the same accent, Ben replied, "Hey, ole dog, dis is da ole CBI agent from Denver."

"Oh, my God! Ben, how ya hangin'?"

"Good, good. Hey, I want to get caught up, but first I've got a favor to ask. Can you look up a name for me and find out if there's a connection to a family in your neck of the woods?"

"Absolutely! Give me the name."

"We know him out here as Jimmy Barone, but there's a chance his real name is Jimmy Bonante. I'm not sure of the exact spelling, but it's pronounced Boh-nan-te. He apparently grew up in the Bronx, and I would guess he may have left in the eighties. I understand he went to school at Brown and became a chemist."

"Got it." They hung up and agreed to speak again after Ryan had done a search.

Within the hour, he received a call from Ryan.

"Ben...it's me. You got a hot one there. Turns out, we are aware of the Bonante family. There was the father, Marco Bonante, who is deceased. He owned a cigar store in the Concourse area. He had two sons, Jimmy and John and we know Jimmy was a smart kid who went to Brown. Marco's real job was being a bookie and running numbers for the Pazzoni family, a mob syndicate. That family is still around and the head guy's name is Tommy Pazzoni."

"That's great stuff," Ben said, elated at this discovery. That's the connection I was looking for. We think this Jimmy Bonante may have been involved in murders of two scientists who were on the verge of break-through discoveries involving street drugs. This could be the tie-in for my cases."

Ryan cautioned. "You may have a problem proving anything against them, though. They're real clever. We've tried going after them a few times, but only the low-level soldiers get caught for misdemeanors, and they have a cadre of shyster attorneys who watch over them very carefully."

"Hey, Ken. Thanks so much. When are you coming out here? We need to catch up."

"I promise one of these days we'll get together. Talk to you soon, Ben."

With this new information, Ben decided to turn up the pressure. He called Cutter to set up a meeting with Doren at the CBI office.

* * *

Ben greeted them the next day when they arrived at his office, "Good morning."

Cutter and Doren took seats without replying.

"Doctor, I'm having real problems with your loan to Barone. Do you have proof of other loans?"

Doren responded quickly. "No, everything was done on a handshake."

"Really? I've got to tell you, I'm having a hard time believing it's a coincidence that your money transfer to Barone occurred immediately following Stevens' death."

Cutter put in, "As my client has already said, that timing was pure coincidence. All we know is that Dr. Stevens died from an allergy shot. Agent Locke, you'll have one hell of an uphill battle with any charges against this man. He's told you everything he knows. If that's all you've got, we're done." Cutter started to stand up.

"Hold on and sit down, Mr. Cutter. I'm not done. Let me ask this question, Dr. Doren. Does the name Tommy Pazzoni mean anything to you?"

Doren's face drained of color. "I need to talk to my lawyer in private."

Locke agreed and he left them in the room alone.

Doren spoke first. "Josh, I need your help."

"What the hell are you talking about?"

"I'll tell you, but what I say can't go any further. It's life or death serious."

"Go ahead, I'm listening."

Pete told Cutter all he knew about Barone and the Pazzoni family, Jimmy's real name, and knowing each other in the old neighborhood.

"This is more serious than I thought, Pete. If you talk to the cops about any of this they can connect you to organized crime, which could switch the investigation to a federal jurisdiction. That can mean a lot more trouble for everyone - you, Jimmy and the Pazzonis."

"I know, but what choice do I have?" Pete's voice trembled. "They have me giving money to Jimmy, and they think I paid for Stevens' death. I have to cooperate and get a deal, or I'll be going to prison!"

Cutter responded. "Keep in mind that you'll be putting yourself and your wife at great risk, if what you just told me about the Pazzoni family is true."

"I know, I've thought about that too."

They called Locke back in.

Cutter said, "OK, here's the deal. Dr. Doren will agree to give evidence about Barone, but we want assurance you'll cut him a break on all charges."

Ben said he'd need approval from the DA's office before officially offering any deal. "Dr. Doren, you'll have to hand over your passport until this issue gets resolved."

Cutter flushed. "That's absolutely unreasonable."

"It depends on one's point of view. Dr. Doren is now a suspect in the murder of Dr. Frank Stevens, so his choice is either be arrested and arraigned, or hand over his passport now."

Cutter backed down. "I need to talk with my client again."

When Ben left the room, Cutter said, "I think we better hand over your passport or this will get messy. I don't want a record of your arrest. If it got out, it'd be bad publicity for you. I can keep the passport issue quiet for now."

When Doren went home, he wasn't sure what he should tell Jacqueline about the investigation. He knew she'd be angry and wondered what she might do if he confessed sending a payment to Barone for taking care of Stevens. There was no way he could spin it differently, other than to admit what he did. Still, he had never asked Barone to kill Stevens. All he'd wanted Barone to do was to interfere in the vaccine research so Stevens would get fired and have to leave town... But who would buy that explanation? It didn't seem plausible, even to him.

Ben Locke met with the Denver DA and members of the Colorado Attorney General's office and told them about his meeting with Doren and Cutter. The attorneys decided there was enough evidence to request a statewide special grand jury to investigate the murder of Dr. Frank Stevens. There would be no deal. They'd give Doren seventy-two hours to talk to them about Barone or they'd arrest him as a suspect in the murder of Dr. Stevens. Ben called Cutter to tell him of the decision by the Denver DA's office.

"Agent Locke, I thought we had a deal already and you were just getting approval."

"Complain to the DA. You've got seventy-two hours for your client to sit down and tell us everything he knows, or be arrested."

"This is BS and you know it. I'll get back to you." Cutter slammed down the phone and then called Doren to relay the terms.

"I don't get it. Why are they changing the deal?"

"I don't know what's behind the change, but I can guess. I think they're playing games, applying pressure to get you to talk."

Cutter's analysis struck home to Doren. "That makes sense. Do you think not cooperating will work?"

"I doubt they have proof that Barone killed Stevens, or anything on the Pazzoni family. Besides, if you testify against the Pazzonis you'll need witness protection, a new identity and relocation somewhere else. You'll never be able to practice medicine again. Is that the life you want?"

Doren shuddered just thinking about the Pazzonis. "No."

"Then it may be better to keep this information to yourself, and take your chances."

"OK, then turn it down, but will they arrest me?"

"I can't answer that. Let's cross that bridge when we come to it."

"OK then, tell them I don't agree to their terms." Doren agreed for another reason. Now he wouldn't have to tell Jacqueline the real story, only that he'd made a loan to Barone.

Chapter Forty-Nine

BARONE WAS LIVING in a rented villa on a picturesque beach in Aruba. It was better than anything he'd ever imagined: one bedroom stucco and a courtyard filled with bougainvillea, a small kitchen, and a comfortable living room with satellite TV. The living room had a bay window looking out on endless crystalline white sands and turquoise ocean waves. He thought he might have discovered heaven.

Jimmy had wired enough money from his bank to keep himself comfortable for a year. At least for now, he'd enjoy scuba diving, fresh seafood, visiting local bars and meeting women who wanted to have a good time - but the idleness of vacation was already wearing thin. Jimmy was actually bored most of the time. He decided to find a job doing the one thing he really enjoyed, working in a lab. He called the local hospital to ask if any work was available for someone with his background. A position in the pathology lab was available, and he set up an interview appointment for the next day.

The woman interviewing him was attractive and tan, with shoulder-length blond hair, blue eyes and a square jaw, all part of the Dutch heritage that was so prevalent on the island. Jimmy figured she was in her early thirties.

"Good morning, Mr. Lerrona, my name is Katarina Veltkampe. I'm the human resource director of the hospital. I'm pleased that you're interested in this position. We've had this vacancy for a pathology tech for quite a while. Do you have a resume?"

"Sure." Jimmy handed her a heavily edited version. He hoped she wouldn't check it out, because it was mostly fiction. He was using a different name, and no one he had worked with would know it was him. His survival depended on not being discovered.

"Please, call me Katarina. May I call you Jimmy?"

"Sure."

"You have a great resume Jimmy. Brown University, impressive! I notice some years of employment are missing, though. Can you explain?"

"Sure, sometimes I get the urge to travel. I want to see the world."

"Sounds like a great life."

"Well, it's easier not having a family to worry about."

Looking interested by that fact, "I understand. Every once in a while I need to get away to visit the Netherlands."

"Sounds like we both have the travel bug."

They spent the rest of the day touring the hospital, the pathology lab, and meeting the hospital pathologist, who was also delighted to have someone apply for the position.

When they returned to her office, Katarina offered him the job without even calling his references, and he accepted without hesitation.

Jimmy started work the next day, becoming familiar with protocols and meeting the other lab crew. In less than a week he was proficient with the microtome, an instrument that cuts thin slices of biopsies embedded in paraffin. All the other procedures were easy for him to learn, and soon he was entrenched in the pathology department. The pathologist couldn't believe how quickly he caught on.

The staff members joked about life on Aruba, how the traffic was getting bad, and the stupid tourists who got drunk and crashed their bikes or autos on a daily basis. When he asked about the celebrated case of Natalee Holloway, they expressed anger because of the bad karma it had given Aruba.

He and Katarina began hanging out for dinners and walks. Katarina had had a dozen or more intimate relationships, and at least the same number of one night stands, mostly with the prototypical Anglo-Saxon type she found attractive. She thought Jimmy was not particularly good-looking, but he made up for that deficiency with his appealing intelligence. Still, she remained hesitant to become intimate, at least until she knew him better.

One night after dinner they took a long walk along the beach, made an outdoor fire, sipped wine and listened to the pounding surf. They conversed about the cosmos, looking at the canopy of stars. Later, they walked back to Jimmy's place where Katarina decided to overcome her reticence by showing him a few tricks she had picked up.

Afterward, while still in bed with Katarina, he decided his life in Aruba was perfect, but that only lasted until the next day when he received a call while working in the path lab.

"Hello, Jimmy Lerrona speaking." After a long pause, Jimmy said, "Hello, anyone there?"

A recognizable bass voice finally answered. "It's me, KC."

Jimmy sat down suddenly, feeling faint. "KC, how are you?"

"Cut the shit, Jimmy. You took off without telling me! What the fuck's wrong with you?"

"KC, I need to explain. COADD was hot on my trail, and Pete told me to get out. I decided I had to go, and I forgot to call you. That's it. That's all it was. Look, KC, please believe me!"

"Asshole. I just found out through my source there's gonna be a grand jury investigation into Stevens' death. They believe he was murdered." He chuckled, and then continued. "Now, where did they get that fuckin' idea, from you?"

"Not me, KC! Why would I tell the cops anything? I know how to keep my mouth shut. Besides, when would I have talked? I've been here the whole time."

"Just get your ass back to Denver, tomorrow! Go see Doren and make sure he keeps his mouth shut, and then go to Stevens' house and find those specs. From what you told us, we think they're still hidden there. Find them, or else. Got it?"

Jimmy sat paralyzed, sweat trickling down his back. "Sure. KC, did they name any suspects?"

"It's supposedly a secret. According to my source, they're sending out lots of subpoenas. And guess who their number one suspect is? You, you a-hole! They also named Doren and some babe whose name is Elizabeth Fink or Fuck, or something like that. Do you know her? Tommy thinks maybe we can pin it on her."

"I don't know, but maybe I can find something out. I—I promise, I'll get back to you."

"I've heard your promises before. Just get it done, now!" Then the phone went dead.

Jimmy left the lab and packed a small suitcase, including a dark brown hairpiece that matched his ID. Before leaving, he called Katarina.

"Katarina, it's me. Say, I've got to leave for a few days. It's a family emergency."

"Oh no, I'm sorry!"

"It's a long story. My uncle is dying and I need to see him. I have to go, but I'll call you later."

"Well, OK, but I'll miss you. Please call."

"I promise."

He boarded the plane and thought to himself. *Nothing is going to keep me from coming back. Nothing, damn it.*

Chapter Fifty

THE FOLLOWING ARTICLE appeared in the morning *Rocky Mountain Tribune.*

New Twist in the Death of Dr. Frank Stevens

The Colorado Bureau of Investigation announced yesterday that they have determined Dr. Frank Stevens' death was a homicide. The CBI officer in charge of the case, Field Agent Ben Locke, indicated the investigation is ongoing and may lead to an arrest of one or more suspects in the next few days. This surprise revelation contradicts the medical examiner's conclusion that Stevens' death was caused by an anaphylactic reaction to an allergy injection he received in the office of Dr. Leonard Haberman, a Denver allergist. Dr. Haberman could not be reached for comment.

Denver radio and TV programs were overwhelmed with discussions about this new revelation. Questions were repeatedly asked: what was the evidence, and who would do such a horrible thing? The speculation was reaching hysterical levels, similar to the famous Jon Benet Ramsey case

Anaphylaxis

that occurred in Boulder, Colorado, which was also fanned by media around the country.

Sol hadn't been updated by Charley, so he set up a luncheon with him at a popular Italian restaurant in downtown Denver.

"Charley, where's this going? Not only are the specs missing, probably stolen by Jimmy, but apparently they now think Frank was murdered. What makes them think that?"

"Ben told me the evidence is solid, but they have to keep it sealed. He insinuated that Jimmy's the prime suspect, but we have to keep that quiet. He couldn't tell me anymore."

"This is beyond real. Would Jimmy actually kill him?"

"I don't know, but Ben and I have speculated there may be a criminal conspiracy trying to stop the vaccine's development."

"But, killing Frank for that!"

"Sol, think about it. Who benefits from people being addicted to cocaine? The sellers, right?"

"That seems right."

Each took a bite of their lunch, and then Sol changed the topic. "Charley, did you ever get in touch with Mrs. Stevens?"

"Yeah, she looked everywhere, including the safety deposit box, and nothing showed up. I asked if we could do a search, but she got real upset. She doesn't want anyone touching his things. She wants everything left in place, almost like it's a shrine. Who knows why? Maybe she just needs time."

"The reason I ask is I've got another problem. The life insurance company called and they decided to hold up payment on Frank's key man policy until the murder investigation is completed. They want to be sure no one here had anything to do with it; but if they hold off much longer, COADD might as well call it quits. We need it to cover the next four months of operations."

Sol paused, and then got to the point of why he'd wanted to meet. "Charley, I wonder if Agent Locke could get a warrant to search Frank's house. What do you think?"

"I'll ask. Actually, I need to meet with him. He wants to know details of our conversation with Jimmy. Both of us may have to testify that Jimmy told us he took the specs."

"Charley, do you think Mrs. Stevens would be more reasonable if we sat down with her and explained why this is important? Not just for us, but for her family, too. Frank had a lot of stock options in the company. It would really be to her benefit to help us."

"I like that instead of forcing a search. You should probably call her."

* * *

Agent Locke had already called Denise to let her know Frank had been murdered. He couldn't tell her the details, but he needed to find out if she knew anyone who would have wanted to kill him. Denise was stunned and couldn't think of any suspects. After the call, she thought about contacting Ted, but decided to call Lenny instead.

"Lenny, it's Denise. I hope you don't mind me calling, but I'm shocked by the news that Frank was murdered! Agent Locke just called."

"Denise, it's unfortunately true."

"I'm so confused, Lenny."

Lenny considered how much he could tell her. "Denise, there's something that the CBI uncovered. I can't tell you what it is, but I know for sure that Frank was murdered. I wish I knew who did it, but that's the reason they're conducting the investigation."

"That means you had nothing to do with it. I'm so glad", she said, really meaning it. "Maybe it wasn't my fault either."

He still thought the propranolol contributed to Frank's death, but knowing her fragility, he decided to agree with her. "I think you're right on both counts." He added, "Denise, you need to stay positive on all of this, and I'll keep in touch with you as developments occur. No one knows where it's headed."

She sighed loudly, "Frank and I trusted Jimmy so much. Then Sol told me that Jimmy disappeared with the plans to make the vaccine. Why would he do that? He was like a member of our family. I just can't believe it."

"I wish I knew more to tell you, but I don't. I do know that Jimmy took the manufacturing specs from COADD and then disappeared. They also think he was involved in the death of another scientist who was working on a research project involving marijuana plants. There's a possible connection to organized crime." He stopped suddenly, realizing he'd inadvertently told her very confidential information.

"What? What do you mean?"

"Just that he may have stolen the specs, and maybe he had something to do with preventing Frank from succeeding." Lenny tried to avoid being too blunt. "Denise, I think none of this speculation is helpful until we know more. Let's stay in touch."

"But Lenny, does this mean Jimmy could hurt me or my kids?"

"No, it means he's a suspect. I'm sure they'll find him soon."

When Lenny met with Dave Sabatha later the same day, he had a lot to talk about, mostly that it now appeared Frank Stevens had been murdered.

"Lenny, I read about it in the papers. What an incredible turn of events. How do they know he was murdered?"

"I can't tell you because it's all sealed for the investigation, but there are several suspects."

"I gathered from the article. I'm surprised, but this should be good for you. Isn't it?"

"I'm no longer responsible for his death, but I'm still involved. They don't have any conclusive evidence of who did it or why they did it, and they need me to testify. So I'm not out of it by a long shot."

"But at least now everyone will know his death wasn't caused by any negligence on your part."

"Yeah, but you have no idea of the nightmare I'm having, trying to clear my name from the malpractice lists sent to hospitals, insurance companies and God knows what. There is one good thing though; the recurring nightmares about Desert Storm and Billy have stopped. So I guess the guilt feelings I've had over losing two friends is lifting."

"Good for you!"

"That may be my only comfort, but get this. I just found out from my attorney that the lawsuit settlement can't be reversed now that Frank was murdered. Can you believe that? My insurance had to pay one million dollars, even though it's been proven that I had nothing to do with Frank's death!... At least my name will be cleared."

"Clearing your name will be very freeing for you."

"I guess but none of it really makes any sense."

"By the way, I never heard from your nurse, Elizabeth Finch. How's she doing?"

Lenny was always amazed at Dave's recall of names and facts. "She still hasn't told us what happened, whether she accidentally or even intentionally gave an incorrect dose of vaccine to Stevens, but as you can appreciate, I can't talk about it with the ongoing investigation."

Dave suddenly ceased talking for several long moments, appearing to be lost in thought. He leaned over to pick up a small object that he began moving around with his fingers, and then looked up at Lenny. "Sure, understood. I think you're doing well given the circumstances, but I don't want to make any changes with your meds until everything settles down. Agreed?"

"Sure, that's OK for now, but I want to get off the anti-depressant as soon as possible."

"Fine. Next time I'll taper it. Let's see how things go."

Lenny left thinking he needed to vent a little more. He headed for the target range to finish his day.

Chapter Fifty-One

JACQUELINE WAS HOME making dinner when a sheriff arrived at the door. He wanted to speak to her husband. Flustered, she ran into the rec room and told Pete a sheriff was waiting for him. Pete knew this would not be good and wondered about calling Cutter, but then decided to find out first what the sheriff wanted. The officer simply handed him an envelope and said, "You've been served."

He opened the envelope and read the subpoena to appear before a grand jury. The letter dropped on the floor.

Jacqueline picked up the papers. "What's this, Pete? What does it mean?"

"I'm not a suspect Jacqueline, he assured her. They subpoenaed me because I know Jimmy Barone. He's the main suspect. I called his apartment manager where he was staying, and they told me he suddenly disappeared. Nobody knows where he is."

"I still don't understand. Just knowing him isn't enough for them to subpoena you."

"Look, they're concerned about some money I sent him. I've lent him money several times when he was short. Jimmy has expensive tastes, a boat harbored in San Diego, and he plays the horses. I sent him fifty grand, and I may as well tell you," he added as he sat down. "I sent him the money right around the time when Frank died, so they're asking questions."

Jacqueline grabbed his hand and sat down with him, not knowing what to say. Her head leaned downward for several minutes.

"Look, Jacqueline, I didn't do anything wrong!" Suddenly sensing a craving for food, he got up to go to the kitchen. He was angry and wondered if Jacqueline's response meant she still loved Frank, even his memory.

She followed him into the kitchen, and calmly said, "There shouldn't be an issue, and if that's all it is, we just need a good lawyer."

"Honey, I have one already, and I'm not worried," Pete said confidently. I have to talk to my lawyer but believe me, it'll pass. I just lent some money to an old friend."

Jacqueline reached to hug him. "Pete, just know I love you."

It was time for Jacqueline to use her ace in the hole. The next morning after Pete left for his office, she called Ted.

"Ted, it's Jacki calling again."

He was surprised to hear from her, but he sure wanted another taste. They agreed to meet at the Broadmoor Hotel in Colorado Springs the following week.

She then called Connie Currier, aka Candy, an ex-escort close friend.

"Hi Connie, it's your old friend Jacki."

"Jacki, it's great to hear your voice. Where have you been? It's been years."

"Didn't you know Pete and I moved to Denver? I've retired and I'm just doing charity work these days."

"Neat I always knew you'd be the first chaste lady of charity."

"Thanks for the vote of confidence. Connie, I have a favor to ask."

"Shoot."

"I need your video know-how." Several clients had wanted Connie to video them having sex with her for a fat fee. She agreed and learned how to use a video camera with some skill. Her new specialty had provided her with an extra three thousand dollars a session that the escort service didn't know about.

"Happy to help out. Send me an email with details."

Jacki reserved a room at the Broadmoor, and Connie came in early to install three video cameras, all carefully hidden, providing different angles of the forthcoming action.

Ted went directly to the hotel room to avoid being recognized. Jacki arrived a few minutes later and excused herself to the bathroom. When she re-appeared she was dressed in lacey black lingerie, high heels, glossy red lipstick and wore an alluring perfume. The only surprise after all these years was Ted's staying power of ten minutes, which was significantly longer than his past performances. Ted had no time for small talk, and when it was over, he left with a big grin, thinking life couldn't get any better. This time he didn't even have to pay her!

Connie retrieved the videos and sent them to Jacki, who printed out a half dozen poses that she thought were the best. She especially liked the compromising shots that showed his naked body and small erection. She had them hand delivered to his office with a request for his signature. Included with the prints was a typewritten letter indicating that copies would be sent to members of the Colorado Senate and House of Representatives, and to his wife, unless he contacted her and did what she asked.

When Larkin received the photos, he fumed, trying to figure out his next move. After some extensive internal debate, he decided he had no choice but to contact her.

"Jacki, you bitch, what do you want? I'm not going to let you black-mail me. I'll have experts certify the photos were doctored by political enemies trying to discredit me."

"Ted, you know I'm a professional. I kept a little black book, like the famous madam from L.A. with details of our trysts. All the details, like when we met, where we met and even receipts for hotel rooms and dinners together. Ted, just in case I have an unexpected accident, those photos will go to law enforcement officials, your colleagues, and your wife."

There was a long pause. Ted didn't say anything, and Jacki continued.

"I also have a fabulous memory for recalling details of my clients' anat-omy. Some people remember faces, but I remember the private parts. I made a detailed sketch and description of yours. Now, Ted, how would someone like me know all those details?"

"You whore! I'll get you for this."

"Now, now, *Just Ted*. Let's talk reality. Short of having major plastic surgery to remove the identifiers of your short extension, I suggest you listen carefully."

She could hear loud breathing, but Ted still didn't speak. "It's real sim-ple. You're a hypocrite. So here's the deal. I need you to get my husband dropped as a suspect in the Frank Stevens' murder."

"I'm not going to be any part of your scheme," Ted hissed. You have as much to lose as I do if these pictures get out."

"Not really, Ted. Pete already knows about my past history with you, but I'm pretty sure your family and colleagues in congress would be real surprised. The high and mighty majority leader, who sponsors legislation to sanction unethical behavior. What a laugh! Once these are sent out, there goes your governorship and any hopes for higher office."

"I couldn't trust you, even if I did help Pete."

"Ted, stop and listen. I'll place all the photos and my notes in a safety deposit box, along with my signed affidavit that the photos were photo-shopped. Only my attorney will know the location, and he'll be instructed to give you the key on my approval. Everything will be in the box for you to destroy. Now, will you help Pete for me?"

"Wait, I need to think it through. How do I know you'll give me the photos if I get Pete off?"

"I thought you'd ask that. I will have my attorney hold a certified check for one million made out to you. If you succeed and I don't give you the photos, all you need to do is show him proof that Pete has been dropped from the investigation and he'll give you the check. I'll send you a copy of a signed letter by me authorizing the attorney to give you the check if I don't release the photos. He has to comply or you can sue him if he doesn't. But don't worry; I don't want to lose a million dollars. If you succeed, just call my attorney. He'll call me and everything will go smoothly."

He paused to think. After a long wait, Jacki prodded him.

"Ted, are you there?"

"Yeah, I'm thinking about what a bitch you are. I don't trust you."

"Just help me and I'll help you."

"I guess I'll agree, but I can't guarantee anything when you're dealing with a criminal investigation. What will you do with the pictures if I can't get them to let Pete off?"

"I haven't thought about that because I know you'll make it happen," she purred.

Chapter Fifty-Two

BARONE RENTED AN apartment with his new ID and called KC to let him know he was in Denver. KC hooked him up with a contact to provide anything he needed, including a hand gun. Jimmy had learned to shoot when he became a member of the Pazzoni family. Tommy Pazzoni was an ex-Marine, and he required all family members to be proficient with guns of all types. Jimmy had taken training and learned quickly, but he didn't love guns and didn't spend a lot of time with the courses. That was OK with Tommy, since he'd hired Jimmy primarily for his scientific skills.

Jimmy knew he had to get back on the good side of the family, and realized to do that, he needed to find the missing specifications. First, he had to contact Doren.

He placed the call. "Pete, it's me, and don't mention my name!"

Pete immediately recognized Jimmy's voice. "Oh, yeah. Where are you?"

"That's not important. Just listen to me very carefully. Our friends wanted me to have a chat with you. They need assurance that you'll keep your mouth shut. Do you get the drift?"

"Jimbone, you don't have to worry about me."

"God damn it. No names!"

"Sorry, look, if you're telling me that I know nothing, I understand. Seriously, I really do know nothing."

"Just in case you forget, remember that everybody knows everybody and where they're at. Got it?"

Pete understood very well.

The next contact would be made in person, when he pulled up in front of Denise's home. There were no cars parked in the driveway and the house was dark. He opened the trunk of his car and went to pull out the handgun given to him by KC's contact. Hesitating, he wondered if he could actually pull the trigger on Denise. Instead, he removed a tire iron, put on thick rimmed dark sunglasses and a black hairpiece. He walked to the front door and rang the bell. He was about to break a window with the tire iron when he heard someone coming to the door. Denise opened the door wearing a bathrobe. She frowned, unsure of who he was. When she recognized him, she gasped.

"Jimmy… why…why are you here? I want you to leave us alone!"

He pushed her back and slammed the door behind him. He dropped the tire iron, placed one hand over her mouth, and twisted her arm backward with his other hand as he pushed her into the kitchen. He forced her to sit down, gagged her, and then tied her arms around the chair. She kept struggling, making the chair rock.

"Denise, shut the hell up." He had picked up the tire iron and held it above her head. "I don't want to hurt you or the kids. Are they sleeping upstairs?"

She nodded yes, her eyes wide with terror.

"OK, here's the deal. I want the vaccine specs. I know they're here, somewhere locked up or hidden away. Where are they?"

She started to cry and shook her head violently. "Denise, I don't want to hurt the kids. Now, where the fuck are the specs?"

She just shook her head, cried harder and mumbled with difficulty, "I don't know!"

"I'll tear this place apart if I have to. Now, for the last time, where are they?" He grabbed her shoulders and shook them. "Do you fuckin' understand me?"

She nodded. He left her tied up and started the search, pulling drawers out, dumping things on the floor, moving carpets, removing pillows from stuffed furniture, opening every cabinet, knocking books on the floor. He went from room to room, to the basement, and then up to each bedroom, even the ones where the children slept. Fortunately, they didn't wake up. When he'd exhausted every possibility, he returned to Denise, who was slumped in her chair, exhausted from crying and struggling.

"Listen to me very carefully. If I find out COADD starts to make the vaccine, I'll know that you lied to me. If that happens, or if you call the cops, someone will come back and hurt you and the kids. Do you understand?"

She nodded yes, shaking and sobbing quietly, watching his every move with widened eyes until he left. Then she fell to the floor, arms still tied. All she could hear was her own heartbeat pounding like a jackhammer. When she was finally able to untie herself, she found her cell and called Ted. He had just fallen asleep, but he sat up quickly when he heard her screaming.

When Jimmy finished, he called KC and told him he couldn't find the specs in the Stevens' home. He reminded KC that Haberman and his son, Jack, might know where the specs were. KC seemed satisfied, especially knowing that Jimmy had told Doren to keep his mouth shut.

Jimmy seemed pleased too when KC said, "Go ahead back to Aruba. We'll handle it from here."

Chapter Fifty-Three

THE COLORADO STATE Grand Jury was called into session. Pete Doren, Elizabeth Finch, Sol Feldman, Ole Bettman, Ben Locke, Charles Blackwood, Denise Stevens, and Leonard Haberman had all been subpoenaed. Jimmy Bonante, aka Jimmy Barone, was on the list of subpoenaed witnesses and was considered the prime suspect, but he had disappeared. An arrest warrant had been sent to state, federal and international authorities. Denise was temporarily excused and under close police protection after Ted Larkin informed the authorities of her horrifying experience with Barone.

Deputy Attorney General William Murphy stood before the grand jury and began by explaining the requirements needed for an indictment. He told them *probable cause* meant there was *reasonable belief* to charge someone with the murder of Dr. Frank Stevens. To make this decision, they would be presented with evidence from his office and hear testimony from subpoenaed witnesses. He emphasized that an indictment did not require the higher standards for a guilty verdict required in criminal trials based upon reasonable doubt. The jury was also informed that witnesses would be permitted to have their attorneys present to counsel them, but their attorneys couldn't object or argue during the proceedings. Lastly he emphasized the need to maintain absolute secrecy, since the hearings would remain sealed from the public until the grand jury had made its final determinations.

First to testify was Lenny. Mark attended, just in case Lenny needed his advice. In response to Murphy's questions, Lenny reiterated everything that had happened following Frank Stevens' death in his office - the prolonged malpractice lawsuit, the discovery that Frank had been on propranolol for migraines, and that this knowledge had led to a settlement of the lawsuit.

Lenny then testified that Agent Locke from the CBI had been reviewing a cold case that made him suspicious about Stevens' death. Locke came to him with concerns that there were some odd coincidences between Stevens' death and the cold case.

"What coincidences are you referring to?"

"It turns out that the cold case involved the mysterious death of another scientist who had been developing a selective herbicide to destroy marijuana plants. The researcher had died from a very odd bike accident caused by tampered brakes, but the real coincidence was that Mr. Jimmy Barone had worked in that lab before he was hired at COADD."

"Who is Jimmy Barone?"

"He was the chief technician at COADD."

Lenny paused to take a drink and then described what happened next. "After thinking it through, we decided an independent lab should analyze the contents of Dr. Stevens' vaccine, to see if something had been added to it, maybe a food he was sensitive to or even a toxin. Agent Locke took custody of the vaccine and it was sent to a lab. The analysis confirmed that the vaccine contained peanut, and Dr. Stevens was known to be extremely allergic to peanuts."

Murphy continued his questioning. "Dr. Haberman, knowing that Dr. Stevens was allergic to peanuts and that it had been added to his vaccine, would you agree that the peanut in his vaccine probably caused his death?"

"Yes, I do."

"So if we know what killed him, the obvious questions to be answered are: who did it, why and how they did it." Murphy outlined this for the benefit of the jury.

"Yes."

"Dr. Haberman, could you tell us how someone could gain access to a vaccine in your office?"

Lenny and Mark had talked about this point and decided that Lenny had no choice but to answer truthfully under oath.

"The refrigerator in my office was not locked."

"Wouldn't locking it safeguard vaccines from tampering?"

"Yes, it would."

"So why wasn't it locked?"

"Almost all medical offices in the U.S. lock up only injectable narcotics. Vaccines like flu vaccines, antibiotics, and allergy vaccines are not routinely locked up. Tampering has never been something that we would worry about. Only narcotics are locked up to keep them from being stolen."

Murphy continued. "So, anyone who gained entrance to your office, let's say after hours, could have easily accessed the vaccine in your unlocked refrigerator. Correct?"

"Yes, that's right."

"Is your office locked up after office hours?"

"Yes." Lenny knew where he was headed.

"Have you ever found it unlocked after hours?"

"Yes, we came in one morning and found the door unlocked. We figured the janitors had left it unlocked. I complained to the owner of the service, and he assured me it wouldn't happen again."

"But there's no way to confirm that, is there?"

"No, unfortunately, there isn't."

"So someone could have entered your office and tampered with the vaccine that killed Dr. Stevens?"

"Yes."

Murphy stepped closer to Lenny. "OK, so how would someone know which vaccine belonged to Dr. Stevens?"

"The vaccines are labeled with patient names."

"How could someone find out that Dr. Stevens was allergic to peanuts?"

"They'd have to find Dr. Stevens' chart, read it, and find the summary of his food allergies."

"OK, now, how would someone have added peanut into a vaccine bottle? They couldn't stuff a little piece of peanut in there, right?" The jury laughed.

Lenny had to smile. "No, they couldn't, but we have a liquid extract of peanut called a reagent, that we use to skin test people for peanut allergy. It could be injected into a bottle."

"OK, and the peanut test reagent, where is that kept?"

"It's kept in the same refrigerator with the allergy vaccines."

"So it would be easy to find if someone was searching for it?"

"Well, it would take some time for someone to do all of this."

Murphy interrupted. "Please answer my question, yes or no."

Lenny shifted uncomfortably, and then answered. "Yes."

"OK, then tell us in detail how someone could add peanut reagent into the vaccine."

"They'd get a syringe, draw some peanut reagent into it and inject it into the vaccine."

Murphy became more intense. "Would the person who read Dr. Stevens' chart require a medical background to understand the information and then tamper with Dr. Stevens' vaccine?"

"Well, not necessarily. Having some scientific background would be helpful, but I guess anyone could have done it. Yet, the person would probably know what would happen if Dr. Stevens was given a vaccine containing peanut, namely that it would cause anaphylaxis and not everyone would know that."

"That's a good point. Could you explain to the jury what anaphylaxis is and what causes it?"

Lenny looked over at the jury. "Basically, it's a severe allergic reaction that can show up as swelling, hives, breathing difficulty and occasionally, shock or even death. Anaphylaxis doesn't happen the first time you encounter an allergen that causes it. Following the first exposure to the allergen, like a food or drug, a person can become sensitized to it. In Dr. Stevens' case, the allergen would have been peanuts. His immune system would have formed allergic antibodies to peanut after he ate them the first few times."

Lenny paused to swallow. "To explain it simply, when Dr. Stevens was injected with peanut in his vaccine, it led to a massive release of chemicals throughout his body. An example would be histamine which can cause allergic reactions. Most people have heard of histamine because they take anti-histamines to control hay fever or other allergies."

Lenny turned his attention back to Murphy and continued. "So when Dr. Stevens was injected with peanut, it would have immediately circulated into his bloodstream and spread to all parts of his body where it would have attached to specific peanut allergic antibodies located on the cells that stored histamine and other chemicals. That in turn signaled the cells to release these chemicals into the bloodstream and tissues, which in turn caused his anaphylaxis. The end result in Dr. Stevens' case was dilation of blood vessels, swelling of tissues, low blood pressure, cardiac rhythm abnormalities, low oxygen, eventually shock and death. The anaphylactic attack that killed Dr. Stevens was like the biologic equivalent of a nuclear reaction that ran amok."

Murphy nodded. "So you're saying histamine and other chemicals would have been released into Dr. Stevens' bloodstream almost instantaneously after he received the injection of vaccine that contained peanut."

"Yes, that's correct."

"So the person who did this had to know that an injection containing peanut would cause a rapid and probably fatal anaphylactic response in someone exquisitely sensitive to peanut. In other words, they likely understood the biology and biochemistry of anaphylaxis."

"Yes. There's an actual medical report of a fatal reaction to an injection of peanut given to a peanut-sensitive patient. The patient was part of a clinical trial to determine if gradual injections of peanut allergen could reduce peanut sensitivity. It turns out this patient was getting placebo during the study, but unfortunately received an injection of peanut by mistake. The reaction was swift and the patient died almost instantaneously."

"Then the person who did this likely had some understanding of anaphylaxis and knew enough to plan this elaborate homicide."

"Yes, that would be my guess"

"Dr. Haberman, who in your office had access to Dr. Stevens' chart, his vaccine and the peanut reagent?"

"Elizabeth Finch had access to all of it, and would have known where the peanut reagent was kept."

"Are there other employees in your office who could have had access to Dr. Stevens' vaccine, figured out he was allergic to peanut, and known where the peanut reagent was located?"

"Sure, probably all of my employees. There's Jane Cross, a nurse, the office manager, Annette White, the receptionist Holly Brown, me, and my partner, Dr. Oliphant."

"Did any of them personally know Dr. Stevens or have interactions with him outside your office?"

"The only one I know of would have been Dr. Oliphant. He sometimes attended parties given by Dr. Stevens."

"Did Dr. Oliphant have any reason to murder Dr. Stevens?"

"No, of course not! They were very casual acquaintances."

"OK, let's go back a bit. Can you tell us how the vaccines are prepared?"

Lenny launched into a description of the process in his practice. His office would purchase allergens in large volumes from specialized FDA approved companies who had collected the raw pollens or other allergens, and then processed their purification, sterilization and standardization. He or Dr. Oliphant would write a formula to reflect the allergen sensitivity for a patient based on review of their allergy and medical history and skin or blood test results. The ingredients would be added in various proportions to make a concentrate and then dilutions from the concentrate would be made, depending on the patient's level of sensitivity.

"Dr. Haberman, who normally prepares the vaccines in your office?"

"Elizabeth Finch makes up the vaccines. When she is on vacation, my other nurse, Jane Cross, would back her up. Both are trained in the procedure."

"Which one prepared Dr. Stevens' vaccine?"

"Based on my record review, Elizabeth Finch prepared the vaccine for Dr. Stevens."

"So you were confident with Elizabeth Finch's technique and expertise. Correct?"

"Yes, I was."

"Can you describe what Elizabeth Finch did when Dr. Stevens collapsed?"

Lenny described what had happened that day, how Elizabeth had become paralyzed, and unable to help. "And then at her deposition she admitted being very angry with Dr. Stevens because he caused an injury to someone named Sam, whom she was very close to. She didn't say who Sam was. She was so distraught, she couldn't finish the deposition. It was suspended and never rescheduled."

"And do you have any idea who Dr. Stevens had injured?"

"I believe that person was Elizabeth Finch's sister."

"Doctor, how would you know that?"

"My attorney, Mark Persons, and I were puzzled as to who she was referring to, so as part of our trial preparation, I asked Charley Blackwood, a P.I., to investigate. He'd been working with COADD, and he was willing to help me on my case." He then related the P.I.'s discovery that Stevens had caused an auto accident twenty years before when he'd been drinking and drove through a red light, T-boning a car driven by Elizabeth's sister, who became a paraplegic as a result of the crash.

Further questioning revealed the volume discrepancy in Dr. Steven's vaccine and confirmed that Elizabeth was the only nurse who administered injections to him.

"Then it's possible that she was angry at Dr. Stevens, may have added the peanut to his vaccine, and administered a larger than normal amount of vaccine in order to kill him?"

"I don't know for sure, but I guess that's a possibility."

"Any other explanations you've considered?"

"Well, I'm not sure I can speculate on anyone else, but I have some thoughts on it."

"Since this is a fact-finding grand jury, if you have reasonable basis for your thoughts, I would like to know what they are."

"Jimmy Barone may have had motive."

"Can you tell the jury again, who is Jimmy Barone?"

"He was the chief lab technician at COADD and worked alongside Dr. Stevens. Apparently the day Dr. Stevens died, Jimmy took some important manufacturing documents needed to make the cocaine vaccine and then disappeared. They found him in a hospital with amnesia after a car accident." Lenny stopped and smiled. "It sounds a little like a soap opera, doesn't it?" Several jurors appreciated the humor.

"Anyway, Jimmy showed up recently and invaded Mrs. Stevens' home looking for another set of manufacturing specs. I understand all of that's in a police report."

"Do you have any idea why Mr. Barone would have done that?"

"I believe Agent Locke thinks Barone may have been part of a criminal syndicate that wanted to prevent development of the cocaine vaccine. I gather he's suspicious of Barone because of the other cold case that I mentioned."

Murphy leaned forward. "Is there any evidence to support this theory?"

"I can't speculate on it. Agent Ben Locke could fill you in."

"Do you have any idea if Mr. Barone would have known about Dr. Stevens' peanut allergy?"

"I don't."

"Did Jimmy Barone and Elizabeth Finch know each other?"

"Not that I am aware of, but he did come to my office several times to discuss the cocaine vaccine trials. I'm the medical director of COADD, so periodically we had meetings on clinical issues that needed my input. Mr. Barone may have met Elizabeth when he was in my office."

"Then it's possible that they knew each other?"

"Yes, it's possible."

"Thank you, Doctor. You may be recalled for more questions."

Mark pulled him aside to congratulate him on his testimony. Lenny smiled and said, "I guess like anything, the more you practice the better you get - but I'd rather be practicing my shooting."

Chapter Fifty-Four

CHARLEY AND SOL subsequently appeared before the grand jury, and gave similar testimony about their conversations with Jimmy Barone and his admission to taking the specifications from COADD.

It was time for Doren's testimony. Jacki had made several frantic calls to Ted, which he hadn't answered. She finally left a desperate voice message for him to *"either help or you'll be sorry."* When he received that call, he immediately called back.

"Jacki, I thought we agreed there wouldn't be any more threats. Look, I'm trying to help you, but I've hit the wall. I've talked to the attorney general about Pete, and he keeps telling me Pete has some explaining to do. I just can't threaten the attorney general. Can you understand that?"

Despite her anger at him, she did understand. "If Pete testifies, is there any way you can prevent his indictment?"

"I'm looking into it, I really am. Trust me, I want this to be over as much as you do."

✳ ✳ ✳

The next day, Doren appeared before the grand jury along with his attorney, Josh Cutter. Doren's testimony was memorialized in a transcript emailed to the state attorney general, who planned to be present to hear this important testimony but couldn't because of a family emergency. The following excerpt was considered to be the most important by Deputy Attorney General Robert Murphy, who did the interrogation.

Q: "Dr. Doren, you have admitted to CBI Agent Ben Locke that you were angry at Dr. Stevens because he had had an affair with your wife. Is that correct?"

A: "I discovered the affair and my wife stopped seeing him. That's about it."

Q: "Really…You had no lingering anger at him after the affair ended?"

A: "When it ended, my wife and I went on with our lives."

Q: "That isn't what you told CBI Agent Locke. Remember you're under oath Doctor."

A: "No, that's all that happened."

Q: "We'll come back to that. What was your relationship with Mr. Jimmy Barone?"

A: "We were good friends"

Q: "Explain what you mean by '*good friends.*'"

A: "We grew up together in New York City-the Bronx, to be specific. Our families knew each other and Jimmy was a smart kid who went to Brown University on a full scholarship in chemistry. I hadn't seen him for years until we both ended up in Denver."

Q: "Does being good friends include giving him money, like the fifty thousand dollars you deposited into his account?"

A: "It was a loan."

Q: "Do you have any proof that it was a loan?"

A: "Nothing in writing, but it's something I've done before."

Q: "Can you explain why you wired the money at the time Dr. Stevens died?"

A: "Jimmy needed cash and I've helped him in the past when he was short. That's what good friends do for each other. Sending it around the time Dr. Stevens died was pure coincidence."

Q: "Why did Mr. Barone need cash? Wasn't he making a good living as a lab assistant?"

A: "I don't know anything about his personal finances, and I didn't know what he was making at COADD. I never asked why he needed money; I just obliged when he asked. He always paid me back."

Q: "Did Mr. Barone have expensive tastes?"

A: "I just said I don't know. I know he lived in a small condo here in Denver, and drove an inexpensive Subaru."

Q: "Let's go back to your testimony on the affair Dr. Stevens had with your wife. Did you wire the money to Mr. Barone as payment for murdering Dr. Stevens?"

A: "No! I already told you I was over that. I don't know anything about his murder. I thought Dr. Stevens died because of an allergy injection reaction."

Q: "Dr. Doren, this grand jury was convened because of new evidence indicating Dr. Stevens was murdered. Are you aware of that?"

A: "All I know is what I read in the paper. They said it was a possible murder. I don't know anything else."

Q: "Do you know what evidence I'm referring to?"

A: "No."

Q: "Let's get back to Mr. Barone. Did you know Mr. Barone admitted taking the specifications to manufacture COADD's cocaine vaccine?"

A: "No, I didn't."

Q: "Did you know Mr. Barone had worked in another lab researching a method to kill off marijuana plants, and in that case, a researcher was allegedly murdered?"

A: "What? No, of course I don't know anything about that!"

Q: "Was Mr. Barone linked to organized crime?"

A: "Not that I'm aware of."

Q: "Does the name Bonante mean anything to you?"

A:" Well, I—I do know a Jimmy Bonante, so yes."

Q: "Is Jimmy Barone an alias name for Jimmy Bonante?"

A: "No."

Q: "Dr. Doren, must I remind you again that you are under oath?"

[Ten minute recess]

Q: "Is Jimmy Barone an alias for Jimmy Bonante?"

A: "Yes that was his alias."

Q: "OK, in questioning I will continue to use the name Barone for consistency. Why would Jimmy Barone use an alias?"

A: "Everyone knew his father took bets on games like football. He made his living as a bookie. Jimmy told me he was embarrassed by what his father did for a living, so he decided to change his name to Barone."

Q: "Who are the Pazzonis?"

A: "I don't recognize that name."

Q: "Wasn't Jimmy Barone's father, Marco Bonante, a bookie for the Pazzoni family?"

A: "I don't know anything about that."

Q: "Don't the Pazzonis control gambling in the Bronx?"

A: "I don't know."

Q: "But you were good friends with Jimmy growing up?"

A: "Yes."

Q: "Well, did you know any Pazzonis growing up?"

A: "I could have met them but I don't remember."

Q: "But you knew Jimmy's father was a bookie?"

A: "Um…yes."

Q: "A bookie, as in taking bets?"

A: "Yes."

Q: "So, gambling?"

A: "Umm, yes."

Q: "And gambling was totally controlled by the Pazzonis? Yes or no please."

A: "Ummm…"

Q: "Dr. Doren. You are under oath."

A: "OK! Yes! But Jimmy's father, Mr. Bonante just worked for them. Jimmy wasn't part of the family, and he left New York to go to school because he didn't want to be involved with them."

Q: "Really. Was Jimmy Barone hired by the Pazzoni family to murder Dr. Stevens to stop development of COADD's cocaine vaccine?"

A: "Of course not!"

Q: "Then did you have Jimmy Barone murder Frank Stevens because you were angry about the affair with your wife?"

A: "I have no knowledge of any murder committed by Jimmy Barone, and I was never involved directly or indirectly in the murder of Dr. Stevens."

Q: "Did you or do you have any association with organized crime?"

A: "No, of course not!"

Q: "Are you aware that Mr. Barone has disappeared?"

A: "Yes, I called the apartment complex where he lived and the superintendent told me Jimmy had left without leaving a forwarding address."

Q: "Do you have any idea where he might have gone?"

A: "No, I don't"

Q: "We found a bus ticket to Chicago in his condo. Do you know why he was going there?"

A: "No, I don't."

Q: "Does he have relatives or friends in Chicago?"

A: "I don't know."

★ ★ ★

On the last day of Pete's testimony, Jacqueline had chilled a bottle of chardonnay and prepared a cheese and olive plate for him when he came home. She poured him a glass of wine. "Honey, how did it go today?"

"I told them I loaned Jimmy the money, but the attorney got hostile. I just gave him short answers. It pissed the attorney off, but Cutter thought I did a good job."

"So what's their concern? You sent him money as a loan and that was it."

As he talked, he kept eating until all the food was gone. "That's the point. There was no reason for me to want Frank dead and they know damn well there wasn't. I'm not the least bit worried."

Pete knew he had to be careful and avoid mentioning anything to her about the Pazzonis. "Anyway, Jimmy took off and they don't know where he is."

"But without Jimmy around, they can't prove anything. You gave him the money as a loan, right?"

"Yeah."

She decided to change the subject and step into more treacherous waters. "Did they tell you how Frank was murdered?"

"No, all they said is that he was murdered. I thought the allergy shot caused his death, but apparently something else killed him."

"Like what?"

"Hell, I don't know. Maybe someone put a poison in his vaccine or something like that....Who knows, maybe something he was allergic to. I had nothing to do with it."

"Oh my God! How could someone do that to him?" She put her hands over her mouth to keep herself from crying.

Her grief didn't seem to faze Pete. "Don't know and it isn't my problem. Say, let's go to a movie or something."

She agreed. While dressing, she thought about Frank's allergy tendencies. He never told her much about his health, other than he had asthma, was on shots and medications for it and that he had some food allergies. It made her wonder what could have been added to Frank's vaccine. Suddenly she sat down, recalling a frightening memory. It happened one afternoon after she and Frank had finished making love in a downtown hotel. She'd decided to eat some caramel peanut clusters that she pulled out of her purse. When she opened it and started chewing on it, he yelled at her.

"Jacqueline! Stop, what you're doing!"

"Why?"

"I can't get close to you. I'm violently allergic to peanuts."

"I didn't know that. Tell me about it."

"I don't want to talk about it. Just some very bad memories."

The memory made her realize how horrible it must have been for Frank if something he was allergic to had been added to his vaccine. It left her with a terrifying thought. *Did Pete have anything to do with his death?*

Chapter Fifty-Five

ELIZABETH FINCH WAS the next witness to testify. She was dressed in a conservative business suit, appearing uncomfortable and unsettled as she shifted nervously in the witness chair. Carthage took a seat in the gallery. After a series of preliminary questions, Deputy Attorney General Murphy began his questioning.

"According to Dr. Haberman's testimony and other patients who were present, you had problems helping Dr. Haberman when Dr. Stevens collapsed. Is that correct?"

"Well, I tried but I just froze. I don't know what happened to me...I was..." Her voice trailed off. "I'm a good nurse."

She sipped some water and glanced at Carthage, who nodded back, encouraging her.

"Ms. Finch, I need to know what happened. Could you explain it?"

Tears began to well up in her eyes. She spoke with a soft voice, almost a whisper. "I had been angry with Dr. Stevens a long time. I knew who he was twenty years ago in college, although I never met him personally. He was a party animal. One night when he was drunk, he ran his car into my sister's car and she was paralyzed after that. It ruined her life and mine. She became a paraplegic, had brain damage and her uterus had to be removed because it ruptured. I—I help care for her."

Elizabeth struggled to regain composure. "She was a beautiful, vibrant young woman, with an aspiring career as an opera singer. Dr. Stevens went on with his life while our lives were destroyed."

Carthage waved his hand. Murphy recognized him and Carthage spoke. "Ms. Finch, do you need a few minutes?"

"No, thank you, I want to finish. She—she became wheelchair-bound, had multiple surgeries, and she needed specialized medical care. She became very depressed because she couldn't have children."

Members of the jury were listening intently; a few elderly women were tearing up.

"I was present at Dr. Stevens' trial and was a witness on behalf of my sister to describe how the injuries changed her life. He never visited her, never called her, never even apologized."

She started to cry again. "I'm sorry." She wiped her eyes and took a sip of water. "He didn't remember me at Dr. Haberman's office. He'd forgotten all about the accident he caused. He wasn't punished like he should've been! Just got a slap on the hand by some liberal judge, fined and a year's probation to do some community service to make amends."

Several members of the jury shook their heads.

"I wanted him to feel some of the pain my sister and our family had felt for twenty years. I started to increase the dose of each injection, just a little each time. Just enough to make his arm swell and be painful. I didn't mean to..." She stopped talking and dropped her head.

The jury remained silent, waiting for her to resume.

Murphy waited her out and then asked. "On the day he died, did you give him a larger amount than his scheduled dose?"

"No, I actually reduced the dose. That day the pollen count was high and I thought, better safe than sorry. I knew what I was doing was wrong, but I didn't want to kill him."

She paused again, this time longer, and shook her head slowly with a look of defeat. "When he collapsed I thought it was because I'd given him extra doses of the vaccine, and that's why I panicked, reacted the way I did... I'm sorry." She broke down completely and sat sobbing.

The deputy attorney general asked for a recess. She leaned on Carthage while leaving the courtroom.

Carthage said. "Elizabeth, as hard as this is, it's important to tell the truth. You know you didn't cause Dr. Stevens' death, so let's get on with it and tell the jury your whole story."

Twenty minutes later, she resumed her testimony.

"Ms. Finch, how many times did you give Dr. Stevens a vaccine dose that was larger than prescribed?"

"I don't know, probably a half dozen times, maybe more. I'm not sure."

"Did he ever experience signs of anaphylaxis?"

"No, he never had a problem. I would check him before he left and he never complained about breathing difficulty or hives. He always waited the required time. He did complain of pain and swelling in his arm, but I knew it was because of the larger doses."

"Ms. Finch, I have just a few more questions. Did you know Dr. Stevens was allergic to peanuts?"

"Yes, he was allergic to a lot of foods and pollens."

"How did you know he was allergic to peanuts?"

"Because I read his chart, as I do with most of my patients on allergy injections."

"That sounds like you knew about every patient's medical condition. Did you know the allergy profile of every patient who was on allergy injections? Answer yes or no please."

She realized she trapped herself. "No, I—I read his medical record in particular, because of what he did to my sister."

"So, you knew he was allergic to peanuts. Ms. Finch, did you know that peanut was added to his vaccine?"

She sat up, startled by the revelation. Then she shook her head several times. "No, I had no idea. Who would do that?"

"But you knew he was allergic to peanuts. You could have tampered with his vaccine by adding peanut to it, and administered a large dose, all with the intention of causing his death."

Elizabeth had a look of total disbelief. Then with both palms facing upward, she pleaded. "No, please... I didn't."

Carthage asked for a moment to talk to his client and Murphy gave approval.

Carthage whispered. "Elizabeth, stay with him. You're under oath. Just answer his questions truthfully. You have nothing to hide. You know you didn't do that."

She nodded and the deputy attorney general passed a note to the court recorder to document that the two were engaged in a conversation. He resumed his questions. "Who else would have known he was violently allergic to peanuts?"

She paused, thinking. "Well, anyone in the office, but besides the staff, maybe Mr. Barone."

"Why would Mr. Barone know about the allergy vaccines or about Dr. Stevens' peanut allergy?"

"He would come over to the office to see Dr. Haberman. While he waited, he watched me give allergy injections. One time he asked how they worked and I gave him a short explanation."

"But how would Mr. Barone know that Dr. Stevens was allergic to peanuts?"

"Well, one time we talked about Dr. Stevens. He said he knew Dr. Stevens was getting shots and then he asked how often Dr. Stevens was getting them. I thought his question was weird, but because he worked closely with Dr. Haberman, I told him it was every two weeks. I probably shouldn't have answered because I realized later that I violated HIPAA confidentiality."

"So you thought it was odd that he asked about Dr. Stevens' shot schedule?"

"Well, not at the time that he asked, but thinking back, I thought it was strange. I'm wondering now if he asked because he might have been planning to do something with Dr. Stevens' vaccine."

"OK, so knowing he was interested in Dr. Stevens' shot schedule, how would Jimmy Barone know that Dr. Stevens was allergic to peanuts?"

"Maybe Dr. Stevens told him. They worked closely together, so Dr. Stevens might have mentioned it to him. I never said anything about it to Mr. Barone. There was no reason to since we were just talking about allergy shots."

"So, Barone could have found out from Dr. Stevens that he was allergic to peanuts? OK, if that's true, then how would he have known where the peanut reagent was kept in the office?"

"He didn't find out from me. Maybe he brought it with him."

"OK, then how would he know where Dr. Stevens' vaccine was located?"

"He watched me pulling vaccines out of the refrigerator, so he could've figured it out."

There were no further questions. She was dismissed but told to be available in the event she was needed for more testimony.

She and Carthage left and stood together outside the courthouse. He told her that her testimony was very credible and he thought she had improved her situation by pointing to Barone as a strong suspect. He asked her to call him later in the week.

While driving home she thought about what Murphy said, *Peanut had been added to Dr. Stevens' vaccine.* At least now she knew his death had nothing to do with giving larger doses of vaccine. But then she thought about something that made her panic. If true, she might unwittingly be connected to Stevens' death.

Chapter Fifty-Six

TED LARKIN AVOIDED the outdoors because of his fear of bees. He also carried his emergency adrenalin kit, ready to inject himself if a bee or any flying insect landed on him. He decided to call Pete Doren, thinking this was a good time to reinforce their friendship. It would provide a signal that he was in Pete's camp, and hopefully Jacki would see it as a sign of support, that he was helping get Pete out of trouble.

"Pete, Ted here."

"Hey, Ted, nice hearing from you. What can I do for you?"

"You recall that terrible bee sting reaction I had a while back?"

"Sure do."

"Remember how much I love to fly fish and golf? I'm freaked out that it'll happen again. It keeps me indoors. Is there anything I can do to prevent it from happening again?"

Doren told him he needed to be skin tested to honey bee venom. Assuming he was positive, he would advise a long-term immunization program of honey bee venom. Ted agreed to the plan, recognizing that it mirrored Haberman's recommendations. He set up an appointment for the following week.

When the day of his appointment came, Ted was the first patient in Doren's office. Doren's chief technical assistant for allergy testing, Tamara Kohler, was in her mid-twenties and a high school graduate who had spent several years as a hair stylist. Despite her lack of medical training, Doren had hired her because she was presentable and because she accepted an hourly rate only slightly better than minimum wage. Doren spent a few weeks training her and then let her take over the allergy department so he could concentrate on his other profitable activities. Tamara enjoyed the independence and felt important because people assumed she was the allergist at the office. She was in charge, which meant she made important clinical decisions, deciding which skin tests were appropriate and selecting allergen ingredients for vaccines.

She got an e-mail from Dr. Doren, telling her to skin test Senator Ted Larkin using honey bee venom. All she needed to do was add saline to the honey bee venom vial in the refrigerator, make five dilutions, and then skin test until a welt and redness appeared. Dr. Doren told her he was confident she could do this by herself. He couldn't be there since he had a full laser and liposuction schedule that day.

Tamara found the vial with dry powder honey bee venom and added the right volume of saline to reconstitute the concentrated test reagent. After shaking it, she made the dilutions from the concentrate. The label on the concentrate indicated one hundred micrograms per ml. She didn't know what that meant, so she just wrote 100 on the concentrate vial and numbered the others by adding a 0 to each dilution to signify each subsequent vial was ten times more dilute.

When she finished making dilutions, she was interrupted by a call from her boyfriend. She returned to the preparation of the bee venom reagents. She sat and thought a minute, *Was 100 more diluted or less?* After a minute she decided 100 meant the most dilute and 100,000 the most concentrated.

Larkin was sitting in an exam room when she brought in the test tray. She had him roll up a sleeve and explained she was testing to honey bee venom, starting with the most dilute to a full dose that would be almost equivalent to a bee sting. He felt anxious, but she assured him she had done these skin tests many times, and had never experienced a serious reaction.

The first test was from the vial with the label 100. She told him she would return in a few minutes to read the results. Within a few minutes, Larkin felt dizzy and his chest tightened. His heart began racing, and he noticed trouble swallowing. He wasn't sure he could get up, but managed to stand while holding onto the exam table. Realizing he needed help, he tried yelling for Tamara, but could only make a faint wheezing sound because his vocal cords were swelling, closing off his airway. Feeling weak, he collapsed to the floor, unconscious.

After finishing with another patient, Tamara went to check on Larkin and found him on the floor. Having no training in CPR, she ran out of the room and called Dr. Doren, who was in surgery.

The nurse in charge of the operating room answered.

"Please, I need to talk to Dr. Doren! It's an emergency!"

"He can't be disturbed, he's in surgery. Can I help you?"

"This is Tamara, his office assistant. A patient is down! Please, I need to talk to him, now!"

"Tamara, he can't speak to you. He's in the middle of a procedure. Call 911 immediately."

Not knowing what to do next, she ran into the office building hallway and started yelling. "Help! Please, someone's dying. Help!"

A female doctor from a neighboring office ran over and found Ted in shock. She administered adrenalin and proceeded to do chest compressions. Tamara called 911 and stood back, wringing her hands.

The paramedics who responded to the call transported Larkin to the ER at Denver Memorial. He was then immediately transferred to the ICU. The staff neurologist confirmed that Larkin likely had total and irreversible brain damage.

When Doren returned from surgery, he went immediately to the ICU and found Larkin on a ventilator, comatose. He read the ICU neurology consultation that diagnosed severe anoxic-induced brain damage from prolonged anaphylactic shock. Panicked at what this meant, he ran back to his office and yanked Tamara into a back room.

"Tamara, tell me exactly what you did."

"I did what you told me. I made the dilutions and started with the lowest number and I tested him just one time, and then he collapsed."

"You started with the lowest number meaning...?"

"You know the 100. That's the lowest amount."

Doren couldn't believe how stupid she was. "Oh, Christ, you gave him the concentrate. I told you, we never test with that dose. Damn it!" He paced around the room, thinking. "Tamara, your story has to change. You actually tested him with the 10,000 dose and then he collapsed," he said carefully. "He was so sensitive that the lowest dilution caused the shock. You agree. Right?"

She looked straight into his eyes. Yes, I do... of course I do."

The next day the *Rocky Mountain Tribune* headline read:

ANOTHER DANGEROUS REACTION IN AN ALLERGIST'S OFFICE

The article proceeded to make a case that allergy care in Denver was dangerous.

When Lenny read it, he knew it would cause serious problems for his specialty. He called the president of the Denver Allergy Society, an organization made up of only fellowship-trained, ABAI-certified allergists. The president agreed that they needed to respond to the article right away. The public needed to know that Lenny's case was a murder, and that the other case did not involve an ABAI certified allergist.

Chapter Fifty-Seven

WHEN JACKI HEARD about Ted's awful reaction, it removed all hope that she could manipulate the grand jury outcome for Pete. She wasn't sure what to do now. She was still wrestling with her suspicions that Pete might have had something to do with Frank's death. She was walking by the living room when she heard a car pull up. She looked out to see a sheriff approaching the front door. The déjà vu made her heart beat rapidly. The sheriff asked to speak to Pete, who was drying off from a shower. When Pete entered the living room, he was handed an arrest warrant and read the Miranda warning.

Pete responded. "What's this about?"

The sheriff replied. "You're under arrest."

Pete told Jacqueline to call Cutter immediately as he was taken into custody and brought down to the county jail, where he remained until Cutter posted a one million dollar bond. He was informed that he had been indicted as a suspect in Frank's murder.

When he returned home, Pete's reaction was complete panic. He started breathing rapidly and hyperventilating until he couldn't talk or stand. Jacqueline made him lie down on the couch, just as he felt dizzy and ready to pass out. She ran to the kitchen to get an ice pack, which she placed under his neck and elevated his legs. She stroked his forehead, held his hands, and talked gently to get him to relax. Eventually he sat up and talked incessantly about how this would impact their lives.

Jacki repeated that she believed in him.

"Yes, but what difference does that make? I'm indicted now."

"But Pete, they have no case .You gave him a loan. There's no one who could prove differently. Isn't it your word against Barone?"

He nodded yes. "I know, but you can never trust the system."

"Then let's get the best defense attorney we can. I'm sure everything will be OK."

Elizabeth was also arrested at her house. The sheriff allowed a call to her lawyer before taking her in.

"Mr. Carthage, this can't happen, I can't go to jail. I have two children to support. They need me..." Her voice trailed off sobbing.

"Elizabeth, you've been indicted. An arrest warrant means you'll have to appear for arraignment, post bail or be jailed."

"Oh, my God. How much will that be?"

"I don't know. I'll find out and call you right back."

Elizabeth was in a jail cell when she was told she had a call from her attorney.

"Elizabeth, the bail is set high and they won't lower it because this is a murder case. It's one million dollars."

"Oh, please. I don't have that kind of money!"

"You'll need ten percent down, and the rest could be collateralized with property, like your house."

"I don't have more than $30,000 in the bank."

"Do you have any family or friends who might help?"

Elizabeth thought for a long moment. "Maybe my brother-in-law will help me."

"All right, we have to appear tomorrow morning at ten for the arraignment. Call me if you have trouble working it out."

She was sent back to her jail cell, where she broke down, unable to clear her mind of a recurring suspicion, but she could tell no one because there might be dreadful repercussions.

Chapter Fifty-Eight

A DENVER CONTACT for the Pazzoni family called KC to inform him of a recent TV newscast that could have serious implications for the family. KC immediately went online to read about it.

The Colorado Attorney General's office has announced that a state grand jury investigation into the homicide of Dr. Frank Stevens has just been completed. Three suspects have been indicted for the murder of Dr. Stevens. Dr. Peter Doren, a local allergist and plastic surgeon; Elizabeth Finch, a nurse who worked in the allergy office of Dr. Leonard Haberman; and Jimmy Barone, who had worked as a laboratory technician at COADD, the company where Dr. Stevens had led research into the successful development of a cocaine vaccine.

Barone aka Bonante is the son of Marco Bonante, a member of the Pazzoni crime family in New York City. The connection raises the possibility that Jimmy Barone aka Bonante was hired to sabotage research on the cocaine vaccine at COADD.

Deputy Attorney General Murphy indicated that the relationships between Doren, Finch and Barone aka Bonante would not be divulged at this time.

✱ ✱ ✱

When Jimmy returned to Aruba, he told Katarina how awful it was watching his favorite uncle pass away from cancer, and how much he appreciated the *now*, especially being with her. They had sex on the spot and every night after that. She was starved, and he was an addict.

One very dark night after she left, Jimmy was sitting on the beach, smoking a joint and enjoying the sound of the crashing surf. He realized he could never go back to work for the family and he hoped he had enough money to stay in Aruba with Katarina. As he began to walk toward his bungalow, he thought he heard footsteps. He looked around but saw no one. Suddenly two large hands grabbed his neck from behind, and pulled him up with his feet dangling in the air.

A deep bass voice rumbled, "Jimmy, I'm sorry."

Jimmy struggled, kicking his legs wildly. His last thought was about Katarina.

The next day when Jimmy didn't show up at the hospital, Katarina walked over to his bungalow. She found him stiff, sitting on the floor, propped up against a wall. She called the police, and wondered if their activities had caused him to have a heart attack.

✱ ✱ ✱

Agent Locke was reviewing a case when he heard his fax turn on. He pulled the sheet and read it.

Attention: CBI

A United States citizen murdered in Aruba has been identified. His finger-prints matched with Jimmy Barone, a former Denver resident who was recently added to the CBI and FBI most wanted list as a suspect in the death of Dr. Frank Stevens. Barone was employed at the Aruba International Hospital as a pathology laboratory assistant. A friend, Katarina Veltkampe, discovered his body. The tentative post-mortem diagnosis was homicide by strangulation.

FBI headquarters, Washington, DC.

Ben called the Attorney General's office to inform them of Barone's murder. That, along with Barone's connection to the Pazzonis, suggested mob involvement in Stevens' death and possibly the mysterious death of the other scientist, Sanford Sontag. Locke thought, *This could swing the criminal case to a federal jurisdiction.*

Chapter Fifty-Nine

KC AND TOMMY Pazzoni decided their next target had to be Doren. He knew too much about the family, and he might talk now that he was indicted. Doren's *accidental death* had to happen before the Frank Stevens murder trial began.

The plan changed when KC received a call from their same Denver contact who told him about an article in a Denver newspaper. It indicated that COADD had just been funded with an NIH grant and would be resuming its research activities on the cocaine vaccine. If that happened, it would become a serious problem for KC and the Pazzonis. The Columbian cartel that had financed sabotage of the cocaine vaccine would be extremely angry, and could cause serious harm to the Pazzoni family. For sure they would want their 5 million dollar down payment back. This made KC nervous, an unusual sensation for him.

KC had to find out if COADD had recovered the missing set of manufacturing specifications. There was still one option left. Lenny Haberman and his son Jack might know something. He decided to postpone the hit on Doren and instead sent an e-mail to his Denver contact: *Put pressure on Haberman and his son to find the specs.*

Lenny had just finished with his last patient of the day, when Jane called on the intercom to announce that a Mr. Lynch was on the line about Jack. He hadn't talked to Jack for a while and felt a twinge of anxiety as he picked up the phone. The call was worse than he'd imagined.

"Hello, Dr. Haberman here."

"Call me Lynch. Doc, I have your son."

"What do you mean, you have my son?"

"Just like I said, I have your son."

"What? Is he hurt? What do you mean?"

"Doc, stop asking questions! Here's the deal. You get the specs that Frank Stevens gave you, and your son will be released unharmed."

"You kidnapped my son?"

"I'll say this only one more time! Get the specs and he'll be released."

"I don't have them, and Jack doesn't either. If I knew where they were, I would have given them to COADD a long time ago."

"Doc, cut the bullshit. You get those specs and meet me tonight at eleven in the parking lot at University and Evans. If you call the police or anyone, Jack's dead. Do you get it?"

"Let me talk to him! How do I know he's all right?"

"Doc, you'll just have to trust me."

"I need time. Please, I don't have them. All I know is that COADD is trying to restart without them."

"I'll be in a black Escalade waiting for you at eleven. We don't play games, Doc. Get the specs or your son's dead in five hours."

Lenny couldn't believe it. He needed to think, but he didn't have time. The only person who might be able to help was Sol. He called Sol at COADD.

"Sol, it's Lenny. I have an emergency. I need your help."

"What's it about?"

Lenny told him about the call. "Sol, I don't know where to go with this. I don't have them, you don't have them, and I can't believe Jack knows where they are either. He would have told one of us if he knew."

He started to choke up. "Sol, can you have someone make up a false set? It might give me more time to find out where Jack's being held. Christ, I can't believe this is happening. And we can't tell the police or Locke. This guy made it clear they'll kill Jack."

"OK, then let's get Blackwood involved. Charley's good at this kind of stuff. Just promise to hand over the specs and let Charley follow this guy."

Lenny decided he had no other choice but to go along, although there was nothing that would stop him from finding Jack. "OK-OK. This has to work."

Lenny met Sol at COADD around seven.

"Sol, I need to get this done now. I only have a few hours."

"I told Beth what's going on. She'll have it done soon."

Just then Charley arrived and they caught him up on the events.

Sol took charge, speaking directly to both Lenny and Charley. "Lenny is not going to follow this guy. He hands over the specs and then Charley takes over. Charley you need to call me after you assess the situation. Hopefully, they'll hand Jack over when you give them the specs. I'll call Locke then and get him to help, but we can't bring the cops in until you tell me Jack is safe. We have to do this right so none of you, including Jack, get hurt. Otherwise I will not condone or support this. Do we all understand?" He then looked straight at Lenny to get his agreement. Lenny immediately nodded yes.

After finishing up some details, Lenny was given a CD that Beth had hastily created. She had to rely on recall since she had no actual manufacturing specs to work from. She knew enough to leave out important components, add false ones, and change concentrations to ensure the formula looked real but wouldn't work.

Lenny and Charley left in separate cars, planning to rendezvous at the location. Both had guns, Lenny a 9 mm Beretta and Blackwood a long barrel 357.

* * *

Lenny waited in his new Toyota RAV under a lamppost in the parking lot. There was no one around. He pulled out his Beretta again to make sure it was loaded, and looked over at the black jeep parked at a gas station a hundred yards down the street, where Charley was sitting low in his seat.

At 11pm sharp, a shiny black Escalade pulled up next to Lenny so the driver sides were facing each other. The driver's head was covered with a full ski mask. At first he didn't speak, just held out a gloved hand and Lenny handed him the CD.

The driver spoke. "Remember, if you or anyone follows me or if you call the cops, you can say goodbye to your son." Holding up the CD, he continued. "And if these don't work, or we find out they've been duplicated, we'll be back for the rest of your family."

"Where's Jack. When will I…?"

"Soon," the driver said, and then the Escalade took off. Lenny sat bewildered until his rage overwhelmed him; the same intensity he'd felt when the sniper killed Billy in Desert Storm. He vowed to himself that this time the outcome would be different.

When the kidnapper drove off, Charley pulled out to follow him. Charley remained far enough behind to avoid being detected. The Escalade drove for about ten minutes into an old West Denver neighborhood of modest single level, yellow brick homes built in the fifties. It was quiet and there was no activity on the street. Charley stayed back a full block and watched the kidnapper drive up to one of the homes. He called Lenny, who met him at a location nearby. They sat in Charley's car, hoping the kidnapper would fall asleep.

Then they walked down an alley behind the house and hid behind a large fence. Seeing that the house was dark and quiet, they crawled up to a privacy hedge in front of a basement window. Charley put on infrared goggles and looked into the basement. He saw Jack apparently asleep, strapped into a chair with his hands bound behind him and a gag in his mouth.

They tried sliding the window open, but it wouldn't budge. Charley took out a cutting device that he'd brought just for this possibility and removed part of the window pane. He put his hand through the opening, turned the clasp and moved the window sideways. Lenny crawled through first, placing his feet on a storage locker, and climbed down quietly onto the floor. Charley followed trying to be equally quiet, but in the process knocked over a box. The noise woke Jack. When Jack recognized Lenny, he slumped in relief and made a loud muffled sound trying to tell him something. Lenny ran to him, removed the gag and whispered to remain silent while he untied the rope.

Suddenly they heard someone coming down the steps. He was barely discernible, a shadowed outline, but light from outside the window glinted off a handgun. Blackwood, still wearing goggles, fired first, but only grazed the gunman's leg. Then Jack pushed Lenny away just as Lynch fired. When Lenny fell, he rolled onto his stomach and fired off two shots in rapid succession. A crashing sound followed as the gunman fell down the stairs. Charley found the light switch, and with total disbelief, realized Lenny had shot the kidnapper twice in the middle of his forehead; two holes overlapping each other.

"That's incredible shooting man!" But there was no response.

Charley turned to see Lenny holding Jack, who was writhing in pain.

Chapter Sixty

LENNY CALLED 911 when he realized Jack had been shot in the abdomen. Jack was bleeding profusely and barely conscious, trying to keep his eyes open as he stared at Lenny.

"Jack, you're going to make it. Just hang in there with me!"

Lenny's eyes welled with tears as he held the back of Jack's head in the palm of his right hand.

"Dad, there were things that didn't make sense…" His voice waned.

"Jack, please, don't worry. It's OK. Everything's going to be fine."

Suddenly Jack opened his eyes wide, and smiled as he struggled to say something that was barely audible. "Dad… I know I've pushed you away many times, but this time it was for your own good."

Then he turned his head, and fell unconscious. Lenny kept pressure on Jack's wound, fearing Jack would bleed out before help arrived.

The paramedics arrived within minutes and took over, starting IVs and medications to support Jack's low blood pressure. It was an amazing display of efficiency, as four paramedics whisked him into an ambulance and sped off to the hospital. Jack was immediately sent to an OR where two gowned surgeons were ready to perform exploratory surgery and stop internal bleeding from what turned out to be a punctured liver.

It was twelve hours before Lenny was informed that Jack's condition was stabilized, although, he remained in critical condition. Lenny walked down to the hospital cafeteria for coffee, the full enormity of what had happened finally hitting him. He called Ben Locke.

"Ben, it's Lenny. Did Sol tell you what happened?"

"He did. How's Jack?"

"Better now, thank God. Does this mean the whole thing was done by Barone and a crime syndicate?"

"It definitely points in that direction. I need to ID the guy you took care of. I gather he told you his name was Lynch. Is that right?"

"Yeah."

"OK. I need to find out who he worked for."

"Ben, do you think we need protection?"

"Definitely, I've already ordered a patrol at your home and an officer to guard Jack at the hospital."

The next day a banner headline appeared in the *Rocky Mountain Tribune.*

DOCTOR THWARTS KIDNAPPING OF SON

Lenny read the article while sitting in Jack's hospital room.

An unidentified assailant kidnapped Jack Haberman, son of Dr. Leonard Haberman, who is an allergist-immunologist and Medical Director of COADD, a company that has been developing an effective vaccine to control cocaine addiction. The attacker, possibly a member of a crime syndicate, kidnapped Jack Haberman as part of a plot to stop COADD from manufacturing its innovative cocaine vaccine. Dr. Haberman informed the Denver police and a shoot-out led to the killing of the kidnapper. Further details are being withheld until the investigation is completed.

Lenny was relieved to read that it sounded like the Denver police had killed the kidnapper. Someone, possibly Locke, had spun the facts to protect Lenny and his family from potential retribution.

Lenny thought about Barone working for a syndicate, and how, through an accomplice, he'd been able to gain access to Lenny's office. Someone knew Frank was allergic to peanuts. This was the piece of the puzzle that he could never wrap his hands around. He thought Elizabeth might have been correct when she testified that Frank could have innocently mentioned it to Barone, but he still remained suspicious that Elizabeth had something to do with it. He also thought it was possible that Frank's medical records could've been obtained from other sources, an insurance application or another doctor's office. The part with Doren remained a puzzle, but his relationship to Barone and personal motive couldn't be ignored.

✱ ✱ ✱

Jack's condition improved each day, and within a week he was moved from ICU to a room on the surgical floor. He was off the ventilator and the drainage tubes had been removed from his abdomen and nose. He was taking clear liquids and meds by mouth.

Lenny received many calls of support from friends and colleagues. One in particular from Denise Stevens was a pleasant surprise. She had read the article in the paper.

"Lenny, I can't believe what you've been through, Frank's death and now this with Jack. I always loved your family... Lenny, I'd like to be friends again."

"Denise, thank you. You don't know how important it is to hear you say that."

They talked for several minutes about their respective families, and then Denise brought up Ted.

"I'm so sick over what happened to Ted, too. His family has decided to stop life support, so he could be with our Lord Jesus. Losing my husband and now Ted has been really difficult."

Lenny tried to console her about Ted, but deep down he suspected that Doren's negligence had caused Ted's anaphylaxis

A week later the paper announced that Senator Ted Stevens had died of complications from an allergic reaction to a test performed in Dr. Pete Doren's office.

Chapter Sixty-One

━━━━━━━━━━━━━━━━━━━━

SOL HAD WAITED to call Denise, especially after Charley told him she wasn't ready to have someone search her home. After a lot of deliberation he decided he had no choice but to place the call. COADD's survival depended on finding the CMV specs.

"Mrs. Stevens, this is Sol Feldman."

"Why hello, Mr. Feldman, what can I do for you?"

"I'm so sorry to hear about your brother's death. I want to extend my condolences to you and your family, from me and from everyone at COADD. I can fully appreciate the depth of sorrow you must feel, especially after losing Frank too. Just know, we all are thinking of you."

"I truly appreciate your thoughts."

"Mrs. Stevens, there's something I need to talk to you about. It may seem inappropriate at this time, but it's very important. Could I come over and talk to you about COADD's future? You know, your family owns a lot of stock and there are things we need to discuss."

"I understand. Would you like to come tomorrow morning about nine?

"Yes, thank you. I'll see you then."

✱ ✱ ✱

The following morning, Denise graciously invited him into the living room. "Mr. Feldman, would you like some tea?"

"Yes, thank you."

As she poured the tea, she asked, "What is it you want to talk about? You know, Frank rarely talked to me about his work."

"Mrs. Stevens, I'm sure you're aware of the problems at COADD since Frank's death. Not only do we miss his leadership and intelligence, but we're at a standstill because the manufacturing specifications are still missing. We need your help to find them."

"Well, I have no idea where they could be. Frank told me very little about the lab. I know he was getting close to something big just before he died." Then she looked away, her voice trailing off softly. "He was so happy then."

"Mrs. Stevens, I'm aware of all the stress you've experienced and I don't want to add any more, but I must ask. Would you let us do one more search in your home?"

She was about to sip tea, and instead put her cup down. "Please, I don't think so... I can't go through that again. There's nothing here. Jimmy almost killed me and my children. He ripped up the entire house. I just don't know if I can handle another intrusion."

"Mrs. Stevens, Barone can't hurt you anymore."

"Yes, I know. Agent Locke told me he was murdered."

"I promise we'll take extreme care not to upset you. This is essential for COADD's survival."

Denise sat thinking, and then decided to request something in return. "Mr. Feldman, as you know, I am a Christian. We've talked before about how much I would like to see you accept Jesus as your Lord and Savior. I have given myself to Jesus. I will consider your request if you will consider mine. If you attend just one of my bible classes, I'm convinced that we can bring you to the Lord."

Sol had thought she might try something like this. "I will do it if you let my staff search your home."

"Yes, without question, sir. I promise on the Bible."

"Good, then we have a deal, Mrs. Stevens."

"Wonderful. We have a deal, Mr. Feldman.

* * *

Sol, Charley and Ole arrived the next day to begin the search. They decided to work as a team, starting in the attic. They went through boxed personal papers, cabinets, dressers, closets, assorted piles of clothing, sporting effects, and pictures of the family. After six hours of exhaustive search, finding nothing, only the wine cellar was left.

Sol said. "This is it, Charley. If we don't find it, it's over."

Charley was looking at Frank's extensive wine collection when he noticed cracks in the floorboard under the wine racks and some deep scratch marks where the racks had been moved.

"Here, you guys, help me move these." They took all the wine off the racks and pushed the racks to the side. Charley slipped a pocketknife into a crack and lifted up a square panel. Under it was a space containing a small metal box. He removed the box and inside it were papers and two CDs. They knew they had found Frank's copies of the specs.

They ran upstairs, and Sol grabbed Denise. "Denise! We found them! They were in a box under the wine cellar floor board."

Sol knew he had saved COADD. He laughed to himself, thinking that all he had to do now was fulfill his agreement with Denise.

Chapter Sixty-Two

LENNY HADN'T SEEN Dave Sabatha for over a month. He made an appointment to have a session at the end of a work day. The psychiatrist had read about Jack's kidnapping and asked Lenny how he was doing.

"He's out of the hospital and staying with us. He's pretty shook up, but he's beginning to sleep better, although he wakes up sometimes screaming for help. Right now I'm sleeping in his room. He seems better when I stay close."

"That's good. Keep doing it, Lenny. It will reduce his fear and hopefully not let it evolve into PTSD."

"Dave, it was just terrifying. Personally I've not experienced anything like it since Desert Storm. But some good has come out of it. We've had some time to talk." Lenny stopped as he began to choke up.

Dave allowed Lenny time to regain his composure, and then carefully changed the subject.

"From press descriptions, it appears a crime family murdered Dr. Stevens to stop development of the cocaine vaccine. It's hard to believe they had to murder him to stop it. He had such a promising career. It's just incredible. I gather the person who set it up was the lab assistant who had ties with the mob. Wasn't he someone Stevens trusted?"

"Yes, very much. The entire Stevens family trusted Jimmy Barone. He was like a member of their family. I'm still trying to get a grip on what he did."

"So he knew that Stevens was allergic to peanuts and added it to Stevens' vaccine. Hard to conceptualize someone could be so evil. The mob's reach is frightening," Dave remarked. "The good part, Lenny, is you don't need to search for answers anymore. You're totally vindicated."

"I know, but it's taking time for it to sink in."

Dave paused for a long moment. "Lenny, I have to tell you something that may be initially distressing, but hopefully you'll understand. My wife and I have decided to move back to New York City. She's been lonely living out here. She misses the culture and her friends back east. I was hoping she might adapt, but it's clear that she hasn't been happy."

Lenny felt a surge of disappointment. "Wow, that's a surprise. I thought you loved Denver."

"It was a trial for us and unfortunately, it just didn't work out. Of course, I'll miss working with you and the rest of my patients. I've made preparations to transfer your file to Dr. Saglen, who in my opinion is excellent, and has a similar psychiatric education and approach to psychotherapy. Do you know him?"

"I've heard of him, but never met him. I don't know if I want to start all over with someone new. I may decide to wait and see how I feel. When are you planning to leave?"

"My plan now is to quit practicing at the end of this month, which will give us a few weeks to tie up loose ends. I do agree with your plan to wait a while and see how you're handling things."

"OK, but what about the anti-depressant? I'd like to stop taking it."

"We'll start that today. I'll write the plan to decrease the dose." Dave was searching for his prescription pad when suddenly he remembered something. "Lenny, I have to take a ten minute break to run over to the hospital. I need to pick up some papers for my malpractice insurer before the administrative office closes. There's no one coming in after you, so we could resume when I get back. Sorry for the interruption. I'll stay until we complete the full hour. Are you OK with that?"

"Of course, no problem. Take your time. I have a journal I can read."

Dave left the office, and Lenny pulled out the latest copy of the *New England Journal of Medicine* from his jacket and read the abstracts on articles of interest. By the time he had finished reading them, Dave had still not returned, so he stood up and casually perused Dave's book collection. There was an eclectic collection of titles on philosophy, psychiatry, art, world museums, travel in foreign countries, and writings in Spanish, German, Russian and Italian. He wasn't sure if Dave spoke all those languages, but it wouldn't surprise him if he did.

Partially hidden behind two books, he noticed a framed photograph. It was a picture of Dave with a woman in a wheelchair. Out of curiosity he pulled it out to get a better look. The picture appeared to have been taken in a European country, with beautiful old ornate buildings, statues, and fountains in the background. The woman was smiling and Dave also had a slight smile as he stood with his hand on her shoulder. She had a blanket covering her legs and her arms were resting on her lap. He replaced the photo on the shelf, thinking maybe he had met her in the past.

He gradually moved to the book shelves behind Dave's chair. As he did so, he noticed a bowl filled with twisted paper clips situated on a table next to Dave's chair. He picked a few of them up, idly shaking them in his fist. Each paper clip was twisted into two rings overlying each other. As he examined them, a sudden recall made him walk back to his chair and search the pockets of his jacket. He felt around and brought out a paper clip of identical shape. He rotated it in his hand as he tried to recall details.

I think it came from my office. Yes, I remember now. I had opened the refrigerator to store vials of blood taken from Frank when I noticed it on the floor. It was lying in front of the refrigerator... on the day Frank died. He repeated the last thought, but this time he spoke it aloud. "On the day Frank died."

He held the clip in his palm, staring at it. Then he walked back to look at the bowl again and noticed dozens of paper clips twisted in similar ring shapes. He picked several up and slid them over his fingers. They were all crafted as if they had come from a precision mold.

Lenny went back and sat down. He kept repeating the same question to himself. *How did this get into my office? It had to be more than a coincidence. If Dave twisted them, then it has to mean he was in my office, and accidentally dropped it; but what was he doing there?*

Then he thought of the picture of Dave with the woman sitting in a wheelchair. He went back to look at the photograph, but this time more closely. She looked so familiar, *but who is she? Who?* She had light blond hair, beautiful large blue eyes and impressive dimples. *Where have I met her?* Suddenly he knew. *I saw her at Elizabeth's house. She was sitting in a wheelchair. Elizabeth was standing next to her. She's Elizabeth's sister. She's the same person in the photograph. Her eyes and dimples resemble Elizabeth. Then why was she with Dave?* He stepped back as the thought hit him. *Could she be Dave's wife?*

Then he recalled the conversation with Dave about the van he drove. *He said he needed it for a member of his family who has difficulty getting into small cars. That person has to be his disabled wife... That's it!*

As Lenny continued to add up the links, the puzzle was becoming clearer. *Finding the twisted paper clip meant Dave was in my office. He had motive-wanting retribution for what Frank did to his wife. He could have entered my office one evening when the suite was being cleaned and added peanut to Frank's vaccine. But how would Dave know Stevens was allergic to peanut? Maybe Elizabeth was in on it, and she told Dave about Frank's peanut allergy. Could this be real? It seems fucking unreal! What about Doren and Barone? How do they fit in?*

Then he remembered what Dave had said before he left. He mentioned that the syndicate probably put peanut into Frank's vaccine. He spoke his next thought out loud. "How would he know? Only a few people knew peanut was added to Frank's vaccine. Only those involved with the grand jury would know. Christ, what does this mean?"

Lenny's mind raced on. *Dave had been defensive about Elizabeth, her reaction to the crisis.* If all this was true, he realized Dave had manipulated him, and everyone else like puppets, pulling strings to get the results he wanted.

Lenny was fiddling with the paper clips when he heard Dave return to the office.

"Lenny, sorry for the interruption, but I had a deadline to pay on my insurance policy." He was referring to paying a final premium on his malpractice insurance to cover potential lawsuits that might be filed after he stopped practice in Denver. "Where were we?"

Dave noticed Lenny holding the clips. "Oh, I see you discovered my peculiar habit."

"Yeah, they're very unusual… Dave, I never asked about your personal life, but now that you're leaving, I'm curious about something."

"What's that?"

"I was browsing through your library and noticed you have quite eclectic reading interests."

"I admit I do. Does that surprise you?"

"No, it doesn't. I always thought you were a renaissance man. I also noticed lots of books on foreign travel."

Dave answered perfunctorily, not sure where Lenny was headed with the questioning. "Yes, my wife and I do enjoy foreign travel."

That confirmed the photograph for Lenny. "There's a photo of you in a foreign country with a woman in a wheelchair. Is that your wife?"

Dave answered. "Yes, Samantha. She was injured when she was younger."

"She reminds me of someone I know."

Dave instantly looked uneasy. "Really, who?"

"I think you can answer that."

Dave frowned. "I don't know what you're asking, Lenny."

"I think she looks like a relative of Finch, her sister. She's Elizabeth's sister isn't she?"

"No, she isn't related to anyone you know," Dave said hurriedly.

"That's bullshit! I actually saw your wife once before. She was outside Elizabeth's house and Elizabeth was talking to her. Elizabeth also referred to her sister as Sam, and we found out that was short for Samantha, your wife's name. Don't deny it, Dave. She's the one who was injured by Frank Stevens, isn't she?"

"What are you talking about?" Before Lenny could control himself, he blurted out, "Tell me, Dave. Does your insurance cover acts of murder?"

Dave's usual psychiatrist's mellow tones returned. "Lenny, calm down. You have it all wrong. Maybe I shouldn't lower your medications just yet."

"I get it. Keep making it look like I need help. Keep the focus off of you," Lenny said, annoyed. "I had time to look around your office and some of the things I found are making me suspicious. Dave, did you kill Frank?"

"Lenny, are you having a paranoid break? Maybe I need to change your meds."

"No way! You've been able to manipulate me, and throw everyone off. Pulling strings for far too long. I've been naïve, but I still can't figure out what would have possessed you to kill Stevens, and why you involved me, a friend, a classmate!"

Dave didn't respond and looked straight at Lenny.

Lenny went on. "I trusted you. I told you about my life, my fears, my anxieties, as if I was in a confessional with a priest… and now I realize you're a con man. Christ, how could you do this to me?"

Dave just continued to stare at him.

Lenny opened his palm. "Here's the twisted paper clip I found on the floor near my office refrigerator on the day Frank died. Now, look in the bowl. They're all alike, bent into twisted double rings. I'd never seen anything like the one in my hand until I discovered these in your office. Dave, this is yours…it's yours!" He threw the one in his hand at Sabatha.

"That doesn't mean anything. Anyone could twist paper clips, Dave protested. "Look, I'm sorry, Lenny. I never mentioned it, but I was in your office one time. I went there to speak to your nurse, Elizabeth, about referring a patient to you. You weren't there. I could've dropped one in your office then."

Lenny wasn't falling for this BS any more. "I don't believe you, Dave. Your wife has to be Elizabeth's sister, and you hated Frank because of what happened to her in the accident."

He had to pause, because his anger was rising faster than he could speak.

"You murdered him for the same reason that Elizabeth injected large doses of vaccine into him. It was revenge, wasn't it, Dave? The clincher for me was when you mentioned that the mob added peanut to Frank's vaccine. No one-no one other than the CBI and police knew that information, along with a few witnesses who testified before the grand jury. Either Elizabeth told you, or you knew all along!" He paused again for emphasis this time. "You're deranged and you were treating me. What incredible irony!"

Dave suddenly reached over into the desk next to his armchair and pulled out a handgun. While pointing it at Lenny, he smiled. "I knew you were bright, Lenny, but I didn't think you'd figure this out. All the leads pointed to murder by the mob. I was hoping that would be enough to close the investigation, but you couldn't leave it alone. Lenny, I always liked you, but now you've created an impossible situation for me."

Lenny focused on the barrel of the gun, realizing he should have been more cautious about openly accusing Dave of murder. Now he was alone with a maniac.

"We're going to walk out of this building quietly. I'll have the gun pointed at your back under my coat. If you say anything to anyone, I'll shoot. I've got nothing to lose ...nothing if I have to kill a second time."

The admission provided Lenny with little satisfaction, especially not with a gun at his back.

Dave went over to a shelf and took down a black doctor's bag. They left the building without meeting anyone and walked to Lenny's car.

Dave spoke quietly. "You drive. Don't try anything." He kept pointing the gun at Lenny.

When Lenny got in, Dave climbed swiftly into the back seat. Lenny had a panicked thought. Jack was coming to pick him up for dinner to talk about his plans to return to college. He glanced at his watch and realized Jack would be arriving any minute. He looked at Dave in the rear mirror.

"Where are we going?"

"You don't need to know that." Dave continued to keep the gun pointed at Lenny's head. "Your analysis is about ninety percent correct. I encouraged Denise to write her letter about propranolol. I thought it would help your malpractice case and settle issues about Frank's death; but I didn't know Elizabeth was giving Stevens large injections. When I found that out, I figured having her confess about the large doses would mislead the investigation. Here's where you're wrong. Elizabeth had no part in any tampering. I had access to Frank's medical record when I took over the practice, and it mentioned his food allergies. I added peanut because of all the publicity about peanut allergy, figuring it would cause a violent reaction. I was actually hoping he wouldn't die, just live with severe neurological impairment, like what happened to my wife. She had no chance for a career or future. Anyway, the reaction ended up being lethal because of propranolol in his system. I don't have any guilt about the outcome. Frank's own wife actually did him in. Kind of ironic, isn't it?"

"That's bullshit and you know it. You killed him! You're out of touch with reality!"

Dave started to laugh. "You apparently didn't do your psych homework. I'm not crazy, just a normal person. I wanted revenge. You would too."

"Dave, you can't really believe what you're saying. No sane person could rationalize what you did!"

"I'm very sane, Lenny. When you took psych 101 you apparently missed the class about revenge. It's an instinct, inherent in all human brains. How can a smart doctor like you, an alumnus of our prestigious medical school, not know that revenge is part of a basic instinct for survival, no different than other instincts, like eating or drinking? You certainly must have read

A Time to Kill, when a black father kills two rednecks who raped his daughter. The best part of that story was the father was acquitted for revenge killing... So you see, Lenny, my actions are not insane. They're just part of a normal self-preservation instinct."

Lenny couldn't believe what he was hearing.

"Lenny, do you think when someone is murdered, the victims' relatives support capital punishment merely to seek justice?" Dave didn't wait for an answer. "Hell no! It's much more basic than that. It's a survival instinct programmed in the genome of the entire animal kingdom. Revenge is merely expressing a basic animal instinct in humans; kill the enemy who threatens your species."

Lenny thought Dave's explanation actually defined psychotic delusion.

"You haven't asked why I waited so long to do it."

"I don't need to hear any more of your insanity."

"Oh, but I want you to know. I'm proud of this part. Samantha wanted to be around children since she couldn't have any. She kept asking if we could move near Elizabeth and be closer to her kids. I wanted her to experience that joy in her life. After we moved, Elizabeth told me Stevens was a patient of yours. He was so arrogant. He loved to tell Elizabeth about his work and how it was progressing, and she would naively tell me what he'd told her. I decided to do it just when he mentioned that the project was close to success. I wanted him to be severely disabled, have a stroke, maybe become paralyzed and unable to work anymore - whatever it would take, so he couldn't enjoy the fruits of his work. From what I hear, I timed it just perfectly."

Lenny interrupted. "Dave, you're delusional. You need help!"

Dave chuckled. "Nice try, but really bad psychiatry, Lenny. I wanted him to have the same experience as Samantha. I wanted him to achieve his ambition of making an effective cocaine vaccine, with all the fame, professional recognition, fortune, and then have it all disappear because he would be a cripple, unable to continue his brilliant career. That would have been the perfect outcome for Frank Stevens. Death was too good for him."

Lenny's mind was racing, trying to find a way to combat this insanity, this evil. He began to focus on the word: *evil... evil...evil ...* and then a spark, an irony. *Evil reversed spelled out live. What a fucking irony... I'm confronted with deranged evil and reversing the word spells live.* Lenny then realized what he had to do, *In order to live, to survive, I need to reverse the evil.*

He turned around swiftly and grabbed onto the gun. For a brief second Lenny thought he finally had the upper hand, until an excruciating pain stunned him. Dave had been prepared; he had removed a Taser from his black bag, and with his other hand shot a bolt of electricity into Lenny's neck.

Dave casually reached into his black bag for a sedative. Using a syringe, he drew up a dose that would be untraceable in an hour, and then injected it into Lenny's arm. He was now assured Lenny would remain unconscious, long enough to implement his plan to make it look like Lenny died from an overdose. He removed pills from the bag, and smashed them into powder using the bottom of a metal thermos. He proceeded to pour the powder into Lenny's mouth.

Being an expert in psycho-pharmacology, he anticipated the drug would be rapidly absorbed in Lenny's mouth. Lenny was already on a serotonin uptake inhibitor anti-depressant and the combination would lead to toxic levels of serotonin that would cause muscle spasms, delirium, high fever, high blood pressure and then shock. He waited for the first sign of toxicity; increased tendon reflexes detected by tapping Lenny's knees and arms. When they appeared, Dave drove off in his own car, satisfied that he had done what was necessary. He practiced his reply if he was asked about Lenny's mental state. *Yes, unfortunately, Lenny had suicidal tendencies from severe depression caused by overwhelming stress over the past year.*

* * *

The sedative effect eventually began to wear off, leaving Lenny confused and groggy. He started shaking his head, trying to get clarity, trying to figure out what was happening. Sensing something odd, he looked into the rearview mirror and noticed erratic twitching of his face. His arms and legs were jerking. Trying to gain control, he grabbed one arm with his other hand, but the spasms continued. Panic surged through him as he tasted something bitter, making him wonder if Dave had put something in his mouth, maybe a toxin, or even cyanide. He looked into the mirror and saw white crystals around his lips and inside his mouth. Realizing he had only minutes to get help before he passed out again, he fought an overwhelming sense of weakness with a sudden burst of energy *to live*. He started the engine and with incredible effort pushed the shift into reverse, allowing the car to move backwards slowly, but he didn't have the strength to turn the steering wheel, and the car backed into the rear of a parked car. Lenny fell forward, slumping over the steering wheel, unconscious.

Jack realized he was late as he drove into the parking lot. He searched for his Dad's car and found it parked at an odd angle against the rear of another car. He pulled over and saw his father slumped over the steering wheel. He got out of his car, jerked opened the door of his father's car and started to shake him. "Dad...Dad, what's wrong!" When there was no response, he pushed Lenny sideways toward the passenger seat. Getting in, he drove to the front of the E.R where a nurse was standing, just finishing a cigarette. Jack yelled, "I need help! He's dying!"

Chapter Sixty-Three

DAVE PHONED HIS wife, "Samantha, something bad just happened. Haberman figured it out. I didn't think anyone would, but he did. We need to leave immediately."

"That's fine. Come home, my dear so we can talk."

Then he called Elizabeth and told her Samantha needed help immediately. He hung up before she could ask what was wrong. He arrived at his house just as Elizabeth drove up. She followed him quickly into the house.

Elizabeth ran to her sister. "Sam, what's wrong? Dave said it was an emergency."

Samantha looked at her oddly and whispered, "Liz, there's nothing wrong. Why do you ask?"

"Dave called and asked me to come immediately. I thought something was terribly wrong with you."

Dave interrupted. "Elizabeth, we're leaving tonight. You may as well know the truth. Dr. Haberman figured it out."

"Figured what out? What are you talking about?"

"Don't act naïve with me. You know what I'm talking about."

Elizabeth looked puzzled. "No, I don't."

Dave responded. "Haberman knows you and Samantha are sisters. He figured out that I was the one who added peanut to Frank's vaccine."

Elizabeth dropped into a chair with a look of total shock. She realized that her greatest fear had come true. *He set me up. I told him Stevens was a patient of Dr. Haberman, and mentioned he was on allergy shots. Now I know why he came to the office to talk to me. He wanted to see where I kept the reagents and the vaccines.*

"Lenny also knew that you made it a deadly reaction by giving Stevens extra-large doses of his vaccine."

Elizabeth stood up, angry at the accusation. "No, God damn you... No, I didn't do that!"

"No one believes that. Everyone believes that Frank Stevens died because of what you injected. Otherwise, he might have only been severely disabled." Sabatha smiled as he said it.

Elizabeth wasn't sure if her sister had also known. She turned to her. "Sam, did you know this?"

Samantha didn't answer. Tears were rolling down her cheeks.

"Did you know he was planning this? Please! I need to know."

Samantha nodded slowly. "Yes."

"My God, why didn't you tell me before he did it?"

"I wanted Frank dead. He deserved to die... but we didn't want you involved. That's why we paid your bail to keep you out of jail."

Elizabeth screamed, shaking Samantha's shoulders. "Sam, that's murder! What have you done to me...and my kids? I have two children to raise! How could you do this to me?"

Samantha began to sob uncontrollably. Dave took Elizabeth roughly by the arm. "We're leaving now. Help me get her into the van."

"No! I'm not helping you anymore!"

"Yes, you will, Elizabeth. You're part of this. You tried to hurt Stevens too. What makes you think you had no part in his death?"

An overwhelming sense of fear gripped her. She thought, *My life is over. No one will believe me.*

Then, another terrible thought struck her. She turned to Dave and screamed, "Where's Dr. Haberman?"

"He got what he deserved, meddling in our lives."

"You bastard! Tell me where he is. What did you do to him?"

"Help me get away and I'll tell you. You might even have time to save him if you do what I ask."

Realizing that she had no other option, she agreed to help move Samantha into the van.

Once she got Samantha belted into the back seat, Elizabeth turned around and saw the gun lying on the passenger front seat. Instinctively, she grabbed it and pointed it at Dave. "Where's Dr. Haberman?"

Dave shrugged, though he was watching the gun carefully. "You're already too late. He's dead."

"You bastard! You're not going anywhere other than to the police."

"Then I guess you'll have to shoot, because we're leaving now."

Dave closed the driver door and started the engine. Elizabeth held the gun while kneeling on the floor in the back. Her door was still open.

"Get out now!"

"I don't think so."

"Turn the engine off... now!"

He stepped on the gas pedal and she fell back into the seat next to her sister, who was yelling as loud as she could, "Liz, no, no... put the gun down!"

Elizabeth's hands were shaking, but at that range she couldn't miss.

A deafening sound resonated as Dave fell forward; the side of his head gone. The van decelerated to a slow halt.

Chapter Sixty-Four

LENNY WAS UNCONSCIOUS when he was rolled into the ER on a stretcher. Several members of the staff recognized him, prompting a rapid mobilization. His blood pressure was low and respirations were labored. He was intubated, placed on a ventilator, and treated with intravenous fluids and medications. Common causes of shock, and respiratory failure were immediately ruled out. A well-regarded intensivist was asked to consult on the case. The intensivist noticed over-reactive tendon reflexes, muscle twitching, dilated pupils, elevated temperature and remnants of a powdery substance in Lenny's mouth. Being suspicious of an overdose, he ordered a stat toxicity screen and gastric lavage with activated charcoal to remove and deactivate drugs that might be in Lenny's stomach. Within a half hour the screen came back, documenting the presence of an anti-depressant and a monoamine oxidase inhibitor. The intensivist recognized that Lenny was suffering from serotonin syndrome and initiated therapy using serotonin inhibitors.

Lenny was moved to the ICU, where Elaine and Jack sat by his side. Gradually over the next day he began to show improvement, and within two days he was moved out of the ICU.

Epilogue

ELIZABETH CALLED THE police right after the shooting. She admitted firing the shot and told them everything she knew about the murder of Dr. Stevens. The DA's office decided not to charge her after all the facts were considered, but the Colorado Nursing Board, having heard her admission that she had intentionally administered incorrect doses of a vaccine, revoked her nursing license. Having a dire need to support her children, she took night courses and became a real estate mortgage broker, but unfortunately she started at the wrong time, and lost her job when the financial crisis hit. Now she was doing odd jobs to make ends meet.

Her sister, Samantha, was institutionalized in a long-term care facility. No one visited her and she died two years later.

Some of Dr. Doren's troubles improved, while others worsened. All criminal charges were dropped by the Attorney General's office after Dr. Sabatha's plot was uncovered. Doren declared bankruptcy after three medical negligence trials culminated in total damages above his insurance coverage. His house and practice assets were sold to pay judgments. The plaintiffs in one of the successful lawsuits against him included Ted Larkin's family, but the reason for the lethal allergic reaction was never publically disclosed.

Pete and Jacqueline moved to Las Vegas where he linked up with an old colleague with a similar practice. He was able to get a Nevada medical license despite his past problems in Colorado. Jacqueline integrated quickly into the Las Vegas culture, and within months became the talk of the town because of her outstanding good looks and abilities as a hostess.

Pete became very popular, making more money than ever, and was back to singing James Brown's song, "I Feel Good."

The Larkin-Scott medical malpractice reform bill had accomplished its goal to compensate victims of medical malpractice with huge judgments. Juries were awarding high damages in all tort cases, not only cases of medical malpractice. Ed Tucker was caught in this litigious atmosphere, and he had to settle out of court with a huge award for injuries to the pregnant mother and her premature infant with severe brain damage. The bill was subsequently repealed a year after Larkin's death, and the settlement bubble for liability claims burst. Trial attorneys had to accept the new reality; owning only one or two leisure homes.

Sol Feldman went to the Bible meeting and actually enjoyed the time with the church ladies. After about an hour of hearing about the need to come to Jesus, he seized the moment and talked about Judaism. All the women were intrigued when he discussed Reform Judaism, especially hearing that women were considered equal to men, could become rabbis, and were encouraged to have education and careers, even if they had children. Denise called to thank him and to ask if she could attend a Shabbat service. A year later, she visited with a rabbi to learn more about Judaism. She had fallen in love with a Jewish doctor and was definitely feeling better about her life.

Sol rehired most of his employees. The studies continued to provide positive results and COADD was preparing to go public in a year. They needed more help and hired Johnny Soto, who had moved from the Midwest, and was considered an excellent addition to the staff. COADD didn't know his real name was Johnny Bonante, but they wouldn't have made the connection since Johnny didn't look anything like his half-brother, Jimmy Barone. Tommy Pazzoni knew the family was under close surveillance by the feds, so he told Johnny to be very careful not to raise any suspicion. Johnny took the warning seriously, knowing how Jimmy had departed from this world.

Lenny went back to work filled with renewed enthusiasm. He was rewarded with glowing responses from patients who warmed to his caring and relished the extra time he spent with them. He wasn't sure why he was experiencing this rejuvenation; he was just pleased to be back to normalcy in his life.

Acknowledgements:

I AM A physician who had never written a novel, only scientific articles. I tried my very best to accomplish this task by seeking assistance from some very talented people. I cannot find words to thank John Paine, an independent editor who guided me. It took courage on his part to keep me as a client after he read the original manuscript. I want to thank others who helped in the editing: Wendy Blake, my daughter-in-law, who was especially helpful because of her background as an avid reader of mysteries, and her scientific and legal education as a genetic counselor and attorney; Beth-Kalman Werner, owner of Authors Connection; and Fred Ruckdeschel, Ph.D., economist. Others who gave helpful commentary included Phil Lieberman, M.D., Clinical Professor of Internal Medicine & Pediatrics, University of Tennessee College of Medicine and leading expert on anaphylaxis; Bobby Lanier, M.D., Executive Medical Director of the American College of Allergy, Asthma and Immunology; Joseph Bellanti, M.D., Professor of Pediatrics and Microbiology-Immunology, Georgetown University Medical Center; John F. Ryan, M.D., renowned pediatric anesthesiologist and his lovely wife Joanna; my son, Robert Blake, M.D., hand surgeon; Robert Woodward, M.D., obstetrician and gynecologist; Richard Asarch, M.D., dermatologist; Charles Kirkpatrick, M.D., Professor of Medicine, University of Colorado School of Medicine; Henry Shinefield, M.D., renowned academic pediatrician; William Berger, M.D., allergist/immunologist and past president of the American College of Allergy, Asthma and Immunology; Sanford Avner, M.D., allergist/immunologist; Eric Weber, M.D., radiation medicine and his wife Lynne; Bart Troy, M.D., cardiologist; Brennan Dodson, M.D., ENT; Anthony

Goodman, M.D., surgeon and author: *None But The Brave; The Shadow of God;* Leonard Hoffman, M.D., allergist/immunologist and his wife Carol; Lu Anne Odt, R.N., manager of clinical drug research site; Melanie Schell, N.P. , specialist in allergy and immunology; Nate Naprstek, occupational therapist and fishing guide; Leslie Carlson, N.P.; Carol Laycob; Steve Zetzer, my son-in-law, intellectual technology and his wife, Kristin Zetzer; William & Beth Sagstetter, renowned Western history authors: *The Mining Camps Speak; The Cliff Dwellings Speak* and my brothers: Richard Wanderer, advertising, attorney and author of novel entitled *The Holiday Party* and his wife Patricia, Warren & Phyllis Wanderer and Paul & Rose Marie Wanderer.

I especially want to thank my past partner, David Goodman, M.D., allergist/immunologist, who while serving in Desert Storm as a physician, experienced two harrowing helicopter crashes and received the bronze medal for valor. Some of his experiences have been modified and incorporated in my novel.

In writing about the malpractice case and the grand jury, I received guidance from the following attorneys: Gary Kalkstein, malpractice law; Wendy Blake, general law; Andy Scherffius, trial law; Robert Novak, business law; and assistance from the Colorado Attorney General's office.

I want to thank my fellowship mentor, Elliot Ellis, M.D., retired chairman of the Department of Allergy & Immunology at National Jewish Hospital. His leadership, teaching skills, intellect and research contributions helped propel the specialty of allergy/asthma/immunology out of the dark ages into the age of evidence-based medicine. I will always cherish his friendship and guidance. I also want to express gratitude to his wife Kathleen Ellis, Ph.D., ARNP, for her helpful critique.

I thank my daughter Jennifer Wanderer (wanderermedia.com) for her excellent graphic art design of the cover, which has received lots of acclaim from readers and editors. And I thank my other daughter Kristin Zetzer for my photograph.

All of my family members were especially supportive and understanding when I sought refuge to write this novel. Lastly a special thanks and hugs for my wife, Patricia, who spent hours reading, critiquing and finally approving the finished product.

CPSIA information can be obtained at www.ICGtesting.com
Printed in the USA
`LVOW121324260413

331125LV00006B/57/P